DEMON DAYS Book One

Richard Finney D.L. Snell

LONO PUBLISHING / ENCINO, CA.

Richard Finney / Lono Publishing
http://lonopublishing.blogspot.com/

First Edition November 16th 2015

ISBN 978-1-938457-29-6

*I found myself in a dark wood
the right way was lost*

-- Dante Alighieri *(The Inferno)*

C<small>HAPTER</small>

1

Everything in the painting was grey.

Tom Hansen ran his fingers through his hair as he stood in front of his canvas, trying to figure out what was missing from his work.

He had a video recording of CNN's coverage of 9/11 playing on his apartment's monitor. The noises and sounds of the day played back on the wall speakers in his living room. Tom hoped it would give him the inspiration to finish the painting.

The video from that day had a reporter interviewing a survivor who had escaped from one of the towers before it collapsed. Tom listened while keeping his eyes fixed on the painting before him.

"We were looking out the window at the other tower when my friend said how the sky went totally black. Then we both saw the plane coming toward our building…"

It was exactly what Tom needed to hear. He snatched his brush and began addressing the color of the sky, turning the grey to black.

Tom was almost finished with his changes when the phone rang. He threw his brush aside and made his way over to the kitchen counter to check the caller I.D. The call was coming from the main doors of the apartment building.

Tom picked up the phone. "Hello…"

"Hello, yes, this is Phillip Potts. I'm here to meet with Tom Hansen."

Hearing the name caused Tom to go mute.

"Are you still there? Hello? Is this the apartment of the artist Tom Hansen? My assistant made an appointment last week with you. Hello?"

A dozen thoughts shot through Tom's head, and he finally latched onto one and spoke into the phone.

"You have the right place. Let me buzz you in."

Tom pressed a button on his phone and hung up.

In less than one minute Phillip Potts, one of the biggest art dealers in New York city, owner of one of the most influential galleries on the East Side, would be knocking on his apartment door.

He looked all around him and saw a dozen easels with his work scattered all around the living room. The contents of each painting flashed across his brain and everything he saw in his mind's eye was unfinished or wrong.

Tom rushed to the nearest easel and grabbed the painting, then moved toward the next easel with the intention of throwing everything on display into the back of the coat closet. But before grabbing the second painting, Tom stopped. What was he doing? Why hide his work now? He had been pursuing this opportunity for years, an effort that had him tapping all his friends if they had even the slightest connection to Potts. More recently, he had become desperate and finally allowed his girlfriend, Sandy, to reach out to someone she worked with at the TV Network.

Just as Tom was returning the painting to the first easel, the sound of his doorbell filled the living room. He wiped his sweaty hands on his paint-covered pants as he moved to answer the front door.

"Mr. Potts, great to meet you."

"You were expecting me, right?"

Potts waited for a response with a suspicious expression on his face.

"I'm sorry, what?"

"Exactly. You weren't expecting me. My assistant screwed up. It's alright, you can be honest with me."

"I don't know what to say. I don't want to get anyone fired."

"Don't worry about that. Firing her is not an option. My assistant also happens to be my daughter. But I do need to know if she screwed up…"

"I've been working from the moment I got up. And I haven't checked my messages all day. It's possible your daughter called to remind me of our meeting, and I never heard it because like an idiot, I haven't checked my messages."

Tom extended his hand hoping that it would encourage Mr. Potts to accept his explanation, and coax him to enter the apartment. Potts was touched that Tom went to the trouble of covering for his daughter and reached out to accept the artist's open hand.

"This is quite the work space you have here," said Potts, as he stepped from the entryway into the living room. The art dealer's gaze was immediately drawn to the floor to ceiling glass running the entire length of the living room. "I bet you have the perfect light coming in here for most of the afternoon."

"I'm sure you're right about that, but I'm a bit embarrassed to admit I can't really say for sure. This is where I work and I keep the shades drawn every day."

Potts turned to look at Tom to make sure he was being serious.

"Every day?"

"Every day," answered Tom. "I guess that will give you a clue as to the type of work I've been doing for the past three years. You won't be seeing any rainbows or cheery sunrises."

Potts sighed as he turned to look at all the easels laying before him. "So, no unicorns?"

Tom chuckled, relieved that, despite his lofty level of success, the art dealer still had a sense of humor. "No, I'm afraid not."

"Well, why don't we take a look anyway? Shall we?"

"First, can I get you something to drink?"

"A glass of Pinot would be nice, but only if you already have an opened bottle. If not, a Chardonnay or a Riesling will be fine."

"I have a Pinot I know you will enjoy, but you have to promise not to move a step until I return." Tom expected his work would end up as road kill once Potts had his way, but he intended to be looking at the eyes of the driver during the moment of impact.

"I understand. And I promise I won't move an inch from this spot until you return."

Tom went into the kitchen and uncorked a bottle of Pinot Noir he and his girlfriend bought on a trip through the Santa Ynez valley three years ago. He snatched two clean wine glasses and was back at the gallery owner's side in less than a minute.

"Cheers," Tom said, offering Potts one of the glasses.

"Yes, cheers."

They both raised their glasses, but Potts moved to the nearest easel without bothering to drink. Tom swallowed half of the wine in his glass before following.

Potts stared long and hard at the first two paintings without comment, causing Tom to steel himself for the inevitable.

One of the most influential art dealers in the city was not connecting with his work.

By the time Potts had reached the fourth painting, and still had not said a word, Tom had already emotionally checked out.

"Of course you realize the Statue of Liberty wasn't physically impacted by 9/11?"

Potts had finally decided to comment on a painting depicting the Statue of Liberty with the flame of her torch no longer gold, but grey.

"Yes, I'm fully aware of the reality of what happened that day, but I chose to go in this direction because I wanted to show, with the use of color, the emotional fallout from the attack. That's what I was…"

Tom's voice trailed off when he could see his words weren't changing the expressionless face staring at his work. One of Tom's mentors in art school had once said to him, "Art is like people. No one should work overtime to convince another person you are worth hanging with or that your work is worth hanging on their wall."

He swallowed the rest of the wine in his glass and shut his eyes, hoping that somehow when he opened them again, Potts would have already left the building.

"Well, I think all the pieces I've seen so far are brilliant. Emotionally stirring work without being obvious. Sublime, if that's possible when painting about such an event."

Tom's eyes flashed open when he heard the words, but was speechless until he replayed in his head what he thought Potts had said.

"Thank you. Your words… mean a lot to me."

At the last easel, Potts seemed to be appraising this final work longer than the others until Tom realized that while the dealer's eyes may have been looking in the direction of the work, his mind was in a totally different place, looking toward the future.

"I'm thinking of the second floor of the gallery for your collection, but it would require three or four more pieces. I'm sure that would not be a problem?"

"No problem at all," Tom answered without hesitation. "I already have several sketches I'm ready to move forward on."

"Excellent. I'm very excited."

Despite the words, and the obvious signs of enthusiasm, Tom still wasn't sure he was reading the situation correctly.

"Excuse me Mr. Potts, are you telling me I'm in?"

Potts finally took his first sip of the pinot from his glass before answering. "How does a winter showing of your work sound?"

C HAPTER

2

The moment Potts left the apartment, Tom reached for his mobile phone to check the arrival status of his girlfriend's flight.

Flight 469's arrival at JFK had been delayed an hour.

For the first time ever, Tom was thankful for the late arrival of a plane.

He switched to another airline's website to check which flights to Hawaii were still available, but canceled the search when he realized he could do it while heading to the airport.

Tom emerged from the apartment building and jogged the couple blocks to the subway station where he caught the next train heading to JFK. The internet connection was dodgy at times during the subway ride to the airport, but he managed to purchase two round-trip tickets before arriving at the international terminal building.

He was running to the gate when something in one of the airport's stores caused Tom to stop and check his watch. Sandy's flight wasn't due to arrive for another ten minutes, allowing Tom to go back and buy the biggest bouquet of roses in the airport shop's refrigerator.

When his girlfriend's flight arrived, Tom was ready to surprise her the moment she stepped off the ramp. He happened to be standing next to another guy waiting for his girlfriend, also holding some flowers, but they were daisies not roses. As the passengers from the flight began to emerge into the gate's lounge, the young man suddenly became self-conscious. "Dude, do you mind standing someplace else?" Tom laughed but did exactly what the guy requested and moved to a different part of the lounge. Tom was very sensitive to what it was like competing for the love of a woman when all one could afford were daisies rather than roses.

Sandy Travis stepped off flight 469 from London with a single thought in her mind: 16:30. She was a segment producer for the TV news magazine show, *24/7*, one of the top-rated programs in the United States.

16:30 was the total running time of the slot in the program her story was expected to fill. She had just spent the last two weeks in Great Britain working with a local crew to cover a parliamentary debate.

"16:30. 16:30."

Helen Curran, an associate producer at 24/7 was dragging her suitcase a few feet behind Sandy when she heard her boss mumbling nervously to herself.

"Sandy, are you all right?"

"No, I'm not all right," Sandy said, looking back over her shoulder. "There's no way we're going to be able to use all the sound bites we wanted to use. Did you look at all the highlight quotes I suggested?"

"Yeah, I saw them. I thought maybe you heard from the network while we were in the air, and they told you we had two slots rather than just one."

"No such luck. I don't know what we're going to do." Sandy sighed, shaking her head as her mind continued to obsess over the situation. "We got so many great bites in with everybody we interviewed. I have no idea what we're going to lose."

"We're too close. We need some time away from what we shot."

Helen was right, and Sandy felt better after hearing her words. The two had been working together for almost three years and they shared an almost telepathic way of communicating with each other.

"You're right, we'll both take some time away."

"I'm talking about longer than just overnight, Sandy."

"Yes, I hear you. We'll sit tight until all the camera discs have been duplicated. Helen, are you sure you don't mind running the discs and logs to the network tonight?"

The two women emerged from the ramp leading from the airplane to the gate terminal and into the crowd of people gathered around to greet the arriving passengers.

"I'm actually excited to run by the network this late at night. This really cute video editor was just hired to work the graveyard shift. Turning in the discs and logs will give me a chance to get in his face."

Helen grinned and winked, but before Sandy could follow up, she heard her name being shouted across the lounge.

"Sandy Travis... Driver for Sandy Travis..."

Sandy stopped to look in the direction of the voice and her eyes found Tom standing nearby holding a bouquet of roses.

"Tom! What... what are you doing here...?"

She rushed up to him as he answered her question.

"I'm here because of you." Sandy was about to embrace him when Tom said, "I'm here because you've always believed in me."

Sandy had always been good at listening to people. Not only to their words, but to non-verbal clues as well. It was one of the reasons she was so successful in the field. Her skills served her well when she saw the look on his face. "Oh, my god, you heard from the 7th Street gallery?"

"Potts was at the apartment, and he saw the entire collection. I have my first gallery opening this winter. Time and date still to be deter—"

Sandy had her lips on Tom's before he could finish.

When Sandy and Tom broke from their kiss Sandy shouted across the terminal. "Helen... Helen... Thanks!" Helen raised a hand in

14

acknowledgement before she disappeared on the escalator.

When he once again had Sandy's attention, Tom said, "I have another surprise."

At first she thought Tom was reaching into his jacket to retrieve an engagement ring and bit her lip in disappointment. Without even trying, Sandy could come up with at least two dozen airports that were a more romantic place to pop the question.

But Sandy went from disappointed to curious when Tom pulled a pair of airline tickets, not an engagement ring, out of his jacket.

"Hawaii? You're kidding right? I mean, I wish I could, but Tom… I can't go to Hawaii. I just got back from covering a story that airs in three weeks."

"I'm talking about getting away for three days," Tom calmly replied. "When you get back from covering a story the first few days are always spent logging what you shot anyway, which Helen can totally handle."

His words had started to wear her down, but she still looked doubtful, causing Tom to draw in closer to her. "You've probably forgotten, but you once said to me that whenever I got my first gallery opening we'd celebrate by going to Hawaii."

"Of course I remember. How could I forget?"

"I'm glad you remember. Because I charged these tickets on your credit card."

Sandy laughed before snatching the airline tickets from Tom's hand. "That's identity theft."

Tom shrugged his shoulders before snatching the tickets back from Sandy.

"If you want to have me arrested, I'll be in Maui."

CHAPTER
3

The Tel Aviv Tayelet is an outdoor promenade running parallel to the white sand beach stretching along the Mediterranean seafront. On a typical afternoon families, tourists, and sun-seekers have the run of it.

But on the promenade courtyard adjacent to city hall, there was a much more diverse crowd. Locals were joined by hundreds of people from all over the world along with media crews who had gathered outside the U.S. Embassy to cover the negotiations for a peace treaty between Israel and seven other countries in the region.

The mob waited behind steel barriers erected overnight in anticipation of Israeli Prime Minister Yitzak Bleiberg and Special Envoy John Wolfenson emerging from a marathon session leading up to the midnight deadline for a final settlement.

Aluf Ginsberg was watching the last of the media crews abandoning their designated area to join the crowd when he received word from the security team inside the building.

"We're standing by with the package at the main doors, awaiting the greenlight to proceed."

"Roger that," Ginsberg answered through his headset. "Okay, everyone, we're about to move the package. Final checks before we proceed…"

Ginsberg scanned the crowd a dozen yards in front of him as the noise began rising in anticipation of seeing the two leaders. When he didn't hear any objections from the other security team members on the task force he spoke into his headset, "We're clear on the perimeter. You have a greenlight to proceed with the package."

The embassy's main doors swung open and the Shin Bet agents emerged, a dozen men and women in dark suits forming a protective pocket around Prime Minister Bleiberg and Envoy Wolfenson. Together they all moved at a steady pace toward the waiting cars in the nearby parking area.

"Okay, everybody, stay in a tight formation." Ginsberg spoke English for the benefit of the U.S. Secret Service agents who were part of the security team protecting Quartet Envoy Wolfenson.

He scanned the crowd as the phalanx of security agents led the two leaders past him and toward the waiting cars.

The entourage had almost cleared the steel barriers when the prime minister spotted someone in the crowd he wanted to greet and stepped away from his agent handlers to approach the crowd.

"Okay, everybody, let's just roll with this," said Ginsberg into his headset. "Eagle Eyes, sing if any of you spot anything."

Wolfenson, the Quartet's envoy to the Middle East, did not follow the prime minister to the barriers. Later, Wolfenson would tell those who were investigating the incident that he wanted to give him a few moments alone in the limelight. If the peace treaty Wolfenson had been working on for years had a genuine chance of succeeding it would take the majority of the Israeli populace supporting the man signing on the dotted line.

The noise from the boisterous mob had drowned out the sound of the sea nearby, but Ginsberg caught glimpses of the blue water in the distance as he continued to scan the crowd. He was looking for any suspicious movement, any strange behavior that would not be visible by the six sharpshooters positioned on the rooftop buildings that surrounded the city hall square.

When Envoy Wolfenson stepped away from the agents surrounding him, he walked past Ginsberg, who followed him as he approached the steel barriers. The change in purview allowed the Shin Bet agent to catch sight of a figure weaving through the crowd.

"I see a potential threat, white male, wearing a red hat, blue jeans, and a beige jacket. He's twenty feet from the barriers, moving toward the package…"

Prime Minister Bleiberg was posing for a picture with a member of the crowd and it looked like Envoy Wolfenson intended to join him for the photograph.

Ginsberg withdrew his weapon and slowly marched toward the crowd while keeping his eyes fixed on the man he had recognized as a potential threat. But then his vision of the man became obstructed by other members of the crowd.

When his sight line once again cleared, Ginsberg wasn't sure he was looking at the same man he had previously sighted. The man he was now tracking had his skin pulled taut over his face, highlighting sharp cheekbones and sunken eye sockets, almost as if the man was wearing a skeletal death mask. He barely bore a resemblance to whom Ginsberg thought he had recognized.

"This is Eagle Nest Two, I have a visual on your threat wearing a red cap…"

But whatever doubt Ginsberg had about who it was he was actually tracking, the agent cast all of that aside as the man reached into his jacket and withdrew a gun.

Three gunshots echoed across the promenade.

Another gunshot came a few seconds later, but this one sounded different because it was fired from one of the rooftops.

It took a few seconds, but the sound of gunfire triggered an eruption of screams and cries of panic. The crowd in the promenade square chaotically dispersed in hundreds of different directions.

After the initial sound of the first three shots, the Israeli prime minister was body slammed so hard by a Shin Bet agent seeking to protect him that Bleiberg was sure he had been hit by a bullet. Both leaders were rushed from the steel barriers to their cars, which then drove off so abruptly the scent of burnt tire rubber was able to mingle with the lingering smell of gunpowder.

Ginsberg finally lowered his gun only when another Shin Bet agent brushed past him to join the other security personnel swarming around the fallen assassin.

As he made his way toward the assassin, Ginsberg encountered a pistol laying a dozen feet from the shooter, kicked away by the first Shin Bet agent who arrived. The gun was a SIG SAUER, .357, the typical sidearm used by the U.S. Secret Service.

The assassin lay on the promenade concrete, still breathing, although a puddle of blood had already begun to surround his body. When his blinking eyes caught sight of Ginsberg, he tried to raise his arm.

The Shin Bet agent dropped down to the killer's side and grabbed his hand.

"Bernie… why?"

The assassin tried to respond, but coughed up blood instead of words.

The Shin Bet agent squeezed the assassin's hand, hoping the pressure would keep him alive longer. But just a few moments later the large, dark pupils in his friend's eyes became fixed, and the hand Ginsberg was holding turned cold.

C<small>HAPTER</small>
4

Palm trees and six-foot tall Tiki statues were strewn throughout the beach area where the Lono hotel held their grand luau. The nightly event took place where a permanent stage had been erected, allowing performers to entertain the diners eating the Hawaiian feast while seated on the sand.

The grand luau waitresses wore grass skirts and tie-dyed sports bras that barely concealed their breasts. For some reason Tom had insisted on having dinner here so Sandy tried to ignore her queasy feeling that they were dining at the Hawaiian version of a *Hooters* restaurant.

"Komo mai. Welcome to the Lono Grand luau."

"Mahalo nui loa." Tom's reply sounded like a native islander and earned him a smile from the waitress.

"You have a choice of three cocktails with your meal tonight." She waved her hand over the choices on her tray. "We have the Maluhia mai tai; the Pele Papaya daiquiri; or the Lono House Special, which has two shots of *Sky* vodka and a combination of guava, coconut, and pineapple juice."

They both went for the Lono House Special cocktails and the waitress transferred the glasses to their table before saying, "Mahalo nui loa na ho'olaule'a me la kaua."

Tom immediately answered, "Kipa mai."

Sandy stared at Tom as he grabbed his cocktail.

"Since when do you speak Hawaiian?"

"I know a few phrases." He drank from his glass before continuing. "I told you when we first met that I spent three years on the Big Island because my father was in the Navy."

"Yeah, now I remember. How old were you?"

"Just a teenager, 17 when we moved to New York." He was about to take another sip from his drink but saw the way Sandy was looking at him and stopped. "Why are you looking at me that way?"

"I don't know… I guess I was thinking that I was seeing another side of you that I didn't know about… even though, technically, I already did know about it."

Tom saw the playfulness in his girlfriend's eyes and lowered his drink. It was exactly what he had been hoping for when he impulsively planned the trip. She was behaving in the way that had initially caused him to fall in love with her.

"Go ahead, I want to hear you say something else Hawaiian."

Her request put him on the spot and it took him a few seconds before he could respond with something that he thought was perfect for the moment.

"Ooee, kakooi, lani."

Sandy repeated the sentence a couple of times before asking, "What does it mean?"

"It's Hawaiian for you are as 'beautiful as the light of the heavens.'"

She was so touched by Tom's words that at first she became embarrassed, then convinced herself that her boyfriend wasn't serious in using such over the top romantic words.

"That's beautiful, but c'mon, tell me the truth, I'm not the first girl on this island you've spoken those words to?"

Tom let out a big sigh when he realized Sandy was implying his romantic gesture was less than sincere.

"I'm just saying that when you were growing up here I bet you used that line on quite a few girls running around the island that you had your eyes on."

"You're way off base," said Tom, after taking a big gulp from his drink. "What I said to you wasn't rehearsed or test marketed. I'm not even sure I can repeat it again if you asked."

He then looked away, toward the ocean water, and Sandy saw he was actually hurt.

"Tom, I was joking..."

He nodded but didn't look back over at her. She tried to think of the right words to get him back. The silence between the two was suddenly filled by the sound of music coming from the band on stage

25

as the performers began the next portion of their dinnertime entertainment.

"Honey, forgive me. Every day I hear what people tell me in front of a camera, half of which turns out to be lies or self-serving bullshit… and when we sat down here on the sand, I guess I forgot to turn off my bullshit meter."

He grabbed his hand because he still showed no signs of reacting to anything she'd said.

"You said something beautiful, in another language! And I reacted like an idiot. I'm sorry."

Tom was about to turn back to Sandy and forgive her, but a man wearing khaki shorts and a Hawaiian shirt stepped up to their table.

"Perfect night for a perfect looking couple. You two look beautiful together. What about a picture to remember this night?"

He was a photographer working with the hotel to shoot pictures of diners at the royal luau and then sell the photos at the end of the evening.

Sandy was irritated by the interruption. She expected an even worse reaction from her boyfriend, but was surprised when Tom was actually excited by the photographer's offer.

"I'd love to have a picture of the two of us," said Tom, as he scooted his chair closer to her.

"On a count of three, how about you both say aloha."

Sandy wanted to grab her brush from her purse, look at her compact mirror for at least a couple of seconds, but the photographer was already beginning his countdown.

"3…"

She looked over at Tom, and saw that for some reason he was unbuttoning his dress shirt.

"2… 1…"

Sandy quickly swept her hair back behind her ears, and wet her lips.

"…Aloha."

The main course of the luau was kalua pig, which was baked in a cooking pit dug into the ground. Sandy tried poi for the first time, which Tom described as an acquired taste, but after only one bite Sandy declared it to be a taste she was not going to acquire in this lifetime. They had three cocktails each while watching the sun set from their table and both enjoyed the performance on stage featuring traditional music and hula dancing.

But during the entire evening Sandy was concerned about Tom. He seemed totally distracted, like something else was on his mind. She was convinced it was over the way she'd behaved earlier even though she had done her best to make it up to him by choosing her words carefully the rest of the evening, and snuggling up to him at every opportunity. She thought that perhaps he was thinking about the gallery showing. She knew he still had at least four more paintings to work on in the coming weeks. Sandy was reaching for other explanations because by the time they had paid their bill and were ready to leave, she still felt emotionally disconnected from Tom.

Leaving the luau area and heading back to the hotel, Sandy noticed a small crowd had gathered near the hut used by the luau staff to greet guests. As they drew closer, she saw the crowd was standing around a bulletin board displaying the printed pictures taken earlier in the evening by the photographer. When the diners saw Sandy and Tom they began to point in their direction.

"What's going on?" asked Sandy.

"I have no idea," answered Tom.

As they whispered and giggled to each other the people who had gathered stepped aside, allowing the couple access to the bulletin board. Sandy quickly scanned the two dozen photographs until she came to the one that featured her and Tom. She needed to lean in closer to see more clearly what her boyfriend had covertly done a second before the photograph was taken – Tom had opened up his Hawaiian shirt to reveal his tee shirt underneath where he had written in magic marker: *MARRY ME!*

She turned to look over at Tom, but he was gone.

Then she realized he was there after all. He had dropped down to one knee and was holding an engagement ring out to her. Waiting for an answer.

"Yes, Tom, the answer is, yes."

The people all around them began to clap and cheer.

Tom leaped up and they kissed.

Their kiss lasted long enough that some of the people watching decided they had seen enough and moved toward the hotel to carry on with their night.

"Hey, Sandy, time to get up…"

His new fiancée didn't move.

It was early in the morning; and Tom had his toothbrush in his mouth, so it was possible his words were garbled and she didn't understand.

He grabbed some water from the bathroom sink, spit, then rushed back into the room and hopped onto the bed.

"We're engaged."

Sandy opened her eyes to see Tom's face a few inches away.

"How do you like me now?"

"I'm in love with you. What time is it?"

He laughed and hopped off the bed.

"It's time for you to get your ass out of bed."

She groaned and rolled over.

"The helicopter takes off in one hour."

The word "helicopter" got Sandy to sit up.

"I have a story to cover today?"

"No story," said Tom, unable to control his laughter at her startled response. "Don't you remember? You booked us on a helicopter tour of the island."

"Yeah, I think I remember."

"Well, the helicopter leaves in an hour."

She hopped out of bed and slipped past Tom into the bathroom. As she looked into the mirror at both her image and Tom she said, "I had the weirdest dream last night. I dreamt that you proposed to me…"

Without missing a beat Tom replied, "Sounds more like a nightmare."

Sandy nodded, playing along with Tom's response, "You're right, it was a nightmare because in the dream I actually said yes…"

He looked at her and smiled.

Then he thought of the helicopter tour and looked at his watch.

"Sorry. I promise I'll only be five minutes," said Sandy.

It was Tom who'd chosen the Ford Mustang convertible as their car rental. The top was down as they sped on the single lane highway toward the airport, with a hint of the ocean in the air as they drove past pineapple fields and coffee plantations.

"I can't find the NPR station on this island."

Sandy was missing all the beauty around her, too busy scanning across the radio dial in a hunt for her favorite station.

"I can't believe we're driving through paradise and you've got your head buried in the dashboard of the car."

"C'mon, Tom, it's not as if I'm looking for my morning dose of head banging music," she quickly answered, not bothering to hide her irritation with Tom's observation.

Her spin across the bandwidth brought in at least a couple of religious stations, three easy music listening stations, and a shocking amount of country music stations, before she was finally able to locate NPR.

The sound of a monotone voice reading the news caused Sandy to lean back in her seat with a serene look on her face as if she was listening to a yoga instructor reciting a meditation mantra.

He looked over at her and saw that she wasn't taking in any of the surrounding sights; his fiancée was instead hanging on every word coming from the radio. Tom endured it for as long as he could before he leaned into the dashboard and turned off the car's radio.

Sandy was so shocked at Tom's action she stopped to think for a moment about what she might have done, and what she might be missing if she responded so quickly with what she wanted to say to him.

"What the fuck, Tom?"

"I should have probably made this clear before we landed, but I was hoping that while we're together on what turns out to be a rather special occasion, maybe we could put some yellow tape around the rest of the world. I was thinking… just you and I for 72 hours."

"That's why I fell in love with you, honey," said Sandy, grabbing Tom's hand in a loving way before she leaned toward the dashboard and switched the radio back on.

"But realistically speaking," said Sandy as she lifted Tom's hand to her lips for a kiss, "I'm going to break every finger of this hand if they come anywhere near the car radio."

"Will you really?"

"Don't test me, Tom. You still have a gallery showing you need to prepare for. How is that going to happen when you can't even hold a paintbrush?"

Tom laughed at her joke, despite the fact he was pissed that she would not leave her work behind, not even for a few hours. Not even after they had become engaged.

"We have more on this morning's assassination attempt on Israeli Prime Minister Yitzak Bleiberg and U.S. Envoy John Wolfenson which occurred just a few hours ago as the two men were leaving the U.S. Embassy in Tel Aviv…"

"So no chance that for just…"

Sandy held out up her hand for Tom to stop talking as she heard the words being broadcast from NPR. Tom stopped speaking, but shook his head with frustration at being silenced like a child.

"A spokesperson for the U.S. State Department has released the name of the assassin. His name is Bernard Rose, an American citizen, thirty-six years old, and a long-time member of the United States Secret Service. The State Department spokesman also went on to say that up until very recently,

Bernard Rose was a secret service bodyguard assigned to protect Envoy John Wolfenson. The assassination attempt threatens to delay the peace treaty signing between Israel and the other seven countries in the region…"

As the news anchor on NPR continued with more details, Sandy reached into her purse and pulled out her mobile phone.

"What are you doing, Sandy?"

"I'm calling into the show."

"Why?"

"I know the guy. I know the assassin, Bernard Rose. I mean, I don't know him, I met him, but just spending a few minutes with an assassin before he kills is gold when it comes to covering something like this. Do you know what time it is in New York? I always forget the time difference. It doesn't matter. Terry should still be in his office…"

"When did you meet him?"

The phone was ringing as she answered Tom, "I met him a few years ago at a dinner party Terry had at his house in the Hamptons. We ended up on in the backyard patio, having a cigarette between dinner and dessert. The thing is we ended up having a substantial conversation."

He had to keep his eyes on the road, but Tom tried to steal some glances at his fiancée to see Sandy's face as she was recalling the details of that night.

"We talked about how hard it was with relationships, meeting the right person. He was a huge fan of the Boston Red Soxes. And that he had a litmus test for every woman he dated that they either had to love the Soxes or willing to be converted. Until he met his girlfriend. She hated baseball. And he ended up throwing out the litmus test instead of breaking up with her." She looked over at Tom. "Seriously, I can't believe he turned out to be an assassin."

And she prattled on about getting involved in a story just a few hours after he had asked her to marry him.

"24/7. How may I direct your call?"

Sandy heard the receptionist's voice, but before she could answer, Tom snatched the phone from her.

"Tom, what are you doing?"

"I'm saving our relationship."

He motioned as if he was going to throw the phone out of the car, but then ended the call before tossing the phone into the back seat.

She began to reach for it, but then saw Tom's clenched jaw and the look in his eyes as he waited for her to react.

"I'm sorry... Did you hear me, Tom? I said I was sorry."

"Three days. Just you and I. Fuck the world!"

He screamed the last three words into the open air.

"Is that asking for too much?"

Tom asked the question at a much lower volume level, hoping Sandy would see he was angry, but not out of control.

She leaned forward and turned off the radio.

"I'm sorry. You're right."

"Just the two of us..." said Tom looking over for her reaction.

"Just the two of us," she repeated. "Fuck the rest of the world."

"I'm serious here."

"Then how come you've got that smile on your face?"

Tom didn't have a smile on his face, but when he looked over at Sandy and saw the same playful look on her face that he had fallen in love with, he couldn't help himself.

He broke out in a smile that stayed on his face the rest of the way to the Maui airport.

CHAPTER
6

There were four passengers on the helicopter tour – Tom and Sandy were riding with a pair of Japanese newlyweds who spoke very little English. The newlyweds sat in front, next to the pilot, while Tom and Sandy were seated in the back. For decades, Hawaii had been a popular destination for honeymooning couples from Japan. The pilot of the helicopter, Stu Rifflen, repeated all of the safety guidelines in Japanese before takeoff.

Despite the language barrier, Sandy was touched by what she observed of the couple. She noticed they had boarded the helicopter holding hands. During the tour, she caught sight of one of the helicopter's small monitors embedded in the dashboard that was picking up the camera pointed at the front seat, and saw the Japanese bride stroking her husband's hand during the flight.

Just as the noise of the helicopter's rotors grew louder, Stu clicked a button on the dashboard and the voice of Bobby McFerrin singing "Don't Worry, Be Happy" was piped through their headsets. Sandy grabbed Tom's hand as the helicopter lifted off from the tarmac.

"This is going to be fun," she said. And Tom looked over and gave his fiancée a reassuring grin.

"I'm totally excited…"

The helicopter tour Sandy and Tom had signed up for was a journey around the entire island. They hovered over rainforests, flew past gorgeous mountains, and circled spectacular sites such as the Haleakala Crater.

"We're looking at the world's largest dormant volcano," said Stu over the headsets.

"It looks like the moon," said Sandy through her headset.

"Yes, I agree with you, Sandy. And yet unlike the moon's surface, the cinder cones we're looking at tower higher than the Empire State building."

Tom was impressed with how the pilot obviously kept in mind where his passengers hailed from. On more than one occasion during the tour, Stu compared the Hawaiian landscapes to landmarks both in New York and Tokyo.

As they flew away from the Haleakala Crater, the pilot looked at his watch before announcing through the headphones, "You folks are in luck. It's almost noon, so we'll be the last tour to see the Wall of Tears up close."

"What happens after twelve?" shouted Tom into his headset microphone. The volume of his question caused everyone in the helicopter to grimace before Stu responded.

"The wind picks up dramatically, making it tricky for helicopters to approach the site. But we'll be just fine at this time of day."

Tom was not comforted by the pilot's words. He reached out to grab a hold of the leather armrest attached to the glass door beside him. The entire flight had gone so smoothly; it was the first time Sandy saw him show any distress.

"Tom, are you all right?"

She forgot that her words spoken in the mic went over the helicopter's interior intercom system and blanched the moment she realized her mistake. Her words immediately caused the pilot to look up at the monitor attached to the camera fixed on his passengers in the backseat.

Tom was aware that Sandy's question had gotten the attention of the pilot and he waved at the camera with a cheery grin.

"Having a great time. No problem. Carry on."

"One more island site before heading back to the airport," said Stu through their headsets.

"Fine. Having a great time," answered Tom.

"Terrific. If anyone has any difficulties, just let me know," said Stu, before steering the helicopter toward their next landmark. "We're only here to have a good time…"

As a journalist, Sandy had flown on helicopters dozens of times over the years. The only problem she had ever encountered ended up being a big one – while covering the Idaho white supremacist siege, one of the cult members shot at their helicopter as she was with her cameraman shooting aerial coverage of the compound. The shots caused the pilot to ditch their helicopter in an onion field a few miles away, with everyone surviving. But she was back up in another copter a few days later to cover the invasion of the compound by federal agents.

She tightened her grip on Tom's hand, while using her other hand to cover her headset microphone.

"Seriously, Tom, are you all right?"

He nodded confidently, then squeezed her hand to emphasize his answer.

After flying across the ocean for a few minutes, Stu veered the helicopter back toward the interior of the island. They flew over acres and acres of taro fields before approaching mountains rising above the flat landscape.

The copter slipped between a narrow gap in the mountain range, and continued flying on a narrow path between steep cliff sides running on both sides.

The sunlight disappeared almost at the same time rain began falling. Stu turned on the wipers so they could still see out the front windshield of the helicopter. The glass was wiped clear of the raindrops as they approached a stunning sight in the short distance.

"This is the Wall of Tears."

When Stu's voice came over his headset Tom had been staring out the window, terrified by how close they were flying as they cut their way through the narrow cliffs.

"Gorgeous sight, right?"

Tom turned to look outside the front windshield of the helicopter and saw dozens of waterfalls flowing from a cliff side, each narrow stream of water descending six hundred feet to the lagoon below. It was a spectacular sight, one that could probably only be appreciated in a helicopter hovering at the same level of the lava holes.

"The source of the water is the interior of the island, which gets at least ten times the amount of rainfall the rest of Maui receives. The ancient lava tubes were created when the island itself was first formed by an erupting volcano."

At the end of Stu's verbal description of the site, a powerful gust of wind shook the helicopter hard enough that the Plexiglas around the passengers vibrated for several seconds.

Sandy saw the pilot tighten his grip on the flight stick, but that was the only sign she noticed as he insisted on not allowing anything from the incident to disturb his narration.

"Legend has it that the gods poked their fingers into the cliff side and made the earth cry and we ended up with the Wall of Tears. Well, what the Hawaiian gods lack in empathy, they certainly made up in sheer beauty."

After finishing his prepared description of the site, the pilot switched off his mic, something he had done numerous of times throughout the tour to allow his passengers the chance to view the sites in silence.

But the wind sweeping through the narrow canyon only allowed a few seconds of silence before it struck again. This time the punch was so powerful, Stu needed some time before he grabbed back control of the copter and was able to steer it back to the middle of the canyon.

"What the hell was that?" Sandy asked once the bird had settled.

The pilot hit several buttons on his dashboard before responding. "That was some of the wind I mentioned earlier, Sandy."

The female Japanese newlywed spoke frantically to her husband, which was captured over the headsets of all the passengers. Her husband replied to his new wife, then leaned forward to address the pilot. Nothing he said was in English, but the panic in his voice was easy to translate.

"Not sure of every word you said, Mr. Osaka, but I'm pretty sure I understand enough," said Stu. "It's time to…"

Another blast of wind slammed into the helicopter before the pilot could finish his sentence. This gale force caused the helicopter to drop a dozen yards before Stu was able to regain control.

The sudden descent caused Tom to feel like his stomach was using his neck as a bridge to swallow his head. He let go of Sandy's hand, then frantically grabbed for the vomit bag next to his seat.

"I'm sorry about that. Is everyone all right?"

Sandy was looking at Tom with concern, but made it a point to respond to the pilot's question.

"We need to leave now."

"Are you both all right?"

She leaned toward the camera to emphasize her response. "Stu, get us out of here. Now."

"I agree with you, Sandy. Time to leave. Listen everyone, our way out of this canyon is going to feel at first like we're going upside down, but don't worry…"

Another powerful airstream slammed into the helicopter, causing pilot and passengers to be violently thrown forward until their belts abruptly stopped them. Tom lost his vomit bag and tried to reach for it before finally throwing up between his knees.

"Just do it," shouted Sandy through the headset.

Stu pulled back on the cockpit stick while simultaneously working the pitch lever and the helicopter responded instantly by angling backwards while rolling over on its side in a maneuver the pilot had performed hundreds of times over the years.

But right in the middle of the maneuver, at a point where the vehicle was the most vulnerable, another fierce gust of wind broadsided the helicopter, causing the engine to immediately shut off.

The sound of silence filled the air as the helicopter began dropping toward the ground.

"Shit," screamed Stu over the headsets after he realized his efforts to pull back on the stick were useless because the helicopter no longer had power.

He lunged toward the dashboard, but the restraint of his seat belt held him back before he was able to finally move forward and frantically stab at several buttons on the helicopter's control panel.

"I can't believe this is happening," Tom mumbled to himself. Seconds before he'd been so sick he'd forgotten where he was. Now, his brain was so crystal clear, his thoughts were scattering in a dozen different directions – *the price of his work would skyrocket after he died... But since he had not finished his last series of paintings would that hurt the selling price.... Sandy was with him... they were going to be married... she had not even picked out a wedding dress... now they were both going to die...*

"Tom, listen to me, when we land, get out of the vehicle immediately. As soon..."

The sound of the helicopter's engine firing up interrupted her words, and everyone in the cockpit held on to their last breath as they hoped the sound meant they were going to be all right.

But then the noise of the engine sputtered out.

Stu frantically hit the same series of buttons in a desperate attempt to engage the engine, but after running through the same routine twice and getting no reaction, the Japanese man began screaming into his headset. Somehow the copter's engine wouldn't turn over, but the electrical power in the cockpit was still working, so they could all hear Mr. Osaka's screams. Stu reached over his wife and grabbed the headphones off the man's head. He then clicked a button on the dashboard before speaking into the mic on his own headphone.

"Mayday, mayday, this is N6037. We're going down. Mayday, mayday, this is Niner6037. We're at the Wall of Tears and we've lost all power. No engine response. We're going down… mayday, this is N6037 near the Wall of Tears…"

The helicopter's impact with a cluster of trees silenced Stu's mayday. The front windshield of the cockpit exploded and a wave of shattered glass shot across the front seat toward the back. Sandy had already raised her arms but saw glass flying toward her like it was a wave of water crashing on the shore of a beach.

The tree line absorbed the initial impact of the helicopter, and then would ease the final descent to the ground. The tail impacted first and then the rest of the helicopter landed upright in lagoon water about three feet deep before beginning to sink into the sand.

Through the shattered Plexiglas, the sound of the water falling from the Wall of Tears could be heard, but none of the occupants in the helicopter's cockpit could hear it.

No one was moving.

CHAPTER 7

Sandy's left eye began to involuntarily blink.

Blood had pooled up in her eye socket and begun pouring in the moment she'd awoken.

She tried to raise her hand to wipe the blood from her eye, but found her arm would not move.

When she summoned the strength to try again, she was successful, but her hand slammed against her face so hard in an attempt to clear the eye socket of blood, it was like she had punched herself in the face.

It took several wipes from the back of her hand before she was able to open both eyes. Seeing with some clarity took even longer as she looked around her.

Tom sat slumped forward against his safety harness. It was hard to see his face because a tree branch had plunged through the windshield and extended to the back seat during their fall to the ground.

"Tom? Tom, are you all right?"

She ripped off her headset and undid her seatbelt, wincing as she tried to move her legs. Doing her best to ignore the pain, she turned her body in the seat so she could face her fiancé.

"Tom! We need to get out of here." Still not getting a response, she shook his arm and his eyelids twitched; he began to stir.

"Sandy..." he said.

"Oh God, you're alive!"

"Yeah, but don't get mad... I didn't get the flight insurance."

She let out a short reflexive laugh.

Tom's voice was clear, but there was a slight pause between each of his words. And as he spoke she noticed his teeth were tinted red. There'd been a longer pause in the middle of the two sentences. Sandy hoped the fact that he was thinking of comedy timing before he uttered the punchline meant he was going to be fine.

Her reaction caused Tom to look over.

Their eyes locked for a few moments before he closed his. But he spoke at the same time.

"How are the others?"

Sandy leaned forward to check.

Tree branches had impaled the pilot and the Japanese newlyweds, pinned them against the front seat like butterfly specimens. There was blood everywhere, splattered all over the twisted metal, still dripping from all three bodies.

"They're all..."

She tried to say the word 'dead' – but it wouldn't leave her lips. After a couple more efforts fell short,

Sandy turned back to Tom. He was ghostly white, looking similar to the bodies she had seen in the front seat of the helicopter.

A drop of blood fell onto her pants leg and she followed it to the source of the bleeding. The tree branch that obscured Tom's face had speared his neck.

Sandy looked back toward the front seat – to the white handkerchief covering the Japanese woman's hair. She snatched it and turned back toward Tom.

"Honey, your neck... There's a branch…. You need to hold still."

She reached for the branch, but found her hand was trembling so bad she pulled it back. Sandy stared at her hand, trying to will it to stop shaking, but when she wasn't able to make any kind of difference, she raised it anyway and grabbed a hold of the knotted branch piercing Tom's neck.

Blood rushed from the wound the moment she withdrew the branch. The white cloth she applied to his neck seemed to turn into a sponge after just a few seconds as blood continued to gush from the hole. Tom did not flinch when she applied more pressure, then raised his own hand to the handkerchief.

"You need to hold this here with the same kind of pressure. That's right Tom, just like that."

His hand stayed on the handkerchief and Sandy's spirits rose with his response.

She began moving around him, toward the helicopter's door.

"Where are you going…"

"We need to get out of here."

"Good. But I don't want you to leave…"

His words prompted her to check his hand on the handkerchief on his neck and the pressure he was maintaining on his wound. He seemed to be holding it tight even though there was still blood dripping, now onto the seat.

She tried to open the door, but it would not budge. She tried again and again, and on the third try the handle disengaged from the frame. Sandy got up from the seat and used her available strength to throw open the door.

By the time she turned back around, Tom had dropped the bloody handkerchief from his neck. She started to go for it, but then stopped.

Sandy unbuckled the seat belt around Tom and pulled him from the seat as she leaned in the direction of the doorway. Together, she was able to yank him onto her, then out of the helicopter they both tumbled.

She quickly scrambled, pulled him up from the ground, and dragged him a dozen yards, through the shallow water, to a place where she was able to ease him down into the dry sand of the lagoon. Sandy then took off her shirt, and applied it to Tom's neck.

Less than two minutes had passed from helicopter to sand, but when Sandy looked down at Tom, he looked a hundred times worse.

"Tom, you need to stay with me. Tom, open your eyes…"

Her words managed to get a response. Tom opened his eyes and looked at her, though there was a vacant look in the irises that was not encouraging to Sandy.

"Sandy… I need... tell you...."

His eyes rolled back to bloodshot whites, then fluttered shut before he mumbled any more words.

"Tom. Tom?"

She tilted his head back, pinched his nose shut, put her lips to his and began to breathe into him.

His chest didn't rise. Sandy adjusted the tilt of his head and tried again; this time she saw his chest rise.

Sandy let go of the shirt applied to his neck and began chest compressions, pumping twice every second.

"Come on, honey, stay with me. You can do it."

After thirty compressions, she gave him two more rescue breaths and kept pumping.

Thirty compressions.

Two rescue breaths.

Over and over again.

She didn't stop until Tom gasped, opened his eyes, and began breathing on his own.

"Tom! Oh my God—don't leave me again!"

He reached up and Sandy grabbed his hand tightly.

"Do you hear me? Stay with me."

Tom shook his head as if he was responding to her pleas. But she was more confused than worried. Some color had returned in Tom's face, and he no longer had the vacant look in his eyes.

51

"I can't hear you…"

She leaned closer to him so she could hear the rest of what he was trying to say to her.

"… over the noise…"

His eyes were looking past her, toward the sky. Sandy finally turned to look up to see what Tom was staring at…

It was a helicopter hovering directly above them.

Sandy stood up and waved at them to make sure they saw them lying on the beach. She fell back down to her knees the moment she saw the helicopter descending down toward them.

CHAPTER 8

One of the two paramedics working in the cargo hold of the helicopter had hooked an IV into Tom's arm and fitted him with an oxygen mask. He was checking his vitals while the other paramedic was doing the same with Sandy.

"How's he doing?"

The paramedic tending to Tom heard Sandy and raised his thumb.

"He's going to make it."

Sandy nodded with relief at the paramedic tending to her. But then she became confused.

The paramedics looked just like each other, like they were twins – both had blond hair, blue eyes, and their faces were smooth, wrinkle free. It was as if they had both...

"You saved his life," said the paramedic tending to Sandy.

She noticed his breath smelled sickly sweet.

"He's going to be fine. You'll both be fine."

The paramedic put an oxygen mask over Sandy's mouth and she took some deep breaths before looking over at her fiancé.

"We'll take it from here."

Tom turned his head to look over at her. She was now breathing oxygen, but rather than allowing her to see more clearly, the oxygen seemed to be causing her to see everything as if the helicopter they were in had ascended into a cloud.

Sandy awoke with a start, grabbing the wrist of someone, but it took her eyes a few seconds to see… it was a nurse removing the IV connection on her arm.

"Where's Tom?"

"You know the answer, Ms. Travis."

It took her a few seconds before she was able to recall. "His room is down the hall."

The nurse nodded.

"I want to see him."

"Yes, of course."

She pulled back the sheets on her bed and held out her hand ready for help standing up.

"How is he doing," Sandy asked, as the nurse helped her from the bed.

"Not as well as you. You're being discharged today. Did you know that?"

Sandy was about to shake her head, but then she remembered speaking to the doctor who had been tending to her for the last several days after the helicopter accident.

"You're fine. There's nothing more I can do for you. But perhaps there's someone else who can help you from here."

She had handed Sandy a card with the name 'Dr. Bess Forulani, PhD' printed in embossed black letters. "Before you are discharged, why not spend some time with her? Have her look at what I can't see with any X-rays?"

The card the attending doctor had handed her fell to the floor as she stood up from her bed with the nurse's aid. There was no need to retrieve the card, or even ask the nurse to grab it and set it aside on her tray cart next to her bed.

Sandy had been through plenty of tough battles over the years. What had happened during a helicopter tour of a Hawaiian island was a freakish event. The idea that the tragic events of that day would cause such mental instability that she would need to spend time with a shrink to deal with the adverse effects almost caused her to fall to her knees, light-headed, ready to vomit.

"How are you doing, Ms. Travis. Are you able to make it to your fiancé's room?

"Absolutely," she quickly answered.

The room was filled with the sound of medical machines operating in concert with a myriad of wires and tubes connected to Tom. He wore a thick bandage around his neck, his hair was matted, and he desperately needed a shave.

Although the doctors assured her Tom had suffered no brain damage from lack of oxygen, she couldn't stop herself from dwelling on the scenario of them being wrong – pushing Tom around in a wheelchair, changing his catheter bag, feeding him. Her hand holding the brush that finished the rest of the paintings that the art dealer would insist upon before he could hold the gallery opening celebrating Tom's work.

"Sandy—Sandy!"

She had insisted that the nurse leave her in a chair next to Tom's bed.

"Honey, I'm here..."

He glanced around, breathing fast and erratically until Sandy was able to get up from her chair and stumble over to his bed.

"Where am I?" he asked.

She grabbed his hand.

"Tom, we're at the Maui Memorial Medical Center."

The grip on her hand relaxed as Sandy's words matched the hospital room around him.

"How are you feeling?"

When he didn't answer, Sandy reached for the alert button dangling from the bedrail. But Tom stopped her a moment before she was about to push the button.

"Before you do… I need to tell you… something first."

Tom's words were sluggish. His skin was ghostly pale and covered in a layer of sweat beads. Tom's pupils were so enlarged they looked like twin moons hanging in a bloodshot skyline.

This caused Sandy to ignore her fiancé's words and push the button alerting the medical staff to Tom's revival.

"Honey, you can tell me anything," said Sandy. "I'm just glad to see you alive."

She let go of the bedside alert button, and grabbed Tom's hand.

"You know I died."

"Yeah, I was there," said Sandy. She stared in his eyes for a moment, waiting for more, but then continued, "I'm hoping there's a reward for bringing you back to life."

He smiled.

At first she thought, everything is going to be fine. No brain damage because Tom reacted to her joke. But then she saw the smile on her fiancé's face seemed to be unrelated to what she had said. The look in his eyes matched with the grin on his face seemed to be a response to something Tom was running through his mind.

"I died and... something happened. I was on... the other side."

"Honey, you're high," said Sandy. "It's the drug they put in your IV."

He gripped her hand tighter. "No, listen to me. I remember you pulling me from the helicopter and laying me on the sand – then laying me down on the grass. The next thing I remember there was this brilliant light, so intense I had to look away."

She turned away from Tom and looked at the open door to the room. But there was no sign of anyone from the medical staff responding to her alert.

"When I looked back," Tom said, "some of the light had been blocked by a figure. I couldn't see his face, but the... light around him... it was beautiful. He didn't speak and I didn't utter a word, but we somehow communicated. Like, you know, telepathy. He called himself 'The Angel of Light.'"

Tom stopped in his narrative to look over at her, to gauge her reaction to what he had said.

"But, honey, you don't even believe in God."

He nodded his head, almost as if Sandy's answer was the words he was waiting to hear from her.

"I do now."

They stared at each other before Tom continued.

"This angel, he told me something. He said, 'It's not your time. There are things you need to do. You need to go back.' I reached out, kind of like in the Michelangelo painting, and the moment our fingers touched, everything seemed to explode like a supernova exploding in space. The brilliant light swallowed me up whole. When I opened my eyes again, there you were, right beside me, having brought me back to life."

Sandy's blank face and non-verbal response caused him to release the grip he had on her hand.

"You believe me. Don't you?"

"Honey, of course I believe you. If you believe you saw an angel... well, then I'm right there with you."

"Really?"

Sandy grabbed his hand.

"Yes, of course."

The noise of footsteps caused Tom to look toward the door where a nurse appeared huffing and puffing like she had sprinted the entire way from the check-in station near the floor's elevators.

"Mr. Hansen, you're…" The nurse couldn't finish her sentence she was breathing so hard.

"Yes, I'm awake," said Tom.

C HAPTER
9

The alarm clock on Sandy's side of the bed buzzed. She squinted at the time before clicking it off. She rolled over to drape an arm around Tom, but he was gone, the covers on his side of the bed rumpled and tossed back.

He was out in the living room, sitting at one of his easels. For once the shades were raised and the morning sun was lighting up the area.

"I didn't hear you get up."

"I didn't want to wake you," answered Tom as she approached him.

"You better not be working. Remember what the doctor in Hawaii said, 'at least'…"

"… one week after you get back to New York you stay in bed and no work." Tom interrupted Sandy, finishing Doctor Permordia's advisory word for word, even adding an Indian dialect.

She laughed. "That was good. But you didn't roll your head at the end of each sentence."

"Forgive me, I still have problems moving my head in either direction, but come back next

Tuesday when the happy hour drinks are free until 5 pm, and I'll do Dr. Permordia's accent, head roll, and medical advisory."

Despite Tom's continued attempt to make light of the situation, Sandy had trouble responding with a smile.

Tom had almost died.

And less than a week later they were back in New York trying to move on like nothing had happened. He could make light of the situation, but she was completely uncomfortable with how fast he was trying to go back to work.

"I'm sorry I couldn't help it," Tom said, setting down his paintbrush as he spoke to Sandy. "Just sitting in the bed for another day. I couldn't do it. I'm not saying I'm feeling great, but I am saying I need to start doing something or I'm going to go crazy."

His words, and the reasonable tone he expressed them in took all the steam out of Sandy's attempt to make him take it easy.

"I understand, honey. And you know what, I totally agree with you."

He seemed relieved to hear her words and picked up his paintbrush to begin working again.

"Let me see what you're working on…"

She stepped past the easel and was surprised by what she saw. The paint on the canvas was still shimmering in the early morning light but it depicted a shadowy figure floating in the middle of the canvas, with bright yellow and white light illuminating his presence in a way that was both striking and vague. There was no obvious source of the light or details on the form it was highlighting.

"This is what you were telling me about in the hospital."

"Yeah, I needed to get it on to the canvas."

He looked over at Sandy, waiting for a reaction.

"I'm glad you got it down before you forgot what happened."

"Well, there's no chance that I would forget what I saw. But I wanted to get it down so I captured all the details."

Sandy looked over at Tom when she knew he had turned his attention back to the canvas. She wanted to see how his eyes were looking at his work. Was his painting the vision he saw during his Near Death Experience therapeutic or… something else. She couldn't answer her own question. Nothing in what she saw in Tom's eyes seemed to be different than before the helicopter accident.

"Do you feel better about getting it onto the canvas?"

He stared at his painting for a few long moments as if he was contemplating an answer to her question.

When Sandy felt like she had waited long enough for a response, she leaned in closer to him, "Tom?"

Tom leaned away from her before standing up and then stepping away from the easel. He stepped away again when Sandy tried to reach out to him.

"Honey…"

"I'm going to go out for a while…"

"Go out?"

"For coffee and a newspaper. I'll be back..."

Before she could say another word, Tom was out the door.

Sandy waited as long as she could before leaving. She had showered, dressed, and put on her makeup. It was her first day back to work since the accident and she had not planned on being late, but changed that plan when Tom still had not returned back to the apartment.

She called his mobile phone before leaving, but a ringing noise drew her back to the master bedroom where she discovered Tom's phone still in the jacket he'd worn on the trip home from Hawaii.

On the subway ride to work, Sandy tried calling the apartment, but both times her calls went straight to the answering service.

As she emerged from the subway station Sandy tried calling again and this time Tom answered.

"Hello."

"Tom, you're back."

"Yeah."

"Are you all right?"

"I told you I was just going out for coffee and the newspaper."

"Tom, we have a coffee maker in the kitchen and I almost tripped over the New York Times and the Washington Post when I left."

"Honey, I'm sorry."

"Are you all right?"

"Yeah, yeah, I'm fine. I just needed to get out. I'm feeling much better now."

She ignored his words, and concentrated on the emotional tone of his voice.

"Are you sure you're all right?"

"Yeah, I'm fine. I'm sitting here, in front of my easel and I just want to work."

There was a flat, detached aspect in the way he was responding to her questions that bothered her enough that she veered off before entering the building where she worked. Tom had always been an emotional guy, sometimes with extreme mood swings in a single afternoon, which Sandy had come to understand was specifically connected to his work and not his general psychological state.

"Honey, I'm really worried about you."

"I know you are. And I feel bad. I realized when I was out that this is your first day going back to work. I'm trying to sound fine so you don't worry about me."

Sandy sighed, relieved to hear Tom's words.

"That's really sweet and it makes me feel better. But, Tom, please, don't work too..."

She stopped talking because the icon in her phone's window had turned red, meaning the connection had ended.

"Tom are you still there? Tom?"

Sandy thought about calling back but instead entered the building. She was already over an hour late.

C<small>HAPTER</small>
10

Sandy entered the Optio Entertainment building and was greeted by the security checkpoint station just a few feet from the main entrance. She waved her passkey across the scanner and pushed through the turnstile and into the rest of the main lobby.

The OptEnt building was the home of the CBB TV Network, and also where the network's flagship show, *24/7,* was produced. One of the journalists who had been part of the show at its inception over forty years ago had come up with the nickname for the seventy floor, all glass skyscraper – *The Glass House*. The moniker was meant as a cursory description of the building, but more a statement of the journalistic integrity intended as a foundation of the show; both would stand proudly despite any size rock that came their way.

"Sandy!"

Sandy not only heard her name but recognized the voice, and quickly hit the button to stop the elevator doors from closing.

Helen rushed inside, and the two women immediately embraced, albeit in an awkward way. Sandy's associate producer was carrying a tray of takeout food from *Harried Healthy*, one of the nearby fast food places specializing in organic food. It was a restaurant Helen regularly frequented for lunch and the sight caused Sandy to feel guilty for arriving so late. Helen was already on her *second* food run of the day.

"Let me see the ring…"

Sandy held out her hand, but Helen's eyes never made it to the ring because she could not get past the sight of a dozen deep lacerations running up and down Sandy's arm, which was still in the process of healing.

"What the… Sandy, what are you doing here?"

Sandy looked at the wounds and was startled to feel an element of shock about what she saw on her arm. For the last three weeks she had seen every cut and bruise on her body hundreds of times. Clearly the difference was someone else, besides doctors, nurses, and her boyfriend, seeing her wounds for the first time.

"I know, right? And across the board, everyone at the hospital kept saying the same thing – 'you're going to have some scars. At least you have a story to tell with a happy ending.'"

She started to drop her arm but Helen stopped her.

"I'm sorry, but I really do want to see the ring."

Sandy raised her hand up so Helen could see the engagement ring Tom had given her.

68

"It's beautiful. Gorgeous. But if I was being honest with you Sandy, what I'm really feeling here is… invidsitorious."

"Invidsitorius?"

"That's right, *invidsitorius.*"

Sandy realized what this was about and laughed as she lowered her hand. Helen was a wordsmith and in her spare time, she would try to come up with new words for the English language. Her dream was to get one of her words included in the Oxford dictionary.

"Okay, so tell me, what does invidsitorius mean?"

"Invidsitorius is a combination of the Latin word, *Invidia*, where we originally got the word envy, and the old French word transitorie, which gave us the word transitory. Invidsitorius describes the feeling of being envious of another person – let's say someone who wins the lottery or gets a beautiful engagement ring from a gorgeous guy –while at the same time your envy is brief, sometimes just a few seconds, because you really care for the person who has been rewarded in ways that seem out of reach, impossible to achieve. Invidsitorious. What do you think?"

Sandy shook her head with a grimace. "Sorry. The word still implies the person is holding a knife behind the smile."

"Damn," said Helen, looking truly disappointed at Sandy's verdict.

The elevator was almost at the 55th floor and it reminded Sandy of a vow she'd made to herself of something she wanted to say to Helen the first moment she saw her.

"Why don't we work together on coming up with a new word because I've been trying to come up with something original to say, but keep coming up empty. It would be a word or phrase that describes the immense gratitude one feels when they are stuck in a Maui hospital and her associate producer ends up transforming their news piece into an amazing segment."

When Helen realized where Sandy was going, she looked away, embarrassed to hear the words of praise.

"Helen, seriously, thank you so much for covering my ass on the piece. Not only getting the story on the air, but doing it in a way that was brilliant. I got an email from Terry. He said it was one of the best pieces *24/7* has aired this year."

The two fell into each other's arms. When they parted Helen was still wiping the tears from her eyes when she asked, "Did my name come up in Terry's message?"

"No, of course not," said Sandy, without missing a beat. "And when I replied to his email, I didn't mention your name either. I knew we would have this moment together and that as long as the two of us knew the truth about what you accomplished in my absence, there would be no reason to share with anyone else what should remain a private moment between two people who care for each other."

"That was a good call," said Helen, also making sure her reply did not miss a beat. "It shows why I have so much to still learn from you."

The bell sounded, indicating their arrival on the 55th floor.

"I'm glad you're back."

"Me too."

"Stop the video there," said Sandy.

Helen hit a button on the keyboard and the video on the computer screen froze. In the middle of the screen was Bernard Rose, the assassin who tried to kill Israeli Prime Minister Bleiberg.

Sandy stared at his face long enough that it was Helen who eventually broke the silence.

"It's him, right?"

"Yeah, it's him."

"Sandy, what is it?"

"He looks different."

"Different?"

Sandy had trouble articulating exactly what she was seeing. "His face… there's something about the skin…"

"I'm not sure I understand?"

"Look, it's been years since I saw the guy, but his face… it looks… different."

"Different how?"

"Like it's been stretched."

"So are you saying it's not Bernard Rose?"

When Sandy didn't answer, Helen hit a button on the keyboard and the video began to play again.

"He looks different – but it's definitely the same guy I met at Terry's dinner party."

Helen nodded, then hit a button that paused the video again.

"Then how come Terry assigned the story of the assassin-bodyguard to another team?"

"To who?"

She handed Sandy a copy of *24/7*'s most recent story assignments.

"Bishop? The same Bishop who thinks a story about the Mideast is about Bridgeport, Connecticut?"

Helen laughed at Sandy's joke, but then quickly stifled her reaction when she realized the words weren't necessarily meant to elicit a laugh.

"Was Bishop there at Terry's house the night you met Bernard Rose?"

"Are you kidding me? Terry would never have Bishop over for dinner. Not in a million years."

Helen puzzled over what she heard while Sandy angrily crumbled the work schedule into a paper ball and threw it on the floor.

"This is bullshit. I'm the one who should be working this story." Sandy stepped on the paper ball on her way to the chair behind her desk.

"What do you mean Terry would never have Bishop over…?"

Sandy shook her head, regretting her words. "Forget what I said. I don't know what I was thinking." She then picked up the phone on her desk.

"Who are you calling?" Helen was hoping her question was rhetorical.

"I'm calling Terry. I'm going to get him to reassign the bodyguard-assassin piece to us."

Helen clenched her fist in triumph.

The in-house company phone number rang only once before an assistant in Terry's office answered.

"Terry Rawlins' office, please hold."

The phone connection then went to elevator music.

Terry's office was constantly flooded with calls, causing the assistants to stack the callers, putting everyone on hold, sometimes for minutes but at times for hours. And when one of the assistants finally did come back on the line, it was usually to only say Terry was unavailable.

Sandy waited while Helen replayed the video over and over again, looking for anything they might have missed the first dozen times they reviewed the footage. Sandy checked her watch and thought about what to do while listening to the Berlin Philharmonic perform their version of "Smoke on the Water."

Then she hung up the phone and got up from her chair.

"Are you all right?" Helen asked.

"I'm fine. But waiting on the phone is a waste of time," said Sandy. "It's 11:38 on a Wednesday. I know where to find Terry." She grabbed a jacket hanging on the door, and before Helen could say another word, Sandy was gone.

73

CHAPTER
11

Sandy stepped off the elevator at the 57th floor of the OptEnt building, the location of 24/7's main soundstage. She weaved her way through a labyrinth of narrow corridors, walking past several crew members and production personnel preparing to shoot the promos and the lead-in segments for the Sunday broadcast.

At the end of one of the hallways, Sandy came to a stairwell, and climbed three flights to the floor that housed the soundstage control room. When Sandy pushed open the solid black door, she was greeted with a punch of cold air that felt like she was venturing into the walk-in refrigerator at a slaughterhouse.

All of the equipment in the control room functioned at the optimum level only when it was kept at a cool temperature. Cool meant cold to video engineers. Sandy always wore a jacket when she knew she'd be spending some time in the room, such as when one of the intros to one of her segments was being produced.

The control room was also dark. But it wasn't too much of a challenge to navigate through the room because it was essentially divided into two areas. One area had a huge computer console running from one end of the control booth to the other. This is where the director and his crew oversaw the production on the soundstage below, their eyes to the activity on stage provided by a dozen video monitors showing the camera feeds from the set.

"Henson, what is the ETA on Ben's makeup?"

Sandy heard Terry's voice and climbed a set of four stairs to the other area of the control room, known as the Producers' Perch. It was the area of the control room where producers involved with the production had their own access to the activity on the soundstage below.

"No Henson, I heard what you said, but I'm curious as to why Ben's makeup wasn't started *before* we called the crew back from their last break?"

Terry was sitting in one of the padded chairs, staring at the monitor in his producer's console showing the feed from a stationary camera attached to the lighting grid above the soundstage. The image showed Ben Peters, one of the show's anchor/reporters, on the set being tended to by a makeup artist and a hair stylist.

"Maybe you lost your watch Henson, but it's 11:23, which means if we don't break for lunch in two hours, we go into a meal penalty with the entire crew, plus the production support staff."

At first Sandy thought Terry had noticed her when she'd stepped onto the producer's perch, but when her boss didn't acknowledge her presence she waited for an opportunity to speak up.

"What I'm saying is now would be a good time to kick Davers and Layton in the ass and tell them to get Ben camera-ready so we can start shooting."

The moment he stopped speaking into the mic, Terry pounded his fist hard on the console table. Sandy looked around and noticed that no one in the control room reacted, as if Terry's outburst was a common, daily occurrence that no longer registered on anyone's radar.

Despite the reaction of everyone else around her, Sandy was not prepared to tackle Terry while he was in such a foul mood. Less than a minute after she arrived, she was stepping back toward the small stairway down to the lower floor – then halted when she heard a voice behind her.

"Travers, you're not only alive... you're live, here, in person!"

Terry stood up from his chair and reached his arms out to greet her.

"Seriously... How are you feeling?"

"I'm doing great!"

They embraced and Terry practically squeezed the air out of her lungs before letting go. Whenever anyone asked about Terry Rawlins, Terry always said that yes, Terry deserved his place on the list as one of the toughest son of a bitches who ever worked in the TV news business, but he was also on the top of the list of people who gave the greatest hugs.

"We were really worried about you," said Terry, as he waved Sandy over to sit next to him at the producer's console.

"I appreciate the concern. But I'm doing great. Ready to get back to work. And hey, I really appreciated getting the card and the flowers."

She saw that Terry had no sooner settled back in his chair that his attention was already back on the soundstage video monitor.

"But the Range Rover you bought for Tom and I, that was completely unexpected and over the top. And I'm here to say thank you so much."

Her words got an immediate reaction from Terry. He turned to Sandy with a confused expression on his face that seemed to be just a few ticks away from the rage he would express if what he thought he'd heard was really what he heard. Sandy knew Terry's assistants handled everything in the office. She knew there was an exploitable gap between what Terry wanted done, and what his staff actually did to make it happen.

Terry burst out laughing when he saw her smile.

"Good one, Travers."

Since the first day Terry hired her as an associate producer, he had always used her last name, like he was her high school gym coach. Sandy ended up falling in love with this personality quirk when she realized that, with the exception of the talent who worked in front of the camera, Terry always used the last name of everyone who worked for him, male or female.

"You looked really scared there for a second."

"So I guess you must be doing all right if you're clever enough to bait me like that."

"Yeah, I feel great Terry. Seriously. No problem at all."

The second the last word left her mouth Terry shifted his attention back to the TV monitors on his console.

"I know you're busy Terry, but I wanted to speak to you about the bodyguard, Bernard Rose."

"Let me ask you a question – when you're out in the field with Ben, how much makeup does he use?"

It was as if Terry didn't hear a word she had said, but Sandy answered his question anyway.

"We apply it with a trowel," Sandy replied. "But it's not my face on camera, so I never rush him, and I certainly never pass judgment. All I care about is that when he's in front of the camera he asks all of the questions I've prepared for him."

"Well, right now he's wearing more makeup than my mother before the family picture at Christmas."

"Terry, are you aware that Ben is older than your mother?"

Her joke got Terry to laugh and his attention back on her. She tried to think quickly of the perfect segue to the bodyguard-assassin story, but Terry beat her to the punch.

"I gave the story to Bishop because I was trying to show everyone that I had a heart. No one around here believes I have a heart. But that's why I gave the story to Bishop."

"C'mon Terry, I have no idea why you believe people think you don't have a heart."

Terry stood up in response and shouted out, "Who in this room believes I have a heart? Raise your hand."

No one in the entire control room made a move. Terry was sitting down when a lone young woman standing nearby raised her hand. Believing she recognized her, Sandy squinted so she could get a better look.

"Is that Lauren… your granddaughter?"

"It is Lauren. She's interning with the show for a few months," answered Terry.

"Oh, my god, the last time I saw her she was… like an embryo."

When Sandy turned back to look at Terry he was staring at her with a very serious face.

"Sandy, I do have a heart. You and Tom almost died in Hawaii."

"Where did you hear that Terry? Look at me, do I look like I just died?"

"How's Tom?"

"He's fine. He just got his first opening with the *Potters Field* gallery on the east side. I was intending to invite you and Ruth to the opening, but now I'm thinking I'll wait until I can see if Bishop can make it."

Just as she expected, rather than feeling assaulted Terry giggled at her joke. A second look at Lauren then got Sandy to realize the last time she really had seen Terry's granddaughter.

"I was wrong. The last time I saw Lauren was four years ago, at your house in the Hamptons. At a wonderful dinner party being held for the newly appointed envoy to the Middle East, John Wolfenson. I don't recall Bishop being there, but do you remember who *was* there? Bernard Rose, Envoy Wolfenson's bodyguard. I actually spent some time with him out on your back porch as we smoked a couple of cigarettes. Any of this ringing a bell, Terry?"

"Yes Travers, I remember it all very well."

"Well, why don't we say you forgot all about it, and now that I reminded you of this dinner you decided to reassign the Bernard Rose story to me?" said Sandy.

"Okay, the story is yours."

She was stunned that it ended up being so easy. Then when Terry leaned closer to her and lowered his voice, Sandy realized there was something she had missed.

"I was going to speak to you later today. My office just got a call from Bishop's partner. He's in the hospital."

"What! Is he all right?"

"We're still waiting to find out," said Terry. "Apparently he was coming to work and someone on the subway attacked him."

"Jesus…"

Her verbal attacks on Bishop earlier in the morning and just a minute ago flashed across her mind and caused Sandy to cringe inside.

"Unfortunately, no matter what condition he's in, we have to move forward. So the story is yours. As long as what you said is true – you're doing all right?"

"Absolutely. You know me. I'm a power drill that runs on batteries." It was what she had said to Terry in her job interview, and it was something that she continued to repeat whenever he asked how she was doing.

"Look, you should know that Bishop had already begun working on the piece and that he ran up against a wall. With another potentially embarrassing lapse in their ranks no one in the Secret Service is willing to talk on record about how one of their own ends up being an assassin. So I'm warning you, you're going to find it hard to get traction on this story."

"I understand," said Sandy.

She stood up because Terry's gaze had shifted back to the TV monitors in front of him. But before she could leave, Terry said, "Rose sat between you and my wife at dinner. I remember him being a Red Sox fan. And I think he said something about being a swimmer, and winning some medals when he was younger. So what did I miss?"

"I'm not sure you missed anything. I mean, if you missed something, I missed it too."

He shook his head after taking in her words, still not understanding how someone he broke bread with could be a killer. Then Terry saw on his console monitor that a second makeup person had joined the two stylists still working on Ben. The sight caused the executive producer of 24/7 to fly into a rage. He stabbed at the button on his control panel and shouted in the microphone, "I've had enough, Henson. Tell everyone to stand clear so we can start shooting. And if Ben says a word, you tell him that if we don't go now, the next person who'll be working on his face will be a plastic surgeon."

Chapter 12

Sandy exited the elevator on the 55th floor, but before she proceeded to the reception area, she heard a voice she recognized, one she had not heard in years. He was in the middle of telling a joke, so Sandy waited until he was finished before she entered the lobby.

"... and finally God said, 'Saul, I'll let you win the lottery, but meet me halfway – first you need to buy a lottery ticket!'"

Helen laughed at the punch line as Sandy made her entrance, walking past the reception desk to the waiting area where her associate producer was seated on a leather couch next to Father Alan Olsen. Even before she could announce herself, Olsen stood up as if he knew exactly who had joined them, an impressive feat given he'd been blind for most of his life.

"Sandy, forgive me for just dropping in you like this."

"How did you know it was Sandy?" asked Helen.

"The combination of Neutrogena body lotion and cigarette smoke. Though I would have gladly been in the dark if it meant Sandy had kept her promise to quit her nasty habit."

Between catching the elevator from the 57th floor back to the 55th floor, Sandy had made a detour, wanting to take some time to think about her meeting with Terry while smoking a cigarette on the 56th floor, which had the best outdoor smoking area.

"I tried to quit," said Sandy, "but what can I say, I'm weak and I just love my Neutrogena body lotion."

Sandy silently mouthed Helen a thank you for taking the trouble to sit with Father Olsen before continuing, "And what about you, Alan, I see you haven't changed. Shame on you, a Catholic priest still telling Jewish jokes."

His milky white eyes locked onto Sandy's voice. "Fair enough. I will admit my own weaknesses as well. But very soon it won't matter what kind of jokes I tell."

Sandy knew it had to be something serious to cause him to pay her a visit after having no contact for several years.

"What's wrong, Alan?"

"The Vatican calls it 'Expulsion,'" he replied.

Sandy was confused because he was still wearing his collar and black frock. "You of course are well aware of the differences I have had over the church about their inability to modernize our practices. But I'm afraid I've finally pushed them so far that there will be a parting of ways. The church calls it 'Expulsion.' I'm not sure what the equivalent would be in the secular world."

"On the show they would call it termination of services before being fully vested," said Helen.

Olsen smiled. "Ah, then we are talking the same thing."

Sandy took Olsen into her office, and after having him sit at her desk, played back a digital copy of the original video profile she'd done on him for *24/7* nearly seven years ago, when she was still working her way up the ladder as an associate producer. Doing a segment on the renegade Catholic priest had been her first story pitch to end up getting the greenlight.

The broadcast of a rebel parish priest in New York City and his crusade to modernize the church had ended up reaching an audience of millions of people overnight. The controversy over his views caused a lot of internal problems within the church and many discussions in the media. And the story led to Sandy showing up on Terry's radar as a possible segment producer for the show.

"It sounds like someone I used to know," said Olsen after Sandy paused the video playback. "I hear him speak, but it feels like it's not me."

At the time she'd done her story, Father Olsen was considered a maverick within the church because he had been pushing the Catholic hierarchy to update their policies on issues he believed were completely out of touch with modern times. In the video story profiling his crusade, Olsen had railed on such issues as female priests, contraception, and even abortion.

"I'm not sure I understand," replied Sandy.

"You would have to confirm this for me, but I'm sure I have less hair and more weight. The point is that I've changed, but the voice you just played for me, that's still the same one that Rome hears, even though I'm now trying to sing a different tune."

"I'm still not sure I understand, Alan. I know the home office was upset when the story aired, but they ultimately didn't take any action. Are you telling me they're kicking you out now, over the same issues?"

"It's not over the same issues." He reached into his cassock, pulled out a photograph and set it on the desk. "I've just returned from Jerusalem. I was there to investigate claims made by parents of a young boy," said Olsen, tapping the photograph with his index finger. "Mom and Dad claimed their son was possessed and… ended up believing their claims."

"Really?" is all Sandy managed to say before picking up the photograph. The picture depicted a young boy holding a soccer ball, with long curly black hair, and a smile that was awkward because he was missing one of his maxillary incisors.

"His name is Ami," Father Olsen continued, "and he had no symptoms of mental illness. Of course with my training I ruled that out before I would even consider any other possibilities. Over a period of several weeks, I met with the boy six times and during these sessions there were things he said to me when he was not under direct control of the demon that possessed him. Some of the words were interesting, new, I guess I should admit that a few of the phrases I had heard before, but they didn't immediately register as words that came from the Bible. The more I looked into what I heard him say, the more troubled I became."

She reached out for his hand, but the moment she touched him, Olsen flinched. Normally he would not have reacted in such a way, but as he was relating the details of his recent experiences with Ami, he had almost disengaged from the reality of being in the office with Sandy.

"I'm sorry, I didn't mean to…"

"No, forgive me Sandy. I am… I have not been myself for a while." He reached out to her and this time they clasped hands.

"Alan, are you all right?"

"I'm mentally sound. That's the answer I'm sure you no doubt want to hear right now. But it's important to me that you believe my answer because I've come here for a reason."

"Go ahead. Tell me why you're here."

Without even catching his breath, Father Olsen said, "I believe that if your show did a story on the situation I've encountered, it would expose what is happening and change everything. Exposure is the last thing these people want."

Sandy wanted to release his hand, not because she didn't care, but because she realized the little comfort she was providing would not be up to the task confronting her.

"There were three phrases that continued to come up whenever Ami was lucid. One was 'The Restrainer'…"

"I'm sorry, I've never heard the term." She let go of his hand. "Let me grab my notebook and write this down."

Father Olsen waited just a few seconds before continuing, "Thessalonians 2:6—'For the secret power of lawlessness is already at work; the Restrainer who now holds Satan back will continue to do so 'til the Restrainer is taken out of the way.' Once the Restrainer is eliminated, Satan will be walking amongst us. The Restrainer's death would unleash Armageddon."

"Alan, I can't go to my boss quoting scripture when I'm pitching him a story."

"Of course. Yes. Absolutely. Let me start over. Ami also repeatedly spoke the words – Har Megiddo."

"Har Megiddo is the place the Bible declares will be the setting for the final battle between Good and Evil."

"Yes Sandy, very good."

But he did not pick up on the tone of skepticism in Sandy's voice when she'd answered.

"Ami kept repeating that I needed to go to Har Megiddo. So I finally went. You may know recent excavations there have discovered ancient Christian texts known as the Diei Demonici…"

"Diei Demonici?"

"Diei Demonic translated from Latin is *Demon Days*. The phrase is a reference to what we commonly refer to as the *End Days*."

He waited for her to react but when she didn't he sighed.

"You're so silent I can hear you roll your eyes."

"I'm sorry, Father… but as I said before, I can't go to my boss and pitch him this. You understand, right?"

"I'm not doing a very good job of explaining myself. Everything I've learned since the attempted exorcism on this boy has led me to believe that we're in danger. Something is happening. Right now."

"So you did an exorcism on the boy. How did that work out?"

"It's the reason Rome is using to throw me out of the church. I did not have authorization."

"I'm sorry. How did the exorcism turn out?"

"It was not complete. Before I could continue with the rites of exorcism the boy managed to flee the place where we were performing the ritual."

The door to Sandy's office opened and Helen stepped in. "I'm really sorry to interrupt. Sandy, Terry is in my office and he says it's urgent and he needs to speak with you." Helen turned to the priest. "I'm so sorry, Father Olsen…"

She felt bad, but there was so much to do. Sandy had sent Helen a text… a 911… that she knew was her cue to interrupt a meeting.

Olson stood up from his chair and said, "Please... there's no need to apologize. I'm the uninvited guest who has overstayed his welcome."

"Alan..."

"Forgive me. That did not come out at all..."

He didn't finish his sentence. Instead he regrouped by reaching into his pocket, withdrawing a business card, and placing it on the desk next to the picture of Ami.

"The number on the card will be good for another week, until I vacate my office at the church. I know how this all sounds. But look at me. Don't I look like the same man you profiled years ago?"

Sandy looked over at Helen, who was waiting at the door to escort Olsen out. She was there because Sandy had used her mobile phone to text Helen the word "stop." It was their agreed upon code word for Helen to break up a meeting with a fake emergency.

"You've lost some hair, and you've put on some weight," said Sandy, "but yes, you look like the same man."

"Please, Sandy, can we talk again?"

"Of course, Alan. I'll definitely call you."

CHAPTER
13

Sandy's shock and concern was genuine when she first heard of Bishop's mishap. Nevertheless, she and Helen ended up spending the rest of the day scrambling to get on top of the story Terry had re-assigned to her. It was only when riding on the subway back to her apartment did Sandy realized she had not once thought about Bishop.

She pulled out her mobile phone to order some flowers, but the subway train was travelling underground and she couldn't get a connection.

"Authentic" was a word Sandy often used as the litmus test for anyone she talked to for the show. She looked for any signs in their behavior that would indicate the person wasn't authentic. Not thinking of Bishop's wellbeing during the entire day made her wonder how she would do on her own litmus test.

At her stop the subway train's doors opened and Sandy exited along with the other passengers. She immediately scanned the platform's surroundings before heading toward the stairs leading to the street. Sandy called the quick search for any potential dangers her "paranoid pan." It was a tactic she initiated years ago on her first visit to the Big Apple when she was just a teenager. Even though Sandy had an aura of self-confidence that led people to believe she had grown up in the city, she came off like a native New Yorker only because she had spent all of her life working to be one. Sandy had in fact been born in Connecticut, but spent all of her childhood in Morristown, New Jersey. And as long as she could remember all she could think about was being a journalist, dreaming of the day she would be part of the city that had always felt like it was in her life blood.

It was a few minutes past eight pm when Sandy's scan of her platform surroundings failed to pick up anything unusual. Walking with the rest of the passengers to the stairway, Sandy stopped before taking the first step.

Her eyes caught sight of a man on the other side of the tracks. He was standing like a statue on the edge of the platform, with a vapid look in his eyes, but his lips were moving as if he was talking to himself, just like many of the mentally ill homeless people Sandy encountered throughout the city.

And yet this one was different, prompting Sandy to veer away from the stairwell. She walked across the station platform with her eyes focused on the man across the way. When she recognized the clothes and the features on the man's face, it was only shock that caused her to lose her voice for a few seconds before reclaiming it.

"Tom! Tom! Tom!"

She waited for a reaction, but when the man didn't seem to hear her, Sandy tried shouting again, but her yelling was suppressed by the noise of a train pulling into the station.

Sandy's feet shifted nervously in place as she anxiously kept an eye out for the man who looked like Tom as he at first was swallowed up the debarking passengers, then seemed to disappear altogether with the crowd of people boarding the subway train. She quickly scanned the windows of the train as it left the station, but couldn't locate the man she had just seen seconds earlier. And after the train departed Sandy saw the platform of deserted.

She rushed from the subway station to the street, then ran the next three blocks to her apartment building. Sandy burst into the apartment screaming Tom's name but was greeted with silence. Tom had always been good at keeping her informed of his whereabouts. When his work wasn't going well, Tom would often slip away for a walk around the neighborhood to clear his head. Sometimes during a particularly acute fit of creative frustration, Tom would disappear for a longer period of time, but he would always let her know he had left with a note attached with a magnet to the fridge or a voice message recorded on their answering machine.

Sandy rushed over to their answering machine on the bar and saw there were no messages. She hurried into the kitchen and checked out the refrigerator door -- Nothing. She called out Tom's name again, but the apartment was empty.

95

Despite her inclination to go back to the subway station, she stayed at the apartment hoping Tom would call or show up. Two hours went by as Sandy ended up pacing back and forth in front of the wall of glass in her living room, ignoring the grumbling noises coming from her stomach from not having a bite to eat since noon.

As she was standing out on the balcony overlooking the street below, Sandy finally heard the noise of the front door opening. She rushed in from the balcony.

"Tom?"

"Hey!"

The single word he shouted out was loud and upbeat, certainly not contrite or low key like was hiding something.

Sandy rushed across the room and was able to cut him off before he had even moved more than a dozen feet from the entryway. She glanced at his clothes, and confirmed he was wearing the same clothes she saw the man wearing in the subway. Her eyes quickly moved to take in her fiancé's face which Sandy was surprised to discover no longer looked like someone who was lost and aimless. In fact everything about Tom as he stood a few feet away from Sandy had any resemblance to the disheveled, hopeless looking homeless man she saw in the subway.

"I'm so sorry. I didn't leave a note or anything. I only realized that just this minute as I was on the elevator. I'm so sorry."

He looked like her Tom, the one she had been with for seven years. She rushed up and almost knocked him down when she embraced him.

"What a nice greeting," said Tom. "I'm going to apologize more often if this is what's on the other side."

"I'm just glad you're home."

Just now when I was walking back did I realize how I had completely forgotten to let you know where I was."

She let him go and stepped back. Sandy wanted to take more look at him before launching into what she wanted to say.

Even with a second look, she could not believe the man standing in front of her was the same man she saw hours earlier in the subway. But there was enough of a resemblance that Sandy had no inclination to forego mentioning the incident.

"I'm so happy to see you because I thought I saw you earlier tonight," she said. "I was coming home on the subway, and when I got off at my stop I saw you, across the tracks…"

Tom furrowed his brow as if what she was saying was not possible. Despite the look, she continued.

"You were sitting there waiting for the train and... well, you looked like... something was wrong." Tom had begun to smile, causing her to struggle with the right words to explain exactly what she saw. "You looked... upset. No, you looked… devastated. You were mumbling to yourself… like you had been traumatized by…"

She stopped before saying what she wanted to say -- "Like a bomb had gone off nearby" – because Sandy suddenly remembered that Tom had actually gone through something similar.

"Really? You mean like a helicopter accident…"

She didn't know how to respond. It wasn't as if Tom was challenging her with an intense look of denial on his face. He still had a smile on his face as if everything she had been saying was a long joke and he was waiting for her to deliver the punch line.

So she laughed… as if he had delivered the punch line to her joke. Tom stepped around her and entered the apartment.

"Hey, I know it sounds crazy, but I definitely saw someone that looked just you."

"When did this happen?"

"A little after eight o'clock."

Tom didn't respond as he made his way to the kitchen. Sandy stopped him just as he was about to open the refrigerator.

"Are you all right?"

The corners of his mouth fell a bit before he answered. "No, I'm not all right. In the mail today we got a bill from the car rental place in Hawaii. Even though they promised they weren't going to apply a late charge to our credit card, they did it anyway. I was so pissed, I just had to get out of here and go for a walk."

She studied his face for a twitching eyelid, a trembling lip, any hint of the anguish she had witnessed in the subway. And though something was definitely different about the way Tom looked, she couldn't put her finger on it.

Tom grabbed a coke from the refrigerator and shut the door.

"Where would you go this late at night?"

"Well, first it started out as a walk around the block, then I ended up grabbing the subway to Central Park. I found a spot on the lawn and laid down for a bit." He took a swig from his coke and was swallowing when his eyes lit up. "I almost forgot, they were shooting *Law and Order* near the reservoir. I stuck around to watch them and thought about you. You would have loved it."

Sandy loved all the *Law and Order* shows. With her busy schedule it was one of the few quality shows she could watch because there was no continuing storyline. And over the years a lot of her friends she went to school with had bit parts on the show. Tom knew all of this, but for some reason she suspected he was only telling her this to change the direction of their conversation.

When she didn't respond, Tom turned to leave, but she grabbed his arm and stopped him.

"I'm serious here," said Sandy.

Tom stared at her expressionless for a few seconds before asking, "Then why are you smiling?"

She couldn't help herself. After a few seconds of just staring at him, her face broke into a smile. No matter what was going on with Tom, he at least had not lost his memory. Maybe he had even acquired a better sense of humor since the accident.

But instead of following up on their connection, Tom turned to walk away.

"Where are you going?"

"To bed. My mad wanderings today have made me feel like I'm going to collapse any second. I'm still taking the drugs from the accident. Maybe that's why I feel so tired."

He walked out of the kitchen and toward their bedroom without Sandy saying a word. She stood there, next to the refrigerator wondering if he would even notice she had not said a word and was not following him.

The noise of Tom opening their bedroom door and closing it behind him was her answer.

CHAPTER
14

The early morning sun peeking through the window in their bedroom allowed Sandy the opportunity to get a good look at Tom as he slept. She was able to clearly see what she first noticed last night -- the skin on his face was perfectly smooth. It was as if during the emergency surgery in the Maui hospital the doctors who saved his life had also decided to slip in a facelift for kicks.

Sandy wondered if the skin on Tom's face felt as different as it appeared. She had been dying to find out the answer, but spent the last hour working up the courage to touch Tom's face.

Then her alarm clock went off.

Tom's eyes flashed open. He caught a flash of Sandy's finger hovering over his face before her finger moved away to silence her alarm clock.

"What's going on?"

"What?"

Sandy rolled back over, now laying on top of Tom.

"Your finger was hovering over my face."

She then did what she had been dying to do all night – touched Tom's face with her hand, and covered her action by saying, "I was going to wake you up by doing this…"

Sandy then kissed Tom passionately.

When they broke from their kiss, she asked him, "Any objections?"

"None." He moved to kiss her again, but stopped. "Wait. I have one. Why are you up so early?"

"I'm sorry," said Sandy. "I forgot to tell you last night that Helen and I are flying to D.C. today. Remember the bodyguard who tried to assassinate the Israeli Prime Minister… the story we heard over the radio in Hawaii?"

"How could I forget?"

"Well, Terry assigned it to me."

"You're kidding me? After almost being killed in a helicopter accident, and on the first day back to work, Terry has no problem assigning a major story for you to cover?"

"I'm not sure I'm getting your point," said Sandy.

She expected Tom to react in the same way he had in the past about Terry's lack of empathy, but her fiancé was not amused at all.

"Are you all right?"

She couldn't believe his question. Ever since that night when Tom talked about his N.D.E. Sandy had run the exact same thought at least a hundred times through her brain, but the context for the question was to get the answer from Tom, not her.

"Are you talking about me?"

"It's just that after what you said last night, about seeing a guy in the subway who looked exactly like me, it got me to worry about you.

"Honey, I went through dozens of scans of my head, but no one did a thing to you. Maybe they missed something."

"Tom, I'm fine. I appreciate your concern. But I'm fine." Sandy looked over at the clock, and seeing the time allowed her to roll off of Tom, and this time he did not stop her.

"Shit, look at the time. I need to start getting ready."

Sandy hopped off the bed to the bathroom.

"How long will you be gone?"

She had started the water running in the shower and never heard Tom's question.

The 24/7 car service picked up Sandy thirty minutes later in the front of their apartment building. Helen was waiting in the back seat with all the research they had accumulated in the last 24 hours about everybody who was involved with the assassination attempt in Tel Aviv. Together they reviewed the information on the way to JFK airport and on their flight to Washington D.C.

After they landed at Dulles airport, Sandy tried one last time to get in touch with the Under Secretary for Political Affairs, Robert Davis, to discuss the assassination attempt in Israel by Bernie Rose. Her latest phone call went the same way the previous attempts had gone, with no chance of contact and Davis' assistant sounding as if she was reading from a prepared script – "Robert Davis, the Under Secretary for Political Affairs, has a press release for all media outlets on the State Department's official website. Beyond the press release, Mr. Davis will have no further comment on the assassination attempt in Tel Aviv. Are there any more questions?"

The only question Sandy had was whether Robert Davis was behaving in a dodgy way because of the specific story she was pursuing… or because he was being dodgy for personal reasons.

Before she met Tom, Sandy had dated Robert Davis.

It happened at a point when she was not the only one who had noticed his attractive qualities. TIME Magazine had just declared Davis one of The 50 Most Promising American Leaders Under Age 40.

Some people absorb such moments in the media spotlight as an accomplish they had not only hoped for, but perhaps had orchestrated.

Robert Davis was not one of those people. This was something Sandy found as an attractive quality when she and Davis began seeing each other. But somehow this attractive quality might have been the foundation behind what she witnessed in the ensuing months – Davis suffering a complete mental meltdown. Any deeper thoughts Sandy had about the situation were basically impossible due to the brief duration of their relationship, which ended up being much shorter than the time and energy the two spent breaking up.

Gaining access to the Department of State without an appointment would be difficult. Sandy had figured an approach and contacted her college roommate, Gwen Parsons. Gwen had gone straight from her graduation at Penn State to a junior advisor position at one of the top lobbyist firms in Washington D.C. The fact that Gwen's father was the major partner at the company had something to do with her entry-level job and her quick sprint up the company ladder. When Sandy called for help, Gwen had no trouble booking a meeting at the Truman building with an official at the State department, listing Sandy as one of her colleagues from the firm who would be at the meeting.

Sandy accompanied Gwen through the ground floor security checkpoint of the Truman building, then they both rode one of the building's 43 elevators to the 4th floor.

Gwen exited the elevator for the scheduled meeting, but Sandy stayed onboard and hit the button for the 7th floor. After the doors opened, she made her way to the floor's designated smoking area.

CHAPTER

15

Robert Davis had a lit cigarette in his mouth as he exited the doors to the Truman building's 7th floor smoking area. He was able to get a few relaxing puffs in before he heard a voice from the other side of the courtyard.

"Hey Robbie, I knew it was only a matter of time before you showed up here."

Davis had missed seeing Sandy standing in the shadows near some tables set up for people to use during their meal break.

"Sandy? What are you doing? Are you stalking me?"

He immediately regretted his choice of words.

"Me… stalking you?"

Sandy took a drag from her cigarette and waited for him to explain dodging all her calls. Davis turned away from her and continued to smoke his cigarette, as if nothing out of the ordinary was happening. He knew there were CCTV cameras positioned all around the smoking courtyard, feeding images to a security room on the basement floor of the building. He had visited the department himself and marveled at how the wall of monitors looked like the security control room at a major Las Vegas casino.

"You probably thought you were being clever here, but the entire courtyard is lined with cameras. So we need to pretend that we just politely said hello to each other before going our separate ways."

For a few moments, Sandy remained silent, allowing Davis to think what he had said was going to allow him to escape.

She then shouted across the courtyard, "I'm working the Tel Aviv assassination story for 24/7. When I was assigned the story I was thrilled because I knew I had a great source at the State Department. Someone who owed me personally... big time."

He shook his head in disbelief, and nervously took a long drag from his cigarette before responding.

"Maybe you didn't hear me," said Davis. "My people know about our prior relationship. If anyone suspects I'm your source about what happened in Tel Aviv, I will get the full rectal."

"I very much doubt they know everything about our past relationship, Robbie. So either you start talking about what you know about Rose and Tel Aviv... or get ready to practice coughing with a rubber glove up your ass."

"Sands, listen to me. I promise, I'll make good on your marker the next round," said Davis, staring in the direction of the flower garden running parallel to the east courtyard wall. "There's too many eyes on what's happening right now."

She took her time with an answer, knowing the longer she remained silent, the more pressure it would put on him to cooperate.

"Here's my problem. If I go back to New York without anything new on this story, I'll feel the compulsion to pitch Terry something else to make up for my failure. And the only other story I can think of to pitch is about a high-ranking State Department official with a credibility problem due to his past inability to handle rejection in his personal life. I think Terry will go for the pitch after seeing the security video I have of this State Department official breaking and entering into a woman's apartment, and then running around naked as he performs lewd..."

"Shut Up!"

He screamed the words so loud, a bird resting on one of the courtyard tables was startled enough to take flight. Davis angrily threw his cigarette down on the ground and stomped on the butt as if it was a live cockroach.

Sandy waited in silence, confident she had finally gotten through to him.

"What do you want to know?"

"Why won't any of my contacts at the Secret Service talk?"

Before answering, Davis pulled another cigarette from his pack and lit it up.

"They won't talk because it turns out Rose had a lot of mental problems, and the professional attention he received was not standard protocol."

"What do you mean?"

Davis turned in another direction as if his interest was the spectacular view of George Washington University.

"When Rose was suspended, standard protocol would have been for him to consult with a staff therapist. But Rose was assigned a shrink from the private sector. No one at the Secret Service will admit how or why this happened. A short month later, Rose was given a clean bill of health from his private sector shrink, just in time for Rose to fly unrestricted to Tel Aviv and wind up standing outside the U.S. embassy waving his service weapon."

"So who was the private sector therapist who ended up treating Rose?" She watched Davis exhale a thick cloud of smoke before responding.

"You'll have to go to someone else for an answer. The shrink's name was redacted from all the briefing reports that came across my desk."

Davis looked at his watch and saw he had gone past the maximum time he normally spent on his cigarette break. If they took too much longer, the security camera feed of him standing in the courtyard would be flagged by the computer program and there would be a standard precautionary search of the footage for any behavioral discrepancies.

"Are we done here?"

"I hope not. If you walk away now, we're both screwed," shouted Sandy. "I can't go back to Terry with only what you've said so far."

There was silence for a few seconds, long enough for Sandy to note the noise of traffic in the near distance.

"Everyone is assuming the target was the Israeli Prime Minister because Rose was guarding John Wolfenson for years and could have killed him anytime, But the truth was that John Wolfenson, the envoy to the Middle East was really Rose's target."

"How do you know this?"

"The C.I.A.'s report on the incident makes a big deal about Rose contacting Wolfenson prior to the Tel Aviv assassination attempt. But the Middle East Envoy refuses to meet with him, and two days later, Rose shows up in Israel, in front of the U.S. embassy, packing his service revolver."

Davis waited for his words to sink in, before throwing his last cigarette into an ashtray, and walking back toward the building.

"If I find out you've lied to me, or you knew more than what you've given me, you won't be happy. The security video I have of you wearing my panties on your head while spray painting nasty words on my apartment walls will be going straight to the sleaziest Internet site I can find. Are we clear?"

Davis raised his hand over his head to acknowledge her threat before he slipped back into the building.

Sandy sat down on the bench and took the last bite of her sandwich. She would need to stay in the courtyard for a few more minutes, but was satisfied that she got everything she could from her source at the State Department.

Chapter 16

For the last hour, Sandy and Helen had been watching the gathering outside the main gate continue to grow. The two women were in their rental car across the street from the Capshaw Capital Preschool, waiting for the classes to let out for the day. Parents, nannies, and guardians had been arriving in droves to pick up their children attending the expensive and exclusive school located near the capital building. Julie Rose, the widow of the assassin in Tel Aviv, had their son attending Capshaw Capital Preschool. Sandy and Helen were waiting and hoping Julie Rose would appear in person to pick up her son.

"I'm embarrassed to admit the bulk of my homework on the assassination in Tel Aviv focused on the Israeli Prime Minister, not the Quartet Envoy to the Middle East."

Helen made this confession in response to Sandy's update about what she had learned from her contact at the Truman Center.

"Don't be embarrassed," Sandy replied. "Only a few people besides foreign policy wonks know about the existence of the Quartet Envoy or have even heard the name John Wolfenson. Let me tell you all I know…"

Helen whipped out a notepad and pen from her jacket, and in less than five seconds was ready to take notes. Unlike many of her millennial cohorts, she was not a tech geek. In fact, her Luddite leanings almost prevented Helen from making it past the first round of job interviews with Sandy when she applied for the position of associate producer with *24/7*.

"If you're looking for someone who can break apart a smart phone and reassemble it in the dark, I can give you my roommate's Facebook address," said Helen during that initial interview. Even though Sandy had intended to hire an associate producer who could compensate for her lack of hi-tech skills, she went with Helen because they both seemed to be rowing in the same direction. When Sandy told Helen the good news, and let her in on why she'd been hired, Helen's response was to say, "You know there's an app you could have downloaded that would have made sure you and your new associate producer were always rowing in the same direction."

"John Wolfenson became the youngest head of the World Bank at 34 years old. Before that achievement, his bona fides included being a member of the Trilateral Commission and the Council on Foreign Relations. Nineteen months ago he took over for Tony Blair as the Quartet's Special Envoy."

Though Helen knew little about Wolfenson, she knew the basic history of the Quartet's Special Envoy. The diplomatic position was created in 2002 in Madrid, with the singular purpose of helping to ease tensions in the Middle East.

"But here's what shocked me," said Helen, "the Quartet is made up of representatives from the United States, the European Union, Russia and the United Nations. Hard to believe that these four groups, who have never agreed on anything, somehow agreed on appointing a special envoy to the Middle East."

Sandy laughed, then asked Helen, "Don't tell me you've become one of those conspiracy nut jobs?"

"Never," answered Helen immediately. "But in the case of the Quartet, the diplomatic office hasn't been a feature of conspiracy theories because it's mostly been a punchline since its inception."

"You're right," said Sandy. "But that's changed when John Wolfenson was appointed as the new envoy. He's been working earnestly for years to bring peace to the region. And before Bernard Rose came along, it looked like Wolfenson was *that close* to bringing Israel and seven other countries in the Middle East together to sign a peace treaty."

"Wow, he must be quite the guy. You know him. What's his secret?" asked Helen.

Sandy shook her head immediately.

"I've never claimed to know John Wolfenson. I've met him, spent some time with him. Look, he's no Martin Luther King. He's not even a Ronald Reagan. John Wolfenson is not who I would pick out of a line of suspects if I was being asked to finger the guy who could bring peace to the Middle East."

"And yet he may pull it off," said Helen. "So what's your theory?"

She thought long and hard before answering. And in the silence, the attention of both women stayed on the crowd of people waiting outside the preschool. They were keeping a close eye on two men who they suspected were connected to Julie Rose and her son. It was not their appearance that gave them away; both were wearing the same type of clothes as the other fathers milling outside the main gate – jeans, sneakers, and a sports shirt. The difference was in their behavior. Neither seemed interested in mingling with the other parents, their attention focused entirely on the activity happening beyond the front gate of the school.

"I met a young woman at Terry's house in the Hamptons," said Sandy, finally responding to Helen's question. "This woman was part of Wolfenson's office staff, not a career government worker, but someone who was really proud of what they were all doing on behalf of the Quartet Envoy. She wanted to show me a picture of her and Wolfenson posing with the President of the United States and the German Chancellor. But when she got out her mobile phone, and pulled up the photograph, it turns out the envoy wasn't in the photograph she wanted to show me. She was there, standing between the President of the United States and the German Chancellor – but no Wolfenson."

"It was like he had become invisible," interrupted Helen.

Sandy looked over at her co-producer and nodded.

"Yeah. Exactly. If Wolfenson gets this peace treaty to fly, it's because he's able to become invisible. He allows the other people around him to shine."

Sandy suddenly sat up in her seat. "I think that's her..." She raised a pair of binoculars to her eyes and looked in the direction of the preschool.

A woman wearing sweat pants, a jacket over her blouse and a Boston Red Sox baseball cap pulled down over her face was crossing the street toward the main gate.

"Yeah, that's Julie Rose for sure."

The two women quickly exited their rental car. They immediately crossed the street before moving in the direction of the pre-school. As they approached the main gate, Sandy saw a young boy move from the supervision of his teacher only to be swept up into the arms of his mother a few feet later.

Sandy made note of the boy's appearance – pageboy haircut, brown hair, brown eyes, black corduroy pants, and a Red Sox tee-shirt underneath a light blue jacket. But then her view became obstructed.

"Excuse me... is there a problem?"

It was one of the two bodyguards Sandy and Helen had been watching. Sandy ignored the question posed by the security guy, keeping her attention on Julie Rose, who was about six feet away, still embracing her son.

"Mrs. Rose, can we speak with you for a moment?"

Julie Rose heard Sandy's overture, and it caused her to tighten her grip around her son before responding.

"What do you want?"

Sandy made sure her answer was both low in volume and serene in tone, "We just want to speak with you."

"About what?"

"We're producers for the TV show *24/7,*" said Sandy, choosing all of her words carefully, hoping to avoid alarming the young boy. "We want to talk to you about what happened recently in Tel Aviv."

Julie Rose stood up while still holding her son's hand. "I've been told not to talk about the situation with anyone."

"Told not to talk by who, the Secret Service?" Helen followed up her question by nodding to the two men who were standing between them.

"These two gentlemen are not Secret Service agents," said Julie. "Mr. Randal and Mr. Lloyd are part of a private security firm my lawyer hired to look after me… and my son."

Helen was surprised. Every inch of the beef standing in front of them screamed Secret Service agents.

"And this cute boy is your son?"

Sandy held her hands out to her side, clearly showing the bodyguards she was not armed, and no threat to their client.

"Yes, this is Bradley," Julie immediately answered with a surprising amount of good cheer.

"Hey, look, your shoe is untied," said Sandy. She used her observation to justify quickly stepping around one of the bodyguards, then falling to one knee in front of the boy.

"It's all right," said Julie, waving off the bodyguard as he reacted to Sandy's security breach.

"I love your shirt, Bradley," said Sandy as she carefully tied the boy's shoes.

"We're not losers. We're the Red Sox. We won the World Series." The boy spoke the words in an adorable but robotic way, as if all he was doing was mimicking what he had been taught… by someone who was a Red Sox fan.

Sandy laughed and then said, "I know your daddy was a big Red Sox fan."

"You knew Bernie?" asked Julie.

"No, I didn't know your husband," said Sandy as she stood up. "But I met him a few years ago at a dinner party hosted by my boss at *24/7*. I got a chance to talk with Mr. Rose for awhile. We were both smoking outside."

Julie shook her head, acknowledging her husband's smoking habit.

"Honestly, I find it shocking… unbelievable really, that the same man I spent time with that night could be the same man responsible for…"

She stopped talking when Julie Rose picked up her son and turned away from her.

"Look, we're so sorry to disturb you during this difficult time," said Sandy. "We understand if you're not interested in talking to us. And if that's the case, I promise you, we won't bother you again."

She waited, but when Sandy did not get a reply, she motioned to Helen, and both women turned to walk away. But before they could even take a step, Julie finally responded.

"You said you work for *24/7*. Does that mean you know Ben Peters?"

When Sandy turned back around, she didn't bother to restrain her excitement at Julie Rose's question.

"Not only do I know Ben Peters, he's been pretty much the only reporter I've worked with since I became a field producer at *24/7*."

"Bernie watched your show every week," said Julie. "His favorite reporter on the show was Ben Peters. Bernie would always say that Ben never took any crap from anyone he was covering for a story. There's a picture of my husband and Ben... hanging in our living room."

Julie choked on the final few words before looking away.

"Mommy, are you all right?"

She wiped her eyes before responding to her son.

"Yes, honey, Mommy is fine." She offered Bradley a reassuring smile before turning her attention back to Sandy.

"I do have something to say about what happened with Bernie. Things I told the Secret Service, before… Tel Aviv, but they didn't want to hear it. I know my husband would want people to know what happened, and if he had a choice in the matter, he'd want to tell his story to Ben Peters."

Sandy stepped closer to Julie and her son so she could lower her voice. "Here's how it works – we're the two people you speak to first to tell your story. Then Ben comes in later to interview you on camera. But that doesn't mean you can't talk to Ben on the phone right now if that will make you feel good about trusting us to tell your story."

"So you're saying I could talk to Ben Peters right now?"

"I can have him on the phone in less than an hour, if you agree to speak with us about what happened with your husband," said Sandy.

Julie Rose fixed her eyes on Sandy, obviously trying to judge whether Sandy was someone she could trust. During this intense, silent scrutiny, which only lasted a few seconds, Sandy made it a point not to look away.

"We're in that red SUV parked up the street. Follow us to our house," said Julie. "We'll park in the driveway. But you need to keep going up the street, then turn and park in the alleyway behind the house."

"Okay, sounds good," said Sandy.

"And I'll be able to talk with Ben Peters?"

Sandy nodded confidently, "We'll have Ben Peters on the phone before we step into the house. How does that sound?"

Julie Rose's response was to tap the shoulder of one of the bodyguards, "Mr. Lloyd, can you escort us to our car? And let's allow these women to follow us home."

She then lowered Bradley to the sidewalk so mother and son could walk together behind the two bodyguards, who led the way to their waiting vehicle.

The SUV with Julie Rose and her son pulled into the paved driveway of a two-story Tudor townhouse, located just a few miles from the Capshaw Capitol Preschool. The bodyguards hopped out of the vehicle and began scanning the perimeter.

Sandy locked eyes with one of the bodyguards as she drove past the home in the rental car.

"I checked for Bernard Rose's permanent residence and came up empty," said Helen. "Either they are staying with friends or family, or the house isn't listed in Bernard or Julie Rose's name."

"Well at least that explains why there is no media camping out in front of the house," said Sandy.

Halfway down the street, she turned right, and in less than a hundred yards turned right again into an alleyway that ran behind the townhouses on the block.

They drove past a man walking his bullmastiff dog, and then parked in the alleyway, next to a waist-high wooden fence running around the perimeter of the townhouse. Julie Rose was waiting in the backyard doorway, while one of her bodyguards stood on the paver stone pathway cutting through the middle of the garden.

Helen handed Sandy her mobile phone before they got out of the car. "Ben's on the line, ready to go…"

The assassin's widow was pacing in the laundry room as she talked on Helen's mobile phone. The two producers from 24/7 waited patiently on the backyard stoop for the outcome of the phone conversation.

Ben Peter's voice was loud enough that Sandy could catch some of what he was saying to Julie. As a player in the journalism game for over 50 years, Ben had become one of the godheads in the industry, a legend in his own time. Only those who actually worked with him every day knew the real human being that existed underneath the marble veneer the rest of the public saw. But what Sandy saw every day made her confident Ben Peters would have no trouble closing the deal.

"I really appreciate you talking to me. Bernie would have loved to have met you. I'm also sure he would have appreciated his story being part of your show."

Julie had a look of relief on her face as she handed the phone back to Helen.

"Thank you for following through with what you promised. Please, the both of you, come in."

Sandy and Helen followed the assassin's widow down the hallway leading from the backyard toward the front of the townhouse. They heard the sounds of a cartoon show coming from the second floor. When they first arrived, Julie had told them that Bradley was in his bedroom watching TV with his nanny. When they came upon the family room, there was no doubt that it was the permanent residence of the assassin. One of the walls in the room was covered floor to ceiling with framed photographs of him.

"Can I get you something to drink?"

Sandy looked over at Helen before responding, "Thank you, Mrs. Rose, we're fine."

"Please, sit down."

Before taking Julie up on her invitation, Sandy noted that one of the bodyguards was standing near the front windows facing the street, peering through a crack in the drawn curtains. The other bodyguard remained in the back of the house, monitoring the yard facing the alleyway.

She sat down in one of two leather club chairs placed next to each other. While Julie Rose took a seat in the other leather chair, Helen drifted to the wall adorned with the framed pictures.

"How do you want to start?" asked Julie.

Sandy pulled out a tape recorder from her jacket. "If you don't mind, we'd like to record this. It helps us when we plan our story."

Julie nodded, but Sandy would need more. She hit the record button on the audio digital recorder and placed it on a coffee table that separated the two leather chairs.

"This is Sandy Travis, and we're beginning an audio interview with Julie Rose in her Washington

D.C. townhouse. She is aware that this interview is being recorded and will acknowledge her agreement by any words she chooses to use, but if you don't mind, Ms. Rose, can you include the words, 'I'm aware of this recording device and agree to have this interview recorded."

"You can both call be Julie." Sandy and Helen smiled, but remained silent, waiting for Julie Rose to say more. "Sorry... Yes, I'm aware I'm being recorded and agree to this interview being recorded. Is that all right?"

"Close enough," said Sandy, pausing long enough to proceed smoothly to the next point in their agenda. "If you feel comfortable, I think it would be best if our discussion was just between the three of us." Sandy motioned then nodded toward the bodyguard standing in the family room.

"Mr. Lloyd, can you give us some time alone?"

"Yes, ma'am," answered the bodyguard. "Do you mind if I keep watch from your master bedroom?"

"That will be fine," answered Julie.

Sandy waited until the bodyguard had disappeared up the stairs to the second floor of the townhouse.

"So, how are you holding up?"

"I'm all right. More angry than upset," answered Julie.

Sandy could not help observing that the assassin's widow looked neither angry nor upset as she said the words. In Sandy's experience, there were three basic emotions exhibited by people who had recently suffered the tragic loss of a loved one and Julie Rose had mentioned two of them. The other was confusion.

"When you heard the news about your husband, where were you?"

"I was here. Actually, in the kitchen. My girlfriend had called me, frantic, telling me to turn on the news. I couldn't really understand what she was saying, but I heard the words 'Tel Aviv' and my husband's name, and I hung up the phone, afraid to turn on the TV. When I did, the moment I saw what was being reported... I knew it was Bernie. He was the one... the assassin."

"How did you know it was your husband?" asked Sandy.

"I just knew. You can barely see his face in the videos, but I knew it was Bernie. I knew it was my husband, lying there."

Even though Julie continued to respond to her questions without showing much emotion, Sandy took her time before proceeding.

"Did you know what husband planned on doing?"

"No. Of course not. But I did know something was wrong with him. Weeks before I had tried to help him, but everything I said, everything I did, only seemed to drive him further away from me. I finally got so desperate that I decided to break the wall of silence."

"Wall of silence?" asked Sandy

"There's a code the Secret Service agents live by – you not only guard the person, you guard their privacy as well. Every agent honors this, never sharing with anyone on the outside whatever is seen or heard on duty. Every agent, Bernie included, knew it and lived it. But over the years I came to understand that this wall of silence didn't just apply to those who were guarded, but also to the agents themselves. No matter what happened, no one was supposed to let the outside world know…"

Julie abruptly fell silent, and Sandy at first thought she was trying to muster the courage to proceed. But then she realized Julie was being distracted by Helen, who had continued to look at the pictures hanging on the family room wall.

"I know what you must be thinking, but my husband wasn't like Martin and Haynes," Julie said to Helen.

The framed photo Helen had been looking at showed Bernard Rose and two other men sitting in the corner booth of a pub raising glass mugs filled to the brim with ale.

"What's been written in the newspaper is not true. Bernie was never much of a drinker. Certainly he was nothing like those two. Bernie would tell me all the time how the two of them were drunk a lot."

That her actions had attracted the attention of Julie Rose right in the middle of Sandy's interview caused Helen to cringe inside. But it was no surprise which photograph had distracted Julie Rose.

The first newspaper story to examine Bernard Rose, his career, and his character, had appeared in the New York Times two days after the assassination attempt in Tel Aviv. Rose was portrayed as a man who had had no problems in the line of duty for his entire career, no official sanctions, only a steady record of reliable service. The article did point out that Rose had a close relationship with two other Secret Service agents, Myles Martin and Lawrence Haynes, who had been dismissed a year ago for drunken and disorderly conduct while protecting the President on a trip to South America.

"Julie, that's why we're here," said Sandy. "So you can give us the side of the story the New York Times missed."

The moment Julie turned her attention away from Helen and back to her, Sandy picked up where she had left off.

"You said you broke the wall of silence. How did you do that?"

"Things got so bad with Bernie, I called Aluf, because I knew Bernie respected him."

"Aluf Kinsberg?" Sandy asked. "The man who shot your husband?"

"Yes, and Aluf met with him because I had begged him for help."

"What happened?"

"Aluf knew there was something wrong, but he couldn't convince Bernie to take himself off active duty. That's why Aluf had no choice but to inform the service of my husband's… mental disability."

"How did your husband react to this?"

"He went crazy. And I had to hire bodyguards to protect me and my son."

Sandy was surprised to hear this. "Are you saying these bodyguards were hired before your husband's assassination attempt in Tel Aviv?"

"Yes," Julie answered without hesitation. "Bernie was not himself. I didn't care what happened to me, but I thought he could do something to hurt Bradley."

"And what was the Secret Service doing about helping your husband?"

"They relieved him of his duties and had a psychiatrist see him. I met with two officials at their office and explained everything I knew about what had happened to Bernie. I even told them about the accident, but they didn't seem to care. As far as Bernie was concerned, he was finished from working in the service. Of course this only made him more angry… and more depressed."

Sandy leaned forward in her chair, "Julie, did you say, 'accident'?"

Julie sighed, obviously from having to tell the same story over and over again.

"I believe it was an accident, a head injury, which caused my husband to change. We were on vacation in Montenegro. Bernie had been a diver in college and he couldn't resist showing off, especially around people who didn't know him. At the hotel we were staying at they had a pool and a diving board. He was trying to do some of his old tricks, and on one of the dives he hit his head on the board before landing in the pool. I thought he was dead. But then one of the guests gave him CPR and he started breathing again."

"But you said he was different after the accident?"

"Something happened when Bernie lost consciousness," answered Julie. "He told me he saw a figure... Bernie called it an angel. My husband said this angel told him that 'his purpose amongst the living was not complete.'"

Helen waited for Sandy to follow up, but when she saw her colleague was not quick to ask the obvious question, she jumped in, "And it was this near death experience that you believe changed your husband?"

"Yes, absolutely. Bernie was totally different. And he became... even more different... every day after the diving board accident. I told this all to the Secret Service, but they didn't care. They ignored everything I said as if it didn't matter at all. But it did matter. My husband... was not my husband."

Helen looked over to get Sandy's reaction but saw her colleague was pale, and that her eyes were fixed like whatever she was thinking about was playing out a thousand miles away.

"Sandy?"

Helen's voice caused Sandy to rise quickly from her chair. "Excuse me, but I need to use your bathroom..."

Chapter 18

"*His purpose amongst the living was not complete.*"

Bernard Rose's words were similar to what Tom said after his Near-Death Experience in Hawaii. All Sandy could think of was calling her fiancé.

Sandy turned on the bathroom faucet before whipping out her cell phone. She was hoping that Julie Rose accepted her excuse that she needed a break as she left the condo's living room. But running the water would do nothing to convince Helen that her exit was routine. Sandy saw Helen's face as she fled the room and her colleague knew something was wrong.

The phone call to Tom's mobile phone went straight to voicemail. "Honey, it's me. I'm in Washington D.C. Call me back when you get this message. It's really important."

She ended the call by tapping a button on the screen, but quickly pressed more buttons and her phone automatically dialed their apartment in New York.

After only one ring, the call went to voice mail. "It's me. I just left a message on your mobile phone. Tom, please call me..." She was about to hang up, but changed her mind and said, "I love you, Tom."

Call Ended appeared on the screen after she hit the smart phone button. Sandy stared at the icon until the image began to blur. She then shut her eyes and took a deep, cleansing breath. It didn't help her head, which still felt clouded by a dense fog of anxiety and dread.

She suddenly noticed the water had pooled in the clamshell shaped sink. Sandy quickly twisted the spigot, and the flow of water stopped before overflowing onto the floor. Sandy couldn't understand how the water had built up. She leaned in toward the sink for a closer look, but jumped back when there was a loud burping sound. The noise was followed by a rush of green and black sewage bubbling up from underneath the drain and in a flash, transforming the standing water into a dark cesspool.

What the hell, Sandy thought to herself as she stumbled backwards in shock.

"Can you tell me why you took this picture?"

Despite the waterworks drama going on in the bathroom, Sandy heard Helen's voice on the other side of the door.

"I was concerned about my husband. I had no idea who the therapist was that was trying to help him."

Sandy took in Julie Rose's response before stepping carefully back toward the sink. What she saw caused her to stop in her tracks, then replay in her mind everything that she thought she had just witnessed seconds ago.

Now the clamshell sink was completely spotless, with no evidence of that there had been any regurgitation of green and black muck flooding the basin from underneath the drain.

When Sandy emerged from the bathroom, Helen and Julie Rose were standing beside each other, looking at some printed photographs

"Are you all right?" asked Helen.

"Yes, I'm fine," replied Sandy, doing her best to sound refreshed after her bathroom break. She closed the door behind her and crossed the room toward the two women. "What are you looking at?"

"I found some photographs on the kitchen hutch. I think we have a picture of Bernard Rose's therapist," said Helen, handing Sandy one of the photographs.

The grainy quality of the photograph revealed it was shot from a distance, and at night. It showed two men standing in the alleyway behind the house, in almost exactly the same place where Sandy and Helen had parked their rental car. The only source of light was an alleyway street lamp, more than two dozen yards away from the focal point of the photograph.

"As you can see on the date stamped on the photo, Julie took the photo, and all these photos just one week before the assassination attempt in Tel Aviv," said Helen.

"And one of these men is your husband," asked Sandy.

"That's Bernie for sure," answered Julie.

But when Sandy still looked confused, the assassin's widow walked over to point out the man in the photo who she was confidently identifying as her husband.

"That's my husband right there…"

Sandy brought the photo closer to her eyes, making a point of checking it again. The skin on the face of Bernard Rose was stretched to the breaking point, exactly like what Sandy saw in the video shot in Tel Aviv.

She stepped over to the wall highlighting Bernie Rose's career and held the printed photograph next to one of the framed pictures. It was obvious that the man in the alleyway photograph looked very different than the man in the picture hanging on the wall.

"So you're telling me this is your husband in both photographs?"

"I know he looks different, but I swear to you, that's my husband in both pictures," answered Julie.

"I believe you," said Sandy, before she lowered the printed photograph from the framed picture on the wall. "Now tell me about the other man in the photograph."

"That's Bernie's therapist. At least that's what Bernie told me when I confronted him about meeting someone in the middle of the night. I didn't believe him. I mean, what therapist sees a patient in the middle of the night. When I heard him come home, I was waiting with a camera upstairs in our son's bedroom. I wanted to shoot pictures of whoever Bernie was meeting with."

Her words tumbled from her mouth so quickly it was as if they were spilled rather than spoken.

Helen put her hand on Julie's arm to reassure her. "Just relax. We believe you." Julie seemed comforted by Helen's manner, but Sandy still waited an extra few beats before proceeding.

"Do you know the name of the man your husband was seeing?"

Before Julie could respond to the question, the floor beneath them began shaking. Sandy had the presence of mind to look over at the wall of photographs, and noticed that none of the pictures were moving. Weirdly it seemed as if only the floor was shaking.

"Was that an earthquake," asked Helen.

"Yes. We've been getting them a lot in the last few weeks," Julie answered calmly.

Sandy and Helen exchanged looks. Both women were media junkies, both obsessive readers of the AP wire, the news service with "stringers" spread across the globe reporting on anything of significance – a verdict in a murder trial; a meteor sighted in Siberia; a baby Panda Bear born in a zoo in France. The look on both of their faces was the same -- neither had read anything on the AP wire about earthquakes striking the Washington D.C. area.

"His name was Dr. Benjamin Fincher," said Julie, finally answering Sandy's last question. "I remember because I looked him up on the Internet, just to see if Bernie was lying to me."

"And was this Dr. Benjamin Fincher a therapist the Secret Service had assigned to your husband?" Sandy posed the question hoping Julie's answer would match the information she had recently received from her source at the state department.

"No, he wasn't. And it that was a problem for Bernie. He was really reluctant to meet with him when he discovered Fincher wasn't part of the staff at the Secret Service. But after just one meeting, that problem went away. And after a couple more sessions, the shrink was like Bernie's new best friend. It was totally weird. My husband, I'm telling you, he didn't trust anyone."

Sandy and Helen were both writing down Julie's words when another tremor began shaking the townhouse. This time not it was not only the floor that rumbled below their feet, a door beneath the staircase also shook violently.

"So how long did you say you've been getting these tremors?" asked Helen, after the shaking once again subsided.

Before Julie could respond, the door beneath the staircase began to shake, this time independent of any other disturbance in the townhouse. After a few seconds, the door's vibration rose sharply, at one point, it shook so violently it seemed like the door would break free from the frame.

But then it suddenly stopped.

Sandy walked across the room quickly and then put the palm of her right hand against the door. She felt nothing, not even a slight tremble. And the wood was neither hot nor cold to the touch.

Helen had her mobile phone out, but just as she began tapping onto the screen, Sandy stopped her.

"Helen, can we wait a beat before we call the police?"

"Are you serious?"

Even though Sandy didn't respond, Helen stopped dialing and lowered her phone.

Sandy turned to Julie Rose and asked, "Where does this door lead to?"

CHAPTER
19

Julie Rose couldn't remember the last time she had been in her cellar and was surprised to discover the key was laying in the front of the drawer rather than in a plastic container with the other keys seldom or no longer used.

Even after using the key, opening the cellar door proved to be difficult. Sandy and Helen needed to throw all of their strength into the challenge before they were finally able to pry open the door.

"Jesus," said, Sandy, quickly cupping her hand over her nose.

"What the hell is that?" Helen asked, looking to Julie for an answer.

"I have no idea." Julie Rose sounded embarrassed and defensive with her reply. "I've never smelled anything like this before."

Opening the cellar door unleashed a wave of stench so rank and nauseating that none of the women had ever encountered anything as disgusting.

"Well, whatever is down there is way past its expiration date," said Helen. She began to shut the door, but Sandy stopped her.

"What are you doing?"

"I want to check it out," said Sandy, still holding her hand over her nose as she answered.

"What? Something is dead down there. We need to call the Sanitation department." When her words didn't seem to be making an impact, Helen spoke up with what she believed was actually a better idea -- "Sandy, we should call the police."

"Don't do that," said Julie, immediately stepping in between the women to get their attention. "Please, don't call the police. That will mean all the news stations will know where we live. My son... we'll both have to leave our home. Please, I'm begging you... begging you both... don't call the police."

Sandy put a hand on Julie to comfort her, and to help sell the sincerity of her words, "I want to hold off on calling the police until I find out the cause of this smell."

"Thank you," said Julie. "I really appeciate it."

"You heard me, right? If I find anything dead down there that has two, rather than four legs, I'll be screaming 911... okay?"

Julie nodded, somewhat calmed, but still facing the strong possibility that she and her son could very well be looking for a new place to live before the night was over.

Before Helen could weigh in, Sandy moved quickly through the doorway, stepping onto a wooden platform connected to a stairway that descended almost straight down into a subterranean cellar dark enough that the floor of the room was not visible.

Helen was surprised by Sandy's action and had trouble responding. The two women had been through a lot together over the years, including working on news stories in war torn Libya and Sri Lanka. There was also an exclusive on-camera interview with a Warlord in Indonesia in which the bodyguards protecting their leader insisted both women wear blindfolds before being driven to the secret meeting location.

And yet, none of what they had been through together somehow compared to the dread Helen felt as she stood at the top of a cellar entrance to a Washington D.C. townhouse.

By the time she finally recovered her voice, Helen noticed a light switch on a wall just beyond the doorway. She anxiously reached over and flipped the switch.

Nothing.

"What the hell is going on?" She turned back to Julie Rose for an answer, but the assassin's widow just shook her head in confusion and dismay. Her reaction did not dissuade Helen from continuing to flip the light switch up and down in an effort to make it work.

As Sandy continued to descend deeper into the cellar, she discovered the hideous smell accompanied by an extreme change in temperature. With each step she took, the more Sandy felt like she was entering the walk-in freezer at a meat slaughterhouse. About three-quarters of the way to the bottom, Sandy stopped, not because of the freezing temperature and pitch darkness ahead of her, but out of annoyance.

"Would you stop playing with the light switch, Helen? Clearly it doesn't work."

"Okay, fine. Then what am I supposed to do?"

"Just stand there and wait. I'll only be a minute."

"Screw that. I'm not just standing here and waiting."

Sandy waited a beat, but she didn't hear any sound that Helen was moving to join her.

"Why are you doing this?"

"That's a great question," shouted Sandy, before grabbing the bottom of her blouse and lifting it up to cover her nose as she continued her descent. The first answer to that popped into Sandy's mind was that opening the cellar door felt like opening a steel vault, one built to protect something. And the rancid smell and arctic temperature only seemed to validate her suspicion. She wondered if what was being protected was… a secret. Something that would shed light on how it was possible that the assassin, Bernard Rose, could have a Near-Death Experience, and describe his NDE with words similar to…

A spotlight suddenly appeared on the wall beside Sandy. She turned and saw Helen moving down the stairway toward her, holding a flashlight.

"Since when do you carry a flashlight?"

"I got the flashlight from Julie Rose. She gave it to me along with the key to the cellar door. I forgot about it when I freaked out watching you come down here." Since Sandy was in the lead, Helen handed the flashlight to her.

"Thanks for coming with me."

"You're welcome," said Helen. "But I don't think you ever answered my question — Why are you doing this?"

"My first-year journalism teacher said that the best stories were hidden in the dark."

Helen sighed. "Okay, well, my first-year journalism teacher said the same thing, but I always understood the phrase to be more of a metaphor."

When the two reached the bottom of the stairway, the flashlight beam came across a light switch on the wall beside them.

"You try it," said Helen. "I don't like my luck right now."

Sandy tried the switch. Nothing.

"I can't believe all the lights are out down there," Julie shouted from the top of the stairs.

Helen looked back, but could not see Julie Rose, only hear her. It was as if a dark fog had mysteriously materialized between the bottom and top of the stairwell.

"It must be a blown circuit breaker," said Julie. "Bernie showed me the circuit box a few years ago. Do you want me to go and check if I can flip a switch?"

145

"Yes, that will be great," shouted Helen. Whether Julie Rose ignored her answer or left to follow through on her words, Helen could not tell.

"We should go back up."

"Why would we do that? We're already here. Let's check the place out," said Sandy. She was shining the flashlight in a slow left to right sweep across the basement. The room appeared to run across the basic concrete foundation of the townhouse, with a floor to ceiling span measuring about twenty-five feet. The flashlight beam highlighted stacks of boxes, old furniture, and garden equipment.

"See anything? I don't see anything," said Helen.

"No, I don't see anything, but I still smell something," said Sandy. The stench was not as overwhelming as when they first opened the cellar door, but the odor was powerful enough that she still had her blouse covering her nose.

"Wait… what was that?" Something written on the wall behind a stack of boxes had caught Helen's eye and she jerked the flashlight back. "There... Do you see it?"

"I see it," said Sandy, but I can't make out the words. What about you?"

Only the top part of what was scrawled on the concrete was visible over the stacked boxes.

"I'm tempted to make something up, so we can leave," said Helen.

"What are you so scared of?"

"Besides the foul smell and the Arctic weather conditions, I'm afraid of whatever Julie Rose said upstairs that caused a look on your face I've never seen before."

"We'll talk about that later. I want to check this out."

Helen regretted giving Sandy control of the flashlight because she was now forced to follow her boss as she moved into the basement.

The two women pushed aside some of the stacked boxes creating enough room for them to see the cellar wall without any obstruction.

Written in red on the wall across from them was: "The Whole World will be in the Power of the Evil One."

It was only after they got to the last line that the flashlight beam revealed more words on an adjoining wall -- "He is filled with fury, because he knows that his time is short."

And on yet another wall: "Woe to the earth and the sea, because the devil has gone down to you! He wants the Perfect Possession."

The last flashlight beam highlighted dozens of carefully stacked glass jars full of what appeared to be urine. A roughly hewn cross-floated in each one.

Behind the containers, there were words written in blood and magnified in the amber — 'The Restrainer Must Die.'"

"It looks like Bernie had a lot on his mind."

"How do you know it was Bernard Rose who wrote this?"

"Fair enough," said Helen. "Perhaps the Roses had a squatter from hell living in their basement."

Sandy started to shine the flashlight around the cellar, which confused Helen."

"What are you looking for?"

"We haven't found anything that explains the wretched smell?"

Helen suddenly snatched the flashlight from Sandy, and then quickly moved toward the cellar stairwell.

"What are you doing, Helen?"

"Let our first-year journalism teachers search for more answers," said Helen. "We're getting the hell out of here."

Chapter 20

"You need to call the police."

The reaction on Julie Rose's face to Sandy's words was transparent – she felt betrayed.

"I'm really sorry to go back on my word, but what we discovered in your cellar is too disturbing to keep to ourselves."

The assassin's widow shut her eyes before turning her back on the two women.

Sandy waited, but when she didn't get a response, she said, "It will look so much better if the phone call to the police comes from you. But, if you don't make the call, Julie, I will."

When Julie Rose turned back around, she had her mobile phone in her hand. "After I make the call, I'm sure you both will be on your way."

"Not true. We need to stay and tell the police everything we've seen," said Sandy.

"And we'll be here after we talk to the police," Helen chimed in. "For you and Bradley."

"My son and I won't be here, that's for sure," said Julie, before hitting some buttons on her mobile phone. "We'll be gypsies, moving from one place to another… trying to avoid the cameras." Before either Sandy or Helen could respond, there was an answer on the other end. "Yes, my name is Julie Rose. I'm the widow of the Tel Aviv assassin, Bernard Rose…"

While Julie Rose spoke to the D.C. police, Sandy used the opportunity to call Bob Harris, the managing editor for *24/7* and brought him up to date about what they had found scrawled across the basement wall, and the decision to call the police. Harris asked a few questions, but made it a point of being supportive and praising Sandy for her judgement in handling the situation.

Just as they were about to hang up, Sandy asked, "Are you going to call Terry?"

"Only if you want me to," said Harris. "I think this can wait until he wakes up. What do you think?"

"I agree," said Sandy, quickly finishing their conversation when she saw Julie Rose end hers.

"The police are on their way." Julie then angrily tossed her mobile phone onto a nearby couch. "I need to go upstairs to pack my son's things so we're ready to leave the moment the police are finished with all their questions." She clearly had no interest in hearing anything either of the women had to say as she stormed past them to the townhouse stairway leading up to the second floor.

Helen waited until Julie was out of earshot, before saying, "By doing the right thing I feel like we just earned our 'Front of the Line Ticket' when we arrive at the pearly gates. How do you feel, Sands?"

"Yeah, I feel super, but after *Good Morning America* runs their exclusive interview with Julie Rose during the May Sweeps, I'm sure we'll both feel differently." Sandy started walking to the back of the townhouse to retrieve their handbags left in the rental car. "We're going to need to show some identification when the police get here."

Helen nodded before following Sandy. "How long do you think it will be before the police arrive?"

"Thirty minutes under normal circumstance, but because Julie identified herself as the wife of the assassin in Tel Aviv, the DC police should be here in less than ten."

Helen waited a beat before asking her next question. "Is this a good time to ask about what happened earlier, when you rushed off to the bathroom?"

So much had transpired since Sandy sought refuge in the Roses' bathroom, it took her a few moments to recall the details. "I was embarrassed to say anything before. However, after what we found in the basement, I'm not feeling like such an idiot telling you the truth. Remember when Julie Rose described her husband having a diving accident that ended up triggering a Near-Death Experience?"

"Yeah, I remember," answered Helen.

"During his N.D.E., there was an angelic figure that spoke to him – 'Your purpose amongst the living is not complete.' Well, here's the thing – those were the exact words Tom told me he heard from an angelic figure during *his* Near-Death Experience."

"Tom had an N.D.E. after the helicopter accident in Hawaii?"

"Yes. I haven't told anyone, until now," said Sandy. "It's also the reason I wanted to check out the basement. I needed to know if whatever Bernard Rose went through before Tel Aviv is somehow connected to what happened to us in Hawaii." She opened the door leading to the backyard waiting for Helen's reaction.

"I know it sounds crazy, but you believe me?"

"Of course I believe you," said Helen, as she moved through the doorway into the backyard.

Sandy couldn't help but feel that Helen was hiding her skepticism behind her words. She noticed how Helen was moving so fast across the stone steps in the backyard it was as if she planned on escaping in the rental car rather than just retrieve their bags.

"Have I ever struck you as a conspiracy buff?"

"No. Never," answered Helen, stopping a few from their rental car, and turned back to confront Sandy. "Is there more?"

"Yeah, there's more," said Sandy, as she withdrew from her pants pocket the key fop for the rental car and hit a button to unlock all the doors. "I've gone my entire life never encountering the phrase 'the Restrainer.' But now those words have crossed my radar twice in the last 48 hours."

"Where else besides the basement wall?"

In my office, when I met with Alan Olsen."

"The priest? I thought he was there to tell religious jokes and talk over old times?"

"I wish," said Sandy. "No, Alan was there to talk about how his recent exorcism showed signs of an impending Apocalypse, as described in the Bible. He wanted to get my help in broadcasting his message."

"And he used the phrase, 'the Restrainer.'"

"Yes, he did," replied Sandy.

"Well, what did he say about it?"

"Honestly, I can't remember. I probably tuned him out around that point because everything he was saying was so off the rails. Seriously, can you blame me?"

"Yeah, at this very moment, I do blame you," said Helen, in a tone that was half joking, and half serious. She walked over to the rental car and opened the door, then turned to Sandy to speak again, but stopped when she heard a nearby noise – something moving across the alleyway gravel. Before Helen could see anything, a Mastiff dog leaped from out of the surrounding shadows, knocking her backwards with such force that the rear side window shattered.

Sandy rushed forward to help, but was too far away when the dog bit into Helen's neck, hitting a main artery, causing blood to spray across the passenger side of the rental car.

CHAPTER 21

Sandy gripped the leather collar around the hound's neck and used all her strength to yank the dog away from Helen. She stumbled across the gravel alleyway until she lost her footing and fell on her back.

"Helen! Helen! Get in the car," Sandy shouted, hoping her friend not only heard her voice, but was still capable of moving.

Hearing Sandy call out to her enabled Helen to step back from unconsciousness. She reached up and managed to grab the front passenger door handle, then used it as leverage to get on her feet. She opened the door and collapsed onto the passenger seat. All that was left to do was pull her legs into the car before shutting the door.

Sandy felt like she was wrestling with a bear as the mastiff rocked back and forth on its back, frantically rolling from one side to the other in an attempt to regain its footing. She was using her legs to keep the dog from rolling over, but it was only a matter of seconds before the weight, size, and the frenzy of the animal would allow it to stand upright.

Helen could hear the furious struggle between the dog and Sandy a few feet away, but her mental will was not enough to move her legs still hanging outside the car.

The leather collar suddenly broke in two, allowing the hound to roll away into the shadows. Sandy sat up, preparing for an attack, but when the canine emerged from the surrounding darkness, the dog was rushing toward the rental car to pursue its attack on...

"Helen!"

Sandy screamed her friend's name as she scrambled to her feet. As she made her move toward the car, Sandy could hear the appalling sound of the dog tearing into flesh, and the sickening silence from Helen, who was unable to put up a fight.

Just a few feet from the car, there was a sound of a gun shot. The mastiff reacted with a yelp, but two more gunshots echoed through the alleyway, causing the dog to fall way from Helen and the car without making another sound.

She looked over and saw one of Julie Rose's bodyguards, standing a few feet from the rental car, with the security lights attached to the townhouse's roof illuminating the smoke coming from the gun he had just fired.

She waited to make sure the bodyguard knew of her presence before approaching Helen. The street lights in the alley barely lit up the interior of the vehicle, but it was enough for Sandy to see the skin on Helen's neck had been almost completely torn away, leaving behind just blood and exposed bone. And everywhere around her was sprayed or splashed red - on the dashboard, the windshield, and on the gearshift console.

The sight triggered Sandy to have a mental flash of the tour helicopter in Hawaii when she first woke up to discover a similar mess all around her.

A moan coming from Helen ended Sandy's flashback, and prompted her to swing into action. Sandy pulled her blouse over her head, then rolled it up carefully before wrapping it around Helen's neck.

"Oh my god, what happened?"

Even though the words sounded as if they were miles away, Sandy registered Julie Rose's voice.

"A dog attacked them and I had to shoot it. Ms. Rose, you need to go back inside the house immediately."

Helen's eyes fluttered open. She took a few moments to focus on Sandy who was inches away from her, kneeling beside the car. "You were right," Helen said in a raspy whisper. Her words were barely loud enough for Sandy to hear as the siren became louder as the police car drew in closer to the alleyway.

"Right about what?"

"Just ten minutes," said Helen. "The police got here…"

Her voice trailed off and Helen's eyes seemed to glass over. Sandy tightened the blouse tourniquet around Helen's neck.

"Helen, you're going to be fine. Just stay with me."

Helen had closed her eyes before saying, "I might need some help."

"I'm right here."

"I know. Good. Now help me think of a new word for what just happened…"

At first, Sandy didn't understand.

"If you help me, I'll share the credit."

Then Sandy realized that Helen was referring to help discovering a new word that would get her creation officially in the English Dictionary.

Sandy saw flashing red lights illuminate the surrounding trees and walls and knew the police were arriving in the alleyway behind the Roses' townhouse.

"I'll help you, as long as you stay with me."

Helen nodded in response, which Sandy saw as a hopeful sign.

The noise of the police vehicle's tires crunching on the gravel behind their rental car was the final cue for Sandy to rise from her kneeling position. She wanted to make sure the police would immediately call for an ambulance. But after fighting through the glare from the headlights, Sandy was shocked to see not a police car, but an ambulance. Sandy was thrilled at the sight for a few moments, but then the skeptical part of her brain took over -

Julie Rose called the police. Why would the first response be an ambulance?

The attack on Helen happened less than five minutes ago, how could an ambulance get here so quickly?

Before she was able to address the questions running through her brain, the first paramedic emerged from the ambulance. The sight of the man caused Sandy to turn in dread at the other EMT emerging from the other side of the vehicle. When Sandy caught a good look at him, it confirmed a horrible realization – the ambulance EMTs somehow looked exactly like the same paramedics who were in the rescue helicopter in Hawaii.

"Your friend's going to make it," the first paramedic shouted out to Sandy.

"We'll take it from here," said the second paramedic, as they both advanced toward the rental car.

There was something else about both EMTs that connected them to the paramedics on the rescue helicopter, a detail she had somehow dismissed in her mind until this moment -- the paramedics on the helicopter in Hawaii, and the pair of men approaching in the alleyway all had the same stretched facial skin Bernard Rose exhibited prior to his assassination attempt in Tel Aviv.

Sandy looked over at her best friend bleeding out just a few feet from where she stood and several thoughts shot across her brain –

Helen was going to die.

But what if she didn't die?

What if... Helen had an N.D.E.
Like Bernard Rose.
Like Tom.
If she didn't die, would she come back to the living...
And still be the same Helen?

Sandy bent down, grabbed Helen's legs, and lifted them carefully into the car. She then slammed shut the passenger door and raced around the front of the rental car to the driver's side. As she was reaching for the handle of the door, the first paramedic grabbed Sandy's arm.

"She's going to be fine. You'll both be fine."

There was a sincere expression on the paramedic's face to support his words, but all Sandy could see was the menace hiding behind the trusting veneer.

Yanking her arm from the EMT's grasp Sandy quickly opened the car door. When the paramedic put his hand on Sandy's shoulder to stop her, she responded by shoving him backwards, then jumping into the car and quickly closing the door.

The other EMT quickly approached the passenger side of the car, prompting Sandy to hit the button on the key fob, instantaneously locking all the car's doors. She then pushed the ignition button on the dashboard, firing up the car's engine.

"Let us help your friend," the second EMT shouted on the other side of the glass.

Sandy's response to his plea was to slam her foot on the accelerator. The rental car peeled out, fishtailing, and spitting gravel as it sped away from the back of the Roses' townhouse.

When Sandy glanced in the rearview mirror, she saw the two paramedics standing, in the distance, lit from above by the alleyway streetlight, looking lifeless, as if they were statues on display in a museum.

Sandy guided her car from the alleyway to the street running in front of the Rose's townhouse. Almost immediately, a police car with its siren blaring and lights flashing sped past them.

She adjusted the rearview mirror, so she could watch as the police cruiser parked in front of the Roses' townhouse.

Julie Rose called the police… and here they were finally showing up as a response to their call.

So how is it possible the ambulance in the alleyway has the same two guys I saw in Hawaii, less than a few weeks ago?

Coincidence? NFW.

Sandy engaged the car's navigation system to search for the nearest hospital. She opted for the first medical facility that showed up on the computer screen — Access D.C., an emergency hospital only a mile away. She hit a few more buttons on the dashboard, and the onboard navigator voice began with guidance instructions to the hospital.

"Stay on this road for the next three-quarters of a mile."

Helen began stirring beside her. Sandy reached up to switch on the car's interior light and was shocked when she saw her friend's alabaster appearance. It looked like Helen had been drained of all her blood.

"Sandy…"

She could barely hear her speak. Sandy unbuckled her seat belt, so she could be closer to her friend.

"Don't hurt the dog. Not the dog's fault…"

"I hear you, Helen. No one will hurt the dog. You just stay with me."

Even though Sandy could see Helen was still breathing, her eyes closed right in the middle of her plea for the dog's life.

"Helen, did you hear me? Everything is going to be all right. Helen?"

On the dashboard screen, a flashing red box with text caught Sandy's eye — Is this a medical emergency?

Sandy quickly pressed the button for "yes," hoping it would alert the hospital to be ready when they finally arrived.

By the time she refocused her attention back on the road, Sandy discovered the car they were driving behind had made a sudden stop, so abrupt that Sandy had no choice if she was going to avoid a rear-end collision. She yanked the steering wheel to one side, causing her rental car to swerve across the middle divider and into oncoming traffic.

Several cars flashed their lights, and beeped their horns as they reacted to avoid hitting Sandy's car. She looked at her side mirror before yanking the wheel in the other direction, steering her car back over the center divider.

The whole stunt caused Helen to fall in Sandy's lap.

"Prepare to turn right in 1000 feet," announced the car's navigation voice.

Sandy cut across two lanes so she could grab the next exit leading to the hospital.

"In 500 feet, you will arrive at your destination. Your destination is on your right."

She followed the signs with red arrows pointing their way toward the hospital's emergency entrance.

"You have arrived at your destination."

After parking, in front of the main entrance, Sandy slammed her fist on the steering wheel to honk the car's horn. She wanted to make sure someone inside the hospital would know they had arrived.

"Helen, we're here at the hospital. You're going to be fine."

She was surprised when Helen responded, nodding her head in her lap and then raising her left hand high enough to get Sandy's attention.

Sandy saw a piece of paper balled up in her fist. She peeled back Helen's fingers and snatched the paper from her hand a moment before the passenger door opened.

It was the hospital's emergency response team on the other side of the car with a gurney ready to transport Helen to the ER.

Sandy quickly scanned the faces of the doctors and nurses who had come to greet them, and when she was satisfied that none of them resembled the medics from the rescue helicopter or alleyway ambulance, she allowed Helen to be pulled from her lap and gently eased out of the rental car.

"What happened here?"

"A dog attacked her."

"Did you see the dog?"

When Sandy hesitated to answer, the nurse moved to the next question, "The dog that bit your friend…"

"Yes, I saw the dog. It came out of nowhere. I fought with it... tried to stop it from attacking Helen."

"I understand. Now listen to me. You need to focus here. Your friend's life may depend on it. Okay?"

"Yes. Okay."

"Was the dog foaming at the mouth, you know… rabid?"

"No. I don't think so."

"When did the attack happen?"

"A few minutes ago. Wait..." She looked at her watch. "Shit. Helen was attacked like... thirty minutes ago."

"Do you know your friend's blood type?"

Sandy couldn't answer. She tried to quickly search her memory for any time over the years that

Helen mentioned her blood type... but came up empty.

"No, I don't."

The gurney smashed through the doors leading to the emergency operating rooms and everyone, including the nurse Sandy was speaking with, disappeared behind the swinging doors.

A security guard appeared just as Sandy took a step to follow.

"You need to go back down this hallway to the admission desk."

She stood there, staring at the doors, wondering if she had failed Helen.

Should she have known her blood type?

I don't even know my own blood type?

I bet Helen knows my blood type.

If the roles were reversed Helen would have been able to tell the surgical team the right blood to use to save my life.

"Ma'am, did you hear me? You need to check in."

"What? No. I need to be with her."

"Sorry, but that's not permitted. What you need to do is walk back down the hallway, make the first right, then go three hundred feet, and turn left. The admission desk will is this round, white thing with a lot of people working behind it. Someone there will help you."

Sandy nodded as if she understood, but when she didn't move, the security guard grabbed his walkie-talkie and spoke into it before turning his attention back to her.

"Miss, I'm going to walk you to the admission desk myself. I just called ahead. They'll be waiting for us…"

After filling out the admission hospital paperwork, Sandy called Tom again. Like the other calls, it went straight to voicemail, and she was forced to leave a message.

"Tom, something awful has happened. Helen was attacked by a dog, and she's seriously hurt. Call me when you get this message."

She then placed a call into the show's assignment desk, and related the basic facts to the show's segment coordinator, Regina Latham. The other top executives with the show left hours ago.

"Regina, Helen has been attacked by a dog. I'm here at Access Emergency hospital in D.C. waiting for her to get out of surgery..."

Sandy didn't tell Regina much more, only that it was obviously important that the managing editor of the show, Bob Harris, call her, so she could bring him up to speed.

As she waited for the call back from Harris, Sandy stood in a waiting area of the hospital that had a glass wall looking out to the parking lot. This allowed her to keep a paranoid watch on the entrance area believing that it was probably just a matter of time before two guys with stretched faces showed up, either in an ambulance or circling in a helicopter.

After more than a few minutes went by, it occurred to Sandy that she had Bob Harris's private mobile phone number and reached into her purse to retrieve it, but then came upon the rolled-up ball of paper she had taken from Helen.

In all the craziness, she forgot to look at it.

She unfolded the paper and discovered a single word had been written in pen – Skenetimeo.

Helen somehow wrote the word on the paper while in the car. Sandy didn't know how this was possible, but a careful study of the word unmistakably revealed, despite the faint and unsteady manner of the script, that it was Helen's distinct handwriting style. And of course the paper was stained with her blood.

It didn't take Sandy long to figure out what Helen was thinking by writing down the word. She knew her friend had a pre-occupation of gaining entry into the Oxford Dictionary by creating an original word for the English language. Sandy didn't know what to think when she pondered Helen's final two thoughts while she struggled to stay alive - the first was about preserving the life of the canine that had attacked her, and the second was attempting to change the dictionary of record for the English language.

Sandy couldn't look at the blood-stained paper any longer and set it aside, pledging to revisit the matter another time. However, after some time passed, and Sandy had still not heard back from either Tom or Harris, she unfurled the paper, with the purpose figuring out the meaning of what Helen had written.

Skenetimeo.

Over the years, Sandy had often been the sounding board for Helen's creative process. She knew when Helen came up with an idea for a new word, she usually turned to the so-called dead languages – Latin, Aramaic, or Sanskrit – for inspiration. She would search for a word that once had a particular meaning, then look for another word that had a different meaning, and combine the two to form a creation that hopefully rolled easily off the tongue, but more importantly, was something original and distinct and could become part of the modern vernacular.

Sandy began with the natural break in the word, Skenetimeo, between the "e" and the "t." Then, using her phone's Internet connection. Sandy looked up "Skene" on an online dictionary. Sure enough she found an entry for the word --

Skene - Greek term for scaena (Latin).
Etymology: Ancient Greek σκηνή (skēnḗ, "tent").
One of the three parts of the ancient Greek theater, the other two being orchestra and auditorium. At first the skene was a temporary wooden structure where the actors changed costumes and from where they made their

entrances. Beginning in the first half of the fifth century B.C., when theatrical action became more complex and second and third actors were introduced, the skene was built behind the orchestra or tangent to its circumference.

Sandy then looked up the word "Timeo" and also found in entry in the online dictionary --

Timeo – Latin term. Greek term for scaena (Latin).
Etymology: From a Proto-Indo-European root meaning "to choke," related to Vedic Sanskrit (tam, "to choke") and Sanskrit (tam, "breathless, difficulty breathing")
timeō (present infinitive timēre, perfect active timuī); second conjugation, no passive
1. Fear, am afraid. The verb timeō is a Latin verb of fearing.

After looking at the definitions, Sandy had to decide what Helen was going for with the creation of her new word. Was her friend trying to express the fear she had for the next stage... the place perhaps one goes after they leave the main stage? Conceivably, this would also be similar to the place where one waits before their entrance to perform on stage.

Or possibly Helen was after a totally different meaning with her word. Perhaps she intended to create a new word to be defined as a warning about something that was about to happen. A word meant to encompass the sounds/signs/clues that await from a separate part of the theatre, away from what the audience can see, but should dread before whatever character or twist of the story was getting ready to make an entrance onto the main stage.

"Ms. Travis…"

It was the hospital security guard addressing her. At first, Sandy thought he had come to the waiting area to check on her, but then she saw he was accompanied by one of the doctors who had worked on Helen in the E.R.

Sandy closed her phone and stood up.

"How is Helen? Is she all right?"

The doctor looked down before answering, as if Sandy's urgent, tearing eyes were too much for him to face straight on.

"I'm afraid your friend lost a lot of blood. We tried our best, but she finally succumbed to her injuries a few minutes ago. I'm so sorry."

Sandy's knees buckled and almost gave out, but she managed to stay on her feet as she began to cry.

CHAPTER 24

When her subway train pulled into Penn Station, Sandy walked across the platform and headed up the stairs leading to the main concourse. As she approached the top of the stairwell, she was surprised to see Tom. He moved quickly down the stairs to help her, but as he reached out to grab her bag, she stepped right past him.

She walked quickly across the marble floor of the concourse until Tom caught up with her.

"Honey, why are you acting this way?"

Sandy dropped her bag before turning and confronting Tom.

"Why didn't you answer or return any of my calls?"

"What are you talking about? Sandy, I answered all of your calls."

Because his negligence was so egregious, Sandy was astonished Tom was taking the approach of complete denial. "Okay, Tom, if you called me back there would be messages on my mobile phone, right?" She reached into her bag and withdrew her mobile phone, then mockingly waved it in his face.

Tom looked at the phone before his gaze back at Sandy, his face showing no sign of shame or guilt.

"That's right, Sandy, if I returned your calls, there would be exactly four messages on your phone."

Sandy turned her phone around to look and was shocked when she saw four voice messages on the main screen. When the plane landed, she had checked for messages, and did the same thing while riding the subway from the airport. Each time there were no messages.

She couldn't accept what was on the screen and hit the playback button for voice messages --

"Honey, I'm sorry I wasn't here when you called. What's going on? Are you all right? Call me when you get this…"

"It's me again. I don't know what's happening, but apparently you didn't get my last message. What's going on? I'm worried about you. Call me back."

"Oh, my god! I just got your phone message about Helen. I'm here. Call me when you can. Honey, I'm here if you need me. I'll catch the next plane to be there if you want. Just let met me know. Call me. Sandy… I love you."

"Honey, I just got your last phone message. I called back as soon as I could. I have no idea why but instead of ringing, my call went straight to voice mail. Listen, I'm going to meet you at Penn

Station. Don't take any chances. I look forward to seeing you. I miss you so much."

After hearing all the messages, Tom could see on her face that he had the green light to move in for a hug. As they embraced each other, she said, "Tom, I'm so sorry. I don't know what's going on anymore."

"Don't worry about it, honey. After what happened with Helen… how can you not feel like you're going a little crazy. Let's go home."

He grabbed her bag and together they made their way across the main concourse at Penn Station to the platform where they caught a train to their apartment.

During the subway ride, Sandy did her best to appear contrite. She wanted him to believe she had been wrong about him calling her back. However, as they exited the subway train together, and made their way to the street, Sandy would not lower her guard. She had no idea how Tom managed to pull it off – get four voice mails onto her phone as if he had really called her back – but she knew somehow all the messages were fake.

If she was wrong, she was wrong... but she knew she wasn't wrong. One of the reasons she was confident in her conviction was the way Tom looked. He couldn't cover-up his face, which in the short time she had been away, had become stretched and taut in a way that resembled the face of Bernard Rose, right before he boarded the plane to Tel Aviv.

The moment they arrived back at their apartment, Sandy took off her shoes and walked barefoot into the apartment. She did this all the time to save the wear and tear on the loft's wood floors. When she emerged from the entryway, Sandy saw the easels scattered around the living room. She wanted to ask Tom about his latest work, but waited. He took her bag into their bedroom and she went through the motions of flipping through the mail on the bar counter.

"I'm so sorry, honey," Sandy said when Tom came back from the bedroom, "I forgot to ask about your work. Show me what you've been done since I left."

Immediately her fiancé leaped in front of the nearest easel, protecting it from her curious eyes.

"No way. You're not allowed to look. Not until I feel good about the work. And the same thing applies for that picture, and that one as well. Promise me you won't look at anything until I'm ready to show you."

"Of course, I'll wait. But do you feel good about the work you did while I was gone?"

"I think so. I'm still not sure."

There was nothing Sandy could say because Tom's behavior was consistent with the way he normally behaved while working on a new collection.

"I have an idea," said Tom, steering Sandy toward the bedroom area. "Why don't I light a few candles, pour you a glass of wine, and get a bath going for you. After everything that's happened, the best thing you could do for yourself would be to just relax. What do you say, honey?"

All his words sounded romantic in content and tone, but there was something missing. And with the stretched look of his face, Sandy couldn't shake the feeling that she was being micromanaged.

"That's so sweet of you, but I think I'm going to pass on the bath and go straight to bed."

"Are you sure?"

"Yeah, I'm positive."

"Come to think of it, that's a great idea," said Tom. "Let's both go to bed."

She quickly tried to process Tom's words before responding.

"So you're coming to bed with me?"

"If you want me to…"

"Why wouldn't I want you to?"

He sighed, before saying, "I'm doing the best I can. To be honest with you, I'm not sure what I should be doing. After what happened to Helen, I want to help, but nothing I do or suggest feels right. I almost feel like I'm in the way."

She closed her eyes before responding. Whatever strategy she had from the airport to their apartment wasn't working. Tom seemed to sense her suspicion and was making sure there was nothing in his behavior that would cause her to worry.

When she opened her eyes again it was to embrace Tom, then whisper in his ear, "Why don't you grab some wine and come to bed with me. However, I'm warning you not to have any expectations. After a couple sips, I'll probably be fast asleep. But I promise to make it up to you in the morning."

"Honey, I'm not expecting anything. I just want to make sure you're going to be okay. But that all sounds great."

"It's good to be home," she said, after they parted.

"Go to bed. I'll be right behind you with the wine."

He then kissed her quickly on the lips before moving toward the kitchen.

C HAPTER
25

True to her words, Sandy had less than half a glass of wine before she fell asleep.

At least, that's what she wanted Tom to believe.

Did she usually snore or make some other type of noise that signaled she was asleep? She had no idea. Tom had always been too much of a gentleman to mention whatever bothersome nighttime habits she might have.

She wondered if she faked any type of heavy breathing, would Tom see right through it. Did he know her better than she knew him? Better than she knew Helen?

Sandy noted every noise and every movement coming from Tom's side of the bed, but gradually all the acute observations became less audible, less noticeable, until everything on the other side of the bed and in the rest of the room seemed to disappear into a black haze.

As several hours went by, and Tom remained in bed, the premise of Sandy's ruse began to turn into reality… she began to drift off to sleep. If he had only waited a few more minutes, Sandy would have lapsed into a sleep deep enough to be mistaken for a coma patient. But the sound of Tom easing himself off the bed caused her to wake up.

She did her best to maintain a rhythmic breathing pattern as Tom slinked out of the room. Sandy heard the rustle of clothing as he dressed outside the door. A few moments later, his footsteps receded from the bedroom.

As quietly as she could, she slipped to the edge of the bed and sat up. The springs creaked beneath her causing Sandy to freeze. When she was satisfied he was not returning to the room, Sandy made her way quietly to her closet and quickly threw on a pair of jeans, a black sweater, and some running shoes. Wherever Tom had been going every night since they had come back from Hawaii, Sandy had no doubt that wearing tennis shoes rather than flats was the way to go.

Outside in the cold, Sandy saw a few people moving slowly in front of the storefronts around their apartment building. She panicked for a few seconds when she didn't see Tom, but then spotted him walking more than a block away, headed toward the Lower East Side.

Sandy had always considered herself a journalist, but as she began following her fiancé, she suddenly realized she really had never had to use the traditional reporter skill of trailing someone without being discovered. Her skills were more along the lines of reading congressional reports and catching a Senator in a lie and confronting him on camera during an interview.

She went with her instincts and followed Tom at a safe distance, choosing to stay in the shadows wherever she could. Then the TV journalist in her kicked in, and she pulled out her phone and began recording her pursuit on foot. If nothing else, she wanted video so Tom couldn't deny the next morning that somehow he wasn't the person she was following in the middle of the night.

After more than a dozen blocks, Tom turned and headed south from East Houston, toward the Bowery. He went a couple of blocks before Sandy watched Tom approach a building that was like most of the city, brightly lit up no matter the hour. The light on the sign was for the YMCA, and she watched as Tom stopped to talk to someone waiting outside the building. She immediately recognized him, but looked away hoping that she was wrong. However, when she looked again, nothing had changed – it was the same man in the photograph Julie Rose had taken of her husband and her therapist — Dr. Colin Fincher. Her fiancé talked with Fincher for a few minutes before the doctor checked his watch prompting them to enter the building together.

She waited a few minutes before crossing the street. Sandy then walked down an alley next to a nearby building that allowed her access to the parking lot behind the YMCA building. After waiting for a minute in the shadows, she cautiously entered the building along with three women who had driven up in an SUV. Sandy stayed just a few steps behind the women as they approached the entrance to the facility manned by a single security guard in the middle of watching a soccer game playing out on a small TV behind the reception desk. His check of the three women flashing their YMCA gym membership cards and Sandy holding up her Metropolitan library card was cursory at best and everyone entered without any problem.

Sandy approached the elevator corridor and realized that her biggest problem was finding where Tom was in the building. There were seven floors, with a lot of activity despite the late hours. She then came upon a row of signs posted on the wall between the elevators that were meant as arrows to the different events happening that evening. When she came across one of the signs, she was relieved to know instantly which floor her fiancé was on, while at the same time deeply troubled to discover what had lured Tom from their bed in the middle of the night.

N.D.E. GROUP THERAPY
Room 33 / 3rd Floor
Dr. Colin Fincher

There was over a dozen people sitting in a circle. One of them, a middle-aged man with dyed black hair, was relating his Near-Death Experience to the others.

"It took a few moments for my eyes to adjust, but then I saw him. He didn't say a word, but still I heard him speak. He said, 'I am the Angel of Light.'"

As Sandy watched covertly from the open doorway, everyone in the therapy group nodded as if they completely understood not only the words, but what was implied, and apparently needed no explanation.

"He told me that my work among the living wasn't done. I needed to go back."

"That's exactly what happened to me!" Tom exclaimed. He was leaning forward as if ready to launch out of his chair. "He said he was the 'Angel of Light', and I needed to go back!"

Tom's enthusiasm caused Sandy to move from the door to the group therapy room. She was afraid that perhaps she would either fall to the ground in despair… or run into the room in raging protest. Either way, it would give herself away as she stood at the entrance to the room, eavesdropping on the therapy session in progress.

"Tom," said Dr. Fincher in a sober, gentle voice, "maybe you feel comfortable enough now to tell the others about your N.D.E.? You know you're among friends."

Tom glanced around at all the expectant faces and cleared his throat before speaking again, "Hello, everyone. My name is Tom."

In unison, the group replied, "Hello, Tom. Tell us about your Near-Death Experience."

She was back in the doorway watching, and what she heard made Sandy shudder. Something about their voices, unnerved her. There was too much uniformity in tone you often hear with a group of cultists sounding off as a group.

"My N.D.E. happened in Hawaii on vacation with my fiancée. We were on one of the island's tour helicopters when there was an accident. I died. But like Peter, I also saw this tunnel, then this bright, beautiful light that ended up being… an Angel. An Angel of Light. I was ready to die, but then he said, 'you are not done with your work. Go back to the living. There is more you can do.' And here I am. Ready. For whatever I should do."

Sandy was stunned, not only by what Tom said, but how he spoke to the rest of the group. Like everything else he had been covering up from her, the secret he was most protective of was his capability for passion and excitement, two emotions she had not seen from him since the helicopter accident.

"That's great to hear, Tom," said Dr. Fincher. "Now let me ask you this - what do you believe is the reason you were sent back to the living?"

Sandy held her breath waiting to hear what her fiancé would say. However, before she could hear Tom's answer, there were the sound of footsteps behind her.

"Miss," said a man wearing a YMCA staff shirt, "is there a reason you are standing out here and not inside the room?"

Sandy looked down and shook her head, but didn't say a word.

A person from the therapy session shouted from the room behind her. "Is there problem, Gerald?"

The question got the YMCA staff member to move to the doorway to respond, "I'm not sure. I was just checking with this woman in the hallway."

By the time the staff member turned back to look, Sandy was no longer standing nearby. She was already halfway down the hallway moving quickly toward a door at the end of the corridor with a highlighted red EXIT sign above the archway.

CHAPTER
26

For fifteen years, St. Jude's had been Father Alan Olsen's home, and he knew every column and pew. During his homilies, his voice filled the church, from stone floor to pointed ribbed vault, mapping the space with sound. Strangely enough, some of the sculptures never fully materialized in his mind until the choir struck up a hymn and delved into those details otherwise lost to him. As in any other structure, he had blind spots, but less here than anywhere else because he'd filled many of them in with tactile impressions, lovingly polishing each oak pew and its leafy fleuron carvings, fixing the hinge on the confessional when it came loose, dusting off the crucifix above the door to his chamber. The church employed a maintenance staff that could have accomplished these tasks, but Father Olsen knew that to care for something was to cherish it. This was his home.

And the Vatican was forcing him out.

On the desk in Father Olsen's chamber, a radio was tuned to a Catholic station, the voice painting in the contents and corners of the room. He listened as he packed his belongings into a cardboard box.

"It is extremely dangerous to simply pick up the Bible, with no exegetical knowledge, no historical or literary contextual lens, and interpret its message," the radio guest was saying. "The Bible's teachings are too complex—and historically there's been a corruption of the language: the Bible was originally set forth in Greek and Hebrew, but the versions we have now are translations—interpretations in themselves, conditioned and influenced by their cultural godmothers."

"Amen," Father Olsen said. He turned to the walls and began to take down the various photos of him posing with his parishioners. At the end of the gallery hung a cross, which Ami's little brother had whittled from olive wood, darkly veined, something to help with the exorcism. Tracing its crude contours, Father Olsen considered leaving it behind, a gift for the next priest, but ultimately decided to place it with his other personal effects.

Scattered and stacked randomly across his desk were documentaries and books on tape, long overdue at the library. Since his return from the Middle East, he had buried himself in everything regarding The Book of Revelation. He had become so desperate for information that he even researched the questionable prophecies of Nostradamus, hoping the quatrains would shed some light on the complex Bible prophecies—anything that might help prevent the End Days. His fervent research had been one reason Deacon Gregg had reported him to the bishop of their diocese, who had then filed a report with their superiors back in Rome.

It was just as well. Father Olsen's research had broken little new ground. Worse, he had found nothing to help identify the Restrainer, and that had been his priority: first find Satan's keeper, then protect him. Because once the Restrainer was swept from the devil's path, Father Olsen would be helpless to stop the dominoes from toppling.

"And I'll put it this way," the radio guest continued. "Picture children on a playground and on one side there's a field of land mines and on the other a field of poisonous serpents, and as you're watching these kids get bitten and blown up, you're thinking, 'Oh my God, this is horrible!' But then picture a fence keeping these children out of the dangerous fields, and you can breathe a sigh of relief and think, 'Okay, those children are out of harm's way now.' That fence is—"

Suddenly, the radio shut off.

There was silence. Then something banged against the wall causing Father Olsen to jump. He waited for a repeat of the sound, and when it happened a few moments later, the priest recognized it as the noise from the shutters mounted on his windows. The wind outside had caused them to swing wildly about. He got up to address the situation but struggled to close and secure the sash because his hand was trembling during the task. The freezing wind blasted against his packing box, and inside, the wooden cross started to dart back and forth, dinging the cardboard and cracking the glass in the picture frames.

He reached for the cross, but it shot through the side of the box, barely missing his head as it rocketed out the window. The sash slammed shut behind it.

Father Olsen stood there, his hair windblown, as he tried to take in what was happening. Immediately he could sense that the church had changed around him. He felt that everything had somehow shifted to the left of where he remembered: his desk, the bookshelves, the door— everything down to the brickwork. And it all seemed darker. Unhallowed.

Outside his door in the eerie quiet, something clanged.

Father Olsen stepped from his office and into the hallway. He could envision the corridor perfectly lit in his mind's eye. Outside, the wind mourned between the flying buttresses and into every crack of the church but Father Olsen heard nothing else. No prowlers. Nothing suspicious. He turned back toward his office.

"Marhaba, Father..."

The priest whirled around. The voice came from the end of the hall.

"Ami?"

"Why did you abandon me, Father?" The boy's voice had a guttural cadence, as if the voice running through his vocal cords were coming from another source.

"I didn't abandon you, son... I tried to save you."

"No, Father, you left me. You let them take me."

Father Olsen took a few steps toward the voice. "Ami, I tried to —"

He walked straight into a wall of stench, a smell so thick it was impassable. The priest tried not to stagger as the pollution impelled him backward.

"Help me, Father, help get them out of me. It hurts..."

A few times during the exorcism, Father Olsen had pried enough of the demon's fingers from around Ami that he had heard the boy's pure, untainted soul weeping, and he believed he was close to saving him.

"I need you, Father," Ami said, doubling over and clutching his belly. "I need you to make it stop..."

Father Olsen nodded and stretched his hand out.

In his chamber, the radio suddenly switched on. Except it was no longer broadcasting the Catholic station he had been listening to. Now it was blaring static, white noise distorting Father Olsen's visual blueprint of the church.

Ami lunged from the shadows and grabbed the priest's arm. Father Olsen tried to pull away, but the boy's hand held him like a vice.

Above them, surrounded by a shriek of radio feedback, something took wing from high on the church. Father Olsen could not only hear the sound of the creature leaving its perch, somehow he could visualize it as he looked up to the ceiling that featured a stained-glass window created for the church more than a century ago. Through his blind

193

eyes he could see the shadow of a large beast diving toward the glass... dropping toward him. With great concentration, Olsen caught a glimpse beyond the darkness of the shadow and saw a beast, a gargoyle, but not a living creature, instead it was a stone statue sculpted from limestone.

The priest jerked his arm from Ami's grasp and leaped from where he had been standing. The stained-glass window shattered and the stone monster landed with a thud into the tiled concrete floor.

Nothing in her life had prepared her for this situation. Everything she had learned growing up, Sandy had tried to use to strengthen her character. But as she stood in the shadows of a building across the street from the YMCA, Sandy felt like everything she had learned had gone M.I.A.

What was happening with Tom? Why was it was happening? Why was it happening to them... to her?

She didn't have any answers.

She had no idea what to do.

While searching her brain for a clue, Sandy saw Tom exit the building across the street. His demeanor was different than when he had first entered. Now he only had a few words for those who tried to speak with him, as if he was aware of the time of the night, and how long he had been gone from his fiancé who he believed was at home in bed. From across the street, Sandy emerged from the shadows and started to follow her fiancé, but after only few steps, she stopped when she caught sight of Dr. Fincher emerging from the main entrance of the YMCA building. Sandy retreated back into her hiding place, then watched as Fincher exchanged some words with some of the patients in his group who were smoking outside the building. Sandy waited for a few minutes, but then grew anxious and decided to resume her pursuit of Tom, but it was at that very moment, Fincher ended his post therapy banter. She was forced to scramble back into the shadows when Tom's new therapist began making his way across the street... walking in a beeline to where she was hiding.

RUN is what Sandy immediately thought as Dr. Fincher approached. She decided to hold her ground when common sense overwhelmed her primal instinct for flight. Sandy told herself there was nothing to fear from a quack with a medical license he probably got online. And she got more courage by planning on running a full background check on Fincher as soon as she returned to her loft.

And yet, the closer Fincher got to where she was standing, she couldn't help sweating and shaking.

Just a few feet away from her hiding place, Dr. Fincher abruptly changed directions, veering off towards the Lower East Side.

After he was out of sight, Sandy crept out of the darkness and poked her head around the building corner to get a look in both directions. She tried to pick up the sight of her fiancé, but could no longer see him heading toward their apartment building.

Sandy turned, looking in the opposite direction and saw Dr. Fincher moving confidently to his next destination. She felt she had no choice of who she should follow, and yet her decision caused Sandy to feel like one of the pathetic women guests who would frequent the daytime talk shows she and her mother watched on TV after she came home from school. They were more like staged confrontations than talk shows, oftentimes featuring a sexual triangle involving girlfriends/wives of philandering boyfriends/husbands and the guy's mistress. The astounding part of the spectacle was watching the girlfriend/wife pull their punches when it came to their boyfriend/husband, but then put on brass knuckles before taking down the woman who had come between them, as if the mistress' act of luring the man away was much more egregious than the guy's lying and cheating. She had decided to follow Dr. Fincher because she needed to see where he was going and what she might discover when he got there. Sandy needed to know how this man could possibly have the power to develop a hold on Bernard Rose, and on her fiancé. And for some reason, it was Fincher that Sandy blamed.

Her pursuit led her across the Manhattan Bridge into the Bowery. During the entire time she had tailed him, Fincher had not once looked back as he walked with a cocksure swagger that Sandy found both nauseating and intimidating.

As they crossed into a dilapidated neighborhood, Fincher suddenly picked up his pace. He then walked even faster as he approached a street corner. The therapist took an abrupt left turn and disappeared from Sandy's sight.

A minute later, she approached the same corner slowly and cautiously, and from across the street realizing that all along Fincher could have been baiting her, leading her into a trap.

A cold draft slithered up her spine as she studied the street where Fincher had turned. There were no alleys, and all the buildings on the block were crammed together, side by side, and were a combination of residential apartments and street-level commercial shops lining the Boulevard.

Without any clue where Fincher had gone, Sandy began her trek down the same block. Halfway up the street, she caught sight of the building on the corner.

You've got to be kidding me, Sandy thought to herself. Tired from chasing two different men in the middle of the night, she had failed to recognize the neighborhood where her second pursuit ended. She had been there several times before, years ago, working on a story. On the corner of the street was the St. Jude church where Father Alan Olsen was the head priest.

She suddenly wondered if somehow things were beginning to come together. She didn't necessary feel closer to any answers, but at least Sandy had a feeling that all the pieces of the puzzle were finally being laid in front of her, so she could have a clear look at how they all might fit together.

Sandy's footsteps echoed throughout St. Jude's as she walked past the pews toward the main altar. Stained-glass windows, opaque in the candlelight, lined the entire church, decorated with tracery in trefoils, circles, and floral designs. The aisles on either side were separated from the nave by clustered columns.

As Sandy approached the pulpit, she noticed two old women with short gray hair, bony fingers pressed together below their bowed heads, and on their knees in the front pews.

She thought about asking them if they'd seen Fincher, but she was distracted when the soles of her shoes stepped on tiny bits of colored glass. Sandy then saw a gargoyle statue embedded in the floor a few feet in front of her. Looking up, she saw where the sculpture had fallen from the building above and crashed through the stained glass ceiling. The church was ancient, so she didn't immediately question why the gargoyle had broken off, but she was worried that no one was around to notice.

Sidestepping the stone beast, Sandy moved to the end of the corridor where a Koa wood carving of Jesus on a cross hung above the entrance to the priest's chamber. Sandy approached the door to the chamber when it flung outward on its own. Rays of light and a figure shot out from the other side of the doorway and before Sandy could react, she was thrown backwards against a wall.

Chapter 28

"Father Olsen! It's me, Sandy—Sandy Travis!"

The light from his chamber allowed her to see the color drain from the priest's face before he stepped back and released her. "Oh my God, Sandy, forgive me."

Sandy stretched out her left arm, which had impacted against the wall when Olsen attacked her.

"It's all right…"

What are you doing here?"

Before answering "I don't know how to say this without going into a full confession. I'm here because I was following someone. Someone who I think is dangerous."

"We need to leave here immediately," said Olsen, grabbing her by the same injured arm and ushering her toward the front of the church.

"So he's here? Dr. Fincher is here in the church?"

"Who is Dr. Fincher?"

She stopped Olsen's forced march before replying, "I think we should both calm down and start all over. I was following a psychiatrist, who probably isn't armed, and if push came to shove, I bet I could take him in a fight. So we're not in any immediate danger… unless you're talking about something different?"

When Alan did not let go of her arm, she knew that it was the latter. "Sandy, we need to leave the church now. And it has nothing to do with whoever you were following. Now do you understand?"

"Yes, I understand," said Sandy. "But tell me what's wrong, Alan. You look terrified."

"I will explain later, after we all leave. Did you see anyone else in the church?"

"There were two old women praying in one of the pews near the altar."

He nodded and gazed out toward the nave. "Okay, let me take care of them. Now, Sandy, you must do what I say, leave immediately. I'll meet you in front of the church. Promise me you will do this." His hand holding her arm was shaking.

"Yes, I promise. I'm leaving now, and I'll meet you in front of the church."

She lay her hand on top of his trembling hand clutching her arm before they split up.

Father Olsen began walking toward the church's main altar. As he came closer to the front pews, he heard two female voices, barely audible but consistent with what Olsen often heard while walking through the church as parishioners mumbled or whispers their prayers aloud.

But as he drew closer, Father Olsen stopped his approach when he realized the words he was hearing weren't being spoken in English, and they weren't prayers. The words were from the "dead" languages of Latin and Aramaic. However, there were phrases he heard that he recognized only because recently the same combination of words came up while performing an exorcism on Ami.

"Hello, Alan," the two women said in unison. , "Have you come to warn us to leave?" Both women's eyes were jet black like the irises of a shark. Their skin was pulled across their faces as if the flesh was large rubber bands secured at the back of each pair of ears. "You must be stupid as well as blind. We're here to make sure you leave. And Alan, we aren't talking about your retirement from the church."

The organ high above the narthex began to play Carl Orff's "O Fortuna," the pipes thundering loud enough to vibrate dust from the walls. The entire church became an orchestra, doors as bass drums, opening and slamming, stained-glass windows exploding like crash cymbals.

"His time has come. Behold the Angel of Light who will save us all from our wretched existence on this planet."

They both stood and raised their arms, then directed their hands toward Olsen.

"Don't worry, Alan, we shall put in a good word for you with the Landlord who controls your next stop."

"Father!" Sandy screamed from the narthex, shouting over Orff's deafening composition. The twins turned their heads, and for the first time she saw their faces, and realized that whatever Father

Olsen had been warning her about, he was obviously not fully aware of the potential danger.

"Just stay right there," Sandy shouted as she started running toward the front of the church to help Olsen.

The twins looked at each other and nodded, every movement synchronized down to the twitch of their mouths, and then their black eyes rolled up to milky whites.

As Sandy ran up the middle aisle of the church, the pews all around her began to vibrate. When they all began to shake violently it caused Sandy to stop in her tracks in fear.

"Sandy, you need to leave. Go now," shouted Alan.

One by one, and then more and more with every second, all the pews in the church shook off the metal that had fastened the woodwork to the floor, sending steel bolts shooting across the church like bullets, shattering the stained-glass windows that lined the walls of the church.

In all the chaos, Sandy had no choice but to turn around and begin running up the center aisle. When she was made it past the congregation area unharmed, Sandy turned and was astounded by what she saw – all of St. Jude's church pews had somehow risen and banded together to form a huge towering stained pine wood beast with hundreds of cast iron rails as limbs to propel it forward like a lumbering predator going after its prey… Sandy.

She ran breathlessly across the marble floor with the thundering noise of the beast chasing after her.

As she approached the doors to the outer lobby area, Sandy saw the pew monster was about to overrun her and couldn't help mentally flashing on her fate of being buried underneath hundreds of church pews. But then there was a loud screeching noise filling the church walls as the iron legs skidded across the marble floor. She turned to see that the pew monster had abruptly stopped the chase and had begun to re-assemble itself into a different shape, spreading out across from one side of the building to the other. It took only seconds, but when it was done, there was a massive wall of pine wood and cast iron separating the rest of the church from where Sandy now stood.

Near the transept and the stairs to the altar, Father Olsen clutched the front rail and climbed to his feet. The twin women whirled on him, their eyes rolling back to reveal again only white irises as drew on their powers.

The hymn books discarded when all the pews rose to form a monster, now began to shake. Then one after another the books flew from the marble floor as if they were projectiles being shot from a canon. The target of each of these leather-bound hymns was Father Olsen.

Despite being blind, Olsen could sense that he was under attack and reacted, avoiding the first couple of missiles that flew at him. But then one of the books hit him squarely in the head, and he became immobilized, which allowed several more books to strike him before he collapsed.

Sandy dialed 911 on her mobile phone, telling the emergency operator that there was a terrorist attack at the St. Jude Church. While still on the phone with the dispatcher, Sandy saw a fire rise and begin to burn across the church's main altar. She was able to pass along this information so the dispatcher would also alert the Fire department.

Just as she ended her call, Alan was struck down by the flying hymn books. She watched as the two witches began to move toward an unconscious Father Olsen.

"Why are you doing this? Stop!"

But neither of the women would acknowledge her screams.

Sandy knew she couldn't wait for the police and fire department to arrive. It would be too late. She thought about entering the church from the back entrance but feared it would take too long, and that when she got there the door would be sealed off.

She turned her attention to the pine wood and cast iron wall erected before her. Now that it didn't look like a wild beast chasing after her, it didn't look as intimidating. She saw gaps in the broken wood and twisted iron. When she located at the top of the wall one gap large enough to squeeze through, Sandy, didn't hesitate. She took a running leap, then began scaling the wall.

After feeling as if he had been stoned by a righteous mob right out of the Old Testament, Father Alan Olsen was feeling at peace. He no longer felt the pain from the dozens of books that had struck him. His body was now comfortably numb, which he believed was a sign that it was finally time to leave behind a body that had been a challenge to his soul and spirit for most of his life. He was laid out on the marble floor of the church he had guided for many years, shocked but very pleased that his final moments alive would be at a place he loved.

After feeling as if he had been stoned by a righteous mob right out of the Old Testament, Father Alan Olsen was feeling at peace. He no longer felt the pain from the dozens of books that had struck him. His body was now comfortably numb, which he believed was a sign that it was finally time to leave behind a body that had been a challenge to his soul and spirit for most of his life. He was laid out on the marble floor of the church he had guided for many years, shocked but very pleased that his final moments alive would be at a place he loved.

It was only when he felt the heat of the fire... and smoke began to fill his lungs that Father Olsen realized he was not yet dead.

And when he heard Sandy's voice screaming his name, it caused him to open his blind eyes. What he saw was not empty black space, but a face he had assigned to Sandy from his imagination soon after they met. It was the face he had for years matched with her voice, the one he was hearing echo in the church as she screamed his name -- "Alan!"

He coughed as he rolled over and tried to stand. He heard footsteps coming toward him after falling back down. Olsen tried to breathe, but it only caused him to cough some more as he slumped to the ground next to what felt like a towering furnace. He summoned his strength and managed to push himself up.

"We're not impressed, Alan." It was the old women, still speaking in unison. "You're dead. Just embrace it and be done the whole bloody business."

They were only a few feet from him, but for some reason, they weren't attacking him, even though it was clear he was beaten, on his knees, ready to be put out of his misery. His mind wandered. He wondered if they were not finishing him off for a specific reason. Were there rules? Rules of engagement."

"Beg the Angel of Light for mercy," the old women shouted together as "O Fortuna" climaxed with a cannonade of drums and organ chords.

Then there was silence.

He tried to stand, but couldn't muster the strength. So he began to crawl. And he kept crawling across the marble floor with the expectation that at any moment, he would be struck down by the two demonically possessed women. Or perhaps it would be Ami, with the demon inside the boy pulling the strings that would force him to deliver the final blow.

He had moved about a dozen feet when he heard footsteps.

"Alan, you're alive!"

He wanted to respond but began coughing.

Sandy slung his arm around her shoulder and helped him up. "We need to get out of here. The whole place is on fire."

As they walked together, he heard the sound of sirens, some were close others coming growing louder. Sandy couldn't help but notice that the heat and smoke from the fire seemed to be causing weird shadows projected on the walls all around them. The dark gyrations seemed to be following them every step of the way.

Sandy felt some relief when through the thick smoke she saw the firemen chopping away at the wall of pews, carving out a place for them to escape the burning church.

"We're almost there. How are you doing, Alan?"

"I'm all right," he said, finally getting his voice back. "I am a little discouraged though that people will think that on my final day I burned the place down."

Father Olsen looked terrible as he lay on the gurney. Strands of gray hair were frayed and sticking up around his bald spot and there was blood staining his face and hands. However, Sandy needed to take advantage of the opportunity to speak with him before he was driven off to the hospital.

"Help me out, Alan. What the hell is going on?"

His milky white eyes stared at her as he took his time thinking about how to answer his question.

"What do you think is happening?"

Thinking was a problem for Sandy. It felt like her whole life had turned upside down, and her analytical brain was not keeping up with current events.

"Honestly, I have no idea. You tried to warn me, but at the time I wasn't listening. You've got my attention now.

"Because of what you saw tonight," said Olsen. The tone of his question showed no sign he felt vindicated that Sandy was finally interested in what he had to say. It took the burning down of his church before he could convert his first true believer.

"Yes of course. But there's been other horrible things that have happened since we last met at my office. I was working on a story about the recent assassination attempt in the Mideast." Sandy waited for a reaction from Olsen, wondering if he kept up with current events.

"You mean the shooter in Tel Aviv?"

"Yes, that's right. I was in Washington D.C. meeting with the assassin's widow. Helen and I were walking to our car when she was attacked by a dog."

"Is this the same the young woman I met at your office?"

Tears had welled up in Olsen's eyes even before he asked the question.

"Yes, I tried to get her to the hospital but I was too late and Helen died."

He grabbed her hand. "Sandy, I'm so sorry."

She nodded, without tearing up herself. Perhaps she was too exhausted to cry.

Father Olsen continued to squeeze her hand as he asked, "And you believe the attack by the dog was unusual, somehow connected to what we just went through?"

"Not at first. But there's more…"

Sandy looked out of one of the van windows. She wanted to scan the group of onlookers on the street who had gathered to watch the church burn down. Sandy wanted to make sure Dr. Fincher wasn't part of the crowd.

"It's Tom. Ever since the helicopter accident in Hawaii… he hasn't been himself. He had a Near-Death Experience. Just like the assassin in Tel Aviv. And both claimed to see the same image during their N.D.E."

"The Angel of Light," said Father Olsen.

"Yes," Sandy said. "When I was coming to help you, I heard those two women use the same words. So, yeah, I believe everything that has occurred is somehow connected. However, I have idea how… why… or what to do about it."

Before Father Olsen could respond, two fire department paramedics stepped into the van.

"Okay, Father we're all set to go."

Sandy had already checked the paramedics out the moment she handed Alan over to them. No member of the crew had any resemblance to the thin-skinned goons she had encountered in Hawaii and Washington D.C. Though she still had not gotten a chance to mention that strange detail to Alan. Everything was happening so fast.

"Sorry, ma'am we need to take your friend now. You can follow us if you'd like. We're taking him to Mercy Heart Hospital just a few blocks up the street."

She nodded to the paramedic and stepped off the van. She shouted out to Father Olsen, "Alan, I need to go home first to see about Tom. I'll come to the hospital as soon as I can."

The paramedic shut the back doors before the priest had a chance to respond.

"No! Sandy, don't go home," shouted Father Olsen. "You need to stay away from Tom…"

But she didn't hear anything Alan was shouting out to her as the van pulled away.

When Sandy returned to the apartment, she was surprised to discover Tom was not there. It was hard to tell whether he had come home after the therapy session and then left again, or whether he had not come home at all.

She waited for a few minutes, just standing there in the middle of her apartment, too tired to think clearly, but still too wound up to sleep. After more time passed, Sandy finally decided to take a shower. She was a mess from everything that had happened.

Tom was still not home when she got out of the shower. She put on her pajamas and called the hospital to check on Alan. A nurse working the reception desk updated her on Father Olsen's status. He was in stable condition, but had three broken bones, multiple contusions all over his body, two that they were afraid had caused some internal bleeding. However, what caused the attending physician the most concern was that X-rays revealed that a head injury had caused the brain to swell. It was the main reason Alan would be staying in the hospital for at least 24 hours.

When Sandy asked to speak with him, the nurse told her that he had been sedated and would probably be asleep for several hours.

When Sandy hung up the phone she thought about sleeping, then going to the hospital, but after getting into bed, she decided that the events of the evening still had her wired. She was often like this while working on a story. That's when it hit her – she needed to do the background research on a member of the medical profession she suspected of fraud. Sandy would do what the staff at 24/7 called the full rectal - a complete and through check on someone using all the resources available to a network TV show. The target of her inquiry was Dr. Benjamin Fincher.

Sandy was at it for hours, eventually recruiting one of her fellow workers in the research department she knew was up and available. Her effort was so passionate and consuming that the first time Sandy noticed the time was when she heard the apartment door open. She closed the file she had been working on with her laptop computer before running to the entry hallway.

"Where have you been? I was worried about you."

Tom closed the door. "I was looking for you."

She turned away and shook her head.

"I woke up last night to do some work," said Tom. "But when I came back to bed you were gone."

"Yeah, right." She turned to walk away, but suddenly Tom was right next to her, his hand grabbing her arm just above the elbow. She had no idea how he got from one part of the hallway to the other in the blink of an eye. But then she thought about the last 36 hours — no sleep... a traumatic experience at a church... and pulling an all-nighter working on a background check. Was it any surprise that her perception of reality had become seriously frayed?

"Where were you?" He was inches away; Sandy could smell his breath, which wasn't pleasant, but it didn't smell of booze or pot. But then there was the skin on Tom's face, which looked like cellophane pulled across a bowl of fruit you were hoping to keep fresh for a week.

"You know where I was," she answered without flinching. "I was following you."

He stared at her with a blank look in his eyes, as if his brain was trying to calculate how to react to Sandy opting for honesty rather than deception, and it was taking some time for the proper response to show up on his face.

"Tom, you've been different ever since Hawaii. So last night, after you got out of bed in the middle of the night, I followed you to the YMCA."

"You followed me?"

She yanked her arm out of his grip and continued. "Yeah, I followed you. And I saw the group therapy session with everyone, including you, talking about Near-Death Experiences."

He finally reacted, raising his hand to his forehead as if he had a headache. "I can't believe you followed me. Why would you do that?" As soon as he looked like he was going to make another move, Sandy backed up in the living room of the apartment. She now had it her mind that it was probably best to keep at least a couple of feet between the two.

"Normally, I'd be supportive about anyone, especially you, reaching out for help. But you lost me when you decided to keep everything a secret. Why keep it a secret, Tom? I thought we were in this together."

"Maybe I was embarrassed about what you would think."

The words were pretty good, but Tom didn't have the contrite look on his face to sell it. Sandy could see he was going through the motions. And it worried her that Tom was no longer even making the effort to sell his lies.

"You should be embarrassed," said Sandy. "Not for reaching out for help, but for reaching out to a guy like Dr. Benjamin Fincher."

He looked around and spotted her laptop on the kitchen counter. He quickly deduced what she had been working on. "I'm sorry, honey. I don't really care what you've dug up on Dr. Fincher. I'm not going to stop seeing him."

"Really? Nothing I've discovered would cause a change? What if I told you that in 2001 Dr. Fincher was asked to resign as the head of the psychiatric unit at Boston Memorial Hospital because an investigation found 'serial actions of unethical behavior. In 2003, he was forced to resign from Orlando Presbyterian for what the board of directors there cited as 'irregular, and unprofessional episodes in which Dr. Fincher refused to deny nor explain during an internal hospital investigation.' I have more. Way more. Are you telling me that none of this makes a difference to you?"

Tom shook his head, "No, it doesn't. But I am curious – why did you do all this?"

"Because I was worried about you!"

"Sure you were..." Tom turned and stormed away from her, toward the front door of the apartment.

She followed after him, "Honey, where are you going?"

"I'm sleeping at a hotel tonight. I can't get over how you invaded my privacy and followed me like... like the target of one of your news stories. I'll call you tomorrow..."

Before she could react, her fiancé threw open the apartment door and rushed out.

"Tom, wait!"

But the door slammed just as the words were leaving her mouth. She waited, but when the door remained shut, Sandy knew he was gone. Things had spiraled so quickly out of control between them Sandy never got a chance to use her last weapon, the one she was saving to close the deal with Tom with his agreement to see another professional doctor who could really him.

I love you. She had planned on using the phrase at the perfect time, hoping that whatever it was that had a hold on Tom, her expression of love would give him the strength to break free. Sandy now regretted holding back because they had parted without her fiancé hearing her say the words.

CHAPTER
30

Family and friends gathered around Helen's grave site. Sandy stood among them, but wished she was invisible as she said goodbye to her friend.

There were things she knew about why Helen was attacked and killed, but she couldn't tell anyone standing with her that day. Not yet. Not until she had more proof. However, everyone's eyes were on her during the memorial service as if she would have something to say.

As the priest concluded the last rites, the mourners bowed their heads and closed their eyes. After a brief period of silence, the people in the procession tossed flowers on the brushed-gold coffin, then one by one paid their respects to Helen's brother Charlie.

Sandy thought about trying to slip away, but she wasn't invisible. Everyone would notice. She also thought about Helen and knew that fleeing her grave site without a word to her brother would piss her off.

"Charlie, I'm so sorry for your loss," said Sandy. All Helen could talk about was how much she loved you… and your kids. I'm so sorry."

Helen's brother nodded before saying. "Thanks for coming, Sandy. My sister spoke so highly of you."

Feeling like it was the right moment, the next person to pay their respects moved forward, but Charlie raised his hand to stop him.

"Do you mind, giving me a minute?" He then turned back to Sandy, "Sandy, can we speak privately?" He began walking away from the grave site, and Sandy felt like she had no other choice but to follow him.

Charlie cleared his throat and adjusted his tie before looking straight at Sandy. "My sister looked up to you, admired you. So it pains me to ask this question — is it true that emergency paramedics arrived at the scene where my sister was attacked, and you refused to let anyone see Helen even though she was bleeding… dying right in front of you?"

Under different circumstances, Sandy might have anticipated the embarrassing encounter with Charlie and been prepared to handle the situation. However, after the last few days of no sleep, her entire belief system thrown into a mental dumpster, Sandy considered her appearance at Helen's funeral a miracle. She certainly was in no shape to defend herself or her actions concerning Helen's death.

She ran every word from Charlie's mouth three times through her head before she finally opened her mouth with a response.

"Charlie, I loved Helen. She was like my sister. I wish I could have helped her. I'm so sorry."

Sandy was not surprised when her answer was not good enough for Charlie. Helen's brother stepped closer to her, not with the purpose of lowering his voice, because as it turned out, he actually spoke much louder, attracting the attention of almost everyone standing at the burial site.

"That's not really an answer, Sandy. I spoke to two of the hospital staff where Helen died, and they both believed that if my sister had received immediate attention after being attacked, she might still be alive. So, again, I'm asking you — did you refuse to allow the initial responders to save the life of my sister?"

Charlie deserved to know the truth, and Sandy geared up to tell him everything that had happened. But as she was about to speak, a man interrupted, stepping in between them like a referee in a boxing match.

"You don't have to answer that," said Terry, Sandy's boss.

"Excuse me," said Charlie, "this is a private conversation…"

"And I do apologize for my intrusion," said Terry. "But I'm afraid this conversation is not in the spirit of the occasion. Take it from someone who's been to many funerals – the goal of the living during these services should be to maintain a mood of tranquility and respect. And everything else should be at least a rock throw away from the burial site."

Charlie turned to Sandy with fire in his eyes, "This must be your lawyer."

"Absolutely not," said Sandy before Terry took over the conversation again.

"Heaven's no. My name is Terry Rawlins. I'm the executive producer of the show, 24/7…I was your sister's boss."

"Terry Rawlins. I didn't recognize you," said Charlie, "Helen spoke about you all the time." Nothing on Charlie's face, or the tone of his voice let on about what Helen probably said about Terry when she was alive. Sandy could see Charlie was focused on just one target, and not interested in anyone else.

"It's nice to finally meet you, Terry. However, if you don't mind, I'd like to talk to Sandy about the night my sister died."

"I understand," said Terry, but rather than backing off, he stepped closer to Charlie. "I see the pain. Everyone on the show feels it as well. But you were Helen's brother, so even though we'd like to believe we're all experiencing the same feeling of loss, there's no way we can understand what you're actually going through."

Terry had a 24/7 business card ready and forced it into the palm of Charlie's hand.

"Take this. It has the phone number of the show's Human Resources Department. Charlie, I want you to call when you are ready to talk. I promise you they'll hook you up with the best grief therapist on the planet. And don't worry about the expenses. 24/7 will take care of it all. No matter how long it takes for you to recover from this tragedy. It's our way of showing you how much your sister meant to us."

Terry did not wait for Charlie's reply; he wrapped an arm around Sandy and pulled her away. The two did not say a word until they were completely out of earshot. And during that time Sandy ran through a few choices of what she could say to Terry, but in her frazzled mental state, she opted to speak candidly.

"I would thank you for intervening on my behalf, Terry... if I really believed that is what you just did. But we both know it was the show you were defending, not me."

"It's your choice to see it that way, Sandy," said Terry. "But it's a viewpoint that has me now worried for the first time about what happened the night Helen died."

"I tried calling you. There's a reason I wouldn't let the paramedics…"

"No, Sandy, I don't want to hear it. However, I do know of a man who is very much interested in everything you have to say. His name is Brian Gooden."

She couldn't help but roll her eyes at hearing the name. "Brian Gooden, the show's in-house lawyer," said Sandy.

"I understand he has put in three calls to you since the incident, and you've not returned a single one."

"I wanted to talk to you first."

They arrived at the long line of black cars parked at the edge of the cemetery.

"I think I've been pretty blunt that your instinct misled you, Sandy. If you had nothing to hide regarding Helen's death, then there would have been no need to call me. You should have returned Brian's calls. If you did something you're trying to hide, why would you call me? I'm not your life preserver. If you drown, you go down alone, and there's no way you will take me, or the show with you. I'm not ashamed of this. I've worked on 24/7 my entire professional career. Why would I let you bring me down? I hope this makes sense to you?"

"Yes, it makes all the sense in the world," she answered without looking at him.

Terry looked back and saw everyone standing at the grave site was watching them. He made a point of hugging Sandy, so there would be no misunderstanding of his and the show's support for her.

"It doesn't matter what you've done, Sandy. This is why lawyers were invented. You know that better than anyone. So play this right. Don't talk to anyone until you and Brian have connected first. Understand?"

"I understand."

Terry motioned to his driver. "Henry, I want you to call the car service and get them to send another car to drive me back. I want you to drive this lady home. Make sure she gets there. Understood, Henry?"

"Yes, sir. Understood." Henry opened the back door and waited for Sandy to get into the car. She looked up toward the burial site, and tried to think of Helen, but her brain was not responding. She couldn't even bring up a mental image of her friend's face before she gave up and stepped into the back of the car. Sandy saw that Terry was already heading back up the hill before the driver slammed shut the door.

CHAPTER
31

"**C**harlie was looking at me with these accusatory eyes as if I were the one who actually killed his sister. And you know something? Maybe I did."

Father Olsen tried to sit up in his hospital bed, but when he had trouble, he quickly gave up trying. Alan did not want to distract Sandy from venting. She needed to get everything that had happened at Helen's funeral out of her system.

"If I had let the same guys who had helped Tom in Hawaii, and miraculously showed up in Washington D.C. help Helen, yes, Helen might still be alive, but she wouldn't be the Helen I knew. Just like Tom isn't Tom."

For the first time since walking into Alan's room, Sandy stopped talking. After she was dropped off by Terry's driver in front of her apartment building, she walked to the nearest subway station where she caught a train to Mercy Heart hospital. Sandy knew the only person in the world who could possibly understand what she was going through would be a blind priest undergoing a battery of medical tests hoping and praying that it would lead to him being discharged.

"And you truly believe this Sandy?"

"Do I truly believe I killed Helen?"

"No. I'm sorry. I wasn't referring to Helen's death. Sandy, you did your best to save her. But right this moment, you're feeling what many people go through when someone dies… guilt. Did I show them enough love, compassion, honesty when they were alive? What you feel is what you would feel no matter the circumstances of Helen's death. Given time, you will see this as the truth. My question was about Tom. Do you truly believe he isn't the same person you knew before the helicopter accident?"

As she contemplated how to answer, Sandy walked over to the hospital room's window. She saw the city streets below had become a mess since she arrived. Something had happened causing the police and fire department to yellow tape the entire block and reroute traffic.

"I've always been a skeptical person, and it's served me well as a journalist. But I think you already knew that about me, Alan. So I hope that gives me credibility when I say I honestly believe Tom has profoundly changed after the helicopter accident Perhaps I wasn't thinking that way immediately after we got back from Hawaii, but I certainly feel that way now. There have been too many Black Swans floating across my pond for me not to notice. And what happened at the church was the final tipping point. I now believe what's been happening to me is somehow connected to what's been happening to you. And that's why I'm here in this room with you."

"You should know, Sandy that I'm relieved to know I'm not alone in all this."

"What's sad, Alan, is that there's a part of me that wishes you were alone. I was... happy with my life."

"I understand."

When she turned away from the window, Sandy's face had the intense look of a prosecuting attorney about to cross-examine a hostile witness in court.

"So let's get to it. In my office, Alan, you used a phrase, 'the Restrainer.'"

"I heard the phrase when it was spoken by the boy, Ami, who I was attempting to exorcise in Israel. He used the phrase the Restrainer during a point of the exorcism when he seemed to be free of the demonic possession. It was as if he was trying to help me with a clue, something he knew about because of his possession. I also took seriously what Ami said because his freedom was fleeting. Only a few minutes later the demon who possessed the boy once again took over control. When I said the words – the Restrainer – the possessed boy spit on me, and then verbally and physically attacked me. I believe the phrase was not something I was supposed to know about."

After his explanation, Olsen's mouth was parched, and he motioned to Sandy to retrieve his glass of water on a nearby tray. As he drank, Sandy said, "I ask because Helen and I came across the phrase in Bernard Rose's townhouse basement. It was scrawled in blood—'The Restrainer must die.'"

Olsen was too excited to keep on drinking, "Was there any other words written on the walls?"

"We saw two other phrases -- "The devil has gone down to you." And, "He wants the Perfect Possession.'"

"And this man, the one who wrote these words, like Tom, there was also some kind of accident which triggered an N.D.E. prior to his personality change?"

"That's right," said Sandy. "How did you know?"

"Ami, the boy I saw in Jerusalem, he also had been in an accident. He was hit by a car prior to showing any signs of demonic possession. I never asked the boy's parents about whether their son had a Near-Death Experience but insisted on seeing the medical reports following the car accident. I was satisfied that the change in his personality had nothing to do with his head injury."

Sandy had been pacing back and forth in the room as Alan talked and ended up at the end of his bed when he finished. The noises from the medical equipment monitoring Olsen's vitals seemed to grow louder in the silence Sandy needed to think things through.

"Father, let me run a theory by you. Imagine that you're involved in an accident which leads to a Near-Death Experience. You see this bright light, an ethereal figure, and because everything looks the way it should look you think, 'Wow. I'm in the presence of an angel sent by God.' And you're sent back to the living with a new purpose, with the feeling that everything that happened was beautiful and transcendent. But now imagine that the experience wasn't what you thought. What if it was actually occurred was the exact opposite of what you believed happened? What if this astral adventure left your body wide open, an opportunity for something else to slip in and become…"

"The perfect possession," interrupted Father Olsen.

"So you're ahead of me on this," said Sandy.

"No, Sandy, I'm still catching up. But what you said... it makes sense. I would only add that if this is happening, then it must be happening for something bigger than the demonic possession of a dozen of people."

"You believe this is about The End Days," said Sandy.

Olsen nodded. "At least give me credit for being consistent in my beliefs. Sandy, its's reason I came to you in the first place."

"Go ahead, Alan, tell me what you think. This time I'm really listening."

"The phrase the Restrainer is from Thessalonians 2, verse 6." Sandy watched as Father Olsen was able to quote verbatim the passage without using his brail bible as a reference, "And you know what is restraining him now so that he may be revealed in his time. For the mystery of lawlessness is already at work. Only he who now restrains it will do so until he is out of the way."

"I'm presuming the words 'him' and "it" are references to Satan," said Sandy.

"That's right," answered Olsen. "The restrainer is like some kind of gatekeeper preventing Satan from ushering in the End Days. Traditionally, the identity of the Restrainer has been a person, but I believe it could be someone or something that Satan must bypass before he can walk among us with the goal of triggering the End Days begin."

"And you believe this is all happening now... why?"

"I don't know. Perhaps because there is something happening that is unique, special, that needs to be taken advantage of. But, again, I don't know."

"And somehow Tom figures into this. Like he's a pawn in some kind End Days Game scenario."

Alan sighed. "I know it sounds like the plot of a video game the kids play in the rec room on Saturday at the church."

She looked at her watch. "Listen, Alan, I need to leave. But I'll be back."

"Where are you going?"

"Back to my apartment."

Alan took the news like he had been hit across the face with a sucker punch. "You're leaving because you don't believe in what we've talked about?"

"No, Alan, that's not true...." When her words didn't seem to sway him, Sandy moved to his bed and grabbed his hand. "Alan, right now, what we talked about seems to me to be the explanation that makes the most sense. Okay?"

"Then why go back to your apartment? Tom may be there."

"I doubt he will be. However, if he is, I'll deal with him. I'm going back to my apartment to get some things that I need because something tells me I won't be there for a while. Then I'm going to check into a hotel nearby this hospital. After I get everything sorted out, I'll be back here when you're supposed to be discharged. My plan was to then take you to the hotel where we'll be together. It'll give us a chance to keep on talking about all of this. Okay?"

He nodded, but as Sandy tried to pull away, Alan would not let go of her hand.

"Sandy, when was the last time you had communion?"

"Are you serious?"

"There's a chapel in this hospital. The priest who runs it, Father Martin, has been nice enough to visit me twice since I arrived." Alan threw aside his covers, as he prepared to get out of his bed. "I'm sure he won't mind if we use the chapel for a few minutes."

"Alan, no."

"Sandy, please, after everything that's happened. Look at it as putting on a bulletproof vest."

She could have pointed out to Alan that his beloved church was in ruin. Whatever holy protection the building had obviously failed. But she chose instead to tighten her hold on Olsen's hand before saying, "Father, I've survived a helicopter crash, a killer dog, and an attack by hundreds of pews chasing me across a church. Whatever I've got going for me; I'll trust will keep me alive until we figure this all out.

CHAPTER 32

By the time the car service had sent another car, Terry was one of the last to leave the cemetery after Helen's service. He was now paying the price by having his car stuck in traffic on its way back into the city. He was trying to make the best use of his down time by watching the network news and answering emails on his laptop computer.

"Reports from the Middle East couldn't be more upbeat as the final minor points have been hammered out leading up to the signing of a peace agreement between Israel and five Arab countries. The landmark peace accord is scheduled for a ceremonial signing this Friday with leaders from all the participating countries in attendance."

On the TV set, footage of Envoy John Wolfenson speaking in front of a gathering of Beltway VIPs rolled underneath the anchor's report.

"Meanwhile, the man responsible for bringing the entire region together for this historical moment, Envoy John Wolfenson, was feted last night in Washington D.C. He called the peace settlement 'a paradigm shift for all of humanity.' Members of the Quartet that appointed Wolfenson have already asked for him to stay at his post for an indefinite period of time..."

Terry turned down the TV and used his mobile phone to dial his office.

"Hi, Diane... well, I'm still stuck in traffic. That's why I'm calling. Yes, you need to reschedule my 3:00, 3:30 and 3:45 meetings. But before you do that can you get Brian in legal on the line?"

The driver of the town car tilted his head slightly, giving Terry the impression that he might be listening. Terry did not hesitate and used a button on his armrest to raise the black privacy partition. While he continued to wait for his secretary to transfer his call, Terry noticed the town car began to speed up. He hoped it was because the stalled traffic had finally started to move forward, but if it was because he'd ticked off the driver with his decision to raise the partition... too bad. Before he could give it another thought, the secretary connected Terry with the head of legal affairs for the show, Brian Gooden.

"Brian, I need to talk to you about this situation with what happened in the field with Helen. I was just at her funeral, and it was a total soap opera. The only thing missing was a commercial break, which would have allowed me to jump in before things got really ugly. I'm calling, Brian, because I think we need to do something about Sandy after all..."

Terry was forced to grab a hold of his armrest when the town car suddenly veered one way, then another, before picking up speed again.

"Excuse me for a second, Brian. It looks like I've got Steve McQueen behind the steering wheel..." Terry leaned forward and tapped the glass. "Hey, take it easy up there. I think you already heard. I canceled my next three meetings. We're not in a hurry!"

Terry settled back into his seat to continue with his call "Anyway, Brian, as I was saying, this situation is serious. I think we may be forced to pay off Sandy's contract and let her go—"

The car lurched to the right, and Terry slammed against the door.

"Goddamit! You need to hold on a second, Brian..."

Terry laid the phone beside him and reached for his seat belt, only to discover that it had been cut off. And when Terry reached to the other side, he found the same thing: a stub.

The privacy partition began to descend, revealing the back of his driver's head.

"What the fuck is going on!" Terry shouted. "These seat belts have been removed!"

The driver ignored him, keeping his eyes fixed on the road as he raced and careened around cars, forcing pedestrians in the crosswalk to jump out of the way.

"I had died. But then I was sent back to the living by the Angel of Light.

Terry gripped the door handle to keep himself from falling forward and from completely losing it.

"He told me that my time with the living was not over. There was still a purpose to my life..."

237

"What the hell are you talking about?! Stop this car! Did you hear me? Pull over right now!"

Terry scrambled to pick up his mobile rolling around on the floor in front of him. But when he finally had it back in his hand, he discovered that the phone call with Brian Gooden in legal affairs had become disconnected. Terry hit the redial button on the phone, but before it could reconnect, the town car jumped the curb and crashed through a department store display window, mowing down mannequins and then real people, before slamming into a support column.

Sandy unlocked the door to the apartment and took off her shoes before she entered.

"Tom?"

As she walked into the living room, Sandy saw that none of the lights were on and that the blinds were shut tight. And the place was even colder than what she experienced at the doorway.

"Tom?"

She made her way to the bedroom, but didn't see any sign her fiancé had returned. His clothes were still in the closet along with all the items he had left behind in the bathroom.

Sandy made her way back into the living room, and stopped at the kitchen bar to check for messages. She lifted the phone off the hook and heard the stuttered dial tone. Sandy hit the button to call in for voicemail, then hit another button that automatically sent the code to playback the recorded messages.

"Hola, Ms. Travis," the housekeeper said on the machine, "I will not be there tomorrow. I have to take my girl to the doctor."

While listening to the message, Sandy noticed for the first time a large puddle of water stretching across the hardwood floor from the guest bathroom.

"I come on Wednesday," the housekeeper said. "Let me know if that's a problem. Good-bye."

"Tom, is that you?" Sandy called, approaching the closed bathroom door. She was still holding the phone in mobile phone unit in her hand as she approached the door. Sandy saw light and more water flowing steadily through the crack under the door.

"Tom, are you in there?!"

"Sandy," a man's voice said on the next voice message, "This is Bob... you need to call in. Terry was in a car accident..."

Her hand froze on the door handle. The voice belonged to Bob Harris, the managing director at 24/7

"We don't have many details, but it looks like Terry is dead. I tried calling your mobile phone first to let you know. Oh, my god, the network news crew just started sending back footage on the Sat-Feed..."

As Sandy listened in shock to Harris' voice message, she stopped paying attention to the fact that she was standing with her bare feet in cold water streaming from the bathroom.

"Sandy, call me when you get this message."

The voice service moved on to the next message.

"Honey, it's me. I miss you. I'm coming home tonight. I'm sorry for the way I've been acting."

Suddenly, Sandy saw something move, a figure crouching in the shadows, near a standing light.

"Baby, we're in this together. I love you..."

The figure touched the frayed end of the cord cut from the lamp, and a blue lightning bolt arced into the pool of water that stretched across the room and underneath Sandy's feet. Instantly she felt several paralyzing jolts shoot through her body, which caused her to go rigid, stopping her in mid-scream. All around her blue electricity crackled and danced.

The voice from the answering service said, "End of Messages."

With the phone still in her hand, Sandy toppled over like a statue pushed off its pedestal.

CHAPTER 33

Sandy's eyes shot open.

She lay in the water but couldn't feel it. She couldn't feel anything. Couldn't smell, couldn't taste.

Like a balloon, she drifted up from the hardwood floor—leaving her body behind. It lay in the puddle, its eyes closed, its chest still, as peaceful and empty as her mother had looked in her casket. Sandy could sense that she was tethered to it though, as if by a string, something easily cut.

A blast of wind buffeted her around, and light began to seep from everything—the water, the walls, the furniture, the blinds—every particle aspiring to be a sun.

In the front room, the man in the shadows was illuminated. He lifted the frayed cord from the water, and with hands gloved in black leather, he pushed back his hood. Sandy immediately recognized the goatee. The man, her executioner, was Tom's guru Dr. Fincher.

The humming sound grew louder, deeper, and the air in front of her opened into a large dark tunnel, suddenly bursting with bright light, forcing

Sandy to shield her eyes and turn away. The luminance appeared manufactured to dazzle, evidenced by a hollow artificial quality. Halogen instead of celestial suns.

A shadowy figure emerged from the tunnel and eclipsed the radiation, save for a brilliant corona. She could see only his outline, no details, no facial features, his profile as black as the dark side of the moon.

"Who are you?" she asked, though her mouth didn't move. The sound seemed to generate from the trembling of the air itself.

"I am the Angel of Light," the shadow replied, his voice majestic and resounding, yet tinny, reminiscent of the Wizard of Oz amplified to deceive Dorothy. "It is not your time. There are things you still need to do."

He reached out to her, and she reached out too, both in slow motion, the corona moving around them in warm swells, but as their fingertips were about to touch, Sandy grabbed the angel by the wrist and pulled him out of his aura, revealing a horned goat skull onto which raw flesh had been melted, one eye socket impossibly deep, and in it a vision—all the world a battlefield bereft of the slightest skittering of life; cities reduced to skeletons of steel, concrete, and rebar; bodies upon bodies decaying in layers, the bottom one oily crude, all overshadowed by a sky of burning coal.

The deceptively divine light flared from the tunnel and enveloped Sandy in sweet blindness, hiding from her the hideous skull. As the brilliance faded, she felt her body reeling in the string that anchored her. The helium that had inflated her now hardened to the density of lead, and a moment later she opened her eyes, gasping for breath.

She woke up staring into Tom's eyes, his lips pressed to hers, performing mouth-to-mouth resuscitation.

"Sandy, are you all right?"

He reached to embrace her, but she pushed him away and scrambled backward, hands splashing in the water.

"Honey, what's wrong?"

She glanced around, her mind spinning. The loft reeked of burnt hair. She noticed the frayed lamp cord in the living room and fixed her eyes on Tom.

"What have you done?

"I didn't do anything, except save your life."

"Tom, did you make the water overflow from the bathroom so that I would be electrocuted?"

He frowned. "Of course not. Why would I do that?"

"I don't know, Tom, maybe so I could have a meet and greet with your guardian angel."

"You had an N.D.E.?!"

"Yeah... And trust me when I tell you that the Angel of Light is fucking Satan."

"Then you didn't see what I saw," Tom said, sitting back on his haunches.

Sandy climbed to her feet, too uncomfortable to lie vulnerable beneath him. She grew dizzy and almost vomited.

Tom moved toward her.

"No." She held up her hand and backed away. She wanted to run but needed time to recover; otherwise, she would just stumble and fall, and he would pounce. She came here with a purpose. Now she would use it to buy time.

"Tom, you need to listen to me. What I saw, what we both saw—it's possessing you. It wants to control you so you will do what it wants. Honey, you have to fight it."

"But I don't want to fight it," he said, taking a step toward her even as she took a step back. Very little room remained between her and the wall. "My purpose in life has never been clearer. Sandy, I want you to join me..."

He lunged at her.

She jumped away and crashed into one of his easels. The painting landed at her feet. It was a watercolor rendering of John Wolfenson.

Sandy darted farther into the painting area, into a funhouse of easels flaunting Tom's latest work: Wolfenson in different death scenes and a unique ribbon of blood unifying the collection, first forming a slash across the Envoy's throat, then looping above his head in a crimson halo and, on the next canvas, glazing a sharp point of glass gripped tightly in someone's hand. The red thread appeared continuous, as if the artwork had all been a single canvas, now segmented, so that when aligned the filament would tie them back together. One painting departed from the theme and depicted a shadowy figure descending from the heavens, but

244

the last one picked up where the blood left off, and in bright-red letters Tom had written, "The Restrainer Must Die!"

Sandy slowed down to absorb the clues, realizing she might only have one chance to see them. Tom, having caught up, grabbed her from behind.

She bucked and writhed and kicked paintings to the floor. Tom's foot punched through one of the canvases, through Wolfenson's face, and his shoe caught in the rip. He stumbled.

Sandy broke away from him and scurried to the door. Tom kicked off the painting and took chase.

The deadbolt—she had locked it before. Now her fingers, seemingly fat and uncoordinated, fumbled to disengage it.

Tom growled, closing in. She jacked back the bolt. He pounced—and Sandy slammed the door in his face.

Barefoot, shoes still inside, Sandy broke out onto the sidewalk, shouldering past a few bystanders who got in her way. She ran for blocks until she realized Tom hadn't followed, and then she stopped, wheezing and stooped over.

After a few seconds, she lurched to the gutter and filled it with puke.

CHAPTER
34

Terry had died. So many things had happened that Sandy had almost forgotten until she entered the Optio Entertainment building lobby. The receptionist, Margot, was crying behind her desk. Sandy moved to her, and they embraced. "I can't believe he's dead," Margot said. Her sobs rocked Sandy, bruised her deep into the bone, yet still she couldn't cry.

Bob Harris, the executive who had left the message on Sandy's machine, walked up behind the two women and waited until they parted. His hair looked more gray than usual, and his face more weathered.

"C'mon, Sandy, we need to talk."

She followed him to his office, chrome- and mahogany-themed. Nothing, not even a scrap of paperwork, cluttered his desk. He settled into his leather office chair, and Sandy seated herself across from him. Unlike his, her seat did not feature a built-in massager.

Bob sighed and folded his hands on his immaculate blotter. "I spoke with Brian in legal. He filled me in on what Terry wanted to do.

Apparently, his last directive was to pay off your contract and let you go." The executive let the statement hang in the air before continuing.

"But something came up this morning concerning Envoy John Wolfenson. He's agreed to an exclusive interview with 24/7 in Jerusalem after the signing of the peace treaty."

"That's a nice get for the show."

Bob sighed, but this time she was hoping his breathy release wasn't his way of questioning her sincerity. Her statement was voiced sincerely, and also made in an attempt demonstrate that she was prepared to leave the network on the most positive terms.

"I know you did a piece on the envoy a few years ago."

"Yes, I did a story on Wolfenson before he was appointed by the Quartet to the post."

"Well you obviously made an impression: Mr. Wolfenson specifically asked for you and Ben to handle the interview."

"Really. Wow. That's flattering," said Sandy, trying not to sound to enthusiastic. She wasn't sure if Harris was using this discussion in some way that still ended up with her getting fired.

He sighed a third time and this time Sandy was sure what it meant. She had learned long ago that Bob only pretended to grapple with tough decisions, would even go through the trouble of weighing the options with you, when, in fact, he had already made up his mind. He scripted everything, complete with suspense and predetermined outcome.

"Here's the thing, Terry's not even in the ground, but I'm contemplating going against one of his last wishes."

"I'm sorry, Bob. I don't understand."

The executive tapped a finger on his desktop and frowned at her, faking deep thought. "I'm the only one in this building without a law degree who is getting paid to make a decision they will need to stand by. I can either go with the safe move that keeps me in this chair for sixty days or the risky move that might keep me in this chair for sixty months." He tapped his desk louder and slowed to a stop, the last beat lending a sense of finality. "So it's settled. Ben will conduct the on-camera interview, and you'll produce the piece. After that, we'll discuss your future with the network. I hope you don't fuck me on this decision, Sandy. It'll be a one night stand for the both of us." He stood up before she could answer, knowing what she would say.

"Thank you for giving me the story," said Sandy. "I won't let you down."

"I know you won't. You never have. I don't know what Terry was thinking." He was leading her out of his office, but at the door, she stopped him.

"Bob, do they know anything more about Terry… how he died?"

He shook his head. "Not really. Apparently, the driver was speeding and lost control. Don't listen to the rumors that the driver was the son of the driver behind the wheel of Lady Di's car. That's bullshit."

"So nothing unusual?"

Bob reached to open the door to his office, but stopped. "I told you Brian was talking to him on the phone when it happened. He told me Terry said something about... the seat belts being cut."

Sandy raised an eyebrow.

"That's totally between you and me and not to be repeated."

She nodded.

"If there's something that's not right about Terry's death, you have my permission to get all Nancy Drew on the situation—but not right now. The interview with Wolfenson airs this Sunday. So I need you to take an extra dose of Ritalin and focus completely on this interview. Capiche?"

"Yes, I completely understand," said Sandy, before leaving Harris's office.

Sandy emerged from the front doors of Optio/Ent and made her way over to the adjacent plaza courtyard.

She panicked when she didn't immediately see Father Olsen sitting at the bench where she had left him before her meeting with Bob Harris. Sandy looked around and was relieved to find him at another bench in the courtyard feeding the birds leftovers from the breakfast they had at their hotel. The priest was covered in bandages, and his right arm was in a sling, but otherwise he had been discharged from the hospital with no threatening injuries.

"You were right. I wasn't fired. And you were also right about my next assignment." Sandy held up her JFK boarding pass she picked up from the 24/7 program coordinator. "I've been booked on a flight to Tel Aviv. Ben Peters and I have an exclusive interview with the Mideast Envoy, John Wolfenson, after the signing of the peace treaty." She lowered her hand holding the plane ticket, suddenly remembering that Alan was blind.

"Are we alone? I mean is anyone watching us," asked Father Olsen. Sandy looked around the plaza and only saw tourists taking pictures in front of the plaza fountain and two nannies talking with each other at a different bench while the children they were watching slept.

"I think we're all right," said Sandy. It was the first time since she picked him up from the hospital that he showed any sign of paranoia.

Father Olsen crumbled up the empty bag and stood up.

"Sandy, can you help me to the nearest garbage can."

She quickly moved to his side, gently nudging him with her elbow. He grabbed her arm, and the two walked toward the nearest trash can in the plaza courtyard. They had now spent enough time with each other that their smooth rapport was similar to what had developed years ago when Sandy first shot her TV story on the priest.

"Of course, I take no satisfaction from being right," said Father Olsen. "Indeed, while you were at your meeting, I was praying that what I predicted last night would end up being wrong. I would have consoled you if you had lost your job, but I would have felt relieved that you were not being used as a pawn in some dark plot."

"So shouldn't we seriously consider that everything else you said last night is probably also true," said Sandy. She stopped in front of a trash can, took the trash from Father Olsen's hand, and threw it in the wastebasket. "Tom's possession was not a random event. He was chosen because of his access to me."

"And now you have a backstage pass to the biggest event in the last couple of decades – peace in the Middle East. Yes, Sandy I believe that there are too many black swans swimming past for us to ignore."

"So then what do we do next?"

"When do you leave?"

"Today. I have a flight from JFK at four o'clock."

"That doesn't give us much time," said Father Olsen.

She looked over at him. "So you have a plan?"

"The key is Tom. If we can remove him from the equation, then there will be nothing to worry about. You can go to Israel and do your job and the forces that have been plotting will need to come up with a different plan. One that does not involve Tom."

Rather than turning back in the direction of the plaza bench, Olsen led Sandy toward the street.

"Where are we going?"

"We need to get a taxi and go to your apartment. We need to act fast. The forces we are up against might already have grabbed Tom. I would not be surprised if he's on his way to Tel Aviv as we speak."

As Sandy entered, she was immediately struck by the awful odor that permeated the entire apartment. Her instinct was to be embarrassed because she had come with a guest, but then Sandy remembered that the guest accompanying her was Father Olsen.

"Sandy, you do smell what I smell?"

"I sure do," answered Sandy. "It smells a lot like the Roses' basement."

When Sandy opened the drapes, the light revealed an apartment that looked as if burglars had ransacked it. Furniture had been tipped over, the couch cushions disemboweled, and all the easels with Tom's work and supplies had been scattered across the floor.

Taking an uncertain step, Father Olsen cracked a picture frame beneath his foot and bent to explore with his hand.

The debris confused his senses, which would be expected, but Alan was feeling tense, not from the mess all around him, but something he felt nearby. A presence lurked in the apartment, a threatening respiration, yet he couldn't zero in on it.

"Sandy, Tom is here."

Sandy touched Alan's arm. "Okay, let's not move from this spot." He nodded his head and tried to look confident about what he was sure was about to happen.

"Tom, are you here?"

"Of course I'm here."

The voice caused Sandy and Father Olsen to spin around toward the kitchen. It was Tom's voice, but Sandy only saw her fiancé after he stepped out of the shadows.

"Why shouldn't I be here? I thought we agreed that I would have the apartment to myself Tuesdays, Thursdays and half-days on Sundays."

"What are you talking about, Tom?"

Before he could respond to Sandy, Alan took a step toward the kitchen.

"Hello, Tom. We haven't met. My name is…"

"Shut the fuck up, Father."

Olsen was no longer wearing his priestly garb, so Sandy was shocked to hear Tom's words.

"Tom, how did you know Alan was a priest?"

"Are you kidding me? I smelled his stench when the two of you were in the elevator. I can't believe you're leaving me for a priest, Sandy."

"What are you talking about, Tom. I love you. I'm not leaving you."

Tom emerged from the kitchen into the living room allowing direct light from the windows to fall upon his face, which was gaunt and completely smooth, the skin pulled back by an unseen force. He laughed as if he had just heard some joke whispered in his ear, then turned to address Father Olsen in words spoken in Latin — "You may not be able to see, Padre, but I know you feel, lusting after my fiancée, the slut."

"What did he say," Sandy asked Alan after Tom had finished speaking. The priest kept staring forward, and when he spoke it was not to answer Sandy but to respond to Tom in Latin.

"Your Latin is very good. Where did you learn this, Tom?"

Tom laughed rather than verbally responding to Alan's query.

Their conversation was interrupted by a knock on the apartment's front door.

Without saying a word, Sandy moved quickly toward the hallway.

"What are you two up to," asked Tom, speaking in English, and without any smugness on his face.

"Believe it or not we're both here to help. Tom. We're worried about you."

"Why are you worried about me, Father? I can take care of myself. For the first time I have a purpose in my life. All I want now is to be left alone so I can achieve my goal. Leave a legacy… something people will remember."

"What about your paintings, Tom. Can't that be your legacy?"

"Nobody cares about art anymore. The artist has to actually bleed for his work or no one cares."

Sandy appeared in the living room followed by two beefy men wearing hospital uniforms.

"Who are you guys?" Tom asked with a sneer on his face.

"We're here to make sure you get the help you need," answered one of the men, a black man with a shaved head.

Tom turned his gaze to Sandy. "What have you done?"

"I've had you committed to a hospital," answered Sandy. "I'm really afraid that you're a danger to yourself... as well as to others."

"You can't just have me committed," protested Tom. "It has to be signed off..."

"By a mental health professional," interrupted Father Olsen. "That would be me. Besides being a priest, I am a board-certified psychologist registered with the state of New York."

Tom kept his attention on Sandy. "I can't believe you're doing this. How can you commit your own fiancé?"

"Because whoever you are, you're not my fiancé."

Tom nodded, apparently at peace with the situation. But then bolted across the living room. The two orderlies grabbed him before he made it to the bedroom. They dragged him out of the apartment with Tom shouting obscenities and threats, and literally foaming at the mouth every step of the way until Sandy shut the door behind him.

When she walked back into the living room, Sandy happened to come across a framed picture laying among the apartment wreckage. Broken glass was still partially covering the photograph originally shot at the luau in Hawaii. Tom was holding his shirt open to reveal a handwritten sign: "MARRY ME."

Alan had no idea that Sandy was close to breaking down and crying. He said the two words that he hoped would comfort Sandy — "It's over."

"Do you really think it's over?"

"I do, Sandy. The dark forces behind this plot went to great trouble to recruit Tom. We've now eliminated your fiancé as their pawn. You'll catch your plane, and I'll check on Tom once he's settled in at the hospital. It's going to be all right, Sandy. It's over."

"Come on, pal," the black orderly said to Tom, who writhed and spit like a cobra as he was escorted to a hospital van idling at the curb. "You're just making this harder on yourself."

"I don't know," said his co-worker, "he's kind of making it hard on me too..."

The orderlies threw open the van's back doors. Together they lifted Tom into the waiting hands of a blond-haired man… with an oddly stretched face.

.

"Okay," Steve said, "I got him. We'll take it from here." Steve guided Tom to the bench and strapped him in. "You're going to be all right."

The black orderly was amazed to see how Tom had suddenly calmed down. "He's like a stuffed animal in your hands. Maybe we should call you... the Looney Whisperer."

259

Steve laughed before yelling to the driver in the front cab, who, aside from the brown hair, appeared to be Steve's identical twin. "We're set. You can go anytime."

The driver nodded before turning to Tom, "Don't worry. You're going to be all right." He then put the van in gear and pulled out into the traffic.

The dining room of the Bedouin Diwan restaurant in Jerusalem had arched ceilings, and walls painted in the color of the desert. The aroma of chicken shawarma filled the air as Sandy, Ben, and Rick Walsh, the press liaison for the Middle East Envoy John Wolfenson, sat at a table grazing on appetizers as they negotiated the terms of the live network interview to follow the signing of the peace treaty.

"So we're in agreement on the time and place and the length of the interview, and most of the other ground rules, but there are still a few sticking points," said Walsh with his distinct British accent. "I thought I was clear on this point before your team flew out here. We will not allow any mention of Mr. Wolfenson's past presidency of the World Bank, his association with the Trilateral Commission, and the Council on Foreign Relations."

"You requested there would be no questions or any reference to any of those groups by Ben during the interview. And we did agree to that point," said Sandy. "But the language in your last email moved the marker on that point and demanded a response. C'mon, Rick, do you really expect that the network news covering the peace treaty is not going to use Wolfenson's resume during their live coverage of the peace treaty signing? We have no control over that. So we can't guarantee that. Sorry."

Walsh nodded without a fight. He obviously expected that he would not win that fight. But then his eyes lit up when he came upon another contested point.

"You've written here that, '24/7 has right at their discretion to re-edit any portions of the interview for future broadcasts. These re-edits will in no way change any word from the original interview?' What the hell is this all about?" asked Walsh.

Sandy waited to see if Ben was going to respond to Rick's objection, but when he made it a point to begin eating the artichoke gnocchi, she knew it was up to her to speak up.

"That's no big deal, Rick. We often re-air 24/7 interviews that have only the cut-away shots of the correspondent, sent through post production to enhance the look."

Walsh got it and moved on. "Okay so here's the final thing I have highlighted. In your last email, you wrote, 'John and his violin.' I don't know what this means?"

When she saw Ben set aside his plate and sit up to respond Sandy relaxed and began to drift mentally away from the table conversation. She looked all around her at the other tables and saw Arab couples—the women modestly dressed in hijab headscarves— eating kebabs and fried kibbeh and wondered what Helen would have said about the surroundings. She had accompanied her on these news assignments for years, and without her there beside her, Sandy couldn't help feeling confused… sad… lost.

"I've seen him play; he's quite good. John played his violin at Terry's house in the Hamptons. He was the hit of the party. Right, Sandy?"

She did not miss a beat, jumping back into the conversation as soon as she heard her name.

"We're talking B-Roll of him playing," said Sandy clarifying their request. "We're not requesting something awkward, like asking him to play during the interview. We want to use it for the prime time presentation, run him playing the violin as we go in out of a break?"

"Rick, we're trying to add some personality to your man," said Ben, "not expose his lack of talent as a violin player."

"I understand," said Rick. "I personally love the idea. I'll talk to John about this and see if he responds to the idea. I'll get back to you after we speak."

Sandy's attention drifted again along with her eyes.

"So, I think that does it," said the envoy's public relations representative. "Unless there was anything else you two were planning on dropping in my lap at the last second?"

Near where the ceiling arch met the brick wall was a recessed window that looked out to the street.

Sandy's eyes caught sight of a man staring into the window, his face sullied with dirt, dust and a half-grown beard.

"Sandy, we don't have anything else for Rick?" asked Ben.

It took her a few seconds to recognize the man staring at her in the window, but then she realized it was… Tom.

"Sandy, anything else?"

She sprang to her feet, banging her knee on the table and almost toppling all of their drinks.

At the window, Tom was already gone.

"What's going on?" asked Rick.

"Nothing," she said, "I'll be right back," and then she rushed away from the table.

The heart of Jerusalem is the Old City—Ottoman ramparts shaped like castle walls. And stretching along the cobblestone streets were small fluorescent lights attached to power lines running above the maze of stone walls.

Sandy emerged from the restaurant and immediately caught sight of Tom before he disappeared into a crowd of people heading toward the Damascus Gate, one of seven open entryways into the Old City.

She was about to take off running when she saw another figure she recognized – Father Alan Olsen sitting at a table in an outdoor café across from the Bedouin Diwan restaurant. Before she acknowledged his presence, Sandy noted tables around the priest seemed to be populated with people who looked nothing like tourists, and were overdressed to be locals. When she spotted the earpiece dangling from one of the people sitting near Father Olsen, Sandy did not bother to acknowledge she saw Alan all. She just took off running toward the Damascus gate.

The Souk Khan al-Zeit was a narrow market street packed with Arab merchants and customers haggling over pomegranates, shoes, and banana bunches. Sandy picked up Tom's trail and continued to follow him through the market place. He was moving at a good pace, but Sandy could not tell if it was because she was following him.

Like the Roman Cardo Maximus before it, the cobblestone street stretches north to south, and from east to west. Together the two thoroughfares divide the Old City into four neighborhoods: the Christian Quarter, Muslim Quarter, Armenian Quarter, and Jewish Quarter, each revolving around their holiest sites. Tom, with Sandy not far behind, turned into the Muslim district. She was able to keep an eye on him for a couple of blocks, then he disappeared near the Madrasa al-Omariya chapel. It was the path where Jesus bore his cross, and the cobblestone street was packed with tourists taking pictures for their Facebook page.

Sandy fought through the crowd until she caught sight of Tom down the street, turning down a dark street that led to the Armenian neighborhood. It was several blocks away from yet another marketplace where Armenians sold pottery and ceramics. For a few streets, Sandy had the light of the bazaar to help keep her from walking down completely dark streets.

She saw Tom standing at the end of one of the streets. He had turned now and was looking at her.

"Tom? What are you doing here?"

He wouldn't respond. She slowly walked toward him.

"Let's talk…"

He suddenly took off again, slipping into one of the nearby houses lining the street.

Sandy raced up the dark cobblestone street to the front door where she had seen her fiancé enter. She tried the door and was surprised that Tom had not locked it after entering.

When she entered she saw the hovel was empty, but there was a fire going in the fireplace providing enough light to illuminate the room. Sandy saw Tom under a wooden beam leading to the hovel's kitchen area.

"Tom…"

She took a step toward him, but stopped when she saw that in his hand was a shard of glass.

"Sandy…"

"What are you doing?"

"I'm not sure anymore," he said.

"Tom, everything's going to be all right." She started to move toward him. "Just stay right where you are…"

But then there was a noise coming from the street… footsteps approaching the hovel. She turned to look at the door and wondered if she should lock it so she had time to speak with Tom before they rushed in. She turned back to tell Tom about her decision to move and lock the door, but discovered he was now right beside her, holding the jagged shard of glass up to her neck.

A pounding noise at the door grabbed their attention. Someone was using force to open the door. The noise caused Tom to release Sandy, and she dropped to the floor. Her fiancé disappeared into another part of the hovel.

A few moments later, the front door flew open and the same people Sandy had seen surrounding Alan in the café were now rushing in wielding guns.

"Where is he?"

She shook her head, not able to answer. They scattered in different directions to begin searching the hovel.

"Sandy?!"

She looked through the open doorway and saw Father Olsen standing on the street.

"Alan!"

He heard her voice and tried to move toward it, but was immediately restrained by one of the men wearing an earpiece and carrying a gun.

"Are you all right?"

"I'm fine," she shouted back. Sandy had lied. But it was impossible to be truthful under the circumstances.

In a shin bet safe house, Agent Aluf Ginsberg watched a bank of video monitors as Sandy Travis and Alan Olsen interacted with each other in another room down the hall. After he and his agents lost Tom in the Armenian neighborhood, the American priest and journalist were driven in separate vehicles to the safe house where they would be interrogated. During the car trip, Ginsberg needed to decide on a strategy. He could continue to keep the two separate from each other, allowing him to judge the veracity of their stories and see if they matched. Specifically to discover if what Sandy Travis' had to say was consistent with the claims by Father Alan Olsen that originally triggered their citywide search for Tom Hansen.

Ginsberg ended up going with the strategy of putting the two in one room and observing how the two interacted once they were together, even if they presumably were smart enough to know they were being watched and recorded. The tipping point for his final decision was the priest's blindness. If the two had something to convey to each other, presumably they would need to verbalize their communication.

"So, he wasn't at the hospital the next day when you went for your visit?"

"Yes, Sandy, but what got me to catch the next plane to Tel Aviv was the discovery that Tom had never been checked into the hospital at all. Whatever arrangements I had made to have your fiancé committed had been thwarted. So I caught the next plane to Tel Aviv and immediately contacted Shin Bet because I knew they would be in charge of security for the peace treaty signing."

"But Alan, why didn't you call me once you knew Tom…"

"I did call, Sandy. Several times. All the calls went to voice mail. And you never called me back."

She thought about all the voices messages Tom had sent that never got to her. "I believe you, Alan. Tom claimed to send me messages, but I know he didn't, and yet somehow they were there in my voicemail. You probably tried to send me some voice mails, and I have no doubt they were prevented from getting to me by whoever is doing this. I have no idea how this is happening. But I know you understand?"

"Yes, I do understand," answered Olsen.

"You sound tired," said Sandy.

He certainly had every right to be tired. The last few days were a relentless attempt to stop Tom from hurting anyone, specifically Sandy. After he discovered Tom had been never checked-in at the hospital, Alan made a mad dash to JFK to catch the earliest flight from New York City. And after a long plane trip across the ocean (with two stopovers in London and Paris), there was a daylong wrestling match with Shin Bet trying to convince the agency about the potential danger of Tom Hansen.

"Weirdly I've been feeling completely wired," said Olsen. "For the last 48 hours, I could feel the adrenalin coursing through my body. Everything I was dreading I thought was going to come true."

"Tom was going to become a killer, just like Bernard Rose," said Sandy.

"Yes, Sandy. I believe Tom is being used by a force that we should never underestimate. We've experienced firsthand the fact that they will stop at nothing to bring their agenda to fruition. Tom is here, in Israel, still walking around this city, because there are forces that are powerful enough to make it happen."

"But why, Alan? What is Tom being used for," asked Sandy.

"On the plane flight over, I did some more research," said Father Olsen. We both agree that Tom's paintings of John Wolfenson makes him the target for assassination. But why the Middle East Envoy? The priest answered his own question by quoting from the bible —*the dragon gave the beast his power and his throne and great authority. One of the heads of the beast seemed to have had a fatal wound, but the fatal wound had been healed. The whole world was astonished and followed the beast.*

"It's from the 13th verse in Revelations."

"I'm sorry, Alan. I'm not sure I understand."

Olsen took a deep breath before saying aloud what he was thinking, "what if Satan were able to possess the soul of the man who had just pulled off the greatest accomplishment in the last one hundred years – peace in the Middle East. Wouldn't his ability to further his dark agenda among the living be so much easier to accomplish if it was coming from the most celebrated leader of our times?"

"If your theory is true," said Sandy, "why have Bernard Rose kill Wolfenson? And why are these same dark forces trying to have Tom once again attempt to kill the Envoy?"

"Think about it Sandy," said Alan. "You know the answer to that question."

She stopped and pondered the situation, and it didn't take long for her to figure out the answer. "Bernard Rose was never meant to kill Wolfenson, only shoot him, so the Envoy would have a Near-Death Experience."

"But when that didn't happen," said Alan, "the forces guiding this plot needed another assassin."

Sandy fell back to her chair looking despondent. "Tom. He's the next one chosen to make sure Wolfenson is shot so he can have a Near-Death Experience."

"I believe Satan is working to have the opportunity for the perfect possession," said Father Olsen, "so he can usher in the End Days while walking among us."

The two sat in silence for a while before Sandy said, "we need to get out of here."

"No, Sandy, we need to tell these people what we know."

"They won't believe us, Alan."

"Sandy, right now, the best we can do is get them to believe us because we will need all the help we can get to stop what is about to happen. Do you understand?"

Before she could answer, the door to the interrogation room opened, and in walked Agent Ginsberg.

Sandy recognized him as one of the agents she had seen in the café sitting near Alan, and then later, after Tom escaped from the hovel. He was one of the agents standing off to the side coordinating the aftermath. Like many Israeli men, his head was shaved because his scalp was already in the process of going completely bald. Earlier when she saw him he looked bigger, probably because he was wearing a coat to camouflage his bullet-proof vest. He was now wearing a windbreaker over a tee-shirt and as Ginsberg sat at the table opposite them, Sandy couldn't help but feel he was too thin, a bit short, and looked very tired. He looked nothing like the hero she imagined was going to come to the rescue and make everything turn out all right.

"You are Sandra Travis, resident of New York city? You currently work for an American TV news show called "24/7.""

"That's right," said Sandy. She noted his accent, definitely Israeli, and consistent with a Shin Bet agent. But oddly hearing him speak got Sandy to remember where she had seen him once before – on the video of Bernard Rose's assassination attempt in Tel Aviv.

"You know the man next to you, correct?"

"Yes, I do. This is Father Alan Olsen."

"And the two of you…"

"I also know who you are as well," interrupted Sandy. "Your name is Aluf Ginsberg and you're an agent with Shin Bet."

Ginsberg tried not to look too surprised or impressed, though he was feeling both as he replied, "That's correct, Ms. Travers. Have we met before?"

"No, we haven't," answered Sandy, leaning confidently toward the agent. "But I saw you before in dozens of different videos shot that day in Tel Aviv. You were the one who stopped Bernard Rose that day, shooting him before he could kill or hurt anyone else."

"Sandy, what are you doing," asked Alan, grabbing her arm. But she ignored the priest.

"I talked to Julie Rose, the assassin's widow, and she told me about your friendship with her husband. That's how I know what you had to do that day in Tel Aviv. You not only stopped an assassin; you ended up killing a friend. This is true, is it not, Agent Ginsberg?"

"Yes, I was the one who shot Bernard Rose," answered Ginsberg without hesitation.

"You killed a man because it was your duty to protect anyone who is intent on hurting other people. And even though you recognized the assassin, you did not hesitate to shoot because... he wasn't the same man you once knew. He looked similar to the man you once knew, but he also looked different. And that's because *he was different*. The man you shot was no longer the same man you once knew as your friend. Am I right, Agent Ginsberg?"

This time Ginsberg didn't immediately respond.

In his silence, Sandy reached over and touched Alan's hand that had been gripping her arm.

"Alan, everything's going to be all right. Oh my God, Alan, you of all people will so appreciate this. As it turns out, we're actually preaching to a member of the choir..."

Ginsberg checked his watch the moment he left the interrogation. It was late and he knew all of his phone calls were going to piss off a lot of people. He started by hitting the speed dial for the chief of Shin Bet. While he waited for his call to be answered, Ginsberg ran through his head what he planned on saying -- *I've just spent the last several hours with two people who are either a pair of religious fanatics who enjoy each other's company because of their shared delusion of an apocalyptic plot. Or the two consistently corroborate each other's sincere belief that a potential assassination attempt will be made during the signing of the Peace treaty at the Western Wall Plaza. As the head of the Shin Bet team in command of security, I need to proceed if the latter scenario is true and take extra security measures. My call is to alert you of the situation.*

"Agent Ginsberg?"

"Chief Cohan, I apologize for calling so late, but there's a security issue that I needed to alert you to. It concerns these two Americans I've just spent the last several hours observing and..."

Thousands of people, representing many different faiths, had come to the Western Wall Plaza to bear witness to an historical moment. Many had come hoping that their dream of peace for the region was finally about to become a reality.

For the signing ceremony, security fencing cordoned the square with a combined force of Secret Servicemen and Shin Bet agents working together. The U.N. Patrol was manning the checkpoints for all those entering the Western Wall Plaza. Sharpshooters were stationed on rooftops, perched like gargoyles trying to discourage evil spirits from making an appearance.

At the back of the plaza stood the Western Wall, taller in cubits than the biblical Goliath. Bushes and plants thrust roots between the building blocks, and prayers on scraps of paper mortared the lower Herodian seams.

Stationed a respectful distance from the open-air synagogue of the ancient retaining wall, an elevated podium held a long table with six chairs, one for each politician signing the treaty.

Sandy waited with Ben and their 24/7 cameraman near the platform, gathered with VIPs and government higher-ups. Rick Walsh, Wolfenson's press liaison, stuck to Ben's side, and Shin Bet Agent Ginsberg hovered so intimately behind Sandy, she could smell the oil used to clean his weapon. His eyes didn't seem as weary as they had in the interrogation room, and she knew he was scoping for Tom with binocular vision.

She had spotted Father Olsen in the crowd— could smell him, like a mass grave polluting the occasional breeze. And though he couldn't see her, he sensed her general location.

He had come with the mission of guarding against Tom, but had been swept up in the excitement of the crowd. If the eternal optimist inside him won out and no tragedy befell the pacifists, this day would ring in unprecedented peace. A feud, centuries long, would finally end and the gates of Old Jerusalem would no longer sustain bullet wounds by the name of conflicting gods. Of course, the Muslims still prohibited Judaic prayer on the Temple Mount, holy to the Jews, but the treaty constituted a momentous step in the direction toward long lasting cooperation between the faiths.

To one side of the plaza, a row of reporters conducted live stand-ups in a roped-off area for the press. From the staging area, Sandy couldn't hear their reports over the fervent Hebrew, Arabic, and English, but she knew what it was like to be isolated from the main stage, not being able to glean anything insightful stuck observing in the gallery. Today, she had a backstage pass. Indeed, Sandy had become one of the main players on a stage that the whole world was watching.

The motorcade parked near the staging area. As Israeli Prime Minister Bleiberg and the Arab leaders exited the cars, security agents assembled into a broad shield around them. Quartet Envoy John Wolfenson stepped out of the last vehicle. As Sandy had always observed with famous people, the man towered the size of God on television but appeared diminished and mortal in person.

With security detail in line, the politicians embraced and exchanged words with their relatives and other people gathered near the platform. Wolfenson approached Ben and Sandy as their cameraman shot the action.

"Ben," Wolfenson said, sharing a warm handshake with the anchorman. "Good to see you here."

"John, it's an honor. Thank you for the invitation."

"I'm sorry to hear the news about Terry. Please give his family my sympathy."

Ben nodded. "We'll see you after the signing."

Wolfenson turned to Sandy, who was pretending not to eavesdrop. They exchanged a hug, but she must have moved in too quickly because a bodyguard stepped closer.

"Sandy," Wolfenson said as they parted, "it's wonderful to see you again. Promise me you'll keep this bulldog on his leash later."

"Don't worry about, Ben," replied Sandy. "I promise you he'll be a pussycat during the interview."

Rick, the press liaison, motioned to Wolfenson to take the stage. The envoy nodded, and stepped into his spotlight, waving to the multitudes who had gathered and were now cheering for him. When the crowd quieted, the envoy began his speech, booming with a richness for which the sound system could not be fully credited. "Where God gathered the dust and breathed into it the life of Adam, King Solomon of the Israelites built the First Temple where they kept the Ark of the Covenant. And under the golden Dome of the Rock, just on the other side of this holy wall, Muslims preserve the stone from which Muhammad ascended to Allah. This land is where Christianity, Judaism, and Islam intersect, and yet it is also where they collide. But on this day, I urge you, brothers and sisters of the planet we share, let us not cling to our differences and harbor hatred. Instead let us celebrate our common ground. Let us usher in a new era of peace and prosperity and, most importantly, let us embrace a time of unity, the well from which eternal hope springs."

After he waited for the audience's deafening applause to end, Wolfenson introduced the Israeli and Arab leaders as each one made their way onstage. The entire group then posed for pictures and waved to the crowd who had gathered. Finally, the six men settled into their chairs, and to the clicking of cameras and boisterous cheers, they distributed the signature documents among themselves.

Sandy was watching the leaders sign the treaty documents when she caught sight a face that she instantly recognized -- Tom.

Her fiancé was slithering through the crowd, looking as if he was driven by the same single-minded purpose as Bernard Rose in Tel Aviv.

"There he is..." Sandy said to agent Ginsberg standing next to her. "I see Tom..."

The Shin Bet agent squinted and followed her finger. Into his headset, he relayed the information of Tom's location, then moved off with his gun drawn from the holster.

Tom continued to weave between people as he made his way closer to the stage. He was unaware that all around him security agents were quickly closing in on his position. As he got about one hundred yards from the stage where the leaders scribbled signatures on multiple copies of the treaty, Tom reached into his coat.

The Secret Service grabbed him. One of the agents confiscated his weapon—not a gun, but a pair of binoculars; the lenses glinted briefly in the sunlight before the device disappeared into the guard's jacket. Then the agents whisked Tom away. Sandy watched it all happen, and afterwards she thought that if she had blinked, there was a good chance she would have missed the entire confrontation.

All the leaders had finished signing the peace treaty and joined John Wolfenson at the center of the stage for one more photo opportunity. Each dignitary embraced the other, and together they all raised their hands triumphantly. The audience roared with their approval at the sight.

All around him Father Olsen was hearing the noise of people screaming with joy. He even heard a few people near him crying, overwhelmed by their emotions now that the peace treaty had officially been signed. Then the priest felt a cold hand fall on his shoulder, followed by a whisper in his ear, "The Angel of Light has risen and will become flesh."

Next to the stage, Sandy had been watching Father Olsen in the crowd, and she saw Dr. Fincher appear beside him. She calmly watched as the rogue psychologist quickly slip away into the surrounding crowd. Sandy then saw everyone around Father Olsen begin to change, become something completely different, right before her eyes. Everyone beyond the stage had become demons, their eyes were glowing red as they jeered and roiled madly.

Sandy felt something sharp in her hand—a shard of glass dripping blood. For a moment, as it changed angle in the sun, the glass reflected Sandy's smooth face. She and Tom could have been twins.

Through new eyes, black as a shark's, Sandy saw she was now on stage, leaving behind the rest of her team from 24/7. Ben Peters had dropped to his knees to help the 24/7 videographer who had mysteriously collapsed next to him. The glass

Sandy had in her hands was from the broken lens of his video camera.

John Wolfenson was the last to leave the stage, following the Israeli Prime Minister and the other Arabic leaders as they all waved to the crowd. At the last second, the Envoy turned as a figure rushed him. He did not recognize the woman as Sandy Travers, because the person charging at him looked so different.

A gunshot rang out from a nearby building. Sandy was hit in the chest by a sniper shot. The punch of hot lead caused her to stop, then stumble back a step, before she continued toward John Wofenson. Sandy raised the shard of glass in her hand and plunged it into the neck of the Envoy.

More Snipers fired, and two bullets struck Sandy, one in the throat; the other hit her again in the chest, just an inch away from the first wound.

Both Sandy and Wolfenson fell; one left, the other right.

It had taken the audience a few moments, but now they began to react. There were screams, followed by a wild stampede.

Amidst the chaos, Secret Servicemen flocked around the envoy, their weapons drawn.

Two paramedics rushed on stage, and Sandy recognized them as they rushed past her as the same men who had resuscitated Tom and had tried to resurrect Helen.

"I'm a priest!" Father Olsen shouted, struggling his way past two security agents. "I need to offer her the last rites!"

The agents glanced at each other, and in their indecision, Olsen rushed past them both. Somehow, he knew exactly where to go on stage.

Sandy's eyes caught sight of the small cross dangling from Alan's neck, then his milky pupils staring down at her.

"It wasn't just Tom," she said, gurgling blood deep in her chest. "He possessed me... to get to Wolfenson..."

Alan brushed strands of hair from her face. "It's okay. That doesn't matter now. Sandy, do you want me to give you your last rites?"

She coughed up red blood as a response.

"May the Lord in His love and mercy help you with the grace of the Holy Spirit. May the Lord who frees you from sin save you and raise you up."

He retraced the sign of the cross over her at the same time her eyes became fixed and dilated.

Father Olsen sensed she had left this world, and cradled her body as he began to cry.

C<small>HAPTER</small>
39

John Wolfenson heard his wife Patricia talking to Dr. Diamant just outside his room.

"Is he okay," Patricia asked, her voice muffled but audible through the wall of his private room.

"I don't have to tell you that your husband is lucky to be alive," Dr. Diamant replied. "In fact, for a minute there he was clinically dead."

"Can I see him?"

The security guard opened the door for her, and Wolfenson's wife came into the room.

"Oh, honey," she said after seeing her husband reaching out to her. "Thank God, you're all right. I don't know what I would have done without you."

She hugged him as best she could with all the wires and tubes connected to his body.

"Are you sure, Pat, this is a good thing. You could have finally gotten the bridge partner you deserve."

"Shut up," she said, before releasing him and getting the first close-up look at her husband since the attack. Patricia was shocked by what she saw.

"I can't believe how good you look." Tears began to run down Patricia's cheek.

"How sweet of you to say such kind words."

I'm serious, Honey," said Patricia wiping away her tears. "It's as if the E.R. surgeons gave you a facelift after they stitched up your wounds."

Wolfenson tried to kiss her, but couldn't raise himself from the hospital bed. She leaned in and kissed him on the forehead.

In the doorway stood five men and a woman. When Wolfenson saw them, he motioned for the security guard to let them enter.

"Honey," the envoy said to his wife, "I want you to get a hold of whoever's in charge of the kitchen and demand that I get a slice of apple pie immediately. Tell them it's for the man who just brought peace to the Mideast."

Patricia nodded and kissed her husband's hand before leaving his side. As she was walking out of the room, she noted the group entering and didn't know what to think. When she got to the hallway, she was immediately greeted by her press secretary, Rick Walsh.

"How is he?"

"He's going to be fine," she answered. She then motioned to the people who had entered her husband's room.

"Who are they?"

"I don't know," Walsh answered. "I've never seen them before in my life."

The last man to enter the room shut the door behind him. Dr. Fincher stepped forward from the group first and knelt before John Wolfenson as if he was in the presence of royalty.

"It is so good to finally have you among us, my Angel of Light."

Wolfenson extended his hand, and Fincher wasted no time in embracing and kissing it.

Another person in the group stepped forward and said, "Someone sent you a get-well card."

It was from Father Alan Olsen -- "'For we walk by faith, not by sight' 2 Corinthians 5:7."

The envoy smiled and handed the card back to his disciple.

Fincher waited for more of a reaction before speaking. "Don't you think the priest will be a problem?"

"No, I don't. I will deal with him," replied Wolfenson, but there was a small pit in his gut that felt different than his words and the Envoy was intrigued. He wasn't accustomed to the feeling because he had not experienced it for hundreds of years. "There are more demanding issues all of you must worry about."

When he saw his words seemed to have caused some distress, Wolfenson made a point of sitting up in his bed and begin to disconnect the wires and tubes attached to his body. He knew it was the perfect time to show his gathering that he did not suffer from any of the pain inflicted on the body he was now possessing.

"Make no mistake about the mission ahead. I ask for your effort because I will lead the way, but I will need each one of you to help me if we are to succeed."

The sight through his room window caught the envoy's attention. The sky had darkened, and it had begun to rain.

"What a beautiful day to be alive."

The Story Continues…

DEMON DAYS Book Two

ABOUT THE AUTHORS

Richard Finney is a Southern California based novelist, screenwriter, writer, and film producer.

pitandpen.com

D.L. Snell is based in Oregon and is an editor and writer in the horror genre.

If you enjoyed meeting Alexander Templeman then why not join him on his very first official mission as an agent of the British secret service. Sent to Vienna on a routine assignment to collect some important documents things quickly begin to go wrong and Templeman soon finds himself fighting for his life.

Download your free copy of *The Man from the Caucasus* now and prepare yourself to join Templeman as he battles for his life in a city he barely knows and facing a frightening adversary with all the cards stacked in his favour.

https://benwesterham.com/landing-page/

You can find out more about Ben Westerham at

www.benwesterham.com

and on various social media platforms.

From the David Good private investigator series

From 'Good Investigations'

"Mr Good," she purred like a hungry cat meeting a blind mouse, "and I do hope you will be." She slid beautifully, effortlessly in to the knackered old punter's chair, and I swear the thing wrapped itself lovingly around her sexy, lithe frame. Then she tempted me with those dark bewitching eyes, calling me closer, closer, closer

From 'Good Girl Gone Bad'

If you ask me, good girls can be the baddest there are, if the fancy takes them. Maybe it's because they save it all up for one big splurge, then go mad bad. I don't know, but what I do know is that anyone who tries telling you some little darling of theirs' wouldn't say boo to a goose is either stupid, misinformed or both. Any goody two shoes type should carry a health warning, 'Danger, Good Girl. May go bad at any moment'.

From the Banbury Cross Murder Mystery series

From 'The Hide and Seek Murders'

Eleanor Golightly never saw so much as a glimpse of the figure that moved up behind her, swift and silent, from the cover of the shrubbery. Indeed, she was only very briefly aware of the immense blow that came crashing down on her head. Just for a second or two, the world seemed to stop in silence, a peculiar sensation that she couldn't quite get to grips with before it had passed and she collapsed on to the immaculately cut lawn.

* * *

Publishing Coordinator – Sharon Kizziah-Holmes

Paperback-Press
an imprint Paperback Press, LLC
Springfield, Missouri

ISBN - 978-1-964559-13-1

DEDICATION

In Memory of my mentor and friend Jeanne Herr Cornwell.

ACKNOWLEDGMENTS

I am so very grateful for the many people in my life both living and passed. Their encouragement, lessons, love, and guidance have been the keys to my being able to put words on a page.

Special Thanks to my son, Eithan, for his humor, support, and encouragement.

I appreciate my sister, Victoria, for her encouragement and willingness to slog through the very first draft of this book.

The extreme patience and dedication of my publisher, Sharon Kizziah-Holmes, who became my editor and then a mentor, made this book possible.

Thanks to Shirley McCann for her proofreading expertise. Jaycee Delorenzo did a great job on the cover. Getting the mule "right" was our biggest challenge and she nailed it.

CHAPTER 1

I have a story to tell. My name is Fenreya Stonehorse-Stern. Yes, it's a funny name. During her pregnancy with me, my mother was intrigued by Norse Mythology in general and Fenrir the Wolf in particular. My daddy always let her have her way.

It was a dark and stormy night in early November. No, really it was. It wasn't just any kind of storm, though. This was one of the rare "thunderstorm turned tornado turned snowstorms" which occasionally rocked the lower part of the Midwest.

(Our community, situated in the Ozark Mountains, is not too far from Branson, Missouri. It's within easy reach of Fayetteville, Arkansas, and Springfield, Missouri and is called Blossom Bluff. It's tiny. The town didn't seem tiny when I was growing up, but time away at college and subsequently going to work in Kansas City changed my perspective.)

Sorry, I digress. Back to the stormy night.

All was well when my teenaged twins, Ian and Arista, got off the bus from school. We did our evening chores then they did their homework while I got dinner around. We had spicy chili made with our own home-raised, grass-fed beef, homegrown tomatoes, and peppers, and ended with brownies for dessert.

Just about the time we finished the brownies, the weather alert radio went off. The wretched screeching sound I've always despised, warned us about an imminent thunderstorm and potentially high winds.

Ian got up to take his dirty dishes to the sink. "Mom, do you think we will have a tornado?"

"Not in November, you goof," Arista chided, with an exaggerated eye roll aimed at her brother's back. She deposited her dishes in the sink.

"It has happened before, honey. Y'all were too young at the time to take much notice. Grams may remember it though." I turned to my mother. "Mom, do you remember the tornado of November 2010?"

"I do," she replied, shaking her head.

She brushed a wayward curl of her snow-white hair from her eye. The twins looked at their Grams, clearly waiting for more details.

"Grams, can you tell us what happened?" Arista asked.

"That was the year we lost the barn and the bull got impaled with a flying two-by-four," she answered with conviction.

The incident my mother referred to actually happened in 1974, not 2010. My twins knew this story, and they shot me a worried look. You see, Mom had been a bit forgetful, okay, she was diagnosed with Alzheimer's a few years ago. There, I said it. That was hard.

Rather than call attention to the error in her story, I subtly shook my head at the twins. "Yep, Mom, that was quite a time indeed. Are you ready to move to your sitting room? Do you want to knit a little before bed?"

"Yes, honey, that would be nice." She pushed herself up from her chair.

I escorted Mom to her combination sitting room/bedroom.

(Fortunately, even to this day she remains mobile and able to do normal dressing and hygiene activities. She just loses focus sometimes on what she is doing. Therefore, we keep her out of the kitchen. She nearly started a fire two years ago because she put bacon on to fry and spaced out. That incident was the last straw in making my decision to move home to Blossom Bluff full-time. Checking on her via phone and driving down from the city once a month no longer cut it.)

Anyway, I returned to the kitchen and found it empty. The kids were in the family room, just off the kitchen. Ian was glued to the TV where our local weatherman earned his keep by standing in front of his weather map, which showed a line of storms from southwest to northeast and across our half of the state. The leading edge was green and yellow. No harm there. Behind it, and advancing at a steady pace, was an orange, red, and purple mass. That was more troublesome.

As I stopped to watch, the weatherman issued a stern warning to the people three counties to the west of us to "Go immediately to your tornado shelter. If you live in a mobile home, please leave at once and seek shelter…"

Ian turned to face me with a concerned expression. "Mom, this is bad."

"Yeah, honey. It's not good, but we will be fine. This is a very sturdy house built into the side of a hill.

Now, go on to your room and get some rest. I promise to come get you if there is a problem."

Ian bade me good night and headed off to his room, albeit rather reluctantly, I noticed. My daughter still stood there staring at me. "What?" I asked.

"Why is he such a dweeb about storms?"

"Don't be too hard on your brother, I'm not sure why he frets over storms. I have asked, but he won't explain it. Maybe he doesn't even know." She plopped down on the arm of the couch, apparently the concept of it being her bedtime, too, was lost to her.

"You *are* going to chant the storm, aren't you, Momma?"

Her tone came across more like a directive. Just then, my phone roared like a tiger, indicating a text message. I read the message from my aunt Louisa, aka Auntie Lou.

"Buckle up, baby. Something's coming."

A kissy face emoji followed. *Oh, just bloody wonderful.*

(My aunt Louisa is a vivacious seventy-year-old, and she texts with the best of them. She can also waterski, ride horses, and cast a spell that will knock you on your south end. You see, Auntie Lou is a witch. Her mother was a witch and her grandmother…you get the idea. Yes, I am also a witch. It skipped my mother for reasons I do not understand.)

"MOM!"

Arista was staring at me again, or probably still, wanting my attention. Shaken out of my puzzled fixation on my phone screen, I glanced at her. "I'm sorry, what were you saying, dear?"

"Mom, I was *asking* if you were going to *chant the*

storm, and would you like me to help you?"

"Yes, my darling girl, I will be up working on the storm, but you will be in your room." I held up a finger to cut off whatever she was about to say. "I will call for you should I require your assistance." The argument my daughter had been formulating died in her throat as she wisely sized up the expression on my face.

She mumbled, "Yes, ma'am," and headed down the hallway toward her room.

(I can't tell you with certainty how it works in other families, but in our family, "the witch gene"—as my beloved daddy used to call it—runs down the maternal side and nearly every female has some abilities. Occasionally, male children exhibit some magical abilities. For example, my brother, Jacob, is very intuitive, but only, it seems, with electronics and business matters. Some have a heaping helping, like Auntie Lou. Arista already shows signs of developing power at fifteen years of age.)

I remembered the ambiguous text message from Auntie. I read it again. *What in the world is she talking about? The storm? Yes, it must be.* I pulled my gaze back to the TV. The radar showed significant advancement of the storm in the last few moments. Sure enough, there was a nasty cell, the kind with the hook, heading right for Blossom Bluff and likely for us, slightly south of town. *Time to get busy.*

My great-grandmother was gifted in all things weather-related. She could call rain forth, turn a storm, and get a good breeze blowing in stifling heat. There were limits, sure. She didn't trifle with the weather just for fun, as that would be disrespectful to the Powers That Be. The chant I would use tonight had been passed down from Great-Grams and taught to me by my auntie Lou.

I drew in a deep breath and pictured white light infusing my being. I took another deep breath then grabbed a white candle from the little drawer under the family altar, essentially a buffet-style oak cabinet on the south wall of the family room. As I lit it, I began the chant. Satisfied the candle was safely in its little sconce on the altar and surrounded by several crystals, I proceeded out onto the deck on the south side of the house. Since the home was a split-level, built into the side of a hill, the deck was a full story above ground level. This made for a serenely beautiful view 99.9 percent of the time. The other 0.1 percent? Yeah, um, that was tonight. It was beautiful but in a terrifying kind of way.

Still chanting, I opened the door and got smacked in the face with rain. This didn't normally happen on our covered deck. Lightning lit the sky from west to east, and a glow hung for a long moment. Long for lightning anyway.

Stunned at the sight of the darkest, most angry roiling clouds I had ever seen, I stumbled over my words. Despite the accompanying roar of thunder, a little voice in my mind said, "Fen, get your head outta your ass!"

(You were expecting something sweeter, angelic even? Nope. I'm pretty sure that's my great-granny's voice reaching from Beyond, and she had a potty mouth).

Oh hell.

I set my feet, raised my arms, palms up, and looked straight into the storm. Auntie Lou had taught me doing so was important.

"You must look that storm in the face," she'd say. "It won't listen if you cower behind a rock. You must be the rock, baby girl."

Although I was rarely scared of anything, at that moment, I didn't feel very rock-like. My palms began to sweat. Regardless, I began the chant again…

Morrigan, Morrigan, in the sky,
Turn this storm, let it pass me by.
Morrigan, Morrigan, hear my cry,
Turn this tempest to blue sky.

~Silver Raven Wolf (Hexcraft: Dutch Country Pow-wow Magick 1995)

A particularly strong gust of wind knocked me off-balance. Even though my heart raced, with positive determination I took another deep breath and kept my chant going. After regaining my stance, the familiar, powerful energy surged within and around me. My heart slowed, and I allowed myself to relax into what was happening. Then my vision changed. I no longer saw the storm from the outside, as one would if looking up at it. I was seeing it from the inside, as if I had moved to its center. The little voice inside my head cheered, "Yes! That is the way, baby girl!"

Now mind you, I had no time to ponder any of this, not what it meant or how it even happened. The storm continued to rage, but it changed, too. It was remarkably quiet where I was.

I kept chanting. Slowly, my vision and my surroundings returned to normal. I noted the angry roiling had stopped. It was still pouring rain and the wind whipped about fiercely, although less so.

My skin tingled, and I felt light yet perfectly grounded to the earth. Intuitively, I knew I could stop chanting. I spoke heartfelt thanks to the Lord and Lady and my guides and guardians.

Movement, caught out of the corner of my eye, drew my attention. Arista peered out the window, her eyes as wide as saucers. I couldn't be mad at her right then. I was too exhilarated and grateful for the grace that settled the raging behemoth storm down.

However, I was a mom, and she still wasn't in bed where she was supposed to be, so I shot her a smile and a wink and mouthed the words "Go to bed." She knew she'd been caught, knew I wasn't mad, but I clearly meant business. She smiled, gave me a "thumbs-up," and off she went in the direction of her room. I was quite certain she would stop at her twin's room to give him the lowdown on what she had seen.

What had she seen? Were there any visible signs of...of what? An exchange of power? In retrospect, that is what it felt like. Hmm, weird, going to have to run that by Auntie.

Suddenly aware of the cold and soaking-wet clothes, I hurried indoors and headed for a hot shower and some dark chocolate. I could hear my pillow calling.

Warmth enveloped me as sleep overtook me, likely because I was sandwiched between a very round calico cat and a petite dog, Isabella, and Sophia respectively. Though my body was asleep, warm, and well protected, my brain was busy indeed.

Howling sounds, cattle bellowing in agitation, a loud male voice, "Hey, what are you doing? Get out of here!" A thud, and pain. So much pain. Then complete darkness.

The dream scene in my head began to lighten. I saw blood in the snow.

CHAPTER 2

I awoke shivering. I had kicked off the bed covers, and my thrashing about had evidently dislodged the dog and cat. I saw Isabella's green eyes glowing at me through the darkness. I could tell she was annoyed. No sign of Sophia. I was certain she went to join one of the twins. "I thought dogs were supposed to be the loyal ones." Isabella hissed at me.

I could see the feline's silhouette when she turned her back to me and curled up on the far corner of the bed. "Geez, Issy, I wasn't trying to offend you, I had quite an awful dream. I hope that's all it was." Memories of past times, when my nighttime dreams had come true in the light of day, made me shudder.

It was apparent going back to sleep would not be possible. I got up and trudged off to the kitchen for some herbal tea. On my way out of the room, I grabbed my dream journal. "I best write this one down, Issy, it was too vivid to ignore." I got no response from the cat. She was either asleep or in a snit. Smart money was on the latter.

As I walked by Mom's room, I heard her voice

coming through the partly shut door. Peeking in quietly to make sure she was okay, I was able to make out the words.

"Black cows, no no, those aren't black cows, horses I like horses, mares eat oats and does eat oats…"

That string culminated with a rather hearty snore. I couldn't help a quiet chuckle, my immediate concern for my mother, replaced by amusement.

I wrote down my dream then returned to bed with my chamomile tea. I finally dozed off while reading. After the restless night, 5:30 a.m. came fast. This time of year, the sun would not appear for another hour, so it was especially difficult to drag myself, and my kids, out of bed.

It quickly became apparent catching the school bus would not be an issue. It snowed overnight. A lot more snow than we normally got that time of year.

"Mom! There is no school today, can I go over to Heather's?" Arista asked.

"Moooommmm!" Ian yelled, "I want to go snowboarding! Where is my snowboard?"

"Oh, my stars, can you people wait until my second cup of coffee." I turned on the TV to the local news. The storm and resultant damage were the lead, followed closely by the announcer's proclamation.

"The earlier than usual, and it might be a record, folks, snowstorm."

"Damage huh," I grumbled to no one in particular.

As the caffeine began to have its desired and blessed effect, it occurred to me that checking for damage to our fences needed to be the priority of the day. After food and a quick check on Mom.

I set out the eggs and bacon, both of which we

produce on our farm, and the store-bought bread (I really should make bread more than once a year). About the time the toast popped up and the eggs hit the plates, Ian came racing in from the garage.

"Moooommmm," (he always draws the word out, go figure) "I found my snowboard!"

"Congratulations, son, but snowboarding is going to have to wait until the fences are checked. The news said a lot of trees came down in the wind last night." I saw frustration cross his face and was pleased he didn't argue.

"I suppose Heather's is out until after that, too," Arista said with only a hint of disappointment.

"Ah, you are correct, daughter, now both of you eat before it gets cold." I sat down and ate with my kids. Once we finished, I checked on Mom, who was sleeping happily. I left her a note in case she got up while we were out. Then the three of us bundled up in our winter wear and went to check the fences.

Our farm has been in the family for several generations and encompasses 468 acres. Being in the Ozarks means a good part of it is on the side of a hill, a steep hill. Real estate developers like to use cute words like "rolling," "sloping," or "great drainage," but make no mistake, it's hilly.

(The cow pastures on our farm are set more toward the interior of the property with a buffer of woods between them and neighboring farms. The woods were fenced off about ten years ago as part of a conservation plan.)

"Essentially, we need to check all the perimeter and woods exclusion fences today to make sure the cows stay on the property. You two take the interior woods exclusion fences, get a head count on the cows/calves, and go ahead and move them to the next pasture to the south since you are already going to be down there," I told my teenagers. "Take the side by side and enough fence tools to fix what you find."

"Should we take the chainsaw?" Ian asked.

"Not today, the ground is apt to be slippery, and I'd feel better if you weren't handling a saw. Just drag limbs off the fence and we can cut them up in a few days. I'm going to take BB out and check the perimeter fencing." I was proud of the way my children minded…most of the time.

(BB is my gaited mule. BB is short for Blondie Boy. Arista named him when she was three years old. Watching my twins run around the yard with a day-old mule was one of the cutest things I've ever seen. It's one of my fondest memories of my daddy, we laughed so hard our sides ached.

I remember he pointed to his grandkids and said, "That is legacy, not money or land."

BB was in his stall munching hay when I got to the barn. "Hey, BB, how ya doing?" I patted the sweet mule's neck then poured a half morning ration of feed into the feed pan. "I need you to work this morning, buddy. You get the other half when we get back. Don't need a belly ache."

I swear BB gave me the stink eye, but he set about eating half his normal breakfast anyway. Brushing and saddling the big mule went quickly. He was a fastidiously clean animal, he never rolled in the mud like some horses I had known.

Thinking back to my childhood companion, a white pony who could find a mud hole in the Sahara and would wallow around until she was covered, I smiled. I really liked that pony, but I didn't like cleaning her up. "Daddy used to say that pony was part pig," I mumbled to my mule, then put the saddle in place.

I set out down the lane on BB. Breezy 30-degree air bit my nose and cheeks. The four inches of snow was already melting since the ground had been relatively warm. BB's feet made a rhythmic splat sound.

Stonehorse Ranch had a perimeter fence line of about 2.5 miles long, give or take a hundred yards. An average mule walks about three miles per hour, but BB wasn't average. As a gated mule, he could cover ground quicker and a lot smoother, a fact I was always grateful for.

Years of fence maintenance and pleasure riding paid off as BB and I made for the north side of the property at a running walk. Aside from a few minor limbs down, there was no visible indication of the storm the night before until I rounded the corner to head down the western edge of the property. A tree lay partly across the lane that marked the entrance to the neighboring Duke farm. "Well dang, BB, that was a nice little pine tree. At least it didn't wipe out the fence."

The Duke and Stonehorse families had been neighbors for years, so sharing a fence line and the required maintenance of the fence was normal. Mr. Duke was quite capable at 75 years old, but he shouldn't have to move the tree by himself if help could be provided. I shook my head. *I'll have to come back later with the kids and move it.*

He would be heading up to see Mrs. Duke at the nursing home at lunchtime if the roads were clear enough. He had gone every day since her stroke left her unable to be home. I loved visiting the Duke farm as a girl. Mrs. Duke never failed to have some sweet treat ready when I arrived in the yard atop my grimy white pony. *Simpler times for sure but I love the life I have now with my kids.*

BB stopped and snorted, jolting me from my memories. "What is it, boy?" I looked around but nothing unusual drew my attention so I urged BB forward. We were about twenty feet past the downed tree when we heard a horse whinny. BB stopped again, his keen ears working overtime. "Oh, silly mule, that's just Jackson, you know Jackson."

BB turned. It was then I noticed tire tracks, deep ones, in the lane. The snow that had covered them was melting. The imprints went around and partly over the downed tree. "Huh, that's weird. It looks like a heavy trailer went out through here. What would Mr. Duke be hauling so early this morning? In this weather?" My trusty mount stomped his feet and started down the curved lane toward the Duke house. "Hey, bubba, work is this way." I pulled the reins toward the path adjacent to the fence and away from the lane. Mules are known for being stubborn. BB was generally very well-mannered and cooperative, but not at that moment.

I weighed my options as I tried to get the mule to walk in the direction I wanted to go. I could fight and probably lose to the 1200-pound mule, or I could acquiesce and take a detour by the Duke house. Jackson, the elderly Belgium horse owned by Mr. Duke, whinnied again. There was something urgent feeling in the sound. BB fought for control of his head and insistently edged down the lane toward the Duke house. "Fine, let's go see what's got you in a tizzy."

A memory of Auntie's voice slipped in.

"Fen, my girl, the four-legged ones and the feathered ones see, hear, and feel things that we humans forgot long ago how to see, hear, and feel."

Something about the whinny, the wayward mule, and last night's dream coalesced, and my stomach began to churn. Allowing BB to turn down the Dukes' lane, I urged him into a faster pace.

The lane culminated in a large circle driveway. The deep tire tracks proceeded to the gate entering the pasture to the north of the house. The gate was wide open and Jackson, the Belgium, stood just outside it. Mr. Duke's 1997 Chevy 3/4-ton truck was parked in the open machine barn and his 1970 Chevy Impala was parked in its usual place. *Weird both rigs are here, what made those tracks.*

I took in the scene. "Oh hell, this is so wrong." I dismounted, hurried to the house and banged on the door. "Mr. Duke! Lester! It's Fenreya, are you home?"

No answer. My heart fell to my feet. The only sound inside was Violet, the Duke's five-pound Chihuahua. She barked and scratched wildly at the door.

Torn between worry for my dearest neighbor, and a desire to respect his private home, I knew I had to do something. I turned the doorknob. It wasn't locked. I pushed the door open a bit. Fearing I'd find the worst, I swallowed the lump in my throat and called again, "Mr. Duke! It's Fen, are you okay?"

Violet shot out the crack in the door, past my boot-clad feet, and made a beeline for the gate. "Oh hell." I poked my head in but saw no one. The lights were on in the living room. "Hello?" *Just a quick look around inside to make sure Lester isn't hurt or ill.*

I kept up a steady stream of talking to announce myself. After all, nearly everyone in rural Missouri was armed for home defense. It was unwise to go poking around unannounced.

Finding the house empty, I went outside. BB stood in the yard alternately snorting and pawing the ground, although he was not tied up. "Stars, where is Lester and where did Violet go? I can't leave her out in this weather." I trotted to the open gate and followed tiny dog prints toward the barn. Tire tracks, mud and snow combined into a mucky mess beside the corral. To the left…blood in the snow.

My dream from the night before came flooding back, and my breath caught. For a moment, I couldn't move at all. My feet were glued to the earth, my eyes to the blood.

A jolt from behind got me moving again when Jackson nudged my back. I began to breathe again. "No, no no no!" I bent to examine the bloody snow. "What the hell?" There were drag marks leading away from the blood, toward the pole barn. I rushed into the barn and stopped short.

I couldn't believe what I saw. Mr. Duke lay dead still on his side, against a stack of straw bales. Violet arrived well before me and was curled up beside Mr. Duke's torso.

There was blood on Lester's head, and it had run into his eye. Blood covered his left hand and wrist. "Oh, please no!" I gasped as I knelt beside the still form of my elderly neighbor. "Mr. Duke, it's Fenreya, I'm here to help." I spoke softly and felt for a pulse. His wrist was cold to the touch. Nothing. I checked the carotid artery in his neck, and there, faint, but there was a pulse. "Blessed be."

I took off my heavy duster and covered him with it. I grabbed my cell phone from my jeans pocket on the way back to BB. "Please let there be signal," I prayed as I unlocked the screen.

Cell signal was sporadic at best in the Ozark Mountains and the smallest thing can matter, like which side of the hill you are on, how many trees surround you. "Two bars better be enough."

I dialed the phone number for the sheriff's office. Nine-one-one didn't work out in the boonies, so I had preprogrammed the number into my contacts as well as Arista's and Ian's phones. If signal bars are an issue, you really can't rely on Google to get you a phone number when something goes suddenly pear-shaped.

"Bright County Sheriff's Office, is this an emergency?"

CHAPTER 3

"Yes, oh please send an ambulance out to the Duke farm, Farm Road 420 on highway OV!"

"Is that you, Fen? What happened? Who's hurt?"

I recognized the dispatcher's voice. "Justine, it's Lester Duke. I found him in his barn just before I called. He is not conscious but has a faint pulse. Please hurry, he is so cold."

"Fen, the EMTs are on their way. Stay with Lester. Cold isn't good, turn up the heat and cover him with a blanket, just don't block his airway."

"I can't turn up the heat, I told you, he's *in the damn barn*. I can't stay with him and on the phone, there is no cell signal in the *barn*."

I remembered Justine hadn't listened when we were in high school together. Apparently not much had changed. "Justine, send the sheriff, too, something's not right out here." I pushed the end button on my cell phone and ran back to wait beside Mr. Duke.

Now that help was coming, I knelt beside Lester to better assess his injuries. There was a fair amount of blood, but it was beginning to dry and there didn't appear to be any new blood seeping anywhere. *Should I move him?* "No, we are going to let you be, help is coming." I wasn't sure if I was talking to myself or Lester at that point. Hopefully he could hear me and knew someone was there with him.

During college, and my subsequent job as a rehabilitation counselor in Kansas City, Missouri, I had taken CPR and advanced first aid training. Reviewing the training now made me more confident. *Try not to move the patient unless absolutely necessary, but if the patient is unconscious place them on their side so if they vomit, they won't aspirate fluid into their lungs.*

Lester was already on his side. I needed to know he was still breathing, so I held my cell phone screen just near his mouth and nose. It fogged up on the weak exhale. Any breath was good, and I was happy to see it.

With the mundane medical stuff as good as I could make it, I turned my attention to the arcane. The cold and low pulse had stopped the blood, at least for now, so a blood stop chant wasn't needed. I scoured my memory for the right chant. Not blood, not fever, swelling maybe, pain most likely. *Not going to chant bone mending until we know a qualified doctor has properly set the arm and any other broken bones.*

"Okay, I got it." I began to quietly draw up energy from the earth. I started to sing a slightly modified version of a healing chant I had learned sitting on Auntie Lou's lap as a young child. The original version was designed to stop blood, but it could be modified slightly to suit many situations. I took his left hand gently in mine, it was so cold and limp. I fought to keep my fears in check while I chanted.

Blessed Wound Blessed Hour
Blessed Be the Day Goddess came to Power
Women's mysteries fine and strong
Heal this man through female song
~Silver Raven Wolf (Hexcraft: Dutch Country Pow-wow Magick 1995)

I sang my chant softly but with a power fiercely infused with love. Generations of my people had used this, and similar chants, combined with other old remedies to stay alive and healthy, safe and fruitful while living in an area with little if any help from what is now considered normal allopathic medicine.

I sensed my ancestors with me as the power built to an almost-palpable presence. Lester began to stir. I heard the sirens. It sounded as if they were turning onto the lane leading to the house. I finished chanting and my focus slipped to Lester's moves and the distant sirens. I bent close to the older man's ear. "Lester, it's Fenreya, try to be still, help is almost here." I tried to sound reassuring, for his sake.

"Wha-what happened, all gone, tried to stop them," Lester mumbled. His slurred words were barely audible even in the quiet barn.

"It's okay, Lester, there will be time to talk later. Save your strength." I desperately hoped there would be time for talking later. "I'm going out to meet the medics. You stay still and be strong, okay? I'll be right back with help." His nod was weak, but affirmative.

I got up, then realized my feet had gone numb from kneeling on the cold ground. I stumbled, caught myself then raced out into the driveway to meet the ambulance. I stood wringing my hands as much from nerves as to warm them up.

The ambulance bumped to a halt in the driveway.

The mule moved a few feet away and pinned his ears in annoyance at the lights and wail of the siren. It was getting on my nerves, too, but at least they were here.

EMTs, Kim Edwards and Jess Falon, hopped out. Jess began getting their gear out of the ambulance. Kim had been a couple years ahead of me in school, and we recognized each other instantly.

"Where is the injured person?" Kim asked.

"In the barn." I pointed. "He was unconscious when I found him, but he woke a little before y'all pulled in," I said as we were joined in the driveway by Captain Jana Smith and Deputy Clyde Young.

Kim and Jess hurried for the barn with the stretcher and medical equipment. Captain Smith and I fell in behind them, Deputy Young brought up the rear.

The EMTs went right to work assessing Mr. Duke. They stabilized his neck and moved him to the stretcher. Kim swapped out my heavy duster for a couple blankets. "Is he going to be okay?" I asked Kim.

"We don't know yet, but he is a lot more okay than if you hadn't found him and covered him up." Kim handed me my duster. "Put this on, girl, you're shaking."

"All gone, all gone, bastards took 'em," Mr. Duke murmured as he began to move on the stretcher.

"Easy now, Mr. Duke, we've got you and we're going to help you," Jess said.

Jess Falon had come home to Blossom Bluff after his college football career was cut short when he shredded his ACL. I'm sure his deep melodic baritone voice soothed Lester. It did me. The man lost his parents in a fire when he was four years old and was subsequently raised by his grandmother. Everyone liked

Jess, the gentle giant.

"Who is all gone, Lester?" Captain Smith walked beside the gurney on the way to the ambulance.

"Cows, my cows," Lester whispered.

"Jana, please wait to question him 'til we get him stable, warm, and in the hospital." Kim hissed.

I noted the sternness in Kim's voice. She meant business. Abruptly, I heard Clyde Young yell at me in a tone I didn't like.

"Fenreya Stern! You said he came to in the barn, did he say anything about what happened? How'd you get him conscious? Some of that whoo-whoo healing crap?"

He fired these questions at me without giving me time to respond. He had always been obnoxious in school, and I never cared much for him. At five-feet-five inches tall and about 180 pounds, the guy was the poster boy for little man syndrome. He rocked smugly back on his heels, thumbs stuck in his somewhat-overwhelmed belt. I could have smacked him.

"Well?" he pushed.

I was shaking in earnest now. The cold, stress, and adrenaline joined my absolute abhorrence for Clyde Young and rendered me momentarily speechless. Before I could gather my wits and give Clyde the earful he so richly deserved, his attention was directed elsewhere. Captain Jana Smith watched Kim and Jess finish loading up the ambulance and said to Deputy Young, "Clyde, please get out the crime scene tape and cordon off the area from the house to the barn. I'm calling Sheriff Peters."

Although Jana's directive should have left no room for argument, Deputy Young visibly bristled. "What the hell for?"

"Clearly Mr. Duke didn't hit himself over his head and make all his cattle disappear."

She was ticked off. I had to smile when she glared at Clyde. She glanced at me and continued more gently.

"Fen, how about you join me in the squad car. You can warm up and tell me everything that happened."

"I'll be right there, Jana, I'm going to call my kids real quick. I'm sure they're fine but I'll feel better once I've talked to one of them." I just hoped they'd be on top of a hill or somewhere they could get a cell signal.

"Sure, Fen, you go ahead and call. I'll meet you at the car."

I made my call, and it went straight to voicemail so I sent a text. "Hey kids, when you get signal call me. Be safe."

At some point, Jana had scooped up Violet. Poor little thing was also shaking. Captain Smith handed the pooch off to me when I got to her car. Truly relieved to be out of the cold, I settled Violet inside my coat and relayed everything to Captain Smith while she took notes.

Saying them out loud made the day's events sound surreal. I filled Jana in on what I'd seen and done since leaving the house earlier in the morning. Sheriff Peters pulled in just as I finished my debrief with Captain Smith.

Sheriff John Peters was a good old boy, in the best sense. He had gone to school with my dad, and they were friends. When my siblings and I were young and got into mischief, Sheriff Peters always found a way to hold our feet to the fire in the kindest way possible. He was like that with all the kids but was tough as nails when he would encounter an actual nasty person. I admired him for that.

"Mornin', Captain Smith, Fenreya." Sheriff Peters leaned down to talk through the window of the patrol car.

"Hi, Sheriff, Fen was the first one on scene and—"

"Sheriff!" Clyde Young cut Jana off.

Violet growled from under my coat when Deputy Young approached the car. It seemed she didn't like him anymore than I did. His mouth was still running.

"Sheriff, she had me cordon off the barn and barn lot, but I really don't see what the—"

Sheriff Peters held up his hand. "Deputy Young, Captain Smith has seniority and my full confidence. If she told you to cordon off an area, then I expect you to do it without a lot of jaw flapping. Is it done?"

"Yes, Sheriff," Clyde replied. The wind had gone out of his sails, yet he shot a glare at Captain Smith.

"Go sit in your car and warm up, Young. I'll be with you in a minute." The sheriff turned back to the window. "Fen, are you up to walking me through the events of the day in detail?"

Going through the details again was something I didn't really want to do, but I knew it had to be done. I exited the car. Violet popped her head out of my coat and wiggled so hard I 'bout dropped her. I had never seen a dog that didn't like our Sheriff John Peters. "Sure thing, Sheriff." I set Violet on the ground.

As a kid, when the sheriff was off duty and would come over to hang out with Dad, my siblings and I called him Uncle John. Today, on duty and at an official crime scene, the endearing moniker would clearly not be appropriate. He smiled. We were on the same page.

I started from the beginning, which, in my opinion, was about the time I turned down the lane along the fence and my mule got fussy. I explained the house being unlocked, how I had gone in, inadvertently let Violet out, and subsequently discovered the bloody path in the snow and Mr. Duke's very still form in the open barn. I repeated every word Lester had said to me but left out my healing chant.

Sheriff Peters knew a lot about my family. He even knew my grandmother was renowned among the old-timers as a Powwow practitioner. I didn't know if he knew those traits, talents, and beliefs had been passed down to me, and I didn't think an active crime scene was the time to bring it to light.

The faint sound of bells chimed. Sheriff Peters dug into his coat pocket and pulled out his phone.

"Sheriff here, go."

I, joined by Captain Smith, waited and tried not to listen. However, that was all but impossible.

"Good, good, thank you for calling, keep me posted." Sheriff Peters clicked off the phone and returned it to his pocket but didn't bother to zip up his coat. He smiled as he said, "That was the charge nurse. Lester has been seen, is resting comfortably, and the doc thinks he will be just fine."

I let out a huff of breath I didn't know I'd been holding as did Captain Smith. I was thankful they'd gotten to the hospital so quickly and Lester was okay.

Deputy Young said, "Tough old coot, I'd thought he was a goner."

When did he walk over and what an insensitive thing to say. I traded looks with Captain Smith. It looked as if she felt about Clyde the same way Violet and I did.

No longer smiling, Sheriff Peters turned to the deputy. "Clyde, go back to the station and do your paperwork. We'll be out here for a while."

Clyde had no real choice but to admit he had been dismissed. "10-4, Sheriff." He trudged off to his patrol car.

Sheriff Peters said, "Fen, you can head on home. Either I or Captain Smith will be in touch as needed, but call us if you think of anything else."

Violet yipped. She was dancing around the sheriff's feet. It was clear she wanted him to pick her up.

"Aw, poor girl, what to do with you? Fen, could you take custody of her until Lester can come home or other arrangements can be made?" Sheriff Peters asked.

I watched Uncle John pick up the tiny dog and called BB over to me. I checked the saddle girth before mounting. A good habit and one that I learned the hard way. "Sure, Sheriff, the kids and I can watch her. I hope she likes cats." I tried to stifle a laugh as I swung into the saddle.

Violet's eyes grew wide when the sheriff handed her up to me but didn't complain when she was safely tucked in my coat. "I'll call if I think of anything."

"Thanks, Fen."

I waved and reined the mule toward my place. The ride home was uneventful. BB had always been unflappable, I loved that about him. Even when Violet poked her head out to bark at a squirrel, he didn't bat an eye. "Jeepers, Violet, I still haven't checked the perimeter fence." Figuring food and drink would be welcome for everyone, I nudged the mule into a running walk and made good time to the house.

CHAPTER 4

The kids were already back from their fence-checking, cow-moving activities. Ian had his head in the fridge and Arista sat at the table texting. They pounced the moment I walked in the door.

Ian said, "Hey, Mom. Whoa, what's with the dog?"

Arista put her phone down. "Mom, what were those sirens? Is the fence damaged? Isn't that Mr. Duke's dog? Oh god, did something happen to Mr. Duke?"

Ian picked up Violet and scruffed her ears. "Yeah, sis, this is Mr. Duke's dog. Mom, where's the casserole from two nights ago? Aw, you're a good pup."

The rapid-fire questions tumbled toward me like an avalanche. I held up both hands. "Stop, kids, please! It's been a day. I will answer all your questions, *please* just give me a minute!"

They gave me almost five minutes. After a trip to the facility, change into warm slippers, and with fresh coffee in hand, I filled the kids in on the morning's bizarre events. They had a multitude of questions but saved them 'til I was done so's not to "slow my roll" as

Ian was fond of saying.

"Who would hurt Mr. Duke? He is such a sweetie," said Arista.

"Apparently the people that stole his cows. Duh." Ian offered.

"You wouldn't know a rhetorical question if it slapped you upside the head. Anyway, the creeps didn't have to hurt him. He could have died."

"Don't start bickering, you two. I agree, in theory, but these were not high-dollar cows. Seems an awful risk for dairy cross steers. They were nice and well cared for but not remarkably valuable." I continued to sip my coffee.

"I don't know, Mom," Ian said, "I saw the blip on Ag Day when I was getting dressed and prices are up. If a guy has no money in a cow to begin with, the money to be made might be tempting."

Arista and I both looked at Ian with raised brows. He knew what the insinuation meant.

"Not tempting to me, geez, you guys, you know what I mean. Right?" Ian blurted out in a rush, his cheeks reddening.

(It's fun to make him blush. Arista, on the other hand, rarely blushes. She has a poker face any Vegas gambler would envy. She inherited that trait from her dad.)

We made it through the rest of the day without drama. The perimeter fence finally got checked in a collective effort by the kids and me. We brought Lester's horse to our house so we could watch over him.

After the events of the morning and subsequent farm work, popping a meal from the freezer into the oven and walking away for a while was exactly what I needed. While dinner was doing its thing, I sat down in the family room. The kids went to their respective rooms to chill. Ian would be gaming online with the boys, and Arista was probably watching videos and texting. Mom was knitting by the fireplace, humming an old song I didn't recognize. "Hi, Mom, what are you working on?"

"Oh, just a scarf. I don't know who it's for yet. Maybe your father."

My heart clenched. Mom didn't always remember Daddy was gone. Had been for three years. The accident that took his life left Mom with a traumatic brain injury.

Although not terribly incapacitating by itself, the injury seemed to kick the dementia into a higher gear. This was how I ended up moving home to Blossom Bluff a couple of years ago. It only made sense to move back.

(My older sister lives in France and has always been something of a free spirit, and my "little" brother has become a very successful businessman in Silicon Valley.)

After supper, I felt unsettled. I didn't understand why, but I couldn't shake it. "Hey, kids, I'm going to drive over to the hospital and see how Mr. Duke is doing. Wanna ride with me? If he is awake, I want to let him know we have Violet and his horse and see if he wants us to do anything in particular at his place." Arista agreed to come along, but Ian was working on some computer thing he wanted to finish.

We arrived at the community hospital around 6 p.m. It was dark and chilly, but I was thankful the sky no longer leaked rain/snow/sleet. Missouri weather can be indecisive.

"Do you smell that?" Arista asked.

"Yes, I smell something hot. Burning trash?" We went inside.

As we were walking down the hall to the nurses' station, an alarm began to blare and staff started to scurry.

The charge nurse remained at the desk and was on the phone. "The alarm is going off. We are checking the building, but you better dispatch a team over." She hung up and looked at us. "Can I help you?"

"We smelled smoke in the parking lot," Arista offered.

"What room is Lester Duke in?" I asked.

"He is a popular guy tonight. Room 113, but be prepared to evacuate. We hope the alarms are at worst a prank, but if you smelled smoke…" The nurse's voice trailed off when her phone lit up and the walkie-talkie on her belt squawked at the same time.

Arista and I hurried down the hall to room 113, intent on completing our mission. If the hospital was going to become uninhabitable, we would scoop Mr. Duke into the truck and take him home with us.

(What we saw next would not make sense until much later.)

When we opened the door to room 113, there was a person leaning over Mr. Duke holding a pillow. The person was about my height, five ten, dressed in dark clothing, including the ski mask that covered their face. "Hey! Get away from him!" Arista and I roared in unison.

The person, I could now tell was a man, whirled around, threw the pillow at Arista's face, shoved me into the wall then hit the hallway running. I grabbed for him as he bulled between us but missed. I slid down the wall and landed flat on my rump.

Arista stayed on her feet, but barely. "Mom! Are you okay?"

She scrambled to help me up, and I gladly took her hand. "Thanks. I'm fine, stay with Lester, call the nurses' station." I took off down the hall after the assailant and caught up with him in time to see him shove a nurse's aide roughly out of his path as he made for the main doors. She banged her head on the wall then fell to the floor. Torn between continuing the chase and checking on the young woman, I hesitated.

Damn it all. I glanced at the running man, then at the girl. She had what appeared to be a baby bump under her unflattering blue scrub top. I knelt beside her. "Miss, are you okay?"

"Who the heck was that?" she asked, rubbing her head with one hand and automatically cradling her tummy with the other.

"I don't know, but if you are okay here for a minute, I will be right back." I took off again.

It was much too late to see where the guy went. The front doors were shut and there was no sign of anyone running outside. I turned and trudged back in to find the charge nurse. She was by Lester's room talking with Arista and the young aide that had gotten knocked down.

"Did you see where he went, Mom?"

I walked up to the group. "No, he got away."

The nurse had checked Lester over and determined he was unscathed by the assault and resting comfortably, evidently oblivious to the drama that had taken place all around him. For a moment, I kind of envied him. Then thought about the fractured arm, big gash on his head, and the killer headache he would probably wake up with, and decided I didn't have it so bad.

Captain Smith jogged up the hall and joined us. We filled her in on what had happened. She told us the fire department had found the fire outside in the dumpster, and their fire marshal was sure it was arson. Captain Smith went on to say that a guard would be posted at Mr. Duke's door for the remainder of his stay and asked the charge nurse if she could provide access to the security footage.

"Oh, I wish I could. The security camera system hasn't worked for six months. We have repeatedly asked the board to approve money for it to be replaced, but they just keep saying it's not in the budget."

We all stood, grimacing at this revelation. Arista and I gave the best descriptions we could to Jana, and then we went in to check on Lester. My heart leapt with joy when we found him awake.

"Hey, Mr. Duke, it's good to see you," Arista said quietly.

"Arista, Fen, where am I? What happened?" Mr. Duke's voice quavered.

Captain Jana Smith poked her head into the room. "Is he awake, Fen?"

"Yes, Jana, do you need to talk to him first?"

"Yes, please, I need a statement from him. You all can stay if you want, just don't intercede."

Arista and I moved back so the deputy could stand next to Lester's bed. "Hey, Mr. Duke, I'm Captain Smith with the sheriff's department. I'd like to talk with you for a few moments if that is okay."

Lester blinked a few times as if trying to focus in on Jana's face. "I remember you, young lady. You and your brother, James, used to come out and pick up hay bales for me in the summer."

"That's right, sir, we did. Those were simpler times," Jana replied. "Mr. Duke, what all can you remember about what happened?"

Lester scrunched his face in thought and winced as though that small movement hurt his head. I felt bad for him.

He said, "I, oh well, let's see. My dog, Violet, started barking and I told her to hush. I was watching my show, tried to ignore the yapping. Finally, I figured I better go see what got her so riled up. I figured there was probably an old opossum nosing around.

"I got my coat and flashlight and went outside. I saw a truck and trailer backed up to my fence. I went running out there and asked the guy, 'Hey what are you doing? Get off my place!' I don't know anything after that. I woke up here in this room."

Deputy Jana nodded, placed a card on the adjustable table by the bed. "Thank you, Mr. Duke, if you remember anything else, please call me."

She shot a meaningful look at Arista and me, and I took it to mean that we were included in her missive. I nodded and thanked her for responding so quickly to the call. I have often thought police people probably don't hear enough gratitude.

As Jana left the room, Arista and I moved up beside

the hospital bed. I took Lester's hand in mine. I don't need physical contact in order to use my empathy, but I also wanted to surreptitiously check his temperature and grip strength. When I worked as a rehabilitation therapist before moving back home to care for Mom, this was a method I used with each client to get an initial read on them before our session.

"Mr. Duke, how are you feeling?" Arista asked softly.

I smiled.

(My daughter, for all her tomboy bravado, is a sweet soul who would give the shirt off her back to someone in need.)

"Arista, good of you to come see an old man. My head hurts." Lester grimaced as if taking inventory of how he felt. "So does my arm. Fenreya, dear, can you please tell me what the hell happened, I can't remember?"

I recounted the story of how I found him passed out in the barn. I left out the more troubling details of bloody snow and how severe his injuries had appeared. He had questions, of course.

"Are my animals all right?"

"Violet's fine. She's staying with us until you recover and return home. Jackson is also fine, and is in with our stock at our place, too." I paused, not really wanting to tell Lester that all his steers were missing, but he had a right to know.

"What about my cattle? They were there to steal them, right? Any sign of them?"

It was as if he read the omission on my face. "Uh, your cattle *are* currently missing." Lester sucked in a breath, and I saw the sadness in his eyes. "But the sheriff's office is doing everything they can to figure out who attacked you and took your cattle," I added, hoping to take some of the sting out of the news.

Lester blew the breath out and seemed to sink into the bed, looking deflated. I glanced at Arista, her eyes shined with unshed tears. She would not cry until after we left the room, it just wasn't her style. I knew they were tears of anger mostly rather than sadness. I knew this because my eyes burned with the same emotion.

Arista said, "Mr. Duke, we are all going to keep our eyes open and find the creeps that hurt you and do our best to find your cattle. Please try not to worry."

I was proud Arista tried to ease the old man's mind. She was a good girl. Lester nodded slightly and his eyes fluttered shut then open. It was apparent he was tired, and sleep would be as healing as anything else, so we prepared to leave.

"Lester, is there anything we can bring you from home or anything we can do to help while you are in here?" I asked.

"If you happen by the house and find my cell phone, I would like to have it. Make sure the house is locked. And if you could check on Mary up at the nursing home, that would mean a lot to both of us," he said.

"Done."

"Thank you, Fen. You all are the best neighbors an old man could have."

"We just want you healed up and back home where you belong. Get some rest, I will pop in tomorrow to see you," I replied with a smile.

As we were leaving, Deputy Johnny Sharp arrived, carrying a chair. He placed it outside the door to Lester's room. Johnny was the youngest deputy on our county's staff, and he only worked part-time. He went to college the rest of the time. He was a gorgeous kid, about twenty years old, with short dark hair and brilliant blue eyes. He was clearly no stranger to the gym.

"Hey, Johnny," Arista said shyly.

I feel confident in saying my daughter had at least a tiny crush on the handsome deputy. Heck, who could blame her?

"Hey, Arista, Mrs. Stern." Johnny nodded to us both with a bright smile. "Captain Smith told me what happened. Are you two okay?"

His smile turned into a concerned grimace. Arista grinned and nodded. It's wholly unlike her to be speechless. I answered, "Yes, Johnny, we are fine, thanks for asking. Are you on watch for Mr. Duke's safety tonight?"

"Yes, ma'am."

"Excellent, he is in capable hands, then. Thanks, Johnny, we'll see you." We started down the hallway. Arista was mostly looking at the floor but managed a tiny wave in parting. I suppressed a giggle.

When we left the warmth of the building, the wind outside the hospital had picked up considerably, stealing my breath for a moment. We bundled ourselves into the truck and I started the engine. It didn't take long for the heater to grace us with warm air.

I glanced at my daughter as I drove out of the parking lot. She stared in the general direction of her shoes and appeared to be lost in thought. Is this a serious crush? I wondered. Both my kids had had crushes before and had the typical middle school boyfriend/girlfriend scenarios, nothing serious. *They are fifteen years old.*

I remembered when I was in high school a couple of my classmates became pregnant at that age. It wasn't cool, but it wasn't the scandal it would have been ten or twenty years previously. Babies having babies.

I had already had "The Talk" with both Arista and Ian. Besides, farm life is ripe with visual aids showing where babies come from, so even if they ignored our discussions, I knew they understood those risks.

They both know how to be careful, but there is so much more to it than the biological stuff. Heartbreak at any age is hard as hell. It is also an inevitable part of being human. It took about three miles for me to think these thoughts. Arista still hadn't said a word.

"Johnny's pretty cute, huh?" I ventured.

"Yeah, I guess," Arista replied after a beat.

I noticed she was trying too hard to sound nonchalant. "Too young for me and too old for you, what a shame," I said with a chuckle, hoping to draw her thoughts out. She glanced at me but said nothing. "What's got you so quiet, my dear? Are you thinking about the incident at the hospital?"

"I'm mad about that, Mom, I mean, isn't it bad enough that some jerk hurt Lester in the first place, now they are trying to hurt him again? Would he be dead if we hadn't gone by? That's what it feels like, and I can't understand it. Plus, they shoved you, *my mother*, down. I'd really like to curse them or punch them or maybe kick them in the nuts." Arista finished her diatribe with a huff. Then added in a softer voice, "But yeah, Johnny is fine, that you think so, too, creeps me out though."

There it was. I laughed for the next couple miles.

By the time we got home, it had started snowing again. The wonderful aroma of freshly popped popcorn greeted us at the door.

Ian yelled, "In here."

We shed our coats and boots and joined my son and his grandmother in the family room. Ian had stoked the fire and was making a second container of Jiffy Pop. The first one sat near my mother, who had set aside her knitting and focused on the TV. NCIS was on and she had a thing for Leroy Jethro Gibbs. There would be no conversation with her until the show was over even though it was a rerun from Netflix.

"How is Lester?" Ian asked.

"Oh man, have we got a story for you!" Arista said over the TV.

"Shush, you," said Grandma.

"Let's take our conversation to the kitchen, I'll make some hot cocoa," I suggested to the kids with a nod toward their grandma. She enjoyed her programs in the evening, and I worried continued talk of Lester's injury and the incident at the hospital would upset her. How could it not? I was mad as hell, and that would not change until something got resolved.

I poured milk into a ceramic-coated saucepan and turned the burner on low.

(Like my mom and her mother, I don't measure anything when I cook, unless it is a new to me recipe. We've made our own hot cocoa mix for years, and it's kept in a quart mason jar in the cabinet where the coffee, teas, and cat treats live. Funny place for cat treats, you say? It's a long story involving a certain naughty door-opening feline. She dislikes the smell of green tea for some reason, so we attempt to use that to our advantage. It doesn't always work. Cats!)

The kids settled at the table and started in on the popcorn. Arista told Ian all about the hospital debacle. Her story was punctuated by the occasional "omg" and "are you kidding me?" exclamations from Ian. I joined them with three steaming mugs of cocoa complete with whipped cream and dashes of cinnamon on top. Arista paused her story to lick the whipped cream off the rim of her mug before it ran down the side.

"Are you okay, Mom? I can't believe some dirtbag pushed you down!" Ian said.

"Yes, honey, I am fine. Mad and worried but unhurt," I assured my son.

"What about Lester?" he asked.

"Oh, he slept through all the drama but did wake up to talk with us and with Captain Smith. They posted a guard at his room overnight," I answered.

CHAPTER 5

It took a while to decompress enough to get the kids to go to bed. It was much longer before I could lose myself in sleep for a few hours.

At 5 a.m., I gave in to wakefulness and got up for the day. I puttered around the kitchen, made coffee and pulled out a roast to thaw for tomorrow, and some burger for later in the day. One of the huge benefits of raising all our own meat was the ready supply of dinner fixings.

I passed by Mom's room on my way to the shower and she was mumbling again. "Gibbs out at the cabin, funny cabin, funny cows."

"My mom dreaming about NCIS and cows, good grief, the subconscious is a weird place," I mused as I lathered up my hair with coconut vanilla shampoo. I chose my peppermint-scented soap hoping it would be as invigorating as the soap maker claimed it would be. It wasn't.

Saturday's dawn was bright and sunny, the last dab of snow had melted overnight. The sun streamed through the windows in my bedroom. I changed into jeans and an oversized lavender Henley top. I heard the kids emerge from their respective rooms and little Violet yapped to be let outside.

I wonder which kid she slept with last night, bet she misses Lester. I should take her with me to town and smuggle her into the hospital for a visit.

"Good morning, how did y'all sleep?"

"Not bad," said Arista.

"Not great, this little beastie snores. A lot," Ian said with a yawn.

Now I knew who Violet slept with. That was an impressive yawn! I laughed.

"What is on for today, Mom?" Arista asked.

"I will tell you over breakfast." I grabbed the eggs, bacon, and cheese out of the fridge. "One of you make toast, the other one get the juice poured and set the table please."

"Is Grandma getting up for breakfast with us?" Ian asked while loading the toaster oven with whole grain bread.

"I'm going to let her sleep, it's pretty early and Yvonne is coming to get her later and take her to the senior center."

(Yvonne is a longtime friend of my mom, the kind of friend that remembers how things used to be, understands how they are now, and doesn't judge the deficit.)

"What do they do at the senior center?" Arista placed three plates and the associated silverware on the kitchen island.

"Hmm, I know they serve lunch, but they also have room for people to sit and visit while they do puzzles or play cards." I stirred the eggs. "Thanks to a generous donation from an unnamed source, our senior center has a pool and there are classes for water aerobics. It's pretty snazzy."

"Gosh, Mom, that sounds cool, bet you can't wait to be old so you can go play, too," Ian teased.

"Oh, I can totally wait, kid."

I watched the kids pile their plates with eggs, top them off with shredded cheese, and divide the bacon evenly between the three of us while I sipped my juice. "So today we must visit the feedstore, the grocery store, and I want to swing by the hospital and check on Lester. I want to take Violet along and smuggle her in for a visit." Both kids grinned, always up for a "covert op."

After breakfast, the twins went out to do the few chicken and horse chores. I loaded the dishwasher then we piled into the truck and headed to town.

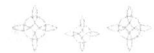

We stopped at the feedstore first since they were only open 'til noon on Saturdays.

The store looked big on the outside but was revealed as an optical illusion because of the large, attached feed storage area. The actual store part was packed with all manner of farm and animal paraphernalia. Everything from over-the-counter medicine for cattle and goats, to buckets, over-the-rail feeders, and assorted fence supplies. It was so full of new items, brought in for the upcoming holidays, it was difficult to walk to the counter without getting distracted.

In the front right corner was a circular rack of

Carhart brand outerwear and hoodies. Ian made a beeline for the rack. I noticed on the drive over that his jacket was a bit short in the sleeves and the elbows were worn nearly through. Sigh.

Arista, who had Violet tucked under her arm, walked beside me to the counter where Rebecca, the number one town gossip, greeted us with a cheerful tone.

"Hello, Sterns, guess what I heard?"

"Hi, Rebecca," we said in unison. Neither of us asked her to continue. But she did.

"Well, you know what happened to Lester because you found him, Fen, but did you know that old Ben Johnson over in Paris was rustled last week?" She continued without a pause for input. "And my cousin's friend told her over in Solehm County that her neighbor lost his cattle two weeks ago!" Rebecca schooled her face into a frown, although her glee at delivering such juicy gossip was evident.

"Wow, how awful," I said.

Arista gaped. "Dang!"

I ordered and paid for our feed and Ian joined us at the loading platform.

"Did I hear right? There were two other cattle thefts in the last couple weeks?" Ian asked Arista quietly.

"Yep," she answered.

I handed the load out ticket to Justin. He grabbed a dolly and began to gather our feed. Justin graduated the year before and was supposedly taking a gap year before he went to college. He always seemed like a good kid, but he looked a bit ragged this morning.

Arista and Ian headed to the grassy area next to the building to give Violet a chance to go potty while "discussing" which of them would drive to the next location. They got their learner's permits two months earlier when they turned fifteen and typically shared driving privileges harmoniously. Occasionally there was a dust up, but I was proud of the way they usually handled it.

I watched them walk away and sighed. *They're growing up so fast, they'll work it out.*

Justin emerged from the warehouse with our feed order and began stacking it in the bed of the pickup. The kids joined me by the truck just as Denny Bowman walked out of the warehouse and spoke to Justin.

Denny was one of three brothers, none of whom had amounted to much, but of the three, Denny held down a job. He had worked at the feedstore for three years. He was around my age, but I recalled very little about him from high school. I didn't know Denny's two younger brothers, but I heard some unpleasant rumors about Randy's proclivities.

"Justin, you better not break another bag of feed…" Denny's words were cut short as Violet, tiny though she was, lunged at her leash, baring her teeth and growling at both men. Arista quickly reeled her in and began soothing the little dog.

"What the hell?" Denny exclaimed as he jumped back.

Justin just stood there looking astonished, and I noticed Denny didn't look too happy. "I'm sorry, fellas. Chihuahuas can be a bit tense. She can't hurt you as long as you have boots on," I ended with a laugh, hoping to lighten the situation.

"There's no damn dogs allowed in the warehouse. They piss on the feed sacks!" Denny declared.

"She wasn't *in* the warehouse," Arista said. She has

never liked any of the Bowman brothers.

Didn't the dumbass know girl dogs don't raise their leg to pee? I shook my head. "That's enough, kids, get in the truck. I will drive for now."

Ian put a protective arm across his sister's shoulder, and they walked down the ramp to ground level. I noticed Ian shot a disgusted glance at the dockworkers. I followed them and got in the driver's side.

"Ian, I saw you checking out the jackets. Did you find one you like?" I asked. Arista was still fuming, and I really did want to know. Christmas was just around the corner.

"Yeah, Mom, they have a few tall sizes in for once. I like the dark green one the best. The arms are actually long enough to go to my wrist," he chuckled.

"Sleeves," Arista said.

"What?" asked Ian.

"Arms are those long things hanging off your body holding the hands you use to shovel food in your mouth. Sleeves are on clothing," Arista corrected Ian with the typical eye roll.

"Whatever! Geez who pulled your chain?" Ian retorted.

The jovial mood they'd started with was slipping rapidly away, and I wasn't in any frame of mind to cope with discord. "Okay, enough, both of you! Can we please focus on treating each other with kindness? If you two start bickering, you can do it at home while you clean out the barn, and I will run the errands myself." I learned when my kids were little that it was best to nip these arguments in the bud whenever possible. Success sounded like a chorus when I heard them in unison.

"Okay, Mom."

"You guys want something to drink? I'm thinking of stopping at the coffee shop. I want to pick up some of those mini-Danishes your Grams likes."

"Yes, please," replied the twins in stereo.

I turned down Main Street heading for downtown. Our local coffeehouse, Cones and Scones sat on the west side of the square next to the local drugstore.

(They have the typical coffee and tea selections, hot chocolate that isn't nearly as good as what we make at home, but their pastries are wonderful. Like *melt-in-your-mouth-habit-forming* wonderful.)

I rounded the corner and drove into the town square. "Oh my! Wonder what is going on here." There were two police cars in front of the drugstore, lights flashing but no sirens. One was county and the other, Blossom Bluff city police. I parked at the nearest spot on the south side of the central parking area, wanting to avoid crowding the police but unwilling to abandon our pastry run. Besides, I also wanted to know what was going on.

"Y'all wait in the truck." I shot them a look that brooked no arguments. I chose to ignore the whiney 'Oh, Mom'.

I crossed the street, heading for the coffee shop just as Captain Smith emerged from the drugstore. Our city cop, Michael Birk, was right behind her.

"Jana, thanks for responding, I've got it from here."

"You're welcome, Mike, we all have to stick together. I guess it's the rush before the holidays, but hair color and beanie babies, really? When a drugstore gets hit, you expect the theft inventory to include pills," Captain Smith said.

"Yeah, but there is no accounting for the stupidity of third-rate thieves. We may find out they are missing more usual items once the pharmacist arrives. He was on his way out of town but should be back in a couple hours. He was none too happy about canceling his plans," Officer Birk said.

"I can relate." Jana turned. "Good morning, Fen."

"Morning, officers." I nodded to them both. "Is everyone all right?"

"Yes, no injuries, the place was burglarized sometime overnight. The girl who opened didn't notice the back door had been broken into until she went out back to sneak a cigarette." It was Captain Smith who answered me, and it earned her a scowl from Officer Birk.

Michael Birk was an outsider to our little community, meaning, he wasn't born here and had only been a resident for five years. It can take a while to be accepted into rural small-town life. He didn't know me at all and was likely puzzled as to why Captain Smith would divulge crime scene details to me. I was kind of surprised, too.

"I'm glad no one was hurt. Seems like a lot of crime for a tiny community all of a sudden," I remarked and reached for the coffee shop door.

"Mike, let me know if our department can be of any assistance. Fen, hold the door, I was heading for my Danish fix when I heard dispatch. That is why I got on scene so fast." Jana grinned at the city cop.

"Who says cops only like donuts?" Officer Birk smiled and headed back into the drugstore.

"Yeah, Fen, you are right about the crime around here, it is busier than usual. Maybe it will all calm down after the holidays." Jana dug in her pocket then pulled out some cash.

We placed our respective orders and walked out. Jana walked with me over to my truck.

"Good morning, kids. Have you all heard anyone talking at school about some pranks or mischief?" Captain Smith asked.

"No, ma'am, but we are freshmen, no one tells us anything. Pranks are usually a senior thing," Ian replied.

Arista nodded her agreement.

"Ah yes, I remember." Jana glanced at me.

"Yeah, me, too," I said.

"I've got to report to the station. You all enjoy the rest of your weekend." Captain Smith turned and headed for her car.

"You, too, Jana, be safe."

CHAPTER 6

I climbed in the driver's seat and passed out the baked goodies and coffee then we headed for the hospital. When we got to the hallway leading to Lester's room, we saw Deputy Young sitting in the chair outside the door. He looked grumpy, but that was nothing new. He'd shown his hand at the Duke farm.

"Oh goody," said Arista with an eye roll.

"Shush, just be polite. I won't let him get under my skin if you don't," Ian told his sister.

I disguised a laugh with a cough and bid Deputy Young good morning.

"What's good about it? Here I sit bored as all hell," he said in response. I heard the terse tone and tried not to let it drag me down.

"Isn't boring a good thing while on guard duty?" I asked as sweetly as possible.

"Hrumpf," he grunted.

We walked into Lester's room, and he smiled at us from the bed. He appeared much better, although still a mite pale. Violet poked her head out of Ian's jacket and began to wiggle so hard I thought he might drop her.

"Easy, little one, here ya go." Ian deposited her on the bed next to Lester, who beamed back at us and hauled the dog to his chest. If the movement hurt him, it didn't show.

"Oh, Violet, bless your tiny heart, I'm glad to see you! Fenreya, Ian, Arista, I'm mighty happy to see y'all, too! Thank you for taking care of my baby and for saving my life the other day, Fen. I don't know how to ever repay you."

"Lester, that's not even an issue. We're happy to help any way we can. We're just glad you are doing better!" The twins nodded and murmured their agreement. Just then, the door opened and the doctor, whom I hadn't met previously, walked in.

"Good morning, Mr. Duke, I'm Doctor Allen. I'll be on shift through the weekend and Dr. Woods has briefed me on your injuries. I'm going to take a quick look if that's okay. What is a dog doing in here?" The doctor's previously pleasant visage morphed into one of terror.

"She is my dog, and I have a right to have visitors!" Lester exclaimed, pulling Violet closer to him.

Violet gave the doctor the stink eye and the man retreated to the far side of the room. He glared at the tiny dog as if she was a cobra coiled to strike instead of Lester's best friend. *Was he afraid of the little ankle biter?* I suppressed my smile.

"I, uh, I don't like dogs, and they are not allowed in the hospital. Dogs are dirty and --"

That was it. I stepped between the doctor and the hospital bed. "Actually, the presence of pets has been shown to speed healing and reduce stress of patients. I will have you know, this particular dog is cleaner than most of the people currently in your ER." I gestured toward my daughter. "Arista, hold Violet while the doctor checks Lester out and then hand her back to him. Doctor," I said, stepping back and gesturing toward Lester, "do what you need to do, and rest assured, my teenagers will protect you from the five-pound pup." Doctor Allen's red face grimaced but he nodded agreement.

After he checked Lester's vital signs and questioned him about pain, he asked Lester if he could talk to him in private. Lester told him we were not leaving yet, and he could talk freely in front of us. I was happy he felt comfortable with us being there. I could tell the doctor didn't, but he continued anyway.

"Your injuries are going to take a while to heal, especially the fractured arm. The sheriff has asked us to keep you as long as possible so he can keep a guard on you. Although this is highly irregular, our administrating physician has agreed. However, after that, I recommend you go to a rehab facility since there is no one at home to look after you. You will need to see an occupational therapist to regain full use of your arm."

Lester visibly bristled. "Now wait one damn minute, you doctor." The last word came out like it tasted bad. "First, you come in here and insult my dog and my friends, then you want to shackle me in some damn nursing home when I didn't do anything wrong except get whacked on the head by some jackass. I can do for myself, thank you very much. I want out of here today!"

I really thought Lester might rip the IV out of his arm just then, so I intervened. "Hold on, Lester, you don't have to go to a nursing home."

"Who are you to tell him—" the doctor tried to interrupt.

Holding a hand up at the doctor, I continued, my tone louder. "You can come to our home once you are released from the hospital, I am a rehabilitation therapist, or I was until I left the city, and we would love to have you there. You would be next door to your place and Violet is already with us."

Lester's face softened and his eyes shown. "You would do that for me? You have already done so much, Fen."

"Mr. Duke, please come stay with us." Arista passed Violet back to him.

Doctor Allen backed up again. I smiled despite the tenseness.

"Yeah, it will be cool if you come stay. Maybe you can talk me through fixing the carburetor on the old tractor. I tried it on my own, but it was an epic failure," Ian added.

Smart kid, my son, giving Lester a challenge and a way to help us. We didn't need that old tractor running but it would be kind of cool if it did.

Lester nodded his agreement. "That sounds like a fine plan as long as I'm no trouble."

I grinned and winked at Lester then turned to Doctor Allen. "Well, Doc, all is settled. Lester will come home with us once he is released. Just let us know what day that will be." I turned back to Lester. Doctor Allen rightly interpreted that as the signal he was dismissed, and he left.

The rest of our visit with our neighbor was pleasant. Ian talked about the old tractor, and Arista added how cool it would be to use it to pull a float in the annual Christmas Parade. Violet snuggled as tightly to her master's chest as she could get but didn't fuss when Ian tucked her back into his jacket in preparation to leave.

We left the hospital and Arista asked what else I had planned for the day.

After the car accident that killed my father and injured my mother, my siblings and I adopted a stretch of road. Although it was a different road than what Daddy was killed on, the commemorative placard was in memory of him.

Daddy hated litter and taught us all to pick up not only our trash but any other trash we saw anytime we went camping or to the lake. It got so we automatically took a contractor-size garbage bag anytime we went on those trips. It was often full when we returned.

"It's such nice weather, let's go home, unload the truck, and head out to the commemorative roadside. We can pick up the litter and it will look nice for Thanksgiving."

It was Arista's turn to drive, and we headed home without incident. Once there, Ian announced he was starving, 'like literally starving,' he said. So, I told them to unload the feed and I headed to the house with Violet on my heels. I made ham sandwiches, making sure to accidentally drop a small piece on the floor for our tiniest house guest. I had them ready when the kids burst in through the back door laughing.

"That was a good sandwich, Mom," Ian said after

pushing back from the table. He gathered his plate and his sister's and carried them to the sink.

"Thanks, honey." I swallowed the last bite of my food.

"So, what's for dinner?" Ian asked.

Arista and I both gaped at him.

"Are you kidding me?" Arista said in an incredulous tone.

"Yeah, I'm kidding, well sort of." Ian grinned.

Eye rolls in stereo from Arista and me. "Let's get ready and go do the roadside clean up. It shouldn't take much more than an hour if we get after it. Be ready to go in about ten minutes." I headed to my room.

Ian drove the five or so miles out to the commemorative stretch of County Road CM and pulled onto the shoulder where a smaller dirt road intersected. It was the safest place to park within fifty yards of our designated half mile of roadway. We always included the area around that intersection as part of our cleanup regimen.

The easement along the road was twenty-five to thirty feet wide, so normally we fanned out in a line and worked from the place where we parked to the end of our designated section. Then we'd grab anything we missed on the way back to the truck. We each wore gloves and carried garbage bags.

Experience had shown the need for extra bags and extra disposable gloves because some of what you may find on the side of the road is really gross. Mostly we found the usual array of soda and beer cans, a few bottles, assorted fast-food bags, drink cups, cigarette butts and feed sacks. Once last year, Ian found a hypodermic needle. We turned it into the sheriff's office but hadn't heard any more about it.

Halfway through our second pass, Arista paused to dig a new bag out of her pocket when the wind caught the bag and blew it across the road where it caught on the fence line about fifty feet away. She ran to capture it and had to navigate a rather deep ditch.

Ian and I stopped to wait for her. We watched as she stood staring down at where her wayward trash bag had been. She began backing away and pointing. Something was clearly wrong with my daughter.

CHAPTER 7

I took off toward her, barely remembering to check the road for cars. It was easy to become complacent about looking both ways this far out in the country. Ian was right beside me when we reached Arista, who had not uttered a sound.

"Arista, you okay?"

"Sis, what happened?"

I looked my daughter up and down, worried that she had been cut or punctured by something when she retrieved her trash bag. *Please, no dirty needles,* I prayed silently.

"There." She pointed toward the fence line. Her hand was shaking.

"Holy crap!" Ian started forward but his sister grabbed him.

"No."

I looked to where she pointed. It took a moment for my brain to register what my eyes were seeing. I heard a gasp then realized it had come from me. My heart fell to my feet and pumped blood quickly through my veins. I stepped between my children and the partially decomposed body of a person and fought the urge to throw up.

I swallowed hard and tried to keep my voice from trembling. "Ian, take your sister and go back to the truck." What the hell was happening in our little community?

"But Mom--"

"Take your sister back to the truck and wait. I'm going to call the sheriff." My tone left no room for further argument. I noticed how bad Arista was trembling and was glad Ian put a shielding arm around his twin and started for the truck. My phone was in my hand. Funny, I didn't remember digging it out of my pocket. I dialed the phone number for the sheriff's office for the second time in two days.

"Bright County Sheriff's Office, is this an emergency?" answered the dispatcher. "Yes, it is." I returned my gaze to the grizzly sight on the ground.

"Ma'am, are you all right? Can you safely talk?" The dispatcher's voice became more concerned than it was when she answered the phone. "Ma'am?"

"Oh, uh yes, sorry." I forced myself to look away from what lay near my feet. "I'm fine and so are my children but we found..." I glanced back to the corpse and the words stuck in my throat.

"What did you find, ma'am?" the dispatcher prodded.

"A-a body. We found a body." I almost whispered the word, like that would make what lay before me not real.

"Oh, my goodness!" said the dispatcher.

In hindsight, I realized this was not a usual response from a professional dispatcher. However Bright

County, Missouri was a far cry from anywhere reports of dead bodies would be considered commonplace. It's sad to consider that the finding of a dead person anywhere would elicit anything less than shocked surprise, but I knew it was true. I had a client back in Kansas City who was a 911 operator. I was her occupational therapist while she recovered from a car accident. The stories she told during our sessions were eye-opening.

"Where are you right now? Are you with the body?" I didn't recognize the dispatcher's voice, but I knew it was not Justine.

"Yes, I am standing about ten feet away from it. We are on County Road CM between the main road and the low water bridge."

"Any chance there is a pulse?" the dispatcher asked.

"No." I looked back at the gruesome sight. That ship had sailed days, if not weeks ago.

"What is your name, ma'am, and can you safely stay with the deceased until the deputies arrive?"

"Yes, I can do that, my name is Fenreya Stern."

"Oh, Fen, bless your heart. This on top of finding Lester the other day! This is Alice, Alice Fowler, but I don't suppose you remember me, it's been years."

"Oh wow, Ms. Fowler," I said, momentarily forgetting the context of our phone call. "It *has* been years! I didn't know you were working for the sheriff's office, I thought you had retired."

Ms. Alice Fowler had been the guidance counselor at the local middle school when I went there, and she had done some substitute teaching at the high school when our English teacher went on maternity leave.

"I did but it didn't take." She chuckled. "Back to the

current issue. I've got the sheriff himself enroute to you as well as the county coroner. Please don't touch or move the body or anything in the area."

"No need to worry about that, Ms. Fowler. My truck is parked on the other side of the road. I will sit in it and put the flashers on.

"Good idea, Fen. Bring your kids and come around for tea. I would love to meet them," she said.

"Thank you, ma'am, I will." We ended the call as I walked back to the truck. I climbed in and was peppered with questions and chatter.

Holding up both hands in the universal stop sign, I said, "We are to wait here for Sheriff Peters, we are not to touch or move the body. That is all I know right now, so let's just wait calmly and catch our breath." The silence resulting from my missive lasted all of ninety seconds.

"I wonder who it is, or was?" Ian mused.

"OMG, I wonder how they died?" from Arista. "It's so sad they died out here all alone."

"Must be a homeless person."

"What if we knew them?"

"Could you tell if it was a boy or girl?"

These last comments all ran together. The cacophony of their voices muddled my ears, and I rested my forehead on the steering wheel. The concept of time melted into the background of my mind as I tried to block out all noise and find a quiet place within myself. The sound I was waiting for finally arrived. The blare of sirens. Thank goodness, someone to take over the vigil for the lifeless remains of that poor person. I raised my head from its resting place on the steering wheel and rubbed my face with my hands.

The twins started to bail out of the truck as the sheriff's SUV pulled up behind us. "Wait, we need to stay put and see what the sheriff wants us to do." Ian shut the truck door with a grimace but no argument.

I turned the ignition key to auxiliary and rolled the power window down when Uncle John approached the driver's side of the truck.

"Hi, Fen, you're having quite a week," he said with a sigh.

"Truer words were never spoken."

"Where is the body?"

"I can show you," offered Ian.

Sheriff Peters peered in the window at my son and then looked at me for confirmation, or maybe it was permission. "Ahh, no, Ian, I'll show him. Please stay by the truck," I said and got out.

I noticed Arista was not chomping at the bit to approach the body but was no longer shaking. I really wanted to insulate my kids from the horrors the world was so readily offering up, but it appeared to be a losing battle. Ian did exit the vehicle and began pacing beside it. Arista stayed inside and scooted over to the window where she had a better view of whatever was going to happen next.

I looked up at Uncle John with a half-hearted smile. "It's this way." I led him to the opposite side of the road and gestured toward the body. "It's over there." I didn't want to go any closer than necessary.

He nodded and surveyed the scene. The body was difficult to pick out if you didn't know exactly where to look. It blended in with the background of fall dried grass, weeds, and a few brambles that were trying to take over the fence line.

"There you are. Dispatch said there was no opportunity for resuscitation, *that* was an understatement." Peters mumbled.

I couldn't tell if his remarks were to me or maybe to himself. I answered anyway. "No, I couldn't even tell if the poor soul was male or female."

The coroner pulled up in his hearse-shaped vehicle. Captain Jana Smith and Deputy Clyde Young pulled up behind him. They all exited their vehicles and walked over to me and the sheriff.

"You again, Fen," said Deputy Young. It was not a question.

"Hey, Fen, tough week." Captain Smith glared at Young.

"Sheriff?" both deputies addressed their superior officer with a question.

"Deputy Young, cordon off the scene, fifty yards in every direction."

"Why do I always have to cordon off the scene?" Young whined.

"Because you are so darn good at it and I say so," said the sheriff.

Young huffed and stomped back to his cruiser for the yellow tape I had seen far too much of this week. Despite the grave circumstances, Captain Smith and I shared a smile.

"Something funny, Smith?" Sheriff Peters asked.

"No, sir, not at all." Jana stopped smiling. "What do you need me to do, sir?"

"I want you to get statements from Fen and her kids. I am going to call the highway patrol. My gut says this scene is going to need more investigative resources than what we have to offer." He turned to the coroner, who had been standing silently by. "Hey, Paul, thanks for getting here so fast. I need you to wait on bagging the body until we get some photos and I've spoken with the state crime lab. They may want something special done, given the circumstances."

I walked back to my truck with Captain Smith where we each gave our statements to her in turn. When we finished, she asked us to wait a minute while she briefed the sheriff and saw if he needed anything else from us. A few moments later, she was back.

"Sheriff says we need to take custody of the trash you all picked up today, even though it was on the other side of the road."

"Sure, Jana." I pointed to the bed of our truck. "All five bags are here. Do you want us to drop them at the station on our way home?"

Jana surveyed the size of the bags. I could see her thinking of the available space in her patrol car. It reminded me of how my sister would stare at her closet and suitcase when she was getting ready for a trip.

"Did you guys find anything particularly gross, wet, or stinky?" Jana asked.

"You mean besides the dead body?"

Arista was getting her sense of humor back, sort of.

"I mean what you collected in your trash bags," Jana clarified patiently.

"No, nothing like that, just the usual stuff idiots toss out of their cars," Ian interjected.

"Okay, they should fit in my cruiser, then. Fen, I need you to sign an evidence release form. It substantiates our chain of custody."

"Sure, whatever you need." I leaned on the truck waiting for Jana to get the form she needed signed from her car. *Chain of custody, evidence, bodies, omg, it is like being in an episode of NCIS. What has happened to my life? How did the kids and I get tangled up in this stuff, and more importantly, how do we get away from it?*

My inner dialog was interrupted by Captain Smith when she handed me a clipboard with the form she needed me to sign.

"Are you doing okay, Fen?" she asked quietly.

I huffed out a long breath and signed the form. "Oh yeah, I guess. I've been through worse. I mean, I don't even know who the person in the ditch is so I shouldn't be upset. Yet I am, it's so surreal. Geez, I'm rambling. I'll be okay. I just want to go home, take a shower, and get some dinner. I am worried about Arista, though. Being the first one to find the body really startled her."

"Arista, and Ian for that matter, are smart and resilient. Just like their mom. I understand you are worried and it's perfectly normal to be upset. Hell, who wouldn't be after finding a corpse. You are human. A caring one. That you cared enough to call this in may give some grieving family somewhere closure. What if the body was never found, or found by someone who didn't bother to call it in? There are people like that in the world. It's okay to feel bad but it's also okay to feel good about feeling bad." She took the clipboard.

"I hadn't thought of it in those terms, Jana, Thank you." Jana walked away with a wave, and I got in the truck and started the engine. I glanced over at my son and daughter. Both were quiet and staring at the passing scenery. The "energy vibe" inside the truck was grim at best. The dashboard clock read 4:15 p.m.

I did a mental inventory of the fridge at home. There

was plenty of food but none of it sounded good, and it all would require more energy than I had at the moment.

"Hey, how about we make a detour to the Pizza Cellar and grab a couple pizzas to carry home? We can binge something not crime related on Netflix and chill the rest of the evening."

Ian brightened up a bit. Pizza nearly always cheered him, and Arista mumbled something sounding like an agreement. It may take a lot more than pizza and a movie binge to lighten up this mood, but it was a start.

We rode mostly in silence all the way to the Pizza Cellar, about fifteen miles. Ian asked Arista a couple inane questions about school, an attempt to draw her out of her funk. I asked her about her plans for her upcoming FFA project. She supplied the most noncommittal answer possible, something about a goat show in March.

⬦ ⬦ ⬦

We stepped inside the "ZaCel", as it was referred to by us local people, at 4:45 p.m. It was just before the suppertime rush and on Saturday night, that would last until around 9 p.m. We pulled up stools at the bar and the owner, Tony, came over to take our order.

"Greetings, Sterns!"

Tony was always cheery and spoiled my kids with free "shots" of flavored soda. He had done this since they were quite young and used to visit with their grandpa. My dad would bring them to ZaCel to play arcade games and drink "shots" with him. "Hi, Tony!" we chorused.

"Let's see, I'm gonna guess coffee for Fen and two shots of vanilla cola for you guys," Tony said.

"Pretty close. I'm going to skip the coffee today, but we need a couple pizzas to go. Both large, stuffed crust with the Works but no olives."

Tony smiled. "So, the *Stern Twin Special* on the fly. I got it. Was I right about the vanilla cola shots at least?"

"Yes, sir," said Ian.

Arista offered only a tight smile.

Tony grabbed the drinks for the kids and headed to the back to make the pizzas. This restaurant was mainly a one-man show except for Friday and Saturday nights when he had a waitress and an extra cook. Tony kept his overhead down and really got to know his patrons by running his business mostly by himself.

Ian challenged his sister to a game of air hockey and, after downing her vanilla cola shot, she accepted. Their game was in full swing five minutes later when Tony came out of the kitchen to check on us. He set a glass of water with lime down in front of me and supplied two more cola shots. I have never been a fan of soft drinks loaded with high fructose corn syrup and rarely kept the stuff at home. But a couple shot-size soda drinks weren't going to hurt anyone. I decided to take advantage of the WIFI and play a game on my phone. I sipped my lime water and glanced around when the door opened a few minutes later.

A young woman I didn't recognize, came in looking flustered and in a hurry. She headed for the back of the building without even a glance at me.

"Sorry I'm late, Tony!"

She passed the kitchen for whatever lay beyond,

probably a staff break room and the time clock if I had to guess.

Tony emerged from the kitchen. "I heard about Lester. Is he doing okay?"

"Yes, he's doing much better. It was a close call though."

"Good. So, what is up with Arista? She looks like someone kicked her dog."

"Ah, well, that is an entirely different story, but I might as well fill you in, it will be in the paper tomorrow." I gave Tony the Cliff Note's version of the last couple hours. I couldn't help but be saddened by the events my children and I had been through the last few days. I hoped the drama would end soon.

We arrived home about 6 p.m. with hot pizzas. There was a note on the kitchen counter. *Fen, your mom had a busy but great time at the senior center today. She was tired and wanted to lie down when we got back. Don't know if she'll be hungry or not, they really put out a good spread up there. Yvonne.*

"Ian, please build up the fire. Arista, please take Violet and Sophia out to potty. I'm going to check on Grandma, then we can eat.

I poked my head into my mom's room. She was sound asleep and looked comfy, so I decided to let her be.

I surveyed myself in my bathroom mirror. *Ugh, were those bags there this morning?* My hunger won out over my desire for a shower, so I splashed some water on my face and headed for the family room.

The fire filled the room with cozy, comforting warmth. The twins were sitting on the couch "discussing" the choice of movies. We watched the first two installments of the Harry Potter films, munched on pizza, brownies, then went to bed.

I worried whether Arista would be able to sleep after what she'd seen earlier. I was exhausted, so sleep would come for me. I hoped it would be dream free.

CHAPTER 8

I fell asleep almost instantly but woke up abruptly when Sophia's cold nose nudged my chin. It was 5:07 a.m. *Are you kidding me, mutt?* "Fine, let's go out and you can go potty." I was trudging down the hallway with Sophia bouncing around in front of me and Violet came racing from one of the kids' rooms. "You, too, Micro Mutt," I said.

The dogs didn't stay out long, it was chilly. Satisfied there was no good reason for me to stay up at this hour on a Sunday morning, I went back to bed. I couldn't go back to sleep, though, so I heaved myself back up at 6:12 a.m.

The kids were bound to sleep in, so I showered, guzzled some coffee, and saddled BB. A ride would clear my mental cobwebs better than anything else.

◈ ⊰⊱ ◈

We took off down the road and turned onto Farm Road 66, a dirt road but was fairly well maintained because it was a frequently traveled shortcut between our road and Highway Z. The cool crisp air felt good, and BB was stepping out in his running walk. He can really cover some ground, yet it feels like floating.

About two miles into our ride, I saw a bunch of trash along and in the road. I kept a couple trash bags in my saddlebags for just such occasions, so I dutifully stopped and dismounted. I'll admit to cursing about irresponsible scum bags tossing their crap out for others to deal with. BB snorted his agreement.

As I started picking up the trash, I realized it was a bunch of empty hair dye boxes and bottles. What the heck? Deputy Jana had just told me about a rash of thefts of hair dye. I called her and left a message. *Should I pick this stuff up or leave it until she looks at it?* I decided to snap some pictures of the area and the trash, and carefully picked it up. Rather than tossing it directly, I would deliver it to the deputy and let her decide.

BB and I finished our ride in peace and after I got him unsaddled, I went into the house. The kids were still not up but my mom was stirring. "Mom, do you want some breakfast?" I asked.

"Yes please, maybe just some oatmeal and toast, I'm still full from yesterday," Mom said with a chuckle.

I busied myself making her breakfast and was grateful she remembered yesterday. *Alzheimer's is so unpredictable.* I got Mom situated with her breakfast and decided to run to town. I scrawled a note for the kids on the small whiteboard we kept on the fridge and hopped in the truck.

◈ ◈ ◈

The Walmart parking lot was pretty empty, so I grabbed a spot next to the cart corral straight out from the door. I like to go armed with a list and during a time that's not too busy. I had finished the produce section and was just starting down the bread aisle when I heard my name.

"Good morning, Fen!" I turned to see a smiling Captain Jana Smith pushing her buggy full of frozen meals toward me.

"Good morning to you, Jana!"

"Fancy meeting you here, Fen. I just got your message and was going to call you later. So, hair dye trash, huh? Weird."

"Yeah, that's what I thought, too. I've got the bag of trash in the back of my truck if you want it, but I took photos of it before I touched it."

"Yeah, I will take the trash, and can you just email me the pictures of the scene?"

"Sure thing, Deputy." I grabbed my phone to forward the pictures right then. "If you get done shopping before me and want to get the bag out of my truck, you're welcome to. Do we need one of those custody chain forms you law types are fond of?" I asked with a smile.

"Actually, yes, but I can send you a form with an imbedded picture of the bag in it. All you need to do is sign it electronically and send it back. Will that work for you?"

"Absolutely. Let's make a plan to go riding soon.

BB loves the cooler weather, and don't you have a new little gelding you got last spring?"

"I do and he is a dandy but needs some miles under the saddle for sure. I would love to get some winter riding in. I will text you soon," Jana said.

We said our goodbyes and I continued my shopping. Since it was paper-supplies day as well as food shopping, my buggy was very full by the time I got to checkout. Just as I was bundling all my groceries into my truck, the after-church crowd started pouring into the parking lot. *That timed out just right.*

The drive home was uneventful, and the kids were up and moving when I got there. I honked the horn, and they came out to help carry in the bags. "Good day, kids. Have you eaten yet?" I asked them as we all set about putting the items away.

"We have," said Arista.

"I could eat again," said Ian.

"Well, of course you could, bottomless pit that you are," chided Arista.

"Okay, how about this, I will start some lunch while you two do the chicken and horse chores, then after lunch we will start decorating for the upcoming holidays. We might as well get a jump on it while the weather is still decent," I suggested.

The twins were more agreeable than usual to my plan and dutifully headed outside as I set about making some lunch, checking on Mom, and starting some laundry. You know how it is, moms can seldom do just one thing at a time.

"Fenreya dear, could you bring my lunch to my sitting room? I'm watching Gibbs and this is a really good one," Mom asked when I checked on her.

"Of course, I will, Momma, I'll be back in a few minutes with a full tray just for you," I replied.

(I worry some about Mom watching too much TV, but she has other hobbies she enjoys. This time of year, it's mostly knitting in front of the tube by the fire. In the spring and summer, she putters in the garden.)

The kids burst through the door with a basket of fresh eggs and mud on their boots. They chucked the boots off in the laundry room, and Ian put the eggs into cartons as Arista fixed the little labels we date the cartons with. Fresh eggs have a long shelf life, but it's good to know when they were collected, and required by the state, if you intend to sell them to other people.

After our lunch of leftover spaghetti casserole, cheesy garlic bread, and fresh baby greens salad, the teeners went to the attic to retrieve the several totes of holiday decorations. I let the dogs outside and was loading the dirty dishes into the dishwasher when my phone rang. It was Auntie Lou. *I better take this*.

"Hi, Auntie, what's shakin'?"

Auntie Lou has always been a free spirit, gifted seer, and a force to be reckoned with. She was also responsible for my training as a Witch and a Powwow practitioner when I was growing up. She has taught me so much, I love her with my whole heart.

"Hi, honey! Just checking in with y'all. Bring me up to date on what's going on there. Why do I keep dreaming about bloody snow, and every time I pull a tarot card, it's a Sword? I'm worried about y'all," Auntie said.

I proceeded to tell her everything that had happened over the last few days, starting with the storm, and ending with the dead body beside the road.

"My stars!" Lou exclaimed when I had finished. "What a lot of drama for our tiny community! Fen, I will tell you now the Sword cards I've been pulling indicate criminal activity, danger, and a shadowy person manipulating everything. So, you be careful, ramp up the protective wards on the property, and make sure my niece and nephew are warded and aware," she said authoritatively.

"I promise I will, Auntie. Will you be home soon? We all want to see you," I replied.

"I'm in Costa Rica right now and don't yet know if I will be home for Thanksgiving, but I will be back for Solstice, Christmas, and New Year's."

We chatted for a few moments about what size clothing the kids were currently wearing, and how Mom was doing then we said our farewells.

I spent the rest of the day with my teenagers decorating the house, inside and out. We would wait to put up the tree until mid-December as it had become a tradition to get a live, potted tree and plant it outside after the holidays were over. We have amassed quite a nice grove of living evergreens west of the house. They are beautiful and make a nice wind block.

The festive family vibe persisted through the making and eating of dinner. We fixed chicken pot pie, homemade but frozen, with baked sweet potatoes and broccoli. After dinner and after Mom had retired back to her sitting room, we remained in the dining room. I filled the kids in about my conversation with Auntie Lou and remembered to tell them about the trash I found earlier in the day during my trail ride.

"Whoa, super weird," Ian said about the trash.

"Yeah, it is," agreed Arista. "Geez, Auntie Lou is

good, but I totally hope she is wrong about the danger and stuff."

"Have you ever known Auntie to be wrong?" asked Ian.

"No," said Arista.

"Rarely, if ever," I said at the same time.

"Mom, what do you think is up with the hair dye thefts? The trash you found has gotta be related, right?" asked Arista.

Before I could answer, my ancient fifteen-year-old, Ian, chimed in, "I think it is just some dumb kids playing pranks. I'm more worried about the cattle thefts. Now *that* could get in our pocket!"

"Plus, they hurt Lester, and what if they killed the guy I found!" Arista exclaimed.

I got up to start my end-of-evening, after-dinner clearing-up chores. I was trying to avoid thinking of assaulted neighbors and dead bodies. The kids and their increasingly macabre conversation followed me to the kitchen.

"Omg, Ian, Lester almost died! I swear all you care about is money and cattle," railed Arista.

"No, sis, that is not all I care about! I'm just saying the motive is money, the method is cattle stealing, and the hurting of people is collateral damage. So, the cops just need to catch the creeps stealing cattle," Ian said somewhat defensively.

"It sounds simple when you say it, honey." I hit the button to turn the coffee maker on automatically at 5:30 a.m., which was probably the best invention ever. Perhaps I exaggerate, but not by much. "Go to bed, y'all. You have school tomorrow," I said.

"Okay, Mom," sounded in stereo.

CHAPTER 9

M onday morning came too early, as Mondays usually do, and the weather was remarkably warm despite the calendar reading the week before Thanksgiving. The twins left for school early when a slightly older friend picked them up. They all had early morning practice of one sport or another or band, they might as well carpool.

I had a calm day planned. The only errand I needed to run would involve a quick trip to town. I felt optimistic about getting to work on my hobby of jewelry making later without interruption.

It's a hobby but it's trying to morph into a business. I make pieces, give them as gifts, people see those gifts, and contact me to make a similar piece.

I checked on Mom, and she was still sleeping, so I left her a note, grabbed a smoothie, and headed for town. The feedstore opened at 7:30 a.m. on Mondays. I got there a few minutes before 8 a.m. and walked right to the jacket Ian had been eyeing on Saturday. It appeared to be the only one in the size and color he wanted, so I grabbed it before it was gone. I got distracted by a new display of leather purses and was examining them closely when I heard Rebecca answer the store phone.

"GGA Feed, this is Rebecca, how can I help you?"

"Oh. Yes, we have thermostatically controlled water trough heaters.

"How long will you be gone?

"Uh-huh.

"Is your water trough filled automatically?

"Uh-huh, okay.

"So, you just want to prevent freezing in case the weather drops while you are out of town.

"Right. I will pull one off the shelf and have it here at the counter for you, Ms. Parks."

Rebecca may well be the biggest gossip in town, but I must say she has active listening down to a science. I approached the counter with the jacket for Ian and a really cute purse for Arista, one for myself, and one for Auntie Lou. "G'morning, Rebecca."

"Hey, Fen, find what you wanted?"

"I did, thanks. I'm so happy y'all have Ian's size jacket. He has gotten so tall this year it's getting hard to shop off the rack for him!"

"He *is* tall, for one so young!" Rebecca said with a laugh. She continued as she eyed my pile of purchases. "Looks like you're well on your way to getting your Christmas shopping started. You know our Pre-Black Friday Super Sale starts today," Rebecca said, grinning big.

"I did not know. How 'super' is it?" I asked.

"Thirty-five percent off everything but an extra 15 percent off anything over $200.00, and I can tell by looking, you're there, girl," Rebecca said with a wink.

"Yeah, I sure am. 'Super' is right! I think I'll grab a couple flannels while I'm at it."

Rebecca held up a finger to pause our conversation, picked up the store walkie-talkie in the other hand, and said into it, "Warehouse, pull me out a thermo-control tank heater and bring it to the desk." Then she said to me, "I heard you and the kids found the dead guy out by the road the other day. What do you reckon happened?"

"Gosh, I don't know enough to venture a guess what happened to that poor person." I was careful to keep my tone and word choice neutral. I didn't want to fuel the rumor mill during an active investigation. I did, however, want to hear everything Rebecca had heard.

In my defense, I never said I was anti gossip, just that I don't actively spread it. "What all have you heard?" I asked with wide eyes. This was all the encouragement Rebecca needed to spill every single tidbit she had heard in the last couple of weeks. For the next ten minutes, she regaled me with several weeks' worth of gossip, centered largely around the cattle thefts and resultant drama, but peppered with who was cheating on who and with whom and how she knew it was true.

During her information dump, I injected the appropriate and encouraging "oh my stars," "wows," and "no kidding," but my brain was trying to collate the victims of the thefts and what they had in common besides owning cows. It wasn't easy to think and keep up my side of the conversation, but one question popped to mind as she wound down.

"Rebecca, do all the victims go to the same church or work off the farm at the same place?" What I really wanted to know was where they bought feed and supplies for their cattle, but taking a circuitous route to that question just seemed like a good idea.

"No, the Johnstons go to First Baptist, the widow Henry is Catholic, and Duke don't go to church. I reckon they all may run into each other up at the nursing home, they all have people in there," Rebecca said as she handed me the receipt for my purchase.

"Hmm, could be. Where do they buy their feed and hay?"

"They all buy feed here but mostly get their hay from Larkspurs over on county line. We can't beat their prices on hay because they can buy it in bulk better than we can."

The store phone rang, and Rebecca answered it. I gave her a smile and a finger wave goodbye. I turned to head for the door and practically ran into Denny Bowman standing just beside the end of one aisle of merchandise. I said, "Excuse me," and was met with a glare. Auntie Lou would describe Denny Bowman as a mouth-breathing, knuckle-dragging dipstick. She would not be wrong.

I got home and stashed the presents in my super-secret hidey hole, aka my closet. Mom had gone to the senior center and the kids were in school, so I had some free time and a quiet house. It had been a couple weeks since I'd had time to focus on making jewelry and I felt "way behind." *Is it really a hobby if you can "get behind"? That seems more like work.* I was pondering the existential differences that define hobbies and work as I got my tools and supplies assembled on the counter.

Soon I was focused on some beautiful fire opals and the design I would use for Auntie Lou's present. Fire opals were a favorite of hers, and I was making a necklace to match the earrings I had given her on her last birthday. Just as I secured the clasp, I heard the kids arrive home from school.

Arista and Ian always enter the house with a loud chorus of, "Hey, Mom! What's for supper? You'll never guess what happened today!" and so forth it goes. Today was different in that only Arista popped through the door to my jewelry studio.

"Hi, honey, where is your brother?"

"He went with Tom and JJ to the electronics store they like. He'll be home soon. Oh, that's pretty, is it for Auntie?" Arista asked.

"Yep. Do you think she'll like it?"

"She totally will, it matches the earrings you made, and she flipped out over them in a good way," Arista said enthusiastically.

I smiled at the memory. Auntie had been vocal about loving those earrings.

Arista helped me gather up and put away my tools and we went upstairs to the kitchen to start dinner preparations.

"Mom, it feels like a leftover night."

"I agree, hon, let's add some quick biscuits and call

it good."

About an hour later, Ian got home with a couple mysterious bags from the electronics store and his two buddies trailed in behind him. "Hey, Mom! Can the boys stay for dinner?"

"Of course, dinner is ready, buffet-style in the kitchen. Eat what you take and wash your hands before y'all dig in." I put some plates on the counter.

"Good thing we made extra biscuits. Did you know he was bringing those bottomless pits home with him?" Arista asked me in a whisper.

"I had a feeling," I whispered back.

"Hey, Arista," JJ said. He glanced up from his feet. I noticed his cheeks were flushed. He was sweet on my daughter.

"Hey, Arista, how's it going?" Tom said. His tone and body language were bolder than JJ's.

"Hey. Fine. Mom, I just heard a car. It's probably Grandma getting dropped off. I'm going to go help her in and get settled." Arista escaped the boy-crowded kitchen.

"Are you two Neanderthals hitting on my sister again?" Ian said accusingly as he came into the room.

Both Tom and JJ blushed and protested. I wanted to laugh but I held it in, not wanting to hurt any feelings inadvertently.

After making sure the boys had enough food, and reminding them when they stay over, it is lights out no later than 10:30 p.m. on school nights, I went to check on Mom. Arista had her settled in her room and they were chatting. Mom telling her about the senior center. Tonight was Bingo night and "that blasted Beverly" won again! Come to find out, Mom had also won but that was not the point. I bade them both good night and left the room chuckling to myself.

A good soak in the tub was exactly what I needed. I ran the water as hot as I could stand it and added Epsom salt and a homemade herbal sachet with lavender, rosemary, and cloves inside. I visualized all seven chakras in turn, allowing the colors to become clear and vivid. I did my best to think of nothing at all, but the events of the last several days and snippets of conversations that I had either had or overheard kept surfacing.

I kept shoving those thoughts back, out of the way for now, and refocused on white light surrounding and infusing my being. If I didn't take care of myself, I wouldn't be much good to anyone else. I had learned this lesson the hard way after my husband disappeared during a mission in the Middle East, and again after the auto accident that killed my father and nearly killed Mom.

I exited the tub and toweled off, immediately followed by a generous application of homemade body butter. Determined to get a good night's sleep, I crawled into the king-size bed with the pillow nest in the center and burrowed under the covers. A few moments later, there was a soft thud as Sophia hopped up on the bed and flopped down along my back.

I watched the strangest scene unfold. Several people with long jet-black hair, and no faces, were trying to load cows of various colors and ages into a trailer. The cows and people were all angry. There was another faceless man wearing green, lying under the trailer. Blood in the snow. Bags of trash. The scene repeated. Blood in the snow.

I awoke with a groan. I'd been sleeping well until the blasted dream. I sat up and grabbed my dream diary and wrote it all down before I forgot it. Only after I was done did I chance a look at the time. 6:27 a.m. That's about right on an average school day, so I didn't even grumble as I headed for the coffee room, I mean kitchen.

✦ ✦ ✦

As mornings go, this one was uneventful. The teenagers hit the kitchen like a hurricane and rushed out the door for school. Mom slept in until about 9 a.m., had breakfast, and settled into her cozy chair to knit and carefully absorb every word Leroy Jethro Gibbs had to say on Season 5 of the current NCIS marathon. The dogs went outside and came back in multiple times. Around noon the hospital called to let me know Lester was being released and asked if I would be picking him up.

"Absolutely, I'm on my way."

I popped into Mom's room and told her where I was going and that Lester would be our house guest for a while. She nodded her acknowledgement and kept knitting, eyes rarely leaving the television screen.

I grabbed a change of clothes for Lester from his house on the way to the hospital. Leaving in those breezy hospital gowns is neither comfortable nor dignified. When I arrived at the door to Lester's room, he was sitting up in bed looking very ready to go.

"Hey, Lester, I brought you some of your clothes, and if there is other stuff you want from your place, we can pop by there on the way to my house," I said by way of greeting.

"Fen, I'm so glad to see you! Thank you for bringing me something decent to wear. I'm truly tired of mooning the entire hospital every time I get up. Not that they let me get up very often," Lester said, "and that's another thing I'm truly tired of, sitting around!"

I handed the bag of clothes to the nurse's aide, her badge said her name was Nancy, and said to Lester, "The staff doesn't want you to overdo it and neither do I. You will have the run of the house while you stay with us, but I will ask you to go slow and not take any chances." I smiled at Lester and continued, "I will be in the hallway so you can get dressed. Don't feel rushed on my account."

As I closed the door behind me, I heard Lester's voice.

"Dang it, Nancy, I can put my own darn pants on."

This made me smile. A little way down the hallway, I saw Sheriff John Peters and Deputy Sharp talking. They glanced up and I waved. The sheriff motioned for me to join them.

"Hi, Fen, I see you're here to pick up Lester. Will he be staying with y'all while he fully recovers?"

"Hello, gentlemen. That is the plan," I answered.

"Fen, the investigation into the initial attack on Lester and all the cattle thefts is ongoing, obviously, but the second attack on Lester's life here at the hospital brings this thing to a whole new level. The only theory that makes any sense is the perps were trying to eliminate a witness. They must think Lester saw and remembers more about the first attack.

"For this reason, I have asked Deputy Sharp to take on a special assignment. I want him to watch your house as long as Lester is staying with you."

Sheriff Peters said all this with a friendly, yet stern, expression on his face, as if he expected me to argue with him. "Thank you, Sheriff and Deputy Sharp. I am truly grateful for the protection detail. We have a fairly good security camera system in place, and Ian will be happy to show it to Deputy Sharp. Hopefully it will make your job a little easier."

We chatted a few more minutes. The sheriff told me they had no new leads in the case and assured me if anything developed, he would be in touch. Just after Sheriff Peters left, Lester came out into the hallway in a wheelchair.

"Dang it, Nancy, I can walk just fine, weren't my legs was hurt," Lester grumbled at the aide.

"I know, Mr. Duke, but if I let you walk out of here, I could lose my job. It's just policy and I know you don't want me to get in trouble, do ya?"

"Oh, fine, then. Fen, can we go? I've had it up to my neck in hospital policy."

Lester said those last two words as if they tasted bad. Perhaps they did.

"Sure, your chariot is this way." I fell into step beside the wheelchair. Deputy Sharp followed along behind us, a bit more like a puppy than a security detail but he was young.

After we were loaded up in the truck and I began to pull away from the hospital, Lester drew my attention.

"Fen, thank you so much for all you're doing for me. I don't think I would do well in one of those rehab places. I really should stop and visit my Mary, I miss her. I just don't want her to see me all beat up like this."

"You are most welcome. Arista and I were talking about that very thing last evening. We have a half-baked plan to help you go visit Mary without showing her your bruises. If you don't mind just a bit of makeup, that is."

Lester chuckled. "That just might work. Hey, why is Deputy Puppy Dog following us?"

I smiled over at Lester after a glance in the rearview mirror. "Deputy Sharp has been assigned to provide a bit of watchful protection to all of us after the episode at the hospital the other day."

Lester and I stopped by his house to get some more clothes, toiletries, and check things over. The gate was still open, and I could see the emotions well up in Lester as he took in the scene of his attack and the absence of his beloved cows. There really wasn't anything I could think of to say right then. I couldn't promise his cows would be found and returned because it really wasn't all that likely.

When we got back into the truck and headed for my farm, I said, "Lester, Ian wants to help protect your place by putting in some security cameras. He is good with electronics and can put in a system that is easy for you to use."

"He's a good kid, Fen. I've lived here for my whole life and my folks before me. Security was never a trouble. I don't know what has become of our world." There was a long pause before Lester continued, "I guess some cameras would be okay, kinda like shutting the barn door after the horse done run off, but it can't hurt. He can't do that for free, though, I'll pay him for it and buy the camera gadgets."

"I'm not going to meddle in whatever deal the two of you work out, Lester, but I can tell you Ian needs some mechanical help with the old tractor worse than he needs money. My son is aces with technology but has had no one to teach him about combustion engines. Just a thought." I planted the seed.

When we pulled up to the house and got out of the truck, Jackson, Lester's old Belgium horse, was standing at the gate prancing and nickering. Lester beamed at him and made his way over for a proper reunion. Several minutes of nose rubbing and neck patting commenced.

BB came up to see me, sweet mule didn't want me to feel left out. I grabbed a few treats from the console in the truck for both equine and gently suggested to Lester that we go inside. It looked like the exertion of the last hour or so might be getting to him. Obvious pain in his arm stopped him when he tried to pick up a container of clothes.

"The kids can bring all your bags in when they get home. How about we make some coffee and sit with Mom for a while?"

Little Violet, Lester's Chihuahua, was in full happy-fit mode when we entered the house. She wiggled so hard she nearly achieved liftoff.

"Hello, little girl, I missed you, too, you're such a good girl," Lester cooed to the tiny dog. "Fen, I'm getting mighty tired. Would you mind if I skipped the coffee for now and stretched out for a bit?"

"No trouble at all. Arista and I got your room ready last night. It's just down here," I said as I led the way to one of the guest rooms across the hall from Mom's suite. The room was various shades of blue with green accents in a pine-tree motif and had a queen-size bed set in a simple cedar bed frame. "I will check on you in an hour or so, just relax and make yourself at home. We are happy you are here, Lester."

"Thank you, Fen." Lester plopped on the bed and kicked his boots off.

Violet hopped up next to him, and it was plain to see some serious napping was about to begin.

CHAPTER 10

My thoughts turned to what to fix for supper. The weather was pleasant enough, but the temperature was brisk, and I had no idea how many people were likely to show up to eat. *A big pot of ham and beans it is,* I decided.

My pressure cooker would turn an all-day affair into less than two hours, however this meal required fried potatoes with onions and a double batch of homemade cornbread.

I was finishing cutting up the potatoes and onions when Mom came into the kitchen. She handed me an empty glass and sat down on the stool at the island. She looked me dead in the eye and said, "The green man died."

I took the glass and gaped at her. "What? What man?"

"The green man. He's dead. Weren't you listening?" Mom tsk-tsked at me.

Her facial expression was one of mild disappointment. *Sigh.* "Oh gosh, I'm sorry to hear that. Would you like some more water?" I gestured with the empty glass.

"Yes, please and some fresh coffee. Do we have any cinnamon cookies?" Mom's expression brightened with the thought of impending goodies.

"I think we do." I fired up the coffee maker and refilled her water glass.

Arista arrived home from school with her friend, Zoe in tow, just as I set a platter of mixed cookies out on the bar and coffee in front of my mother.

"Hey, Momma, hey, Grandma!" She delivered hugs to her grams and me in turn.

"Hi, honey, you're in a good mood!" I smiled at both girls. "Hi, Zoe, it's good to see you again."

"Thank you, Ms. Stern, it's good to see you, too," Zoe replied.

The girls headed for Arista's room. Mom grabbed a cookie and dunked it in her coffee. I flipped the oven on to preheat for the cornbread and gave the potatoes and onions a good shake in the air fryer basket.

Ian, Tom, and JJ came in with a rush of cold air and a flurry of greetings all around. Ian gave his grandma a hug as he went past and stopped short when Arista and Zoe appeared in the doorway.

"Hey, Sis, what up? Hey, Zoe."

"Hey." Arista raised an eyebrow and gave the three boys a once over.

I hid my grin when I saw Zoe's cheeks redden because my son said hi to her. She gave him a shy smile before she spoke.

"Hi, Ian,"

JJ ran into Tom from behind when he stopped to greet Arista. There was some grumbling between the boys. Arista looked at me with a momentous eye roll.

"Omg, Mom, do they live here now?" She spun around without waiting for an answer and headed back to her room.

Zoe appeared torn between following her or staying to talk with Ian.

Tom smacked JJ in the arm and said, "Dude, what'd ya do that for?"

"Ouch, what'd I do?" JJ whined, rubbing his arm.

Mom and I shared an amused look and I said, "teenagers!" She gave a knowing nod of agreement and grabbed another cookie.

Ian snatched a snickerdoodle. "Mom, do you care if me and the boys work on the white board and map in the office?"

"It is 'the boys and I' and of course you are welcome to work in there." I handed him the platter of cookies. "You might as well take these with you."

"Thanks, Mom, you're the best!" Ian and his two-person posse headed out of the kitchen.

My mother looked stricken. "Was that all the cookies?"

"No, ma'am, we have more. You raised me right." I winked and deposited a small plate of sweets, fruit, nuts, and cheese beside her freshly filled coffee cup.

Mom beamed at me. "Ian's right, you are the best and I did raise you right." She grabbed her snacks and coffee, then stood.

"Where are you going?" I asked.

"Back to my room. Break is over, Season 6 is starting, and those hungry kids might take my snacks if I stay out here." She shuffled off down the hallway.

I knocked on the door to Lester's room. A two-hour nap was probably sufficient, and he would want to freshen up before dinner. "Lester, dinner is in about thirty minutes. Are you doing okay?"

"Oh yeah, I'm fine, that was a good nap, just what I needed. Fen, you got any coffee?" Lester opened the door, simultaneously wiping sleep from his eyes. Violet remained on the bed looking sleepy and annoyed.

"Sure do, come on in the kitchen I'll get you a cup." After getting Lester set up with some coffee, I wandered into the office to see what the boys were up to. They had a list on the whiteboard of names and addresses, one of which was Lester's, and the county plat map was taped to the wall with several small red Post-it notes on it. "What're y'all doing?" I had a pretty good idea.

"Plotting the locations of the victims on the map, looking for patterns. If we can figure out how to predict whose cattle are next, we can put some trackers on some cows and find out where they are going," Ian explained.

"Trackers? That sounds potentially dangerous. I don't want any of you chasing after stolen cows. Whoever is doing this is nasty enough to have nearly killed Lester." I worried they would come face to face with the culprits if they tried to follow them. I was impressed and proud at the ingenuity of their plan, however freaked out I may have been by the implementation of said plan.

Arista and Zoe entered the room about halfway through the exchange. "What tracker, who's chasing stolen cows? Oh cool, a map," my daughter said in a flurry.

There was a chime and Zoe reached for her phone. She gasped at what she read on the screen. "Omg, y'all, my aunt and uncle's place got hit. They weren't home but most of their cattle are gone! Momma is really upset, she says Uncle Don, that's her oldest brother, had a heart attack when they got home and the cattle were missing. Like, for real, he went to the hospital and everything!"

There was a chorus of "omgs, dangs, and sorry to hear that" from the teenage audience.

I laid a hand on her shoulder. "Zoe, that's awful! Do you need to go be with your family? I can run you home."

"No, ma'am, just the opposite. Momma says she is up at the hospital and wants me to stay with y'all if it's okay. Daddy is on the road, and she doesn't want me home alone." Zoe's voice shook.

I wrapped the girl in a hug. "Of course, honey, you stay as long as you like. Please tell your mom if there is anything they need to let me know."

She had become Arista's first and best friend when we moved here from Kansas City, and she was like an extra daughter to me. I felt the same about Ian's friends, Tom and JJ.

Ian leaned on the edge of the desk. "Zoe, where is your aunt and uncle's place? We can add it to the map."

Zoe walked over to the wall with the map and began to figure out the placement. I told them dinner would be ready in fifteen minutes and left them to it.

Once all eight of us were settled around the dining table with rimmed plates filled with ham and beans, fried potatoes, and cornbread, the conversation turned to school projects, holiday plans, and antique tractors. I had asked the kids to please avoid talk of the thefts and the associated violence and the "dead guy in the ditch" while around Lester and my mother.

"When does school let out for Thanksgiving?" Lester asked.

All five teenagers replied, "One week from today." Then Arista expounded with, "We could have gotten out next Tuesday, but we are in session to make up for the snow day we had this week. A lot of parents are grumpy because it messes up their travel plans."

"I can see where it would." I visualized the calendar in my mind's eye.

Lester gestured with his fork. "Back in the day, no one went away for days at a time this time of year because the stock tanks would freeze up and your critters would be out of water 'til ya came home."

Ian grabbed another piece of cornbread and passed the basket to JJ. "The thermostatically controlled water tanks have taken care of that mostly. You still need to check them often to be safe, but it is way better than staying home and chopping ice."

Mom, Lester, and I settled in the family room. There was a cozy fire and I elected to read while they played a few hands of gin rummy. I left the kitchen cleanup to the five teenagers. Either many hands would make light work or would result in a fight, it was anyone's guess.

A couple hours later, Mom and Lester went to their respective rooms to turn in for the night. I let the dogs out to go potty and double-checked the locks on the doors and windows before heading down the hall to my own room.

I heard voices in the den and when I peeked in the

open door, I saw five teens poring over the map and fiddling with some small gadgets that appeared to be electronic. *Could those be the "trackers" Ian mentioned? Keen young minds may change the world someday.* I smiled to myself and left them to it.

I finished brushing my teeth when my phone roared like a tiger. It was a text from Deputy Sharp. He said that he had gone home for a few hours' sleep, but he was back and would be in the driveway for the entire night.

I texted back my thanks and asked if he needed coffee or snacks.

The reply came: *No, ma'am, I'm good to go.*

Okay, come to house in morning for breakfast, I texted.

10-4, came his reply.

CHAPTER 11

F or the first time in what seemed like weeks, I slept very well. There were no weird dreams, no strange noises, no pets waking me up to go out. I blinked and rubbed my eyes. *Jeepers, what time is it? I better get going, hope everything is okay.* I rolled out of bed and donned my robe and slippers. I listened at Lester's door. All seemed good with soft human snoring and even softer tiny dog snoring. Mom was sleeping peacefully and not talking in her sleep (thank goodness), and I could hear teenagers starting to move around since it was a school day.

I'd done the preparation for a large breakfast casserole called Swiss Eggs the day before, so I got it in the oven, grabbed some coffee, and went to poke the fireplace awake. After the first cup of coffee, I hit the shower and by the time I got out, the casserole was done. I tossed a big tray of "cheater biscuits" in the oven and grabbed some more coffee. There was a knock on the kitchen door and Sophia started barking.

A peek out the window revealed Deputy Sharp standing on the back entry. I opened it. "Good morning,

Deputy! Are you hungry?"

His eyes lit up and he grinned. "Good morning, ma'am, and yes I am!"

"Come on in, then, there's coffee,"

"Awesome." He settled at the kitchen counter.

We were chatting amicably when all the teenagers burst into the kitchen. The girls stopped abruptly and both blushed when they saw the handsome deputy.

Ian donned a worried expression. "Mom, did something happen? Why is he here?" Ian looked at Deputy Sharp and added, "No offense, man."

"None taken," said the deputy.

"Sheriff Peters wants some extra protection on the house after what happened at the hospital. The second attack on Lester and all. So, Deputy Sharp has been on duty all night," I explained.

Ian let out the breath he was holding. "Thanks, man. That's cool."

Arista and Zoe edged into the kitchen, got some coffee, the tiniest servings of breakfast I had ever seen, whispered something to each other and zipped back down the hallway. Giggles erupted once they were out of sight. Jeez, you'd think they had never seen a handsome twenty-something guy eat breakfast before.

Lester emerged from his room with Violet, who wanted to go out. He joined Ian and the boys at the table. I got him some coffee and he helped himself to the food.

Deputy Sharp thanked me for breakfast and assured me he would return in the evening. I was happy he'd be back. I was sure I could take care of things, but the added protection made me more at ease. Before he left, he gave me instructions.

"In the meantime, if anything seems amiss, call the dispatch and they will send someone out."

"Will do, and thanks again." I watched him get in his patrol car and leave.

The kids headed out for school and Lester gathered up our kitchen knives from the knife block and magnetic holder then started for the office. I wondered what that was about, but Mom called to me from her room, so I went to check in with her.

"Good morning, Mom, what's up?"

"I've got to get ready. I can't find my ice skates."

"Hmm." *Ice skates? She doesn't have any ice skates. I need to change the subject.* "Okay, Mom, I'll help you search for them." I wondered where, or perhaps when, her mind was. A few moments passed before I said, "Hey, Mom, how about some breakfast and coffee?"

"Oh, that sounds lovely, dear." She headed for the kitchen. Evidently the thoughts of ice skates passed.

While Mom ate a hearty breakfast, I remembered Lester had taken off with all our knives, so I went to investigate. He was seated in the den with the whetstones and the pile of knives. Focused on sharpening, he only looked up when I cleared my throat. I didn't want to startle him.

He grinned. "Fen, I can't be useless any longer, so I asked Ian to show me where the sharpening tools were. I figured you would nix me going outside to work on anything, but this is something I can do, even with a messed-up arm."

"Lester, you are far from useless and if sharpening our dull knives makes you happy, go for it. Just don't overdo it. Gentle movement is better for healing. Let me know if you need anything." I left him to it.

Around noon Yvonne popped by to pick Mom up for a trip to the senior center. They were having an open fiber arts circle and snacks.

I considered calling Jana to see if she wanted to go riding but decided leaving Lester completely alone may be unwise, so I turned my attention to my jewelry making.

I kept dinner simple by tossing a couple casseroles into the oven from the freezer. Add a salad and some bread and boom, food for an army. Only four teenagers arrived from school. JJ had gone home early due to an orthodontist appointment. Mom came home full and tired, so she took a snack-size portion in her room and went to bed early. The kids decided to play Pictionary and insisted Lester and I join them. That was fun and I could tell Lester genuinely enjoyed that the kids had included him.

⊹ ⋄ ⊹

During breakfast, the next morning Arista, Lester, and I decided it would be a good day to take him to see his wife, Mary, in the nursing home. His bruises were still visible, but Arista assured him she could cover them. And no one would know, least of all Mary, he was "wearing makeup like a girl." Arista only had half days, afternoons, at school on Thursdays that semester because she volunteered at the nursing home as part of an outreach project.

I dropped Arista and Lester off at Shady Acres and went to run some errands. Not surprisingly we needed a bunch of stuff from the grocery store. We needed some bagged minerals for the cattle from the feedstore, too.

The feedstore parking lot was empty when I pulled in. Rebecca looked bored behind the desk, filing her nails until she noticed me come in. She perked up and got that 'gossip' glint in her eyes.

"Fen, did you hear the latest?"

"I doubt it, this is my first stop." She was going to fill me in no matter what I had already heard.

"Well, the Davis's got home the other night and nearly all their cattle were gone!"

The Davis's were Zoe's aunt and uncle. "Wow, how awful!" Another hit on a local.

"There's more, I heard the Parks got home from a quick trip to Kansas City and half of *their* cows had vanished. The other half is so wild no one could catch them. Those people have always had the rankest cows, that's what my daddy always said," Rebecca rolled on, like a verbal freight train.

I had stopped listening. Something she said was trying to wake up a memory and snap into place. *Parks...Parks... What?* Then I remembered. "Rebecca!" I said, a little more forcibly than was polite. She stopped talking and looked at me. "Didn't you get a call from Ms. Parks the other day when I was here?"

"Yes, I sure did, that's right, I'm glad you reminded me, Fen. She told me they were going to Kansas City to see her sister's new baby."

A new theory had started to take shape in my brain. I paid for my minerals and got out of there as fast as possible. While I was waiting in the warehouse for Justin to load my minerals, Denny Bowman walked out of the store and glared at me. *Jerk.* I made a quick stop at the grocery store and headed back to the nursing home to pick up Arista and Lester.

I decided to send a quick text to Jana. *I've been hearing some stuff and want to run something by you.*

K, meet at Special Kay's Bowling Bar & Grill? 6:30 pm? I got league.

K.

I dropped Arista at school. Lester and I headed home. I put the groceries away and had dinner ready when the kids returned from school. I had to get a move on if I was going to be on time.

✦ ✦ ✦

A few minutes after 6 p.m., I left to meet Jana. I noticed a vehicle fall in behind me about half the way to town but forgot about it by the time I sat down across from her in the noisy bowling alley.

Jana had chosen one of the tall booth-type tables along the wall in the pool table room. The tables would provide enough noise that we could not easily be overheard, and along the wall in the corner no one could come in behind us.

We both ordered iced tea with lemon and waited until the server set the drinks down. She walked away before we spoke of anything beyond general pleasantries.

"What's up, Fen?"

I was excited to tell her. "I heard about the cattle thefts from the Davis's and the Parks. The weird thing is I was in the feedstore on Monday when Ms. Parks called in asking for a thermostatically controlled water heater."

"Wait, how do you know what she asked for?"

"You know how Rebecca is, and she's the one who

answered the phone. Anyway, I wasn't the only one listening to the conversation. Denny Bowman was lurking behind a display and heard all of it. I also asked Rebecca in a roundabout way if all the victims bought their feed there. They do, by the way. What if—" the rest of my sentence was cut off by a rude interruption.

"Hello, pretty ladies!"

Steve LeBlanc pressed himself against our table, pool cue in one hand, drink in the other. He always gave me the wiggins, ever since high school.

Jana and I looked at each other, both wanting to roll our eyes, but we settled on pained grimaces instead. We both instinctively moved our drinks farther away from him and said reluctant "hellos."

He looked like he wanted to wedge into the seat beside one of us, and he didn't seem to care which one. *Gross.*

"What are such lovely ladies doing out without some men to keep you company?"

I glared at him. "Actually, Steve, I was just leaving."

"Hey, me, too, maybe we can go together," he slurred.

Double gross. Jana chose that moment to "accidently" place her clip-on deputy badge briefly on the table and said, "Gosh, Mr. LeBlanc, you're not driving, are you? How much have you had to drink?"

Bless her.

Steve began to protest the insinuation that he was not fit to drive. I slid out of the booth and mouthed "thank you" at Jana. She nodded and held up the universal sign for "call me."

About halfway home, an oncoming vehicle with extremely bright lights swerved into my lane. My heart jumped into high gear. Was I fixing to die? I knew we were going to hit. I swerved to the right and my tires lost traction on the muddy shoulder of the road. I steered into it like my dad taught me, but my truck began to fishtail. It may have spun around entirely for all I know. It happened so fast and yet it seemed to take forever for it to stop. The other vehicle swerved back out of my lane but not before it hit my rear quarter panel, or maybe, technically, I hit it as my truck spun. My world faded to black.

CHAPTER 12

I woke up clutching my handbag in my right hand. I don't know how long I was out. I found my phone and opened my messages. Jana was the last person I texted. That would do. *Help.* I managed to enter the word before the world went dark again.

The next time I knew anything, there was a lot of activity around me. I was being loaded into an ambulance and Captain Smith was beside me.

"Hey, Fen, you're going to be okay. They're taking you in to get checked out," Jana said.

My breath caught and my gaze darted around. Panic clutched my stomach. "Where are my kids? Are they okay?" I couldn't remember where they were when I wrecked.

She took my hand and gave it a gentle squeeze. "They're fine, Fen, they are at home. You were alone when you had the wreck. Do you remember what happened?"

I began to cry. "They're okay? My kids are safe?"

"Shush now, yes, they are safe. Breathe into it now, you're going to be fine, your kids are fine."

Another voice said, "She's going into shock, Captain, let us transport her, you can talk at the hospital."

A warm heavy blanket landed on me.

The lights in hospitals were so bright. Painfully bright when you have a concussion. The medical staff wouldn't let me sleep and the lights hurt my eyes. Sheriff Peters arrived with Arista and Ian. The kids hugged me and cried.

The sheriff patted my arm. "I brought them so they didn't hitchhike. They were coming to see you one way or the other, Fen."

"Thank you, Uncle John," I croaked out. Formalities be damned.

Jana stepped alongside her boss. "Can you tell us anything about what caused you to wreck?"

I scrunched my face as I thought. The movement created a fresh round of pain, but the memory started to come back. "Someone with their bright lights came over to my side of the road. I swerved to the right. The truck went crazy and there were some thumps. I woke up here. No wait, I think I woke up in the truck. Did we already have this conversation?" I was rambling and I knew it. The kids exchanged a look and Arista started to cry again.

Ian peered at everyone except me. "Is she going to be all right?"

Sheriff Peters spoke up first. "The doctor says she has a mild to moderate concussion and they are going to keep her overnight for observation, but she will be just fine."

"We're staying with her," my twins said in unison.

The next morning my head still hurt, the lights were not as painfully bright, and it warmed my heart to see my twins asleep, leaning on either side of my hospital bed. Bless them, but they should've been in school. That was not a winnable battle.

Dang it, I need to pee. And I'm thirsty. I surveyed the room. There was the typical hospital tray table by the bed with one of those ginormous mugs on it with a straw sticking out the top. *Please let there be cold water in that thing.* Sure enough, there was. *Humph, city water is not as good as our well water. At least it's cold and wet.*

Arista woke up first. "Momma, you're awake! How do you feel? We did the chant after everyone else left so you would feel better faster. Do you feel better?"

I tried to smile. "Hush, baby, one question at a time please. I do feel better. Thank you for doing the healing chant, I'm quite sure it helped." The door opened, and Sheriff Peters poked his head in. "Good morning, y'all, I want to see how you're doing and give you an update."

Ian woke up and rubbed his eyes. He took a long drink of my water which earned him a glare from Arista. He made a face, presumably due to the taste of the water, shrugged, and took another long drink.

Sheriff Peters cocked an eyebrow at Ian, cleared his throat, and said, "So how ya doing, Fen?"

"I'm okay, thanks for checking on me. Where's my

truck and how bad is it?"

"Your truck isn't too bad considering everything. There is impact damage to the left rear quarter panel with paint transfer from a dark vehicle. The theory is that when the truck spun around, you hit your head on the side door. The impact damage is moderate and there is no damage to the frame, although getting an alignment would be wise since running off and back on the road may have knocked it out. I've impounded it so we can get a sample of the paint transfer and protect it from any other damage or tampering.

I groaned as the implications of having no vehicle to drive settled in.

My son took my hand in his. "Don't worry, Mom, I called Uncle Jacob last night and told him what happened. He arranged for a rental to be delivered today and he said he would try to fly in early for the holiday so he can lend a hand."

"Well done, honey,"

Even Arista smiled proudly at her brother.

Uncle John cleared his throat. "In other news, Deputy Sharp reports all is quiet at your house. I called Yvonne to go by and hang out with your mom, and Jana spent the night in the hallway watching this room. She and I discussed it, and we agree that getting run off the road may not have been a completely random event."

"Thank you so much, Uncle John. I am well and truly blessed to be watched over by you and your people," I said. "Yeah, it didn't feel random or accidental when those bright lights were coming at me in my lane."

A doctor came in and announced that everyone must leave. I started to get up.

"Not you, smarty pants," the doctor said, pointing at me.

The twins smirked at me and rolled their eyes.

"Nice try, Mom." Ian walked out first.

Once the sheriff and the kids had stepped out of the room and shut the door, the doctor said, "Let's have a look at your eyes."

He shined his tiny flashlight in one eye then the other. Doc inspected the left side of my head and said the stitches looked good, the swelling around the cut had already receded, which seemed to perplex him.

Healing chants are good, I thought.

Doc put the wee flashlight back in his pocket and clasped his hands in his lap. I figured I was fixing to get the low down.

"Fen, you might have some headaches for a few days, try to take it easy. You've seven stitches on your left frontal bone near the coronal suture. Keep them dry for a minimum of five days." I reached up to feel for the stitches, wondering about my hair and then I realized, someone tried to kill me. I suddenly felt like crying, but I pushed the tears back, swallowed the bile in my throat and focused on the doctor's voice.

"Don't touch them either," said Doc with a grimace. "Clean and dry. If you're worried about your hair..." He handed me a mirror. "I had to shave a little, but I promise I kept it to a minimum."

I grabbed the mirror and looked at my head. *It could be worse.* I handed him the mirror and tried to calm my trembling hand. "When can I go home?" I needed to be close to my mom and children for my peace of mind.

"This morning. We have some discharge instructions to print. I want you to follow up with your primary care physician in ten days to get the stitches out. Call with questions or if any symptoms worsen."

Doc patted my arm and told me to stay out of trouble then he left.

Arista came in with a nurse who was pushing a wheelchair. "Hey, Mom, Ian is pulling the rental car around to the door. We're getting you outta here!"

My clothes from the night before were poorly folded on the wide windowsill and they smelled like sweat and fear, but they were better than a drafty hospital gown and would do for the short ride home.

❖ ❖ ❖

Home was such a sweet sight. I couldn't wait to get inside and find something to eat. I didn't have to look too hard. With Yvonne's help, Mom had set out a bunch of sandwiches and made a double chocolate cake (my favorite) and had a fresh pot of coffee made. *Thank goodness for my family and friends!*

Lester tried to tease me about our matching head injuries and commented that at least I managed to avoid breaking my arm. I took the teasing for the friendly comradery it was intended to be. Although the twins were not amused, they held their tongues.

After lunch I put on a shower cap and took a long hot shower. It felt good to feel clean again, but nervous energy still swirled around me. I tossed on my warmest, softest yoga pants and favorite hoodie. Some mindful stretching and another chakra meditation should set things right. I dozed off while meditating and woke up confused. However, I always woke up confused and grumpy after a nap, so I knew it wasn't from the head injury.

I lay there for a few minutes letting the memories of the last twenty-four hours wash over me. I shivered and shook off the fear that threatened to overwhelm me. *What time is it? What are the kids doing? Who ran me off the road and why?! Ugh, I better get up and get some answers.*

Isabella and Sophia had snuggled against me during the meditation/nap, and they both looked as if their feelings were hurt when I got up and headed for the main part of the house. I found Arista, Ian, and Lester in the office talking about the rash of cattle thefts and poring over the map. That reminded me of what I wanted to talk to Jana about at the bowling alley. We had been interrupted by that dipstick Steve LeBlanc.

"Hey, y'all," I said when I entered the room.

There was a chorus of "Hey, Mom," "Hi, Fen," and "How are you?"

I leaned on the arm of the wingback chair. "I'm fine. I've gotten up from a nap I didn't mean to take. I feel like I've missed everything. Is there a plan for dinner, and do you know how many people are apt to be here?" Arista shook her head and peered at me. "Ahh, you probably needed the sleep, Mom. There is a mess of oven fried chicken planned for dinner. Miss Yvonne and Grandma got it all set up before they left. We're making mashed potatoes with it, and she made up a big salad, too."

Ian fidgeted with a dry-erase marker. "It's only going to be us for dinner. Tom and JJ are skipping tonight because they have other obligations. Hey, sis, is Zoe coming over?"

"Yeah, she'll be here sometime around 6 p.m. She had to do her time with the committee getting the decorations up for the dance tomorrow."

I chuckled. "Doing time? You make it sound like a jail sentence."

"Meh, not far from it if you knew the rest of the committee," Arista said with an eye roll. "Oh shoot, it's time to put the chicken in the oven. Miss Yvonne was very specific." She hurried out of the room.

Ian got up to leave, too. "I better help her, my twin could burn water."

Lester laughed and said, "Fen, those are some dang fine younguns. Worth their weight in gold."

"Yes, they are special. Thank you for saying so, Lester. I think I'll keep 'em." I turned toward the door. "I'm going to invite Jana to join us for dinner.

I went in search of my phone, and Lester resumed his knife-sharpening project. I was glad it was taking him a while. That meant he wasn't overdoing it with his arm. *Wow, all our knives are going to be sharp enough to use. What a concept,* I thought as I dug through the pile of dirty clothes I had left on my bathroom floor. *Jeez, I'm getting as bad as a teenager. No, they wouldn't lose their phone. Ah there it is!* I mused to myself as I snatched up the phone and deposited the stinky clothes in the hamper.

Hey, come over for dinner and finish convo? I texted Jana.

Sure, time?

Anytime. Eat at 6ish.

sys (which is text talk for "see you soon").

Jana and Zoe arrived around 5:30 p.m., and Zoe helped Arista and Ian put the finishing touches on dinner. Jana joined me by the fire in the family room. Lester wandered in a few moments later. He wanted to hear what the deputy and I were going to say. He did have a dog in this race after all.

"Jana, do you remember last night, right before Steve LeBlanc butted in, I was telling you how all the victims are customers of the feedstore?"

"Yes, but I can't figure out the importance of that. It seems like a symptom rather than a cause. The victims all have cows, cows eat grain, and therefore owners shop at a feedstore. In a small community with essentially one feedstore, it would be more remarkable if the victims didn't shop there."

"I see your point but hear me out. According to Rebecca, all the victims shop there, and last Monday, I was standing there when Ms. Parks called and told Rebecca they were going out of town."

Lester gestured with his good hand. "Come to think of it, I called up there and ordered some feed a few days before my farm got hit. I was planning to go up to Springfield for a couple days for my brother's 90th birthday. I told Rebecca I would pick up the feed on my way home. I ended up not going because the big storm came in. You know Springfield got it worse than we did."

The kids came in and announced that dinner was ready. We migrated into the dining room and tucked in. They had done a lovely job of setting the table and the food was delicious. Zoe carried the dinner conversation with stories of the decorating committee. The annual Fall Dance was set to happen the next night in the school gym and there had been some drama over whether the disco ball was going to "work with the theme." The detractors argued that a disco ball didn't have anything to do with Time Travel Rock of Ages, and the disco ball proponents said that the spinning lights symbolized the very passage of time. Evidently the pro-ball team won because Zoe reported that before she left, the disco ball was securely hung from the beam in the center of the gym.

I looked at Jana and said, "Remember when a school dance was a boom box and we kicked off our shoes and danced?"

"Yeah, I do, but I also remember prom and homecoming dances were more elaborate and generally filled with drama."

"Too true." I agreed.

Lester told a story about the barn dance where he met Mary. There was no disco ball, and everything came out fine. The kids were mesmerized with his account of "real music" with guitars, fiddles, banjos, and mandolins.

"There were no drums?" Zoe asked innocently.

Lester grinned. "Nope, no drums. One old guy did play the spoons though." He then launched into an explanation of what "spoons" were in this context and attempted a demonstration which resulted in several spoons on the floor and giggles all around.

I got up to start clearing plates and Ian stopped me. "Mom, we'll get those, don't worry, just chill." Arista and Zoe popped up and began gathering the food to be put away.

"Yeah, Mom, chill for a while," Arista said.

I smiled, proud that my children were such supportive, responsible young adults. "Thanks, y'all. Jana, Lester, would you like to 'chill by the fire' with me?"

We settled onto the poofy furniture surrounding the fireplace, with steaming mugs of hot chocolate.

Jana wiped some whipped cream from the corner of her mouth. "I want to hear more about your theory on how the victims are related, and one of the kids mentioned a map. I'd like to see it."

I nodded at Jana. "Lester, you were telling us before dinner that you had told Rebecca at the feedstore about your plans to be gone for a couple days. I hate to say it, but I'm beginning to wonder if the link connecting the thefts is Rebecca."

Lester shook his head. "No, I didn't talk to Rebecca. She wasn't there that day, which is unusual. I talked to some guy. If he told me his name, I don't remember it. It wasn't Denny though. I would know his voice."

I grimaced. "That kind of shoots my theory down."

Jana held up her hand. "Not necessarily. What if the link isn't Rebecca but someone else that works there, or someone she knows that could be pumping her for information. It's no secret Rebecca likes to talk. She doesn't ever not talk to anyone and doesn't know the meaning of the word discretion."

Arista, Ian, and Zoe joined us in the family room. "What'd we miss?" Arista asked.

Jana rose from her chair, mug in hand. "We'll fill

you in while you show me the map y'all made." The kids and Lester took Jana to the office and were still perusing the map twenty minutes later.

My phone roared with a message. My brother Jacob texted to tell me his flight had been late getting into Springfield, did I know it was snowing there, and not to worry about picking him up. He was in a rental heading our way. In fact, he was about thirty minutes away. *With everything going on I forgot he was coming in today. I get a pass because of the head injury.* I heard Jana.

"Ian, can we add the location of the body to the map? I can't help wondering if that poor John Doe is not somehow connected to the cattle thefts. We just don't have this much crime in this county usually."

"That's a good point, Jana, yeah, we were picking up trash along this road." Ian traced a line on the map with his finger. "We parked about here, and Arista found the dead guy about here." He popped a pin in the map at the location he identified. "Sis, would you agree?"

I watched Arista back away at the mention of the dead guy. *The memory's still freaking her out.*

She took a breath, stepped up to the map, and after a moment, nodded her agreement. "Yep, that looks right." She continued, pointing at the map. "Check this out, there is this dirt road, and if you follow it this way, it leads right to this victim. Who lives there, Ian?" Arista was tapping the map.

I was proud of my girl for dealing with her fear.

"That is the old Montgomery place," Ian answered.

Jana stepped closer to the map and peered at my boy. "Montgomery? That rings no bell. Our department didn't get a report of cattle being stolen out there. How do you know about it?"

Ian blushed and replied, "Uh, I heard it from a friend who knows their grandkid. He was talking about it on the school bus. Sorry, Captain, I thought y'all knew."

I watched my son. There was more to his story, I could tell, but I decided not to bring it up then.

Jana was watching him closely, too. "Ian, I think you're holding something back. I'm going to let it go for now, but know that if it becomes important, the sheriff and I are going to need you to spill. Got it?"

Ian hung his head. "Yes, ma'am."

Lester was watching his boots and not making eye contact with anyone. *Curious.*

Jana noticed, too. "Lester, do you know these Montgomery people?"

Lester didn't look up. "Yep."

Jana narrowed her eyes. "Is there some reason they would suffer a major robbery and not call the police to report it?"

"Yep."

Jana was beginning to look impatient. "Would you like to tell me what that reason might be?"

Lester looked up but didn't make eye contact. "Not really. I will say that the Montgomerys are good people. They keep to themselves and never go lookin' for trouble. If trouble finds them, they generally take care of it in house. They've always been that way. Ever since Prohibition."

CHAPTER 13

A light came on in Jana's eyes. "Moonshine! Are you telling me these people neglected to report a cattle theft because they make moonshine?"

He shook his head. "No! I'm not telling you anything about moonshine at all. You came up with that on your own."

"Oh, good grief! Some homemade 'shine is the least of our problems at the moment. Some of these rustling victims could lose their farms, not only their cows. And the violence! Look what happened to you, Lester. And now Fen has been hurt, caught up in all this. Anyone with information about this case has a duty to come forward. I expect you and you..." She pointed at both Lester and Ian, "to pass that back through your respective grapevines."

Both Lester and Ian looked sufficiently chastised. Arista wore a disapproving expression and Zoe looked amused. Jana was still fired up and I decided it was time to change the vibe. It was getting late, and Jacob was due to arrive any moment.

"I vote we have some more hot chocolate, and there

should be more double chocolate cake left over from earlier today." Jana agreed chocolate sounded good and took a couple photos of the victim map with her phone before we all filed out of the den.

Jana settled onto one of the kitchen island chairs. "You kids did a good job on the map."

Ian ladled some hot chocolate into her cup. "Thank you."

Arista cut the cake and Zoe delivered the plates to everyone.

"Jana, do you really think the dead guy is, or was, involved in the thefts somehow? Like maybe he was a bad guy and got in a fight with other bad guys and they left him to die?" Arista asked.

This was the first time she had initiated a conversation about the body she found. I took this as a good sign. Keeping it bottled up wasn't healthy.

"That is one theory and as good as any other I suppose," Jana answered. "Once we have a positive identification and can piece together who his known associates were, we will be in a better position to answer those questions. We don't even know the cause of death yet."

We all let that information settle as we enjoyed the warmth of the hot chocolate and the velvety, rich cake.

Jana's phone rang. It sounded like one of those sirens from Britain. She blushed and explained, "I needed a ringtone that would get my attention no matter what. This is the sheriff's line. They only call my cell when we don't have a radio dispatcher." She answered, "This is Captain Smith.

"10-4, Sheriff, I'll be right there.

"Twenty minutes or less.

"Will do." Jana clicked off the call and put her jacket on. "I've got to roll, there has been another cattle rustling."

As Jana was going out the door, my brother Jacob arrived, and they nearly ran into each other.

"Hi, and excuse me," Jacob said brightly.

"Hi, sorry, gotta go." Jana brushed past him.

Jacob delivered hugs to me, Arista, and Ian then shook hands with Lester and Zoe.

"Are you hungry, Uncle Jake?" Ian asked.

Jacob nodded. "Famished, kiddo, I'll eat whatever you bring me."

Lester excused himself and retired to his room. The kids fixed Jacob a plate of leftover chicken, mashed potatoes, and a big bowl of salad. I helped myself to another piece of cake. It had been a rough week. Jacob and I settled at the kitchen island and he looked me up and down.

"You don't look nearly as bad as I thought you would, Sissy."

"Gee thanks, I think. I heal fast. Thanks for coming in early, Jacob, it means a lot. The scariest part of waking up in the hospital last night was not being here to watch over Mom and the kids. Heck, my kids were watching over me at the hospital. That was a weird feeling." I shivered at the memory of those fears.

"I'll bet it was. Ian told me some on the phone, but I'd like to hear the entire story from you, if you're up to it," Jacob said between bites of chicken.

I filled my brother in on everything that had happened since I found Lester injured in his barn, and after he was done eating, he followed me to check out the map. Ian, Arista and Zoe were in the office.

Together we told him the information we had shared with Jana earlier in the evening.

"Is Jana the lady that was leaving when I was coming in?" Jacob asked.

"She's not a lady, she's a deputy," Ian said and looked embarrassed a moment later. "I mean, she isn't just some lady, she is a deputy sheriff. But, you know, she isn't *not* a lady. Does that make sense?"

Arista shook her head. "Not a bit, brother, stop digging yourself into a deeper hole.

I couldn't help but smirk. "Jana's not only a deputy sheriff, but a captain in fact, and a very nice lady whom I consider a friend. She's most definitely not a lady to be trifled with."

Jacob put on an innocent face. "What does that even mean? I don't trifle with ladies."

Cue the stereo eye rolling.

The next morning dawned bright and cold. The snow had missed us by staying to the north. Deputy Sharp popped in for breakfast around 7 a.m. and reported a quiet night. I was feeling somewhat guilty that this darling young man was spending all night every night watching over our house so we could sleep peacefully. Guilty but grateful. I made him an extra-fluffy loaded omelet and sent some chocolate cake home with him.

Ian and his uncle Jacob gobbled up some breakfast, did the chores, and were poring over the map in the office by 8 a.m. It warmed my heart to see my son and brother working together. Arista and Zoe slept in but were up and halfway through the to-do list I gave them by 10 a.m. Mom was staying with Yvonne for another day.

I felt lost. My head hurt just enough that I didn't feel like making jewelry. I wanted a break from thinking about thievery, violence, murder attempts and dead bodies. It was too cold to make going for a ride seem fun. We had a small home gym set up in the basement. I went down there to work out some of my frustration. I was a mile into my elliptical session when the dream I had a couple nights earlier came flooding back to me.

Several people with long jet-black hair and no faces were trying to load cows of various colors and ages into a trailer. The cows and people were all angry. There was another faceless man wearing green lying under the trailer. Blood in the snow. Bags of trash. The scene repeated. Blood in the snow. Something Mom said out of the blue came back, too. *"The green man died."*

Fabulous, I was trying to avoid thinking about all this stuff. Why was Mom talking about a "green man" and I dreamt about a "green man?" What makes a man green? Green could be a name. The Green Man was a pagan archetype. People were said to be green with envy, and jealousy was associated with green. Military fatigues were green. Jeez, it's not as if I could go to the sheriff and say, "Hey, y'all might want to search for a missing person that is either named Green, a pagan, super jealous, or a member of the Armed Forces." I scolded myself. These thoughts felt disrespectful.

Two miles on the elliptical was plenty. I took a few swings at the heavy bag out of frustration, but the impact made my head hurt worse, so I went upstairs to clean up. The den was empty. There was a note that read, *We have a theory, going to test it. Be back soon.* It was signed simply *J & I.*

I grabbed a shower and wished I could wash my hair. When I emerged from my room, Arista and Zoe asked if I could take them to Walmart.

We piled into the little rental car and drove to town. The girls were talking about the dance and what they needed to do to get ready for it. I missed my truck and wondered what would need to happen before I could get it back.

The store was packed as expected. The Saturday before a major holiday was always chaos. The girls headed for the makeup aisle, and I decided I should grab some groceries. Already tired of the noisy, bright store, I checked out and went to the car. I sent Arista a text to tell her where I was and to please be done in the next twenty minutes.

I decided to read my Kindle app while I waited. I hadn't had time to read for what seemed like weeks. I was just getting to a good part when the car door flung open, and two giggling girls plopped down in the seat.

"Did y'all find some fun stuff?" I asked.

"Yep! We ran into Heather and her mom, and they told us that the problems last night were over at their neighbor's place. Shots were fired! Heather said they heard the shots, and it was super scary."

"My stars! That's awful, was anyone hurt?"

"No one we care about. Mr. Dawlin saw some people messing with his cattle and he shot at them. Apparently, no cattle were actually stolen, just scattered. The bad guys got away, but Heather says her daddy said that it looked like one of them was hit.

There was some blood over by where they were seen. Mr. Dawlin got scolded by the sheriff for discharging a firearm toward a person, but he said those such and so's would think twice before trying to steal his cattle again."

"Wow, I wonder if the sheriff and Jana have any new suspects. This community is becoming like the Old West, cattle rustling, shootings, I don't like it one bit." I started the car.

"Yeah, but if you think about it, Mom, it's still less violent than a big city."

Zoe cocked her head to one side. "I think it will simmer down once the jerks are caught. Things will go back to the normal, quiet we're all used to."

"I hope you're right, Zoe. Any other stops before we head home?"

"Can we go by my house and get my dress so I can get ready with Arista at your house?"

I put on my turn signal and eased into traffic. "Sure. Will you kids need a ride to the dance? This rental is tiny, but I can take three kids comfortably."

"Tom's mom has offered to drive us. She has a Yukon that seats six. They will pick us up at 6:30 p.m.," Arista announced.

Ian, Jacob, and Lester were in the kitchen eating sandwiches when we got back to the house. Ian stopped long enough to help us get the groceries in from the car. The girls grabbed a few snacks and headed for Arista's room with Zoe's dress bag and their Walmart treasures. I wouldn't see them again until it was time to leave for the dance.

I made myself a sandwich and thought about how grown up my children had become. It was bittersweet. I didn't want to get bogged down in the emotions these thoughts were bound to bring up. I joined the guys at the island. "What was the errand you guys were on this morning? I'd love to hear about the theory you were testing."

"Remember the trackers I mentioned the other day?" Ian said.

I did remember him talking about putting trackers on cows. I nodded.

"Uncle Jake helped me work out the kinks and we have it so that the location shows on an app. It's really cool."

"Awesome, but how does it help find cows that are already missing?" I was genuinely perplexed about how the trackers would help. "And I've already told you I don't want you chasing after anyone."

Jacob stretched. "Don't fret, Sissy. We're not planning to actually track down any stolen cattle or intercept any bad guys. These devices are prototypes. However, if they work we can sure share the data with the sheriff.

"You're right, Mom, they won't find the missing cattle. The trick is to get the trackers on cows that haven't been stolen yet and then track them when they are stolen. The hurdle I couldn't figure out was how to pick which cattle to plant trackers on, and that is where Uncle Jake is a genius."

I grinned at my brother. "Don't tell him that, son, his head will get so big there will be no living with him."

Jacob made a faux hurt face.

Ian resumed talking and placed the few plates in the sink, "We pored over the data of the victims, the type of cattle, then he made an algorithm to predict the next most likely victims. Then we went to the feedstore, and he sweet-talked Rebecca and got a list of people that are supposed to be gone over the next few days. We cross-referenced those people with the list from the algorithm and came up with three most likely farms."

Jacob picked up the story from there. "We contacted two of the three ranch owners and explained we wanted to put a tracking device on some of their cows. There was no one home at the third farm. We were given permission to place them on the cows at both places and the owners even helped us."

"How do you get it to stay on the cow? Is it a microchip like for a dog?" I asked.

Ian smiled and shook his head. "No, it can't be implanted because at some point, the animal may go to slaughter and then you've got microchips floating around in the animal. This is where Arista and Zoe came up with the idea to use nail glue or jewelry glue, it dries fast, isn't toxic, and it's waterproof!"

"We decided that just inside the ear would be a good placement. They're about the size of your thumbnail so they shouldn't be visible. We placed fifteen trackers today and we have ten more ready to go as needed," Jacob said.

I was proud of my son and brother for their ingenuity. They were so clever with technology. "Good work, gentlemen, I'm proud of y'all. Do you both promise not to use these ingenious doodads to ferret out the bad guys?" They each held up their right hands and nodded. They were grinning but I believed them.

"Great. what is the next step?"

Jacob gestured with his hands. "We set a parameter on the app that if any of the cows move more than one mile, it sets off a notification on our phones. Then we can watch the app. It shows a dot moving in a direction. We haven't figured out how to overlay it on a map yet, but it does track distance and direction based on GPS."

Lester looked from Jacob to Ian and shrugged. "I don't totally understand everything y'all just said, but I can tell that there is a potential to help farmers stop the thieves and that's something I can get behind."

"Have you let the sheriff know about the trackers?" I asked.

"Not yet, do you think he will be mad?" Ian asked.

I shook my head. "Mad? I wouldn't think so. It's a tool just like a Lojack. Hey, you could call it Moojack."

They groaned and shook their heads.

Jacob's phone buzzed, he glanced at the screen, and quickly excused himself. Lester said he wanted to check out the tractor Ian was wanting to rehab, so they bundled up and headed for the machine shop.

A couple hours later, the girls rushed into the kitchen. "Omg, where is Ian? It's almost time to leave for the dance!" Arista said.

I looked up from my book just as Ian came in from the machine shop. He was covered in grease.

Arista glared at him. "Ian, what have you been doing? It's time to leave, we're going to be late!"

"Settle down, Ari, it won't take me long to get ready. Tom won't be here for another forty-five minutes." He headed for the shower.

"Boys!" the girls said in unison and stomped out.

I laughed and went back to my book until Jacob came in and announced he was going into town to have dinner with "an old friend." I heard "an old girlfriend" and figured I wouldn't see him until much later or possibly tomorrow.

Tom arrived with his mom in her Yukon. None of the teens had their actual driver's licenses yet. I greeted them at the back door. When my son entered the kitchen he high-fived Tom.

Wow, my little boy had disappeared and been replaced by a young man. A good-looking young man if I do say so myself. "Ian, you look very handsome. I'm sure your sister will approve." Just then, the girls bustled into the room. "See, Arista, your brother cleaned up fine. You girls look very nice, too." My babies weren't little anymore. I fought back a tear when I hugged them goodbye.

There was a chorus of "thanks, Mom, bye, Mom, love you," and out the door they went. I checked the clock on the stove, it was 6:11 p.m. I was a little hungry. Nachos were the only thing that sounded good. I made a large platter, thinking that when Lester came in from tinkering with the tractor, he could eat the rest. Mom had gone to the center with Yvonne again and wouldn't be home for an hour or so. After I finished my nachos I settled on the couch in front of the fireplace with my book, and a glass of Moscato. Yep, I was living large.

Around 7:30 p.m., Mom came home and went right to bed. Yvonne came in with her and she looked tired, too. Who knew hanging at the senior center was so tiring? "Did you ladies have a good time?"

"Oh, my yes, our team won the pitch tournament this week!" Yvonne placed Mom's tote bag on the chair. "It's just bragging rights, but if we win three weeks in a row, we get to pick the movie of the month."

Lester came into the kitchen and exchanged a few pleasantries with Yvonne then scooped up some nachos. He settled at the kitchen island and began to munch.

After Yvonne left, I turned my attention to the older man. "Wow, Lester, you're not nearly as grimy as Ian was, how did it go with the tractor?"

He laughed. "Yep, I had Ian do all the dirty work, that's how the young ones learn. He showed me how to look up parts on the interweb thing, so I did that and made a list. Even so, this old man is tired. I'm going to eat this snack then turn in for the night."

I went back to my cozy spot by the fire with my book but no wine. This time I had a freshly made cup of tea. I must have dozed off because a noise startled me awake. Isabella and Sophia had snuggled up to me on the couch and Issy was purring. No wonder I had fallen asleep. *What time is it?* I fumbled around looking for my phone. 2:07 a.m.! I slept for six hours, geez, I was more tired than I thought. I noticed my message notification bubble was lit up, announcing two texts.

One was from Ian. *"Momma, Arista went home with Zoe and I'm going to Tom's, hope that's ok. Luv U."*

Huh, that's weird. Ian never calls me momma and never abbreviates words in his texts. Dang, I hope they haven't been drinking.

The second text was from Auntie Lou, *Things are not what they seem. A curse is a fine thing if properly placed.* "That's not cryptic at all." I huffed a breath.

I was righteously miffed that the kids hadn't called to get permission to sleep at friends' houses, but it was the first time this had happened, so I decided to let it be for now. I would deal with it tomorrow when they got home. I took a shower and went to bed.

Our house tends to be quiet on Sundays. I like to sleep in, and everyone knows it, so I was astonished to wake to Sophia barking incessantly at someone banging on the kitchen door. I threw on my robe and rushed to see what was up. Captain Smith was standing on the doorstep with a worried scowl on her face. My mind went immediately to my children, but they were safely ensconced with friends, weren't they?

CHAPTER 14

Fear clutched my chest. "Jana, what's wrong? Are my kids okay? Why are you here?"

"Fen, as far as I know your kids are fine. It's Jacob. Someone ran him off the road last night. He is in the hospital."

My heart fell to my feet. Had someone tried to kill him, too? What was happening? "Oh my god! Who would do that? How bad is it? Is he going to be okay?" I rapid fired the questions.

"The doctor said he'll be fine, can I come in? It's twenty-five degrees and I've been at the accident scene for hours." Jana rubbed her hands together.

"Of course, come in. I'll make some coffee while you tell me everything. Then I'll head to town."

"Jacob has a pretty big bump on his head from hitting the window of his car. It was a side impact and it spun him around and off the road. His arm is believed to be broken. He was just going to get X-rays when I left to go back to the scene. I happened upon the wreck while on patrol, no one called it in. He was awake on scene but had misplaced his phone because of the impact. His door was jammed shut and the other door was up against a tree. Lucky thing is, the headlights were still on, that is why I saw it."

"I need to get over to the hospital. I need to call the kids. Are you sure he will be okay?" I paced about the kitchen and patted my robe pockets for my phone. The coffee was not made. I felt Jana's hand on my shoulder. She gave me a reassuring squeeze.

"Fen, I'm as sure as I can be based on what Doc said. How about you change clothes, find your phone, and let me make the coffee? Just take a beat and make a plan."

"Yes, good idea. Thanks, Jana." I headed for my room to follow her advice. I emerged a few minutes later dressed in jeans with layered tops on. In the Ozarks, the weather usually warmed up throughout the day unless it didn't. I held my phone up. "I've already tried Arista and Ian, both their phones go directly to voicemail."

"Where are they?" Jana asked.

After I explained they had spent the night with friends, but I was worried about them, she tried to make me feel better.

"I'm sure they're fine, then. Their batteries probably died, and they don't have their chargers since it was an impromptu sleepover."

"Yes, I'm sure you're right. I will just run by their friends' houses after I see Jacob at the hospital."

I don't remember the drive to the hospital. My brain was swirling with "what-ifs and should haves," not to mention worrying about the kids. I asked Jana to call Yvonne and see if she could go stay with Mom, and I had left a note for Lester.

When I got there, I rushed into the hospital and stopped at the nurses' station. "Excuse me, I need to see my brother, Jacob Stonehorse, which room is he in?"

The nurse looked up from her paperwork. "I remember you from a few days ago, you're Fen Stern."

"That's right. My brother?"

Yes, your brother is in room 111 and you can go right in. I just did vitals, and he is awake."

I hurried down the hall, past the cafeteria, and burst into room 111. Jacob was sitting up in bed. He looked pale, his arm was in a cast and rested in a sling. He had a black eye and a contusion on his brow bone. "Hey, baby bro, you look like hell. How do you feel?" I decided to try to keep things light.

"Thanks, Fen, you aren't exactly a vision this morning, either, and I feel like I look." I relaxed as much as I could. If he could banter with me, I knew he was going to be all right. "What do you recall about what happened?"

He took a deep breath and related the events of the night before. "I'd been to dinner with Ginny, we stopped and shot a couple games of pool at Earls Pub, then I dropped her off at home. I was headed back to your place when a big truck swerved into my lane. I swerved to miss it, but whoever was driving must have swerved back a second before impact because they hit the rear quarter panel of my car and spun me. Everything went haywire and the next thing I knew, I was trapped in the car. I think I got knocked out. When I woke up, my head hurt, and it still does. I couldn't find my phone to call for help. Jana said she would check the car for it and bring it over if she found it."

"Wow, Jacob, that could have been a whole lot

worse. So, the person hit you and didn't stop." It was more a statement than a question because Jana already told me the other vehicle was at large and her department was looking for it. "What is going on in this community lately?" My hands shook and I wanted to punch something. My brother could have been killed.

"I know right? It wasn't this way when we were growing up here." Jacob shook his head and winced.

There was a tap on the doorframe of the open door and Jana walked in. "Hey, Fen. Jacob, I found your phone, it was on the back seat floorboard."

Jacob took the device from Jana. He woke it up and entered his security pin. "Thank you for finding it and bringing it all the way down here, Deputy. Battery's low." He clicked it off.

"No trouble and you can call me Jana."

Is she blushing? I think she likes my brother. Huh, I wonder if he likes her back. I quickly filed these thoughts away in the mental file titled "things I wonder about that are none of my business" and smiled to myself.

"Jana, Jacob was just telling me about the wreck. Is there any word on the person that hit him?" I focused on my friend and waited for her answer.

"Not yet. There was some significant paint transfer and samples have been collected. We will have them sent to the lab to see if we can get an idea of the make of the vehicle. The state lab is way behind, though, so for now, we must keep our eyes open for freshly damaged vehicles and possibly an injured driver. Although no one has checked into the E.R. with injuries consistent with a motor vehicle accident, except for Jacob."

The doctor came in and Jana excused herself. "I'm going back to the station and finish my report. Fen, Jacob, y'all call me if you need anything and if we turn up the responsible party, you'll be the first to hear about it." She closed the door behind her.

The doctor was the same one who had treated me a few days ago. He appeared surprised to see me until he ascertained I was Jacob's sister.

"Mr. Stonehorse, you are a lucky man, the injuries you sustained could have been a lot worse. Evidently you have good bones. Your left arm has a non-displaced midshaft fracture of the Ulna and treatment will not require surgical intervention. You will be in the current cast for four weeks, then we will do another set of X-rays and go from there. You do have a mild concussion and will, therefore, have a headache for a few days. We did a CT scan and found no apparent internal bleeding so it should resolve on its own with no ongoing issues."

Jacob and I both thanked the doctor and we visited for a few more minutes, then I stood and started for the door. "Jake, I'll be back later. I need to go find my wayward kids. Is there anything I can bring you when I come back?"

"I could use a phone charger and a cheeseburger," Jacob said with a grin.

I left the hospital and tried calling the kids again. Both phones went directly to voicemail. I headed for Zoe's house first since it was closer.

Mary, Zoe's mom, answered the door looking

sleepy. "Hey, Fen, what's up?"

"Hey, Mary, I apologize for popping by unannounced on Sunday morning, but I need to speak with Arista, and she isn't answering her phone."

"Arista isn't here, Fen. Zoe came home last night by herself, and she is still asleep. I can wake her if you need me to."

My heart sank. *She isn't here? Where is she?* My mind screamed. The other woman's facial expression changed when her mom-brain came online. It hit her that my girl was not where I thought she was. My shock and worry must have shown on my face. I felt it deep in my stomach.

"Come in, Fen, I will go get Zoe."

"Thank you, Mary." I stepped inside. A rope of terror tightened around my chest. My stomach churned and the room spun. I called Arista's phone, then Ian's for probably the twentieth time.

Zoe came into the warm kitchen, rubbing sleep from her eyes. "Hey, Ms. Stern, what's up, where's Arista?"

"I was hoping you could tell me. I got a text from Ian last night that said she came home with you, and he was going to Tom's house. Now neither of them will answer their phones."

"Oh geez, no. Before the dance was even over, I got a text from Arista that said she wasn't feeling well and Ian was taking her home." Zoe pulled up the text on her phone. "I asked her how since we all rode together but she never texted back."

"Oh my god, where could they be?!" Tears welled in my eyes and began to leak down my face. I couldn't bear it if something happened to my babies.

"I will call Tom's house, Fen, why don't you call a

couple of their other friends. They're most likely just out being dumb kids."

Mary said the words like they were supposed to make me feel better. I called every parent of every friend I could think of and none of them had seen my children. I called home and Lester answered. I asked if my children had happened to come home while I was out. They hadn't. I told Lester what was going on. He promised to have them call me if they came home.

Once Mary got through to Tom's house, she put Tom on speakerphone and his story matched Zoe's to a T.

I couldn't sit here any longer making idol phone calls to friends. I called the sheriff's department, and the dispatcher transferred me to Clyde Young. *Oh goody, as if this day didn't already suck.* "Hello, Deputy Young, this is Fenreya Stern, I need to report that my children are missing."

"Well, Ms. Stern, if they haven't been gone forty-eight hours, I can't file a report. I wouldn't worry, they are probably just out partying. Be patient, they'll come dragging in later."

His tone was dismissive and quite honestly, he pissed me off. I knew my kids and they weren't 'just out partying'

"My children are not like that, they are in some kind of trouble, and I need your department to help me find them." I knew I sounded like a panicked mom. Hell, I *was* a panicked mom, and I was getting madder by the minute because he wasn't taking me seriously. The urge to curse the doofus deputy was becoming difficult to resist. "Fine, if you won't help me, I will call your boss directly."

Clicking the "end" button on a cell phone wasn't nearly as gratifying as slamming down an old-time receiver. I placed a panicked call to Uncle John and explained the situation. He knew my kids well enough to know that this behavior was completely out of character, and I was relieved when he said he was going to take action.

"Fen, I'll get my people busy looking for them. We can't file an official missing person's report yet, but they are minors, so I will ask for an Amber Alert. I'm so sorry y'all are going through this right now, and on top of Jake's accident, too.".

"Thank you, Uncle John. I'm going home to check the house and forward our landline phone to my cell phone. Then I'm going out to look for them myself." We concluded the call, and my phone wasn't even back in my pocket when Jana called.

"Fen, are you okay? The kids weren't where they said they'd be?"

She sounded almost as panicked as I felt. I filled her in on what I knew, which was a big fat nothing. I waved goodbye to Mary and Zoe then left and headed for my house.

"I'm technically off work now, Fen, so how about I meet you somewhere and we will go together to look for them? I know we would cover more ground separately, but I really think you shouldn't be alone just now."

I was grateful for the support and the growing friendship with Jana. "I need to take Jake his phone charger and a cheeseburger, so let's meet back at the hospital. Thank you, Jana."

"No problem. I can grab the burger if you want. I

was going to get something for myself anyway and I don't suppose you have eaten, either."

"I'm not hungry."

"I didn't ask if you were hungry, my friend, you need to keep your strength up. I'll see you in Jacob's room in about thirty minutes"

Jana clicked off before I got another word in.

I rushed through the back door of my house. Lester was sitting at the kitchen island drinking coffee and munching on some toast.

"Is there any word on the kids, and how is Jacob?"

"Jacob is going to be okay. He will likely get released later today. The kids are still missing. Oh god, Lester, I don't know what I'll do if they're not okay!" Now that I was home, I burst into tears.

Lester stepped around the kitchen island and poured me a cup of coffee, added cream, and then took a flask out of the pocket on his bib overalls and poured just a touch of its mysterious contents into the coffee.

"Here, Fen, drink this. It will bring you back to steady. The kids are smart and resourceful, they will be fine. Tell me what I can do to help." He pushed the cup toward me.

I eyed the brew suspiciously through teary eyes. "Lester, I have to drive, it's not a good time for me to hit the sauce. His voice was calm and steady when he replied.

"It's not enough to mess you up, just a dab for medicinal purposes. You'll be fine. Now drink up and tell me how I can help."

I sipped the coffee. It was really quite pleasant and warmed me throughout. Lester sliced a small piece of banana bread and put it in front of me. I began to pick at it. "Lester, if you could stay here and just hold down the fort, call me if they show up, and help Yvonne with Mom if needed. That would be super helpful. I have to meet Jana at the hospital, and we will go out looking from there. I've got to grab Jacob's phone charger before I leave."

"I'll feed the horses, pets, and make sure everyone has water. Don't worry about anything here. Just be safe out there."

Lester patted my arm and made another pot of coffee. I grabbed the phone charger and headed out into the gray mid-morning air. It had not warmed up at all and the thick clouds did not inspire optimism. I was late to meet Jana. I broke the speed limit and at least a couple other traffic laws on the way. Auntie Lou says they are "speeding suggestions." We wondered how she kept her license all these years.

CHAPTER 15

I slid into the best parking spot I could find and rushed into the hospital. Jana was already in Jacob's room, and he was munching the last bite of the cheeseburger she brought him. I gave him the phone charger and helped him plug it in. He looked tired and I suspected he would be dozing before we reached the main doors leading out of the hospital.

We climbed into my dinky rental car and headed out of the parking lot.

"Fen, don't take this wrong. I know your Arista and Ian are good kids and not known for partying, but let's drive out and check a few of the common spots so we can be thorough."

"No offense taken. Let's face it, I was a good kid and so were you, but we both know where the party spots are, unless they have moved since we were in school."

"All the same except there are two new ones, I'll show you. By the way, Jacob's nurse said they will release him later today, probably between 2:30-3 p.m. He is going to call so one of us can swing by and pick him up."

"I'm glad he didn't get hurt worse and can be released." We drove to all the known spots favored by kids for impromptu parties. Jana called Sheriff Peters and asked if he had any new information. He didn't. He shared his theory that if it was a kidnapping, there would have been a ransom demand by now. The concept made sense but didn't make me feel better.

Around 2:42 p.m. my phone rang, and I answered through the car's Bluetooth speaker, it was Jacob.

"Sis, I need you to come now. I have to show you something."

"Have you been released yet?"

"No, the nurse swears she's working on it, but that isn't why I called. I have to show you. It's the tracker application Ian and I made."

"I think it's cool that you guys invented a cow tracker, but, Jake, I don't give a fig about missing cows right now. I would trade the entire farm and every animal on it to get my kids back safe and sound." I had to clench my teeth to keep from cussing. The fear, anger and fatigue had combined into an emotional tsunami. I didn't have time to pitch the fit the situation deserved.

"I don't think it's tracking cows. Just come to the hospital. Where are y'all now?" Jacob asked.

"We are in the next county over checking out one of Arista's favorite places to trail ride. It was a long shot, but we were out of places to search. We'll be there in thirty minutes or so." I ended the call. The only reason my hands weren't shaking was because of the death grip I had on the steering wheel. I turned the car around and headed back to town. Could the trackers be the answer to finding the twins? My soul filled with hope.

Jana's phone chirped just as I was pulling into the hospital parking lot. I held my breath, hoping if it was about my kids, it was good news. I couldn't tell from Jana's side of the conversation, she wasn't giving anything away.

"That was the sheriff. He needs me out on Route 5 for an accident. It's not your kids." Jana hurried to her truck and left the hospital using her magnetic emergency light and siren.

The sheriff trusted her with this equipment on her personal vehicle. The other full-time deputy, Clyde Young, was not allowed to have lights and sirens on his. It was the common belief that he would abuse the privilege. Clyde was mad about it.

When I got to Jacob's hospital room, he was partly dressed. He was trying in vain to put on the shirt they mostly cut off him.

"I'm sorry, I should have thought to grab you some clothes when I was at the house."

"It's okay, it's not like you don't have more pressing things to worry about." He patted my back with his good arm. "Check this out." He shoved his phone at me.

"What am I looking at? I don't understand."

"This is the tracking interface Ian and I made. It's live and it's showing all the trackers, but we only implanted twenty in cows. I think Ian has the other trackers in his pocket. Look here," he said, pointing at the screen. These are all in a clump and haven't moved since I pulled the app up."

My heart hammered. "Haven't moved? Oh, my Goddess, does that mean Ian hasn't moved? Is he hurt or worse? Can we use this gizmo to find them?" Nervous energy bubbled over, and I began to pace.

Jacob wrapped me in a one-armed hug. "Yes, Fen, we can track them with the gizmo. Let's leave now, where is Jana? I'm not much help with one arm in a sling."

"She got called in to an accident out on the highway. We will call her from the road, let's just go. It will be dark soon and it is already cold and getting colder." Neither of the kids were dressed for the weather, and unless they were inside a warm building...I stifled the thought. You navigate, I'll drive."

✦ ✦ ✦

We got in the car and Jacob told me to head east on the main highway. After we had driven about seven miles, we turned down County Road 104. Although it started out paved, it switched to gravel after five miles or so. Jacob's cell signal vanished. He started tinkering with it. He always had the latest tech.

Meanwhile, I was about to come undone. "Jake, I'm terrified for my kids, we are low on gas, and I have to pee. Can we find them with that thing or not?"

"We can, provided I can get a signal. Living in the city has spoiled me. I forgot what it's like to have zero bars. I have a solution, but we need to go back to the house. I've got a portable satellite internet module there."

"A what? Never mind, I believe you. Is there no way we can find them now? It feels like we are so close." I knew the answer and was already turning the car around.

About thirty minutes later, we slid to a stop and rushed into the house. We had a plan. Jacob went to get the satellite thingy and change clothes. I went to the bathroom and quickly grabbed some warm clothes and blankets for the kids. I wasn't sure they were out in the weather, but I'd rather be safe than sorry. If they were, they'd be freezing.

Lester followed me around, peppering me with questions, and we were nearly out the door when the house phone rang, then Jacob's cell in quick succession. My brother swiped the green button and immediately held it out to me. It was Auntie Lou.

"Auntie, we are going to find the kids! Have you seen something?" I said into the receiver Jacob still held.

"Jacob, put me on speaker."

Jake pushed the speaker button.

"Fen, stop! I've been trying to reach you for two hours. Honey, you don't have all the information, so you need to listen."

Auntie wasn't yelling exactly but her voice held the kind of power that is not easily ignored. I sucked in a deep breath and let it go, resigned to the fact this was an unavoidable delay. "What is it, Auntie?"

"When I heard the kids were missing, I threw some cards and worked a scrying. Everything indicates that they are fine and unhurt but not safe and not alone. I do not believe you can reach them entirely by car. You must take your mule or horses. The tarot turned up several Sword cards and the Tower. The stakes are high, honey. I kept seeing a blocked road, though not what it was blocked by. Please, Fen, trust me and listen to your instincts, too."

"My instincts say to go get my kids!" I gritted my teeth and glared at the phone. My auntie had always been well-known for her psychic skills. She's helped many police departments with various investigations. I heard the sternness of her voice but it was laced with a pleading tone too. I hadn't heard her plead for anything at anytime. *Dammit.*

Jacob laid the phone on the counter and headed for the door. "Lester, would you mind giving me a hand hooking up the trailer to the old farm truck and tacking up a couple critters? I don't think it will go well one-handed. Together, we have two working arms."

"I'm right behind you, kid."

My aunt continued talking, "Fen, you need to call Sheriff Peters or maybe Jana. They should at least know where you are going, but I can see that waiting for them is not an option. I love you, Fen. Remember when I taught you how to conjure protective wards? I hope so because you're going to need them. Next time I call you repeatedly, pick up the damn phone."

Auntie clicked off before I could respond.

I gathered Jake's phone, the clothes and blankets, grabbed a few bottles of water and headed to the barn. The trailer was already hooked up and they were discussing whether Lester should go along.

"I would feel better knowing you were here keeping an eye on the house and Mom." I climbed behind the wheel. "Jake, do you have your satellite doohickey and is it going to work?"

"I got it and have faith it will work. Let's roll. Did

you grab my phone?"

"I did." I handed it to him. "Take mine, too, and call Jana and Uncle John. Tell them where we are heading and why. Maybe leave out the part about Auntie Lou and her super-psychic vision stuff. It's no secret but I really don't feel like explaining it all right now. Hey, check the tracker thingy and see if they have moved."

I drove in the general direction of where we lost signal before, and after a few moments, Jacob reported that the tracking app was still showing the same location. Then I listened as he called Jana and told her where we were headed. He said something about "dropping a pin" to her phone. I still don't know what that meant. *Whatever, let's just get there already.*

"Jana said she'll be there as soon as possible. She's just finishing up at the accident scene, but it is on the far west side of the county. She also said it is beginning to snow over there, and it should hit us within the hour."

Great, pulling a trailer full of horses with a crappy old farm truck, in the snow down a crappy, dirt road to rescue my children from Goddess knows what. What could go wrong?

I drove the next several miles in silence, thinking of all the things that could go very wrong. I heard my phone roar.

Jacob read it to me. "Auntie sent a text, it's in all caps 'FEN, FOCUS YOUR ENERGY ON POSITIVE THINGS. HAVE I TAUGHT YOU NOTHING?' I am ever astonished at our Auntie Lou."

"You and me both, Brother." I sighed. Had our circumstances been different I would have been amused by my aunt's message. Now, it just made me tired.

We passed the place where I'd had to turn around earlier, and Jake was fiddling with his tech. He told me to turn down the next road to the left.

In about 500 feet, I stopped the truck and pointed. "You want me to turn there? Jacob, that is not a road, it may have been at one time, but it is most definitely no longer a road." The path was lined with dense vegetation. I doubted it was even visible during the growing season when everything was leafed out. The first hard freeze turned the brush and brambles into skeletons. The trees were devoid of leaves.

Jacob showed me the tracker screen. "Do you see another way? I've overlaid a satellite view from Google Earth, and I don't see any alternatives."

"Are we really relying on Google to set the course for the rescue of my children? Do you know how many times that Google lady has led me on a merry chase trying to find a simple yard sale?" I met my brother's gaze. "I thought you had a verifiable way to find my kids!"

"Google lady, as you call her, is perfectly reliable. I think you are experiencing operator error. You need to ask better questions."

"Shut up, now you sound like Auntie." I swung the truck onto the stupid little road. I was certain it was a bad idea and under other circumstances, I would never have attempted it. It began to snow.

I drove at a snail's pace. I could feel the horses fidgeting in the trailer. Scruffy trees along the road scraped the sides of the truck. The wind began to howl, and the snowflakes got larger.

A memory came flooding back from around the time

I was ten years old, and Auntie was teaching me about protective magick. She had said whenever I was in an unforgiving place and needing to get somewhere else, I should "Conjure a Footman." It sounded silly at the time. "What the devil is a footman and why would I want one?" I had asked. She had explained that in the old days, a coachman was the person in charge of handling the team of horses or mules and the footman was like an assistant, there to handle whatever problems came up that would be outside the purview of the driver.

If ever I was in an "unforgiving place needing to be somewhere else," it was now. If only I could remember the chant she taught me. I was thinking hard, trying to remember, when there was a loud crash behind us.

Jacob said, "Stop a minute and let me check the horses and see what that noise was." He hopped out and headed to the rear of the trailer.

I took a deep breath and let it out. *Just let it come to you.* I stared blankly out the window at the snow and the trees bending in the wind. Then a chant popped into my head. I wasn't entirely sure it was the one Auntie had told me years ago but figured it was worth a try.

Footman, Footman, I conjure thee
Get me where I need to be
Afterward I set thee free

I was finishing the third round of the chant when Jacob got back in the truck.

"What are you doing?"

"Conjuring a footman, I'll fill you in later. What was the noise and are the critters okay?"

"They are fine, just nervous about the weather, and the noise was a very large tree falling across the road behind us. We won't be driving out of here anytime soon, nor will anyone be driving up behind us." The snow is sticking to everything, it's so wet. I heard branches cracking all around us. It reminded me of the 2007 ice storm."

"Dandy." I put the truck in gear to continue down the road as far as we could. "Can you tell if we are still going in the right direction? Is your tracker gizmo working?"

"According to the available data, we are good to go. In fact, if the weather and the trail weren't so awful, we would already be there. It's only about two miles to where the trackers are sitting."

Just then, the truck lights illuminated a large deer in the road, I stopped to allow it to cross. It was a beautiful buck with an enviable rack of antlers, at least twelve points on it. He stood there watching us watch him. There was a loud cracking sound and about twenty-five yards up the road, another tree crashed down, covering the road. The buck ran off into the adjacent field.

CHAPTER 16

J acob and I stared at the tree, the retreating buck, and then looked at each other. Even in the dim light of the truck's dash lights, we knew we were thinking the same thoughts. *Were it not for the buck, we would have been under that tree when it crashed down.*

"Holy crap!" I said. I will not repeat the words that came out of my brother's mouth, but I will say they were accurate. "Uh, I guess Auntie was right about bringing BB and the horses, let's get them unloaded."

"Yeah, she was right again. It feels like the Universe is trying to trap the truck here. I just hope there isn't a tree on top of it when we get back. Oh hell, how are we going to get home?"

I stared at my brother. He had a point. We were trapped. "Let's worry about that after we find the kids. Jana and Uncle John know where we are so surely help will come eventually."

We decided to leave the extra horse in the trailer. Leading it in the dark in bad weather with tree limbs crashing all around us would have been over complicated at best and extremely dangerous at worst.

My blessed mule BB seemed to know he was on a mission. He took off at a trot and hopped over the fallen tree. The horse Jacob rode, although a very good horse, was less enthused by the conditions. It took Jacob a minute to get over the tree. He had to dismount, lead the horse around it, and remount, all with his arm in a sling. (What can I say, my brother loves me and my kids.) His phone chirped and startled all of us except BB, who just kept moving.

"Your phone is still working? How?" I asked.

Jacob pointed to the pommel on his saddle. He'd clamped his little satellite thingy to it. He grinned. "Cool, huh?" He checked his phone message and said, "Hey, Fen, hold up. Jana said she will be here in twenty or thirty minutes."

"No, Jake, I am done waiting. I want my twins. Now. Please call her and let her know about all the obstacles and offer her the extra horse. I locked the trailer but there is a hideaway key under the hitch. I'm going, wait if you want."

Jacob made the call and loped to catch me and BB. "Sis, I get that you're in a hurry, but can you slow down just a little? This is not a gaited horse. It's like riding on a jackhammer and I'm down to one arm."

He was right. I was in a hurry, but if he fell off his horse and got hurt, he'd be no good to me at all. I slowed BB to a flat walk, which is faster than a normal walk. I didn't want to seem ungrateful to my brother. "Doesn't the wet snow mess up your satellite doohickey, like short it out or something?"

"Nope, that is one of the cool things about this design. It's waterproof and small enough to fit nearly anywhere. It's a prototype my R&D guys came up with and I'm testing it. Wait until they hear what I put it through on this trip. I can't wait to show Ian how it works."

The excitement in my brother's voice about the success of the gizmo was evident. Although I was proud of his technological prowess, and that it was helping us, I wanted, no, needed, to get to my children. "That is very cool, Jake. Can you tell how much farther the kids are from us?"

"About a mile closer than the last time you asked." Jacob squinted into the distance. "What is that up ahead?"

As we rode closer, we could see a car on the side of the overgrown road. It seemed to be stuck, but who knew for sure? I saw Jacob reach inside his coat. What was he doing? Then it hit me. "Jake, did you bring a gun?"

"Yes. Not everyone can toss curses around like candy like you can. It is legal. I have a permit to carry."

He sounded defensive, but I let it go. "Okay, fine with me." I reached into my saddlebag for a flashlight and cautiously approached the vehicle ahead. The light revealed the car was empty. I wasn't sure if that was good or bad. We kept riding and my mind was going around and around "Jake, that car seems familiar, but I can't figure out where I've seen it."

I kept trying to remember while we rode farther. When we rounded a bend in the road, we could see the outline of a rather large building. There was a flicker of light in one window, otherwise, the structure was dark. A light-colored pickup truck was parked near the door. I was about to race up and barge in, but Jacob grabbed my sleeve.

He whispered, "That could be the truck that hit me. Let's sneak up there and get a closer look. Do you know who owns that truck?"

"No, just like the car, it looks vaguely familiar but that could only mean it's local. Why would the truck that hit you be here, and where are the kids? Jake, you can't think they were driving it and hit you." I forgot to whisper.

"No, I don't think they were driving it. They would have stopped even if they were out doing something stupid. I'm going to creep up there and take a closer look."

Jacob dismounted and led his horse over to an area heavy with shadows. He looped a rein loosely over a branch and looked expectantly at me.

I got off BB and told him to "stand." I didn't bother to tie my mule. He would stay put because I asked him to and if he really didn't want to, no rope tie would hold him for long. I walked quietly up to my brother, and together we crept toward the mysterious building.

Jacob and I crouched in the shadows under the only window that emitted any light. We were near the suspicious truck. We could now see that it was a white pickup with a king cab and a large "cow catcher" style grill welded to the front. The grill looked homemade and very solid. There was no visible damage to it, but there were some scrapes to the left front fender and the turn signal light cover was broken.

"I'm 99 percent sure that is the truck that hit me last night," Jake whispered.

We stood slowly, one on either side of the window. and attempted to peek to see who might be inside. I heard raised voices and motioned to Jake to get back down.

"Dammit, why the hell would you bring those stupid Stern kids here? Why even take them? Now they know who we are for sure, and we will have to deal with that. Their mother is a nosey bitch. It's only a matter of time before she gets up in our grill."

I did not recognize the voice, but he'd just called me a nosey bitch. In front of my children no less. *Jerk.*

Jacob tapped me on the shoulder, his voice barely audible. "I figured out what this building is. It used to be a mill. I think I was here a couple times as a teenager. If I'm right, there are two large doors on either end. It is a split-level so the grain could go in the top, be gravity-fed into the grinder, and then into the hopper on the lower level to get bagged up."

I made a "get to the point" motion with my hand. Any other time this would have been fascinating information.

Jake glared at me. "The point is, there should be multiple ways into the building if they haven't all been boarded up. I'm going around to the backside to find us a way in. Wait for me and see what else you can hear."

I nodded agreement to the plan and watched my brother creep silently to the end of the building and around the corner out of sight.

The feeling of aloneness hit me. My children were in this building somewhere, evidently held against their will. I wanted to burst through the door and take my children back. The idea that I didn't have all the information nagged at me and made me hesitate. I stood to get closer to the window and could hear them speaking again.

"I took them dumb kids because they saw me and Randy breaking into the drugstore last night. We had to get back to Bobby with the bandages and drugs after that old bastard Dawlin shot him."

I gasped as several things fell into place. Randy and Bobby? Come to think of it, one of the voices did sound like Denny. Did the Bowman brothers take my children? If Bobby Bowman was shot by Mr. Dawlin, then they must have been the cattle thieves. I raised up slightly to peek through the window. I saw Arista and Ian over in the corner. They had gags in their mouths and were tied to a support pole.

Some crates were stacked up on either side of them and someone, I guessed it was Bobby Bowman, was lying on a makeshift bed on top of the crates. I couldn't tell if he was alive or even conscious, and I didn't care that much.

I saw Arista look right at me, her eyes got wide as saucers, and she nudged Ian. I ducked back down. If she could see me, then that idiot Bowman could, too. I needed to find Jacob and tell him what was going on.

I turned to creep around the building after Jake and came up short when something cold and metal poked into my neck.

"My brother was right, you are a Nosey Nelly. Come with me and don't try anything funny."

The man poked me with the barrel of the gun again. He grabbed my arm and yanked me toward the door. I recognized Randy Bowman. He opened the rickety old door and shoved me inside. I lost my balance and landed on my hands and knees about ten feet into the middle of the room. Randy strutted up to me and kicked me in the side. "Hey, bro, looky what I found poking around outside. I always thought she was a looker, can I keep her?"

I felt nauseous, maybe it was the kick to my side that knocked the wind out of me or more likely it was the idea that Randy Bowman found me desirable in any way. Whatever the reason, I wanted to puke, so I did. All over Randy's boots. *Keep this jerk.*

"You stupid bitch!"

I saw both my kids begin struggling and pulling at their ropes. It looked like Arista might be trying to talk, or maybe it was a chant. Denny Bowman struck Ian with a backhand blow and said, "You two best simmer down or I'll give you something to fuss about."

Denny turned to his brother. "Randy, what the hell is wrong with you? We got so many problems right now, way too many people know about this, we sure as hell don't have time for you to play your kinky games. Bobby is shot and we gotta get out of town."

Denny looked toward the other corner of the room. "Leblanc, we will be needing our money early. We gotta go."

Another man stepped from the shadows. Steve Leblanc walked over to where I lay on the floor clutching my side. He nudged me with his shiny show-off urban cowboy-type boot and when I rolled to my back, he put his foot on my chest.

"You, Fenreya Stonehorse, have been a thorn in my side for years. Did you come here alone tonight, or is that uppity brother of yours with you?"

"Nah, I put Jake the Jerk in the hospital last night." Randy Bowman looked really proud of himself when he said it.

At least I knew who ran Jake off the road. If we got out of this, Randy would get his.

"His cute little sports car was no match for a real man's truck. I figure it's a total loss. I heard he was in bad shape."

I didn't dare look directly at the kids for fear I would give something away. I was going to have to lie to these men if we would have any hope of getting out of this. I could see Arista out of the corner of my eye. Tears were streaking her face. Hearing the news about her uncle Jacob and watching me get kicked around was tearing her up.

Ian had schooled his face into a scowl. His eyes were as cold as I'd ever seen them. In that moment, he looked so much like his father, Michael.

A flood of memories hit me. My Michael, carrying me after another attack, teaching me how to protect myself. My Michael at our wedding and riding horses through the woods, getting on a plane the last time I saw him.

Pressure on my chest from Leblanc's boot brought me back to the present moment. He was speaking.

"I asked you a question, you dumb wench, answer me!"

I coughed and sputtered, "Alone, yes alone." I yielded to the pressure of the boot and closed my eyes. I needed these men to believe that I was not a threat, and I needed a moment to think. Jacob was out there somewhere. Hopefully, he didn't get caught, too. Jana was coming, but she would have no idea what she's walking into. Oh goddess, what if... *Nope, focus on what you want not ifs and buts.*

"Well, Randy, you did something right for once. Good job putting Stonehorse in the hospital. He was the only one even more obnoxious than my older brother in high school. It didn't matter that he was my age, my brother would rather hang out with the high and mighty Stonehorse than his own flesh and blood." Leblanc smirked.

"As for getting paid, Denny, you boys have not finished the job, and you've made one hell of a mess."

Leblanc looked down at me and the weight on my chest increased again.

"What are we going to do with the three of you?"

He glanced at my children and around the room in general. I was certain I wouldn't like the answer.

"Look, Leblanc, we done the best we could. You owe us." Denny's voice was taking on an edge that alluded to danger.

Maybe if I could get them to fight among themselves, it would be enough of a distraction, and we could get out of there.

"I don't owe you diddly 'til the job is done, and I'm deducting 10 percent for the extra trouble and all these loose ends," Leblanc said, gesturing with a sweep of his arm.

"Why you crooked son of a bitch!" Denny Bowman started toward Leblanc with clenched fists.

Here we go! My heart thumped so hard in my chest I thought it might jump out, but I had to do something now. I grabbed Leblanc's foot with both hands, twisted and shoved to take him off-balance. Leblanc stumbled toward Denny Bowman just as Denny took a swing at him. I started to get up, but Randy tackled me back to the ground. Denny's swing didn't connect as well as it should have since Leblanc was falling toward him, but it did cause him to hit the floor.

Leblanc got up and pulled a gun from inside his coat. He pointed the gun at Denny. His face was approaching a furious shade of red. "You ignorant hillbilly, don't you ever put your hands on me again. If you do, I will blow a hole in you big enough to read through."

I was on the ground and Handsy Randy was straddling me. I now knew exactly why his nickname was "Handsy Randy." I tried in vain to throw him off me. Denny had squared off with Leblanc and was staring down the barrel of the gun. I watched them faceoff and willed myself to focus and think. That escape strategy was an epic failure. Where was Jacob?

Randy reached for the gun in the back of his pants.

LeBlanc turned the gun on him. "Don't even think about it, Randy. Toss your piece over here, nice and easy like."

Randy's eyes were filled with hatred, but he did what he was told and slid the gun across the floor to LeBlanc's feet.

Outside, a horse whinnied. "What was that?" Leblanc stared at me.

"Gee, Steve, it sounded like a horse. Get this perve off me and I'll be happy to go check it out for you." I glared at him. Randy slapped me but I refused to flinch.

"Why is there a horse out there?" Steve asked.

"Because the road is entirely blocked by falling trees. Have you not noticed the snowstorm raging outside? You will be lucky to get any vehicles out of here for a week or more." My tone indicated that I thought he was even dumber than the Bowman brothers. *Yeah, tick off the only whacko in the room holding a gun. Great strategy.*

"Randy, get your ass off her, go out and check the road. Look around to see if she is telling the truth," Leblanc ordered.

Randy leered at me. "I'll be back for you."

I shivered with disgust. Once I was free of Randy's weight, I got on my feet. The pain in my side where I was kicked had let up. Leblanc was still pointing the gun at Denny.

"Fen, I have to wonder how you found us all by yourself when we are out in the boonies like this. The old phrase about needles and haystacks comes to mind." Leblanc gazed at me expecting an answer.

This lie was going to have to be a good one. *Don't mention the trackers.* That will implicate Jacob and he is my ace in the hole.

"I'm waiting, Fenreya. Perhaps you need some motivation." Leblanc turned the gun on my children.

I opened my mouth and the truth fell out. Some of it anyway. "Uh, my Auntie Lou is psychic, and she told me where to find them, see she uses a scrying bowl and a pendulum and—"

"Stop! You actually expect me to believe you found us out here, in the dark, because of some mumbo-jumbo hoodoo crap you got from your aunt? Come on, Ms. Stonehorse, I suppose that is also why you brought a horse? You magically knew the road would be blocked." Leblanc was looking angrier by the moment, he absently turned the gun on me. "Unfortunately for you, there are seven people here, six if you subtract poor Bobby. He doesn't look like he will last much longer. Six people and one horse, and I have the gun. A gun with at least nine bullets in it."

I did *not* like his math. I saw a look of realization come over Denny Bowman's face. He just caught up. "That's right, Denny, he doesn't expect you or your brothers to be anything more than collateral damage. It's not too late to help me, Denny. Together we can save your little brother, Bobby, and my kids."

"Shut your mouth, Stonehorse!" Leblanc leveled the gun at my chest.

There was a scream outside and a thump. Denny lunged at Leblanc, and Leblanc spun the gun in his direction. The gun went off and Denny slumped to the floor. I saw the kids' ropes fall away and they dove behind the crates Bobby Bowman was laid out on. Steve pointed the gun at me, his face purple with rage.

He pulled the trigger and nothing happened. The kids popped up from behind the crates. Arista pointed at Leblanc and chanted.

The realization that Steve Leblanc just tried to shoot me stunned me. I froze for a moment. That the gun didn't fire would be something to ponder later.

My husband, Michael, had been a Mossad special agent assigned to work in the United States. He taught me Krav Maga, a no-frills martial art that focuses on completely disabling your opponent, by whatever means are available.

I ran to him, grabbed his arm with my left hand to push the gun down and away from me and anyone else I cared about. I struck his throat with the heel of my right hand. I grasped his right arm with both hands and slammed it into my knee until he dropped the gun.

In rapid succession, Leblanc was kicked in the groin, kneed in his nose, and then I put him on the ground. I landed on his torso with both knees. The fear and anger I had been bottling up since this whole mess started ignited somewhere inside me. I pounded his face with my fists. I was losing control, but I didn't care. He had pointed a gun at my children, tried to shoot me, he would pay.

Three hands grabbed me from behind and I came up swinging.

"No, Fen, it's us." Jana ducked my swing.

"Take it easy, sis." Jacob wrapped his good arm around my waist and held tight until I stood still.

Leblanc was gasping for air on the ground and trying to cover his face and his groin at the same time.

I felt feral and ecstatic. My body shook from the adrenalin coursing through my system. I broke our captor's nose and it spilled blood everywhere. It was ugly and beautiful at the same time.

Ian and Arista grabbed me into the best hug ever, and all my anger and fear fell away. My heart was sated by their presence, and I drank in their love like it was the best medicine. All the talking started, the "Are you okays?" and the assurances of being fine.

"Wow, Mom, you really hammered him." Arista grinned.

"Mom, Arista knew this chant to keep a gun from firing, we did it together and it worked!" Ian said.

"Ian, our tracker works, we used it to find you." Jacob held his phone out toward his nephew.

"Steve Leblanc, you are under arrest for kidnapping, assault with a deadly weapon, and a bunch of other stuff that we will figure out later. You have the right to remain silent…" Jana read Leblanc his Miranda Rights and cuffed his hands behind his back.

Denny moaned from the floor where he fell after Leblanc shot him. My heart lurched. I had forgotten about him. He hadn't moved so I thought he was dead. I went over to him and searched him for weapons. He was bleeding badly from a wound in his left side.

I couldn't think straight enough to remember what organ might be there, but stopping the blood would be a good choice no matter what. I begrudgingly began to apply pressure to the wound. "Jana, have you called for backup and EMT dispatch?"

"Yep, I called the sheriff and filled him in when I headed this way. He was going to get some guys to clear the trees off the path but that may take a while. That was smart leaving a horse for me up the road. How did you think to do it?"

"That is kind of a long, weird story. Can we tackle it later over coffee?"

"Sure, those are my favorite kind of stories." Jana laughed.

I put pressure on Denny's wound and hoped it would help. His blood was now covering my hands and it was unsettling. I needed a distraction. I peered at Jacob. "How did you get inside to free the twins?"

"The lower-level door wasn't boarded up. Once I was inside, I crept up the stairs. The hardest part was untying the ropes with one hand."

I looked around the room. Something or someone was missing. "Uhm, guys, where is Randy? He was in on this whole thing. He went out to look at the road and never came back."

Jacob grinned and pointed out the door. "Oh yeah. Your mule took care of him. I had just finished loosening the ropes on the kids and was about to pop up with my gun when the horse whinnied outside. I figured it was Jana arriving on scene, and I didn't want her to rush in and get shot because, by that time, Leblanc was waving his gun around. I crept out to intercept her and fill her in so we could form a new plan. Randy came out and started walking down the road. He saw Jana riding up, but before he could warn his brother and Steve, your mule ran over him."

It was good to hear laughter after all that had happened. I couldn't help but chuckle myself when Jake finished his tale.

"BB held him down with a front hoof. I am not kidding, Fen, I watched your mule sniff Randy. He laid his ears back and bit him on the arm. Randy screamed and BB stomped the ground beside his head. He's probably still there. I suppose I could check on him."

"Yes, Jacob, would you? Here, take this with you." Jana tossed a large zip-tie to Jacob. "I only carry one set of handcuffs, but this will work in a pinch. Tell him to behave or we will let the mule have at him." She and Jacob shared a smile.

Yep, they like each other. I would investigate this development later.

"Mom, Bobby Bowman is feverish, and he is starting to talk," Arista said.

"Could one of you kids record what he says with your phone? If he dies before we can get his statement, the recording should be admissible in court," Jana said.

"They took our phones. We need to find them." Ian frowned.

"Here, use mine. There is a shortcut widget on the first screen for the recorder." Jana tossed her phone to

Arista then nudged Leblanc with her toe. "Where are the kids' phones?"

"I want a lawyer," Leblanc said.

However, it sounded like "ah wa a oyer." I supposed it was because his nose was broken and he was stuffy. Evidently the blood had begun to coagulate, and he couldn't breathe right.

"Okay, Leblanc, have it your way. You will get a lawyer either way and I will add two more counts of felony theft to your growing crime resume, or you could just tell the kids where their phones are." Jana's singsong voice spoke volumes.

Leblanc blew his nose and cleared his throat. Bloody goo landed on the floor in front of his face, and he tried to squirm away from it. "I don't know, ask those idiot Bowmans, they are the ones that took the kids."

"Wow, wicked gross." Arista eyed the snotty goo by LeBlanc. She had passed Jana's phone off to Ian and he was holding it near Bobby just in case the dying kid said anything useful.

Jacob came in with Randy by the arm. Randy was scuffed up pretty bad but didn't appear to have any broken bones.

"Randy, where are my kids' phones?" I glared at the creep. Had I not been so busy trying to keep his brother from bleeding out I would have kicked him in the groin. Heaven knows he deserved it.

He leered at me. "Why should I tell you anything?".

I whistled and called for motivational backup. "Come here, BB mule, come here, boy."

"We tossed them out along the road, couldn't tell you exactly where." Randy spewed the words and looked at the door.

When BB stuck his head and shoulders through the opening and snorted, Randy peed his pants.

✦ ✦ ✦

A few minutes later, a new voice said, "Whoa, mule, good mule. Budge over and let me in there."

It was Uncle John. He moved the mule and came in, followed by two teams of EMTs. He surveyed the room and walked over to my kids. I watched him wrap them both in a bear hug.

One team of EMTs went to Bobby and went to work, checking vitals, starting an IV, and getting him loaded onto a gurney.

The other team came over and relieved me of the burden of trying to keep the despicable Denny from bleeding out. My hands were soaked in his blood, and I really wanted to wash it off.

I was suddenly so tired. My head spun and the world around me started to fade. I couldn't let myself succumb. Not even under the weight of everything that had happened. Thankfully, Jacob caught me before I hit the floor. Jana produced a bottle of water from somewhere and made me drink it. My kids hovered over me with worried expressions on their faces. Someone had grabbed a crate for me to sit on.

Uncle John, ever the voice of common sense, stepped up and said, "Everyone back up and give Fen some space. She needs a moment to get her bearings."

My beloved mule, BB, forced his way into the room and came to me. He gently placed his head on my shoulder and just stood there while I breathed in his earthy, horsy scent. It was like a balm for my soul.

Randy, his hands zip-tied, retreated to the farthest side of the large room, away from the mule. I saw BB gave him the side-eye look that said, *"I know where you are, don't be stupid."*

I got so tickled and started to laugh. The kids and Jacob started to laugh, too, and the EMTs looked around at the mayhem, blood, and their two injured patients. They exchanged puzzled, worried glances but went on about their work.

Two reserve deputies came in and took Steve Leblanc and Randy Bowman away. I heard one of them before they went outside.

"Oh man, I don't want this guy in my car, he smells like piss."

Those words brought me a new round of laughter.

"Fen, I hope you don't mind, but I had to move your truck and trailer so we could get through with the ambulances and patrol cars."

"How did you get the way cleared so fast?"

"All I can say, Fen, is we have an awesome fire department crew. They know how to use a chainsaw."

I should have known Uncle John would know exactly what to do about the fallen trees. Funny that I didn't hear the chainsaws, but my mind was on the safety of my family.

"I drove your pickup myself and it is parked outside." Sheriff Peters motioned to the general area outside the mill. "I need to get complete statements from all of you, but there is no reason we can't do that tomorrow at the station."

"Yes, all good. Thank you, Sheriff." I smiled though I was weary to the bone. I stood up and hugged BB. "You're such a good boy, yes, good mule, let's go home, big guy." BB nickered softly, which I took as his agreement.

"Can I get a ride back to my car? I was going to ride with the reserves but there isn't room, and their car smells like urine." Jana snickered.

I noticed the shy look that passed between Jacob and Jana. "Do you want a lift, too, Sheriff?"

"No, thanks, though. I need to stay here and wait for the tow trucks to come get the Bowman's truck and Leblanc's car. Deputy Sharp and two reserve deputies will be here soon to help me secure the scene." He held up a hand at Jana. "Don't say you'll stay and help. Captain Smith, I believe this was your day off, but you have done more work today than some of my deputies do in six months. Go home, get some rest, come in tomorrow. You can help me sort these witness statements out."

"Yes, sir."

I noticed how relieved she looked. *She must be every bit as tired as I am.* "Where is Clyde anyway?"

Uncle John grimaced. "He is on desk duty 'til the end of the month. I noticed some inconsistencies in some of his reports and I am monitoring the situation."

That was cryptic. *I wonder what the doofus did.*

I put an arm around each of my twins. "Let's go home, kids. Everyone that is riding with me, load up. You, too, BB. Come on."

Once BB and the two horses were secured in the trailer, we all piled into my crew cab. Neither kid wanted to drive this terrible, tiny road in the snow pulling a trailer, but they did manage to argue over who got "shotgun".

I noticed Jana and Jacob quietly got in the backseat

and scooted together to make room for Arista. Ian won the shotgun argument.

We dropped Jana off at her car, and I heard Jake tell her to text him when she got home safely. *My brother has a crush on my good friend. I hope he doesn't screw it up.*

It was approaching 2 a.m. when we pulled up to our barn to unload the equine. Lester came tottering out of the house to help. Bless him, he waited up for us and I hadn't even called to let him know. I found out later he had been texting Jacob periodically throughout the evening.

The kids went directly toward their rooms, each wanting a shower before they went to bed. I wanted the same thing. Fortunately, each bathroom had its own instant water heaters. I was never more grateful for that fact than I was then. Jacob said he was going to sit by the fireplace for a short while. I suspected he might be texting with a pretty deputy.

Yvonne was still at the house with Mom. She had dozed off in a recliner after Mom went to bed. I let her be.

Lester patted me on the back. "Thank goodness y'all are okay. I'm glad you're home, it felt so empty." He went to his bedroom and closed the door.

When I passed his room on my way to my room, I heard him muttering to himself, or maybe to God.

I didn't know if I had the energy to get undressed and into the shower, but I forced myself into action. I stood under the hot water and scrubbed my hands so much I thought my skin might bleed. All visible signs of Bowman's blood were gone. I was trying to scrub away the memory of the sight and feel of it. Realizing those memories would be exorcised with time not soap, I dried off and crawled into bed in my favorite jammies.

My body ached and my mind swam through the violence of the evening. There was a soft plop on the bed. Isabella, my very round calico cat nestled along my side and began to purr. The combination of the purring vibration and the warmth generated by the fluffy little soul at my side began to work. I focused my attention on the sweet humming sound. I drifted off to sleep and by the Grace did not wake or dream until well past daylight.

CHAPTER 18

Isabella woke me around 9 a.m. by sitting on my, somewhat sore, torso, doing her toes vigorously. Some folks call it "making biscuits," others call it "kneading," but in my family, a cat was said to be "doing its toes." Grandma always said if someone kneaded or worked their dough that much, the bread would be inedible and tough. Thinking of her, how she spoke and gestured with her hands the entire time, her opinions were well thought out and she was passionate about them.

"Okay, Issy, I get it. You want out of the bedroom, your food, and a spot in a sunny window, in that order." I hugged the fat cat and moved her off my chest so I could get up. A quick peek out the window revealed an overcast sky, pale light, and about two inches of fresh snow. "Good luck finding a sunny spot today, Issy."

Issy answered with an impatient, "Meow."

I grabbed my fluffiest bathrobe and headed for the kitchen. "I hope there's coffee."

"Mirp," Issy said, trotting out the bedroom door and down the hall.

Jacob, Jana, Lester, my mom, and Yvonne were all in the kitchen when I got there. Jacob and Jana had breakfast cooking and were bantering about the virtues of hashbrowns vs. American fries. Only Arista and Ian were absent. Being teenagers, they were probably still sleeping.

Lester handed me a cup of coffee. "Morning, Fen, let me know if you want some 'special sauce' for your coffee."

His eyes twinkled mischievously with the obscure reference to the flask of homemade brew in his pocket. I laughed. "I think I'm good right now, Lester. Thanks, I'll keep it in mind." I settled myself on the only open stool at the kitchen island and poured cream into my cup.

"Good morning, Fen, I hope you don't mind I came over and helped Jacob take over your kitchen for breakfast." Jana smiled.

I noticed she looked downright perky this morning. "Not at all, y'all cook 'til your heart's content. Jana, I'm truly grateful for your help and friendship over the last few days. Thank you." I smiled back at her. I felt quite certain I looked anything but perky.

"My pleasure. I like hanging out with you, too. Let's skip the attempted murder and kidnapping stuff in the future though." Jana winked.

"I hope so!" I said, but there was a quivering deep in my gut that hinted of future troubles. I suppressed a visible cringe. The house phone rang and I went to answer. Auntie's voice came over the receiver speaker.

"Good morning. I didn't bother calling last night because I knew everyone was okay."

"Thanks to you and Jacob's gadget. I appreciate you,

Auntie."

"I know, dear. I won't keep you, just wanted to hear your voice."

"Okay. Love you."

"Love you, too.

At that I hung up just in time to hear Jake.

"Breakfast is ready, y'all." Jacob placed a stack of plates on the end of the counter.

Yvonne fixed her plate and one for Mom then settled at the dining room table. Everyone tucked into the food with enthusiasm. Except for the "mmm, this is good" and "thanks for cooking" comments mumbled around full mouths, there was no talking.

I sat down next to my mom at the table.

She tapped on her coffee cup with her spoon. "I'm so grateful to you all for rescuing my grandchildren. It's good to have them home where they belong. Fen, I'm proud of you for kicking Steve's butt. He was always an obnoxious child. I knew he wouldn't make for much as an adult." She beamed at me and pushed her empty plate away.

"I've got to get to my TV. Leroy Jethro Gibbs will be on in ten minutes, it's a marathon day." Mom got up and tottered toward her room, her coffee in hand. Her friend Yvonne trailed behind her, ready to help if needed.

I was astonished. We had tried to insulate my elderly mother from the scarier events of the last few days. I hadn't told her the kids had gone missing and certainly hadn't filled her in on the events of last evening. "How did she know about any of that?" I asked the room at large.

Jacob chuckled. "I think our momma hears a lot

better than she lets on and is not shy about eavesdropping."

Just then, Ian and Arista came into the kitchen. Arista was bright and had a bounce in her step.

"Good morning."

Ian shuffled sleepily behind her. "Hey, everybody. Oh dang, is breakfast gone?"

"We saved you some, dude, it's in the oven. Last ones in have to clean up, right, Jana?" Jacob winked at her.

"Sounds right." Jana blushed.

"Whatever," the kids said in unison as they scooped up the remaining breakfast.

I could hear the eye roll and I suppressed a laugh.

✦ ✦ ✦

After breakfast and an adequate application of caffeine, we all decided to go into town to the sheriff's office and get the official statements out of the way. It wouldn't get easier the longer we waited, and I told the kids that Uncle John had been kind enough to let us wait 'til today. We shouldn't take advantage of his kindness.

It took three hours for Arista, Ian, and me to give our statements to the sheriff. I was present during Arista's and Ian's debriefing since they are both minors, but I was not allowed to ask questions or interject information.

During their statements, I learned that Randy Bowman had abducted them during the high school dance by luring them outdoors one at a time. He had taken and restrained Arista first then used her as leverage against Ian. I really didn't think Randy was that smart. Had he tried to capture and contain them simultaneously, it would have been much more difficult.

They were tied and gagged in the truck when Randy ran their uncle Jacob off the road and left him for dead. The kids saw the entire thing.

Randy had driven them to the abandoned mill. Denny was already there with their injured little brother, Bobby. Steve LeBlanc showed up around an hour before Jacob and I got there.

The Bowmans were hatching a plan to hold the kids for ransom then get out of town. They were stuck on trying to figure out how to move Bobby without killing him. Arista said she overheard them talking about how to escape the area and were leaning toward just dropping Bobby off at the hospital entrance. They were afraid he would "roll on them to the cops" if he made it. Not a fine example of brotherly love for sure. Both Arista and Ian had worked out for themselves that their ability to identify the Bowmans to the police put their lives in imminent danger, so they spent their time in captivity looking for ways to escape.

Ian told the sheriff when Steve LeBlanc showed up, he was livid that his lackeys had kidnapped two kids, knowing full well that "their mother was a busybody with friends on the police force." I suspected he cleaned up the language a bit for my benefit.

Once they finished talking with Sheriff Peters, I gave them some cash and told them to go over to the coffee shop. "Grab some snacks and think about replacement phones."

We would go procure some on the way home. The

thought of new phones perked them both up, although neither were happy about lost photos and so forth.

The sheriff closed the conference room door behind the kids as I took a seat at the table. He said, "I'm so glad you and the kids are safe. It may be a while before y'all feel okay, so if there is anything you need, I hope you will let me know. For a rural county in Missouri, we do have some counseling resources available for victims. I'm always around to talk with you and the kids."

"Thank you, Uncle John. I appreciate you taking our statements yourself. I will keep counseling in mind. I hope you and Clarissa will come to the house for Thanksgiving."

"Gosh, that's this week. Will you be up to putting on a feast so soon after the string of ordeals your family has had lately?"

"I think filling the house with good friends, family, comfort food, and fun is just what we all need to work past the stress of the last few days."

"I'll have to check with Clarissa, but I feel sure that we would love to come." Sheriff Peters adjusted his hat and motioned at the tape recorder sitting on the table. He was now in full sheriff mode. "Are you ready to give your statement, Fen?"

"Yes, I am, Sheriff, let's get it done." I glossed over the part about us having taken horses with us to the mill based on information gleaned from my psychic aunt. I had coached my kids on leaving out any talk of chanting, conjuring, or visions.

After I finished giving my statement and the recorder was turned off, Sheriff Peters looked me in the eye. "I suspect there are a few more details to the events of last night that you left out. I am willing to assume you have good reason, and I further suspect I know what those reasons are. I'm fine with that. It's not like a jury would understand or believe the more unusual aspects of how you and now your kids navigate the world.

"What I really want to know for myself is how you got the mule to disable Randy Bowman before he could warn Denny that my deputy was riding up." The sparkle in his eye amused me. I was struck by how unusual my mule's behavior had been. I laughed. "I didn't do anything physically, mentally, or magically to make that happen. He is just a darn good mule and the smartest animal I have ever known." I held up both hands and shrugged.

We said our goodbyes and I left the station and went to meet the twins at the coffee shop. I passed Jacob and Jana as they were leaving, cups in hand and a small carry-out box of pastries. Jacob said he was heading to the station to take his turn talking with the sheriff. I thought they made a cute couple and managed to keep my mouth shut about it for the time being.

When I got to their table, the kids were discussing the pros and cons of various cell phones. We headed for the store and after the initial sticker shock, walked out with two shiny new phones complete with protective cases, extra chargers, and expanded memory chips. "Good grief, I'd once bought a car for less than those phones cost. It even ran!" I was pleased that got a laugh out of my son and daughter.

It was so good to finally get home and be able to snuggle in by the fire and not have to be anywhere the rest of the day. It had stopped snowing, and the main roads were mostly clear. The backroads remained a mess.

Yvonne was still at our house. She, Mom, and Lester worked together and set out a nice spread of food. I was so grateful I nearly cried.

✦ ✦ ✦

The following day was Tuesday. I was surprised the roads were clear enough for school to be in session. I would have allowed the kids to stay home after their ordeal, but they were excited to go. They had a lot to gossip about with their friends. The rest of Tuesday was remarkably calm. We had leftovers for supper and turned in early.

Wednesday morning, I got up late. The house was empty and blissfully quiet. I put on a pot of stew and spent the morning puttering with my jewelry. Auntie Lou called around noon to tell me she would be coming for Thanksgiving.

Fortunately, it was a big pot of stew because the house filled up with people again. Ian brought Tom and JJ home with him, Arista had Zoe with her and a new girl named Brandy. Jacob and Jana came in looking flushed from the cold. Or perhaps another reason? *They really are a cute couple.*

Lester spent the day in the machine shed tinkering. I hadn't even missed him in the house. *Hmm, shows how tired I am.* Mom was jovial, and her memory was vacillating between 1970 and present day.

During the pre-dinner conversation, Jana said she had been granted the day off since she had, essentially, worked straight through her real day off with no break. She and Jacob had met early in the morning and driven over to Branson, MO to play tourist. *Jacob despises that touristy stuff, he must really like her.*

Just as we were sitting down to eat, someone knocked on the door. Ian went to see who, and he came back a couple of minutes later with Sheriff Peters.

There was a chorus of, "Hi, Sheriff, good to see you, Sheriff," and my mom asked him what her brother had done now.

She was speaking of my uncle James, the black sheep of that generation. He had died a decade ago. Yep, Mom's mind was somewhere in the past.

Sheriff Peters greeted everyone in general and assured my mother that her brother James was not in any trouble, in fact, he hadn't seen him "for a while."

I asked him if he would like a bowl of stew, and Arista went to grab another place setting.

The talk over supper was minimal as everyone gobbled up their stew and the hot cheddar biscuits. I began to worry we would run out of biscuits. Two boxes worth was not enough for this crowd. One by one, people pushed their bowls away, and Uncle John told us the reason he popped by.

"Fen, I didn't descend on y'all at dinnertime on purpose but I'm mighty glad I did, that was delicious. The reason I came by was to give everyone here an update on the case. I don't usually discuss open cases with civilians, but virtually everyone at this table had a hand in bringing down the Bowmans and LeBlanc." He looked at Zoe, Tom, JJ, and Brandy as if seeing her for the first time. "You four are not to repeat anything you hear tonight to anyone outside of this room. Is that clear?" Sheriff Peters could look and sound very imposing when he wanted to.

Tom, JJ, and Zoe answered immediately with, "Yes, sir."

Brandy looked as if she was hit with a stun gun and only answered after a not-so-subtle elbow in the ribs from Arista. "Yes, sir," she stammered.

Poor girl, she must wonder what kind of people she was spending the evening with.

"Okay, so neither Denny, Randy, nor Steve are talking, they have all lawyered up. Denny is still in the hospital, under guard, until he has recovered enough from his gunshot wound to be moved to jail. The bullet hit him and went straight through without hitting anything vital. Randy and Steve are in separate cells down at county. Both are whining about the injuries they sustained in their respective fights with you, Fen, and your mule."

This got a few laughs and "atta girls" from the group. I rolled my eyes.

The sheriff went on. "Bobby Bowman was transported to a Springfield hospital due to the severity of his condition. It wasn't that the initial injury, which you may recall, was a shotgun blast of birdshot, was so severe. The problem was that his older brothers failed to get him appropriate and timely medical treatment after he was shot. He developed a nasty infection and is on some very potent antibiotics.

He did wake up this morning, and I drove up to Springfield to read him his rights and interview him. Since he is technically a minor, his brothers will be charged with neglect and endangering a minor in addition to the long list of felony theft, aggravated assault, attempted murder, kidnapping, and a few other things we are still investigating."

"Wait, Bobby is a minor? He doesn't go to school with us," Arista said.

Peters nodded. "Yep, he won't turn eighteen until next summer. He stopped going to school two years ago after his mother died."

"When I met with him in the hospital and explained the situation to him, in the presence of a court-appointed guardian, he rolled on his brothers. His exact words were, 'I wanna cut a deal like they do on TV.'"

Ian pulled back the cover of the biscuit basket and frowned. "Since Bobby got shot by Mr. Dawlin during the attempted cattle theft, does that mean the Bowmans were behind all the cattle thefts?"

Lester sat up straighter and pushed his bowl away. "Have you found my cattle?"

"Yes, and almost," answered the sheriff. "Yes, they were the cattle rustlers. According to Bobby, his brothers were contracted by Steve LeBlanc to steal as many cattle as possible from a specific list of ranchers. Bobby didn't know exactly why there was a list, but I have some suspicions. I don't want to go into details on that until the corroborating evidence is sorted out.

"They were just supposed to steal the cattle and take them to be sold, LeBlanc would get 40 percent of that money. It was Denny who came up with the idea of dying off-color cattle black because black cattle bring higher prices at the sale barn." Sheriff Peters paused to allow for the round of exclamations and questions which erupted.

"Why would that LeBlanc guy get any money? Was he out there stealing cattle with them?" asked Zoe.

"They were using black hair dye to dye *cattle?*" Ian shook his head.

"You mean those idiots painted my beautiful cows black?" Lester smacked the table.

It struck me as absurdly funny that Lester seemed more upset about his cows being dyed than he was about getting knocked in the head and left for dead. I kept my amusement to myself.

"Why do black cows cost more money at the sale? That is some messed-up discrimination."

This comment came from Brandy. She forgot to be shy for a moment.

I stood so I could reach the pitcher of tea. "Whoa, y'all, one at a time. This is starting to feel more like a press conference than an after-supper conversation. I'm sure the sheriff will answer all these questions if we give him a chance."

"Thank you, Fen. Yes, due to a clever advertising campaign by the Black Angus Cattle organization years ago, black cows bring more at the sale than other colors of cows. Those of us who have been around cattle for years know it's ridiculous.

Lester, it remains to be seen if your cattle were dyed yet. Bobby gave me directions to the abandoned property where they were stockpiling the cows until sale day. I'm going out there early tomorrow morning to look the situation over. Deputy Sharp is going with me and, Jana, I need you to go along. Lester, you are welcome to come if you're feeling up to it."

Lester nodded his agreement.

Jacob took the pitcher, refilled his glass then passed

it to his right. "I'd like to come, too, if it's okay with you, Sheriff."

"Me, too," said Ian and Arista simultaneously.

As if reading my mind, Sheriff Peters addressed both teens. "I appreciate you both wanting to go, but I must decline. The place will be a crime scene, and there is no telling what we will find there. It is no place for minors. Besides, tomorrow is Thanksgiving, and your mom shouldn't have to prepare the entire feast with zero help. If tonight is any indication, y'all will have an even fuller house for the holiday."

A look passed between my twins. The understanding that a) the sheriff was right and b) even if he was wrong, it wouldn't do any good to argue, was written on their faces.

"Okay, Sheriff. What about the money LeBlanc was splitting with the Bowmans and what about the dead guy I found?" Arista asked.

I noted my daughter's terse tone, and I'd have been embarrassed had it not been for the extreme stress of the last week or so. She was emotionally invested in all of it.

"Ah yes, the money. Leblanc was pulling the strings on the Bowman brothers' rustling activities. He gave them the names of the families he wanted them to hit and, no, he was not out there stealing cattle with them. I cannot currently comment on LeBlanc's motive for selecting the victims.

"The dead guy, as you call him, has finally been identified using dental records. His name is Anthony Andrew Greeman, a.k.a. Bad Andy. He was a collection specialist for a very bad man who shall not be named right now.

"He was sent here to collect a significant gambling debt from Steve Leblanc, who, it seems, gambles a lot. It has become a problem for him since he is apparently very bad at it.

"The details that led to 'Bad Andy' ending up dead in a ditch are unclear at this time, but I suspect his collection efforts met with some resistance from LeBlanc. Someone killed Bad Andy and the remains were dumped out where you found them. Bobby Bowman claimed to have no direct knowledge of the murder or the disposal of the body." Sheriff Peters concluded his lengthy report, took a deep drink from his glass of tea, and got up to leave.

"Wow, Sheriff, that was a lot of information to take in. Thank you for bringing us all up to date." I walked him to the door. "I figure you will need us to testify when this goes to court?" I hoped I was wrong.

"Yes, Fen, you will be called to testify if any of this mess goes to court. Given the number of charges against the Bowmans and LeBlanc, I expect some plea deals to be made eventually. Between you and me, it would be better if it never saw a courtroom. The guy the collector was working for has ties to the Dixie Mob. Too much press and this could all go pear-shaped. The DM doesn't like their name in the paper or mentioned in court.

"I better go, Clarissa said she would hold supper for me. I will have to make like I haven't eaten yet, so don't you tell her." He winked and patted his full stomach.

"Your secrets are safe with me, Uncle John." I closed the door after his departure and returned to the dining room. It was buzzing with conversation. Only my mother wasn't talking, she was looking very tired. "Hey, Mom, how about we get you comfy in your chair? Do you want to knit a while before bed?"

"Not tonight, honey. I'm sleepy and I have to get up at 4 a.m. to milk the cow."

Oh dear. "Okay, Mom. I will do it if you want to sleep in tomorrow morning." Then I reminded her that tomorrow was Thanksgiving and she always watches the parade. Mom hadn't had to milk a cow for at least thirty years. She was asleep moments after I got her settled into bed. *Is she wearing herself out by being too busy?*

By the time I rejoined everyone, they had migrated to the family room, except for Ian and Tom. Arista told me they had lost at rock, paper, scissors and were cleaning up the supper dishes. I couldn't help but laugh.

Tom's mom arrived to pick up him, JJ and Brandy. Relief flooded me when I realized I didn't have to leave the house to take them all home. I thanked her and we chatted for a few moments before they left.

Zoe's mom had called me earlier and asked if Zoe could stay another night. Her brother was still hospitalized after his heart attack. I told her that Zoe was welcome to stay for as long as they wanted. Silently, I wondered if her brother died if there would be additional charges brought against the Bowmans and LeBlanc. Then I scolded myself for the crass thought.

I reminded Arista and Ian regardless how late they stayed up I needed them awake and functioning in the morning to assist with the cooking, cleaning, and anything else that had been forgotten due to recent, more pressing events.

Jana said good night to everyone, and Jacob walked

her to her car. I headed off to bed. Isabella, the round mound of feline perfection was already there, keeping my pillow warm. I knew Sophia was ensconced with Violet and hoped Lester didn't mind.

Morning was not nearly far enough away, and my last thought of the day was wondering whether or not the turkey would be completely thawed.

CHAPTER 19

Despite a decent night's sleep, I awoke on Thanksgiving morning feeling foggy. The reality that it was 5:50 a.m. and the turkey HAD to be in the oven by 7 a.m. if we wanted to eat at a reasonable hour jolted me into action. I tore through the house to the kitchen, only to find Arista and Ian already there. She was tearing up two loaves of bread for the dressing.

Ian was wrestling the twenty-five-pound turkey in the sink. It was unclear who was winning. I stopped just short of the island bar. "Wow, good morning, kids, whatcha doing?"

"We got up to help, figured you could use some downtime." Arista brushed breadcrumbs off the counter.

"Yeah, Mom, we didn't say thanks. You know, for coming for us at the mill." Ian heaved the huge turkey out of the sink and into the roasting pan.

"I'm your momma, I will always come for you." My eyes started watering. A lot.

Arista dried her hands on the dishtowel. "Since

you're up, can you tell us what to do next? I was about to Google how to cook a turkey, but I figure you have some tricks."

I laughed. "My turkey tricks come straight out of Betty Crocker, but I will gladly accept the help and provide the plan."

With the kids' help and some much-needed coffee, I got the turkey in the oven by 7:30 a.m.. *Close enough.* Then I showered to finish waking up.

Around 11 a.m. Auntie Lou breezed in. (She arrives everywhere like a mini cyclone, one that brings gifts and good wishes. How she travels so much, yet always has so much "stuff" with her remains a mystery.)

"Hello, my lovelies!" Auntie said as she distributed hugs to everyone assembled in the kitchen.

The flurry of activity caused by Auntie's arrival created a traffic jam in the kitchen. The "turkey out, baste baste baste, turkey in" and the shuffling of various pans into the other oven and subsequently to a place on the stove where they could remain warm, took up the next two hours.

Sheriff John Peters and his wife, Clarissa, arrived a little after 1 p.m. Clarissa and Auntie Lou had some catching up to do on the topic of New Orleans. Clarissa was from NOLA and Auntie had recently spent a couple months there.

By the time we all sat down to eat around 2 p.m. I was truly tired of looking at turkey, and would happily have smashed a cheeseburger and gone to bed for the day. But now that the cattle thieving was cleared up and I knew my family was safe, I wanted and needed to spend time with them. Sleep could come later.

The cacophony of chatting changed to "mmm so

good" and "please pass the butter" once the meal began.

We were finishing the pie and coffee when the sheriff's phone rang. He apologized as he checked the caller ID explaining that he had to take it.

I had a funny feeling about the phone call. Auntie Lou must have felt similarly, as she caught my eye. We both did our best to overhear the sheriff's phone call but were unsuccessful. His voice sounded suspicious as he prodded the caller for details.

Once he hung up, he said, "That was the jail. Steve Leblanc claims he received a death threat, and he is demanding protection. I have to get over there now. I'm so sorry to eat and run."

I walked the sheriff and Clarissa out to their car. "Who would want to kill Leblanc at this point?"

Uncle John opened the car door for his wife. "If it's a credible threat, any number of people could want him dead. Steve may know more about the criminal organization than he has let on and someone wants to silence him. The Dixie Mob have one rule only, 'Thou shalt not snitch to the cops ever.'" Sheriff Peters got into the driver's seat, then he and his wife drove away.

I walked back through the kitchen door and practically ran into Auntie Lou. She was holding a tarot card out toward me and said, "Buckle up, baby, we haven't heard the last of this mess."

ABOUT THE AUTHOR

Jen Kenning was born in Iowa and has called Southwest Missouri home for "the important part of her entire life." She always loved hearing and reading stories growing up. Her love of stories slowly morphed into a desire to spin her stories.

Jen has been a maid, waitress, cook, horseback riding trail guide, insurance adjuster, fire and theft investigator, customer service technician, and a reference librarian, among other things. Her favorite jobs were trail guide and librarian.

She currently lives on a family farm with her son and too many pets. When she's not writing she grows microgreens or makes jewelry.

A NOTE FROM JEN:

Hi, I truly hope you enjoyed Steered Wrong, the first book in the Magickal Mule Mystery series. The second book is well underway, although it does not yet have a title. Please check out my website

JenKenningAuthor.com

for updates, fun content, including the occasional recipe for food mentioned in the stories. Until next time Be Well and Be Blessed. ♥ J